FREMONT PUBLIC LIBRARY

3 3090 00653 8914

W9-CKI-103

ALL THE DIRTY SECRETS

ALSO BY AGGIE BLUM THOMPSON

I Don't Forgive You

ALL THE DIRTY SECRETS

AGGIE BLUM THOMPSON

A TOM DOHERTY ASSOCIATES BOOK

NEW YORK

WITHDRAWN
FREMONT PUBLIC LIBRARY DISTRICT
1170 N. Midlothian Road
Mundelein, IL 60060

This is a work of fiction. All of the characters, organizations, and events portrayed in this novel are either products of the author's imagination or are used fictitiously.

ALL THE DIRTY SECRETS

Copyright © 2022 by Agnes Blum Thompson

All rights reserved.

A Forge Book
Published by Tom Doherty Associates
120 Broadway
New York, NY 10271

www.tor-forge.com

Forge® is a registered trademark of Macmillan Publishing Group, LLC.

Library of Congress Cataloging-in-Publication Data

Names: Thompson, Aggie Blum, author.
Title: All the dirty secrets / Aggie Blum Thompson.
Description: First edition. | New York : Forge, 2022. | "A Tom Doherty Associates
   book." | Identifiers: LCCN 2022008315 (print) | LCCN 2022008316 (ebook) |
   ISBN 9781250773982 (trade paperback) | ISBN 9781250834478 (hardcover) |
   ISBN 9781250773999 (ebook)
Subjects: LCGFT: Novels.
Classification: LCC PS3620.H6477 A78 2022 (print) | LCC PS3620.H6477
   (ebook) | DDC 813/.6—dc23/eng/20220225
LC record available at https://lccn.loc.gov/2022008315
LC ebook record available at https://lccn.loc.gov/2022008316

Our books may be purchased in bulk for promotional, educational, or business use.
Please contact your local bookseller or the Macmillan Corporate and
Premium Sales Department at 1-800-221-7945, extension 5442, or by email at
MacmillanSpecialMarkets@macmillan.com.

First Edition: 2022

Printed in the United States of America

0 9 8 7 6 5 4 3 2 1

FOR FRED

AUTHOR'S NOTE

This story contains content that some readers might find disturbing, including sexual assault and references to death by suicide. Please read with care.

CHAPTER 1

LIZA

If your friends won't lie to you, who will?

"Seriously, Liza. You do not look a day over thirty." Shelby takes a big swig of her whiskey sour and crunches down on an ice cube. "I mean, you still got it."

"Uh-huh." I blink. I look every day of my forty-six years, and she knows it. Shelby has been my personal cheerleader since we met at Washington Prep in sixth grade, and I don't know what I'd do without her slightly deluded optimism. Especially this past year.

"I agree." Todd leans across the small table so he can be heard above the din of the bar. "I'd date you."

"Gross." Shelby punches him in the shoulder. "You mean if you *weren't* married to her best friend, right, hon?"

Archer lets out a howl, and Todd rubs his arm with exaggerated care. I laugh, too, maybe for the first time in months. The four of us have been friends since high school, and when we're together, some subtle alchemy happens that melts away all of life's problems.

Washington, and all the frenzied hustle of our complicated, busy lives, is less than three hours away, but crossing the Bay Bridge this afternoon was like traveling back in time to when we had nothing to worry about but how we would fill a long weekend.

Together, here in Dewey Beach, we are forever young.

"Remember when we needed fake IDs to get in to the Cork-board?" Todd asks.

"*We* didn't need fake IDs." Shelby gestures toward me. "'Cause we were cute."

If anyone doesn't look a day over thirty, she doesn't. While Todd's hair is salt and pepper now, and Archer has a few smile lines at the edges of his eyes, Shelby looks virtually the same. Thanks to an annual self-care budget equal to the GDP of a small nation and some good genes, she has the same glossy blond hair, smooth skin, and compact body she had in high school. I'd be jealous if I didn't know how much damn effort it took. I enjoy my nightly half pint of ice cream too much.

"Here's to Dewey." Archer raises his glass. I raise mine. The Corkboard hasn't changed. It's still the perfect beach town bar—dark, divey, and ripe for anonymous make-out sessions. And there's a pretty good crowd for a Sunday night. I watch as a woman nearby takes an oddly angled selfie that clearly includes Archer.

It always amuses me to see how people react to having a celebrity near them. And not a politician but a real celebrity like Archer. He's even better looking in life than on TV, where his makeup smooths out the variations in his brown skin and gives him a plastic perfection. And fame like his makes people act weird. In D.C., most try to act stoic, as if acknowledging fame is a personal weakness. And Washington is nothing if not a town of overachievers with iron wills.

But we're not in D.C. tonight.

The woman appears at Archer's elbow. Up close, it's clear from the way she is wobbling and having trouble keeping her kohl-rimmed eyes open that she's drunk.

"Can I get a pic?" She gestures to the two women behind her, who wave. "We're from Balmer."

"Happy to oblige." Archer scoots one way, and we all lean back the other way to provide them room. Even back in high school,

Archer had that effect on people. He wasn't voted God's Gift to Women senior year for nothing.

"You're so cute," she says. "What's your name again, hon? I know it's not Don Lemon."

Archer laughs. "Archer Benoit."

"Oh, I knew that." She wobbles away as our table erupts in laughter.

"Oh. My. God." Shelby squeals.

"That was a great Baltimore accent," Todd says. "*Balmer?*"

"And I love how she's like, *I know you're not the Black guy on CNN . . .*" Shelby laughs.

"Right? Why not just ask your name?" I sip my drink. "Why drag Don Lemon into it?"

"You would be surprised how often that happens. Sometimes they straight-up ask if I'm friends with Don Lemon. I'm like, no, he lives in New York, I live in D.C., and we work for competing news channels."

Todd looks at his watch, then raps the table with his knuckles. "We'd better get going. We're going to try to catch up with Chris tonight. Last chance, ladies."

"Chris de Groot? Really?" Chris was part of our crew in high school, but has since drifted away. According to a *Washington Post* profile I read, he's keeping busy churning out his Kurt Jericho: Rogue CIA Agent series. But I wonder if copious amounts of scotch, and a few DUIs, don't also play a role.

"He's at his beach house now?" I ask.

"Yeah, we're going to head down there."

"I keep trying to get him to return my emails." Over the years, I've reached out to Chris, hoping he'd agree to let me write a profile on him for the school's alumni magazine, where I work. In high school, he, Archer, and Todd were an inseparable trio. But if we do get a correspondence going, it peters out before I can get him to commit to anything. "He's up to what—novel fifteen at this point, right?"

"Those books are crap," says Shelby without looking up from her glass.

"And you've read them?" Archer raises an eyebrow.

"What? I read books." Shelby tosses back her drink. "Anyway, I don't need to read them. I read the Amazon reviews. Too many heaving bosoms and explosions."

"Heaving bosoms and explosions," Archer repeats and winks at me. "Good name for our band."

I laugh. We've had a running joke about potential band names since Mr. Mooney's civics class in tenth grade, when we first decided Penal Offense would be a great name.

"Forget novels," Todd says. "Apparently, Netflix is making a series out of the books."

"Oh, really?" I ask. My boss, Geoff, would go nuts for that. I can see the headline now: *Wash Prep alum takes on Hollywood*.

"Look at you all excited." Archer smirks, but I can actually sense an undercurrent of competition. You don't get to be a cable news star by being laid-back about other people getting more attention than you do.

"Well, I can't keep writing about you, Archer." I give him a wicked smile.

Shelby and Todd laugh. Because I do keep writing stories about Archer, and he loves it. I don't add that it's in large part because my boss is starstruck by Archer and always leaning on me to exploit my personal friendship with him.

Todd stands up. "All right." He gives Shelby a long kiss on her mouth. I have to look away. Even though I know that their relationship has seen its ups and downs over the years, this display of affection stings me like lemon juice on a cut. In the wake of my recent divorce, I don't need to see someone else's marital bliss up close. Not too mature of me, but there's no denying it.

Archer leans in for a friendly peck on the cheek. He's like a second brother to me, and save for one drunken and horribly awkward attempt at a hookup during college spring break in Florida, we've never been tempted to try anything romantic. "We still on for coffee Tuesday morning?"

"Yup. See you in D.C." I have to interview him for the article, although I don't think there is much I don't already know about Archer.

"Don't you girls get into too much trouble," Todd says, and they're off. I watch them push through the crowd that has gathered to listen to a nineties cover band that is tuning up. When I turn back, I notice that the phone on the table is Todd's. It has a gray case. Everything Shelby has is pink.

"I think Todd grabbed your phone by accident," I say.

She makes a pouty face and picks up Todd's phone. "Dummy. I'd better let him know." She types quickly into the phone and then turns to me.

"Of course you know his password." Daniel never shared his with me. That should have been a sign.

"We share everything!" Shelby makes a cutie-pie face and then laughs. "Sooooo, see any cute guys here?"

"We're not here to pick up guys for me," I say. "We're at the beach to spy on your kids." She and Todd have boy-girl twins, Brody and Kinsey, who have just graduated from Washington Prep, and like the majority of recent high school grads in the D.C. area, they're spending this week partying at the beach, just like we did when we were their age.

"Spy? You're going to do the same exact thing when Zoe's a senior."

I laugh. "I know. But I have two more years until I have to think about that."

Back when we were in high school, our parents sent us to Beach Week in cars loaded with beer, or in our case, Shelby's mom bought us Zima so we wouldn't have to drink our calories. But the overall experience has not changed: the Delaware and Maryland shore is inundated with drunk, horny teens whose cerebral cortexes are not yet fully formed, making them a danger to themselves and others.

So last fall, when Brody and Kinsey entered their senior year, Shelby asked me to mark off this week to spend at her family's beach house. The twins would be renting houses with their friends, but we would hover in the wings just in case. Neither seen nor heard, we would be but a few minutes away if things got hairy. *A girls' getaway,* Shelby called it, even though we both knew that we were really here because she would be climbing the walls with anxiety if she were back in D.C.

"You do need to get out there again!" Shelby shouts above the Toad the Wet Sprocket cover. "You've been divorced more than two years."

"Separated more than two years," I correct her. "Divorced one year, as of last month."

Shelby waves the distinction away. "Whatever. Who have you slept with, besides that guy from the gym? Who was that guy? Oh yeah, Deltoid Doug."

"Please don't remind me about Deltoid Doug." I hadn't realized that you could take the guy out of the gym, but you couldn't get him to stop talking about CrossFit versus Orange Theory.

"Look around—there's got to be some decent guys here." She sweeps her hand around the packed room. But I'm not checking out guys. I'm pulling out my phone to check on Zoe. Shelby puts her hand over mine.

"Yeah, I don't think so. Zoe's at home watching *Dance Moms.*" She gives me a challenging look. "Daniel's got this. I dare you not to check up on her."

"It's just this constant buzzing in the back of my brain—what is Zoe up to? Is Zoe safe? Is she where she said she was going to be?" I sigh. "I'm surprised I've been able to turn it off for as long as I have today."

"I'm the same," Shelby says. "If you weren't here distracting me, I'd go nuts."

"And it hasn't been good lately." Even Shelby doesn't know how bad it's been with Zoe recently. When Daniel moved out,

I thought we might get closer, just the two of us in the house together. But the opposite happened. She's pulled away. Lately, she absolutely vibrates with anger.

"Anything in particular?"

I laugh. "Let's see. According to Zoe, I embarrass her. I smother her. I annoy her. I don't get her. Should I go on?"

"Honey, these teenage girls are witches. I tell you. Thank god I have my Brody. Even though the twins are exactly three minutes apart, they're so different developmentally. Kinsey can't wait to get away from me. Meanwhile, Brody is all, *Mama, can I fill up your gas tank before you head out with Liza? And the tires need air, so I'll get that, too.*"

"So sweet."

"Thank god I did not have two girls."

"Well, I don't have a son. It's just Zoe and me. And Daniel. And he gets to be the fun one, who let Zoe get a nose piercing and took her to see Phoebe Bridgers the night before midterms." I pull my hand, and my phone, out from under Shelby's palm. "The type that would let his sixteen-year-old daughter roam the streets of D.C. after curfew."

"Don't check, Liza. Let Daniel be the parent. You're off this weekend."

"You're never really off, though, are you?" I know she just wants to protect me, but I also know she's the same way about her kids. We both know what can happen to teenagers when parents aren't paying attention.

Just look at what happened to Nikki.

"You're such a Capricorn." Shelby sighs and rolls her eyes. "Fine. Just one quick peek. And then put it away."

I go to the Find My app and look for Zoe's phone. We all do it. Every parent that I know. We lament our kids not having the freedoms we did when we were their age, and then we track their every move.

It takes only a millisecond to register that Zoe's avatar isn't there.

CHAPTER 2

ZOE

I used to be a good girl.

An actual bona fide Girl Scout.

I can still recite the pledge. My mom was our Scout leader, and she made me memorize it.

Honest and fair.

Friendly and helpful.

Considerate and caring.

We earned all these little badges, which my mom ironed onto my sash. I have no clue where that sash is now. It might've moved into my dad's apartment, or maybe it's in a box in my mom's attic. Things get lost during a divorce.

No one would call me a good girl now.

"It's mango," Emery says, passing me a slender can of White Claw. "You love mango." She leans forward when she says this, competing with the whoops and hollers of a group of guys behind her. The heat from all the bodies packed into the living room and kitchen is oppressive. Beyond the open sliding doors, more bodies fill the deck overlooking the ocean. I recognize some faces from Washington Prep, but there are so many bodies jammed in so close that I can't really get a sense of who is here.

Emery winks at me, and a warm, gooey sensation spreads within me, smoothing out my nerves, which have been jangly since we got to the party. I know Parker Mallon's parents rented the beach house for him and his friends. I also know Parker never invited me to this party.

"True. I do love mango." But what I love even more is how Emery remembers all these little random things I've told her. That means I exist to her. If I can't be her—tall and beautiful, confident and brave—if I can't make people look at me the way they look at her, well, then I could be near her. I could be important to her. So if she needs something, I try to give it to her. Even if it's something like taking my mom's car behind her back and driving out to Beach Week.

"Drink up. You're supposed to be having fun, you know. This *is* a party."

"You sure?" I crack the can but don't take a sip. The room is filled with all the people I normally try to avoid at school, all collected in one place. It's mostly seniors, but there are juniors and a handful of sophomores.

Before Emery, I'd float through the halls at school, never connecting. Everyone at Washington Prep talks about inclusivity and diversity, but if you're even a little different, they let you know.

It's not blatant like in the movies, like other kids won't sit with you. No one says anything anti-Asian or anti-Japanese. There's no bully who trips you in the cafeteria so your tray of food goes flying. It's subtler than that, but it sucks just as much. It's pity bombs that people drop, like when I got a C on a math test and this girl next to me peered over at my grade and was all "Poor Zoe, it's so racist that Asians are expected to get good grades."

"So where are we going to sleep tonight?" I ask, trying to sound like I think it's totally cool we haven't really planned this out.

Emery rolls her eyes. "Such a granny."

"Am not."

"Then drink."

I take a sip. It's not technically my first drink—my dad has let me sip his beer before—but it's my first time *drinking*.

"We'll figure it out. Worse comes to worst, we can just crash at someone's house," she says. "It's Beach Week—no one will even notice."

I'm about to point out the potential problems with this plan when I see Olivia and Kinsey heading straight toward us, wearing identical outfits of super-short cutoff jeans and white spaghetti-strap tanks.

"Hey, guys," Olivia says, barely glancing up from her phone. I wonder how she doesn't bump into things when she walks, because I literally never see her *not* looking at her phone.

"Be here now, Liv," Emery says. It's what our headmaster always says at the end of every weekly all-school meeting.

"Ha ha, funny." But it does make Olivia look up.

Kinsey turns to me, her mouth twisted in a half smirk. "Didn't know you were coming to Beach Week, Zoe." Her tone is light, and any grown-up would think she was being nice. But she's not. Her message blares as clear as a neon sign. Beach Week is for seniors. Correction, *cool* seniors. Not for sophomores who do orchestra like I do.

When we were little, we were all friends—Brody and Kinsey and I. On Sundays, my family would go over to the Smythes' house. Todd and my dad would watch football. Mom and Shelby would drink wine in the kitchen. We kids would jump on the trampoline in the backyard or watch movies in the basement theater. For a long time, I actually thought Todd was my uncle and Shelby was my aunt. That feels like a million years ago.

"She came with me." Emery's voice matches Kinsey's in sweetness, but the way she's making eye contact with Kinsey is no joke. It's like watching two lionesses square off on the savanna. Kinsey falters and blinks hard. Emery is choosing me over her. Dorky sophomore over Kinsey Smythe. Not that the two are friends. It would all have been so much easier if they had become friends this year; then Emery and I wouldn't have to mess with Brody at all. But Emery said that when she showed up at school last fall, Kinsey was a cold bitch to her. *That's okay*, Emery had told me, *boys are easier.*

"Okaaaaaayy." Kinsey draws the word out. "Very cool. Just surprised that Liza was down with that."

"It's fine." I take a gulp of my White Claw to hide the tremor of fear running through me. The last thing I want is for Kinsey to contact my mom, or her mom, which is basically the same thing. The whole plan was to go to Beach Week and come back without anyone ever knowing I left D.C.

"Bitches! Hello, I've been looking for you." We all turn to see Amina sashaying toward us, her glossy curls bouncing as she moves her body to the music. Up close, I can see she's applied highlighter to every visible inch of her dark brown skin, making her look like she was carved from one of those bouncy balls with the gold glitter stuck inside. Amina jerks her head toward Olivia and Kinsey. "I need someone to come with me so I can talk to you-know-who." I have no idea who *you-know-who* is, but I'm guessing Kinsey does because she rolls her eyes. Amina grabs Olivia by the arm. "You. Come with me."

"You're pathetic!" Olivia squeals, clearly delighted to be chosen.

Amina stops short for a moment and looks at Emery and me like she is seeing us for the first time. "Oh. Hi! Bye!" She grabs Kinsey with her other arm. "Sorry, but I need these two."

As soon as they have gone, I can breathe again, as though something heavy on my chest has been lifted.

"They're so annoying. *Hi! Bye!*" Emery says, imitating Amina.

"Do you think Kinsey's gonna tell my mom I'm here?"

Emery waves away the question. "No way. She's just messing with you." She twirls my mom's spare car key, on a chain with a big red *W* for the Washington Nationals. This makes me nervous. I want her to put it away for safekeeping. "Don't let her get to you."

Easy for you to say. I take another swig of the White Claw. Everything bothers me. I wish it didn't, but it does. It bothers me that my dad barely looked up from the documentary he's editing when Emery showed up at the apartment and I told him I was going to spend the night at her place. On the other hand, Mom would've practically made a copy of Emery's ID before she let me leave with her. And that would have bothered me, too. Sometimes I wonder if I can *not* be annoyed.

"Do you see Brody over there?"

We both turn our heads toward a group of guys yelling, "Drink! Drink!" One guy grips a silver keg with both hands while two of the Ledge Boys hold his legs in the air. That's what they call themselves. The Ledge Boys. Between classes, most of the lacrosse team, and some football players, would hang out on the low, brick wall at the edge of the Washington Prep quad. Last fall, they ranked a bunch of the girls in the school based on hotness and willingness to do anal and oral. Emery ranked in the top-five hottest girls at Washington Prep. Of course, I didn't make the list at all.

"*But they're such good boys,*" I say. It's what a lot of their moms said when the boys got busted.

"*And you don't want to ruin their future.*" Emery bats her eyes at me.

"C'mon, let's check out the deck. Maybe Brody is there." She plunges into the crowd, and I follow her unquestioningly. The crowd parts for her, but then they swallow her up, leaving no room for me. She's tall, with hair halfway down her back like a mermaid's. But it's not only that she's pretty. There are lots of pretty girls at Wash Prep. It's how she carries herself. Like she's daring you to challenge her. Even though this was her first year at the school—and she came as a senior, no less—she walked around campus with the confidence of one of the popular girls. Which of course made her one.

I struggle to keep up with Emery as we head toward the deck, but when I get outside, I can't see her. Maybe if I find Brody, I will see her, but the deck is just as noisy and packed with bodies as inside. Out here, everyone seems taller than I am. In the semidarkness, all the guys look alike. T-shirts or oxford button-downs, baseball caps, chino shorts. I wiggle my way to the splintery old railing and stare out at the black ocean, wondering if coming to this party was such a good idea. All of a sudden, what we came here to do seems crazy. The surf is loud and sounds rough, almost mechanical, like cars on a highway. The beach is empty and uninviting. I can't picture my mom and her friends—or anyone, really—wanting to dive into that dark, cold water.

But my mom did. And Nikki did.

I know the story the way most children know the story of Little Red Riding Hood, having heard the cautionary tale my whole life. Nikki Montes is why, even now, my mom won't let me swim in the ocean without an adult.

"Hey, there you are."

Startled, I turn to see Emery standing there, eyes wide. "Where were you?" I ask. "I couldn't find you."

"I have to go." Her voice is frantic. "Just stay here, and I'll be back."

"What do you mean, you have to go? Where?" A chill goes through me. That's the thing with Emery. She's always changing plans, keeping secrets.

"I have to meet someone."

"Who? We just got here. Is it Brody?"

She shakes her head but keeps her lips pressed together, as if by opening them some information might accidentally spill out.

"Who are you meeting?"

"I can't say. I won't be gone long. Forty minutes, maybe—an hour tops."

"An hour?" I say, alarmed. "Let me come with you. I'll stay in the car."

She shakes her head. "You can't. I'm sorry, Zoe. I have to go alone. But I'll be back, I swear." She grips my arm. "Just stay here, okay?"

"Where are you going?"

"Some lighthouse."

"Yeah, but where?"

"I'll drop a pin when I get there. I promise."

I swallow the lump in my throat. "What about me? What am I supposed to do while you're gone?" I know I sound sulky, but I'm lying to my parents to come with her, and she's bailing on me to meet someone else.

"You," she says, drawing out the word, "are going to do something really important."

She reaches into her bag and pulls out a plastic envelope.

I gasp. "You want me to do it?"

"Please? I need you to."

"How? I can't just walk up to him and ask for some blood."

"Give me your phone." I pass it to her. She knows my password, just like I know hers. I look over her shoulder as she opens Instagram and taps until she's pulled up a picture. She takes a screenshot of it and saves it to my phone. "This," she says, "is all you need."

I zoom in on the photo. It's a picture of a guy's hand, with multiple Band-Aids across the knuckles.

"Mountain biking wipeout. It's all over his Instagram. The good news is you just need one."

"I can't do this." I shake my head. "I'm not like you. I can't just walk up to someone and take a Band-Aid off their hand."

"Yes, you can. He'll be drunk. It'll be easy. I know you think you can't do it, but you can, Zoe. And I need you to do this."

Her words pierce me but also pull me closer to her, like how I imagine one of those whale harpoons we studied in history class does. She needs me. And I'm the only one who can help. I know she feels alone in the world, ever since her mother died last year. She's an only child, like I am, and she barely knows her dad, and isn't close to her grandparents. I'm the one who knows her secret, what she's trying to do.

"Okay." I take the bag. "I'll try. But be careful, okay?"

"Don't worry, Zoe. I got this."

She hugs me tightly, and I breathe in her smell. Then she's on her way, slipping through the crowd. Once I can no longer see her, I turn back to the ocean and take a deep breath. Emery needs me.

Opening up my phone, I stare at the picture of the scraped-up hand. Could this hand really hold all the answers? It's up to me now to find out. I promised Emery.

Back in D.C., my dad is lost in his editing world. My mom and Shelby are at Shelby's beach house, probably drinking and watching a rom-com. If there is one upside to divorce, it's being able to slip through the cracks like this.

No one is watching.

And when no one is watching, anything can happen.

CHAPTER 3

LIZA

"It says she's offline." My chest tightens. "That's impossible. She doesn't exist offline."

"Don't freak out. I'm sure her phone died or something. Check with Daniel. I'm sure she's in her room."

I text Daniel: *Zoe's not on the app. She there?* I know this will annoy him. It was a running complaint during our three-month stint in couples' counseling. My micromanaging of his parenting. But I can't help it.

Three dots dance across my screen, tantalizing, torturing me with the promise of a response.

Finally: *She's out with a friend.*

"He says she's out with a friend. Which friend?" Zoe has never been the most social kid. When she was at the lower school at Washington Prep, her closest friend was a quiet, sweet-natured girl named Agneta, whose parents worked for the Danish embassy. The family moved back to Denmark right before high school, leaving Zoe without a best friend. Freshman year was lonely for her. She was friendly with Hyun and Ira, who were also in orchestra. But halfway through the past school year, Zoe abruptly dropped violin, and this year, she's been almost antisocial. If she is hanging out with friends, she doesn't share that info with me. Every suggestion I make—to invite Hyun or Ira over, or to reach out to one of the nicer girls in one of her classes—is met with derision. "And if she is with a friend, her Find Me app should be on. That's the rule."

Shelby nods. She's been my sounding board this past year when I have struggled with Zoe.

"Maybe I should just call her."

I start to respond to Daniel. *What friend?* But then I stop as one word appears on my phone from him, as if he can read my mind.

Chill.

Shelby straightens up and plasters a fake smile on her face. I turn to see Prentiss Crosby weaving her way through the crowd, holding a wineglass aloft. I'm not surprised, exactly. Her daughter, Olivia, and Shelby's daughter, Kinsey, are inseparable. And there is no way on God's green earth those two girls would miss Beach Week. Every high school party that has taken place in the past four years—whether a formal at a country club or a rager at someone's house when their parents were away—was practice for the big game: Beach Week. Here, recent grads' social standing is measured not just by which parties they're invited to but whose house they're bunking at, and how big said house is and how close to the ocean.

"Did you tell her we were here?" I whisper.

"I had to. You know she signed the lease on the house Kinsey is staying in."

"I just don't feel like comparing white picket fences right now."

"Me, either." Shelby nods. She knows what I mean: those women who immediately trot out their accomplishments. Kids at swim regionals! Vacation to St. Barts! Running the Boston Marathon for the second time! *How about you?*

Shelby throws her arms open wide, and Prentiss lets out a little whoop as she hugs her, sloshing wine onto me.

"So glad I found you guys. I was getting worried." Prentiss takes a seat between us, but not before kissing the air near both my cheeks. She is the ultimate praying mantis, my name for the sticklike and identically dressed blond women who dominate the

Washington Prep parent scene. This time of year, it's turquoise and pink Lilly Pulitzer. They show up in droves at restaurants in Spring Valley to drink heavily, gossip, and drop humblebrags like napalm. *"Poor Emma, she was all set to go to Stanford, but then she was recruited to Brown's field hockey team. She is so stressed out. I told her, 'I can't make this decision for you, honey.'"*

"This is my first Beach Week. So fun!" Prentiss claps her hands. "Is this what parents do? Hang out nearby and drink?"

"In our day, we would have died if parents showed up at Beach Week. Right, Shel?" I ask.

"Oh, for sure. But also, like, my parents did not care. And we care. That's why we're here."

"But we're not really here." Prentiss tips her wineglass at Shelby for emphasis. "I'm staying at the new Marriott Ocean Suites in Bethany. It's divine. I have it all to myself, a fabulous view of the ocean, and best of all, I can lie in bed and watch Bravo all day! I mean, it's not cheap. Even with points, it's like twelve hundred a night. Where are you all staying?"

"We're staying at my parents' place," Shelby says. It's her place now, and I'm guessing she's calling it her parents' to play down the fact that she did not invite Prentiss to stay.

"Oh." Prentiss pulls her lips into a round little pout. "I see."

"I think Olivia and Kinsey are headed up to Parker Mallon's house," Shelby says brightly. She's trying to change the topic, and I watch Prentiss to see if she falls for it.

"Oh yeah?" Prentiss's eyes widen. In a former life, she was a top-notch litigator for one of D.C.'s most prestigious firms. She renews her law license each year, she once told me, to keep her "toes in the pond." But the only signs of lawyering I see her do are interrogating other parents. "Did you hear? Parker had his offer to Rice rescinded because he made an off-color joke on TikTok. Isn't that awful?"

"Depends." I shrug. "What was the joke?"

"Oh, I don't remember," Prentiss says, scrunching up her

nose. "The point is that it was a joke. You can't even make a joke these days."

I take a big swig of my drink and roll my eyes at Shelby.

"I agree," Shelby says. "Liza gets real upset when I kid her how she controls the Wash Prep media. You know, 'cause she's Jewish and all."

The sight of Prentiss's horrified face almost causes me to spit out my drink. "Shelby, you're terrible," I say. "Tell Prentiss you're kidding."

Shelby wiggles her eyebrows. "I'm kidding, Prentiss."

Prentiss lets out a trill laugh. "Oh, thank god! I was like, *Oh no she didn't!*"

Shelby points her near-empty glass at me. "But I got you to smile, didn't I?" It comes out *dinn-eye*. When Shelby drinks, her ancestral North Carolina accent erupts like a natural hot spring bubbling to the surface.

"You did." I stand up. "And to reward you, I'm plying you with more alcohol."

When I come back a few minutes later bearing drinks, I can tell the mood has shifted. Prentiss has her frowny face on, and as soon as I sit down, she gives my arm a squeeze.

"You poor thing," Prentiss says. "I can't believe Daniel lives above a tattoo parlor in Adams Morgan."

I shoot Shelby a look. She gives me a *what could I do?* shrug.

"He's having a midlife crisis," I say in an offhand manner, but it's not really true. He's always been this way. Senior year of college, we were having breakfast together at Tom's Diner when he referenced *Reality Bites*. "Liza, this is all we need—a couple of smokes, a cup of coffee, and a little bit of conversation." At the time, it seemed so sexy, the way he didn't worry about anything. And for a while, we didn't need to. But life got harder—we had Zoe, and my father died—and Daniel's effortless approach to life began to look like not making an effort at all.

Coffee and conversation will only take you so far.

"Midlife crisis?" Shelby guffaws. "A really fun one."

"Well, no wonder you're worried," Prentiss interjects. "Zoe could be roaming Adams Morgan as we speak."

Shelby snorts. "She's not roaming anywhere. If Daniel says she's with a friend, that's where she is." Shelby plucks the phone from my hand and places it on the table facedown. "You need to let go."

"Zoe wants to move in with Daniel," I blurt out. It is the first time I've said it out loud. But Shelby doesn't look surprised.

"Oh no." Prentiss makes a sad face. "That's hard."

"We agreed she could do a trial run this summer." I look down at my glass, embarrassed that I've just admitted this to Prentiss. More than anything in the world, I want to be close to my daughter. My own mother had left by the time I'd hit high school, and I promised myself I'd be a great mom to Zoe once she was a teenager. It's been brutal to learn that I don't really know how to do that. Prentiss is the last person I want to reveal any weakness to, but the alcohol has loosened the latches in my brain. My thoughts are flowing out of my mouth before I can stop them.

"Well, I say, if she wants to live with Daniel for the summer, let her." Shelby slaps her hand on the table. "You're off the hook, Liza. It'll be great for you. You can enjoy life. And frankly, it's about time Daniel stepped up."

"You might have a point." I know she's trying to put a positive spin on things. But I can't find the positive in my daughter not wanting to be around me.

"Trust me—one summer with him and she'll be begging to move back in with you in the fall. You think he's going to re-member to buy her oat milk? Heck, I don't think she'll even last the summer."

"Shelby's right. It could be a blessing in disguise," Prentiss says.

"Exactly." Shelby's enthusiasm, fueled by drink, seems almost manic. "You can use the summer to focus on you, Liza. Maybe a personal shopper at Nordstrom? A new haircut?" Shelby is ticking off her fingers all the ways in which I can be improved. "'Cause FYI—that side part is not working. The Zoomers are right about that. Side part's gots to go."

"Hey." I touch my hair, knowing that she is right. It's been years since I spent time, or money, on myself.

"This will be the summer of Liza. The new Liza."

Maybe that is what I need. All I've been doing this past year is worrying about Zoe. Her grades, her moods, her silences, her anger. Walking on eggshells to avoid triggering an outburst. Trying to cozy up to her to show I'm her friend, not just her mom. And then coming down hard when she pushes back against my rules. Or fails French, like she did this spring.

"Summer of Liza, huh?" I ask. I recently found a photo of myself in my early twenties, taken at a crime scene when I was a police reporter. The photographer at the paper had taken it. In it, I'm scribbling into my notebook, interviewing witnesses behind yellow crime scene tape. I used to be so brave. Is there any of that brave girl left in me? Maybe this is the summer I find out.

"Now, enough of the pity party!" Shelby shouts. "This is supposed to be a fun night. No more talking about kids. And you"—she points to me—"are officially off the mommy clock. And we're going to have fun even if it kills you."

We raise our half-empty glasses.

"Let's get crunk!" Prentiss shouts.

"I don't think people are saying that anymore," I say.

"I love this song!" Shelby begins belting out the chorus of a Jane's Addiction song.

Prentiss sighs. "I miss the nineties."

"Don't we all, girl," Shelby clucks. "Don't we all."

Soon we're in the thick of the crowd, losing ourselves in the music. Most of the other dancers are in their thirties and forties. We're all here, hoping to temporarily loosen ourselves from the grip of adult responsibility. I let the music and alcohol transport me away from the headaches and heartaches of marriage, financial woes, and kids, and back in time to the nineties, when things were simple and my life lay ahead of me.

I open my heart to the possibilities of what lies ahead. That the best might really be yet to come.

This weekend will be:

Salty, humid nights.

Cold wine in the afternoon.

Walking on an empty beach at sunrise.

Laughing so hard with Shelby that my sides ache and I pee a little.

Prentiss leans in close, her breath hot and boozy. "That guy is totally checking you out."

I look around the crowded bar and find him in the darkness, his face barely visible. We make eye contact, and he gives me the tiniest nod with his chin. My face gets hot, and I turn away, seeking refuge in the dancing crowd. He's younger than I am and too hot for me. But I'm smiling now. This is a good night.

Shelby comes toward me, her hand outstretched. I reach to take it, to spin her into the middle of the dancing throng, but then I see it. She's not reaching out to me; she's trying to pass me a phone.

My phone.

"It's the police," Shelby says once she is close enough for me to hear. "They have Zoe."

CHAPTER 4

LIZA

Shelby's already started the car, and I'm climbing into the front seat when Prentiss runs out of the Corkboard. "Do you need me to come?"

"You don't have to come," I say. It's bad enough that she knows this at all, which means every Wash Prep mother will know by morning.

"Are you kidding?" She climbs in the back, her face shiny with excitement. "I'm here for you, Liza."

Shelby rolls her eyes. But there's no ditching Prentiss, and there's no time to argue. Shelby pulls the SUV out onto the road super slowly, the way you do when you're a bit tipsy, and it occurs to me that she really shouldn't be driving at all. Especially since we're heading to meet the police. But I need her to. I have to call Daniel. I take out my phone and dial, but it goes straight to voice mail. I hang up and stare out the window. We head south on Route 1 toward Fenwick Island. The road grows darker as we leave the lights and crowds of Dewey behind.

The Dewey Lighthouse. What is Zoe doing there?

This is Sergeant Harris from the Dewey Beach police. We have your daughter.

"I just don't get it," Prentiss says from the back seat. "What is Zoe doing in Dewey?"

"No idea." I hope the terseness in my voice shuts her up.

My emotions bounce around like a pinball—fear for my daughter's safety, anger at her recklessness, fury at Daniel. I fume as I dial Daniel's number again. Straight to voice mail, again.

"I could kill him."

"No answer?" Shelby asks.

"It was bad enough when we were married and I couldn't reach him, but I told him, when Zoe is with you, you have to answer your phone."

"Breathe, Liza. You're going to hyperventilate."

I let out a long breath that makes my chest ache. On some level, I've been expecting this call all year. Even going so far as to play it out in my mind. Catastrophizing. That's what my therapist called it. Daniel hated that about me, that I could jump to the worst conclusion in a matter of minutes. Zoe a few minutes late from school meant she could be kidnapped. A late-night fever might mean meningitis.

At a stoplight, Shelby squeezes my arm. "She'll be fine. Remember the kind of trouble we used to get into? The Columbia golf course?"

I smile despite myself. Our senior year, Shelby, Whitney, and I sneaked onto the private course and took a golf cart for a joyride before crashing it in a drainage ditch. Shelby's father, who was on the club board, wrote a big check and made the whole thing go away. I dutifully told my father about it, and I remember him telling me sternly, *I hope you realize you're not Shelby Covington. No one is going to bail you out in life.*

I try Daniel again, and this time, I don't hang up. "What is Zoe even doing in Dewey?" I say after the beep. "You're supposed to be watching her. You need to call me as soon as you get this." I hang up and groan. "He makes me so angry. He had one job, *one job* this weekend. To watch his daughter. Is that so hard? I leave town, I'm gone for what, less than twenty-four hours?"

"Okay, calm down," Shelby says. "Right now, let's just focus on Zoe. We'll deal with Daniel later."

We pass the sign that says *Dewey Lighthouse* and turn into a small parking lot. I hadn't been here since I was a child and visited with my father.

"How the heck did she end up all the way down here?" Prentiss asks. "We're halfway to Fenwick Island."

No one answers her. We're all thinking the same thing. No houses nearby, no restaurants or stores. Shelby heads across the vast empty parking lot to a cluster of cars and blinking lights.

"Shit. There's an ambulance." My throat tightens. "Why is there an ambulance?"

"Don't panic. Remember, if she were hurt, she'd be at the hospital and someone would have called you from there."

I glance at Shelby. I want to believe her. Instead, I'm thinking of that night twenty-eight years ago. There was an ambulance then. And it wasn't all right, was it? How can she not be thinking the same thing?

As soon as Shelby puts the car in park, I jump out and run toward the commotion. Momentarily confused by the lights, I look around wildly, trying to make sense of the scene. And then I see her, sitting in the back of an ambulance, her legs dangling off the edge the way they did when she was little and couldn't reach the floor.

"Honey, baby."

She looks up, red-eyed, vulnerable. She lets me wrap her in a real hug, not the kind she's been giving me lately where she backs into my arms and allows herself to be hugged, but the real thing.

"Mommy." It almost cracks my heart wide open. She's taken to calling me Elizabeth when she addresses me these days. As in, *All right, Elizabeth. Whatever you want, Elizabeth.* Zoe buries her face in my neck, and I inhale the sweet scent of her hair.

"Sweetie." I don't ask why she is here or what happened.

No questions for now.

There will be plenty of time for questions.

A beefy EMT with strawberry-blond hair and a sad attempt at a soul patch tells me he must take Zoe's blood pressure.

"Mommy, I want to go home." Her voice is slightly slurred, and that's when I realize she's not acting quite normal.

"Zoe, have you been drinking?"

She shakes her head.

"Is she all right?" I ask the EMT.

"She's physically fine," the guy says, all the while staring at the reader in his hand. "All her vitals are normal. But she was agitated, so we gave her a mild sedative to calm her down."

"And how long will that last?"

"About six to ten hours."

I jump as he rips the Velcro cuff off Zoe's arm. My nerves are shot.

"We're done here," he says. "She's good to go."

My heart feels so full it might burst. My girl is all right. I'm going to kill her tomorrow, but tonight she is all right, and that's all that matters.

For the first time since Shelby handed me my phone in the bar, I let myself fully exhale. I take in the surroundings. The empty parking lot, the small keeper's cottage that's seen better days, the white lighthouse. We're a good ten-minute drive from downtown Dewey, from the parties and the bars. How the hell did she even get here? Then I see it. A Subaru with a Washington Preparatory School sticker on the back.

"Zoe, is that my car?" She doesn't answer. The car is old, a stick shift. Zoe can't drive an automatic, much less a stick.

"Do you know how my daughter ended up here?"

"No clue, ma'am." The EMT gestures toward the police. "You really should ask them."

"Can we go, Mommy?"

"I'm not sure." I wipe a string of hair from her face. My sweet, drugged-up little baby. Who may have stolen my car. "Did you drive my car here, Zoe?"

"I'm sorry." She buries her head in my shoulder. "Don't hate me."

"Shh, shh. Of course I don't hate you."

A middle-aged man in a blue windbreaker walks briskly toward me. He stops a few feet away. From here, I can see he is about my age, but he has bags under his deep-set eyes, and his sloping shoulders lend him a defeated air. "Detective Gaffney. Are you the mother?"

The mother. I sit Zoe upright and straighten up, proud. I'm the mother, and a mama bear at the moment, ready to do battle. "Yes, I'm Zoe's mother. Elizabeth Gold."

He frowns. "Your daughter said her last name was Takada."

"That's right. That's her father's last name."

An almost imperceptible twitch of his lip. I can't be the first woman he's ever met who kept her maiden name.

"I'm with the Delaware State Police," he says. "Do you mind if we have a word in private? Why don't we chat over here for a moment." He takes a step back, not waiting for my response. A crackle of panic runs through me. It was someone from the local police who telephoned me earlier. Why are the state police involved? Why a detective? I know from my years as a cops reporter that the state police get called in for serious crimes. Not teenagers who borrow their mothers' cars.

Zoe stares at me imploringly. I don't want to leave her alone. I see Shelby standing by her car and wave at her. She jogs over in her short, white miniskirt and low-cut top. The EMT's jaw just about drops to the asphalt.

"What's up, hon?" She immediately takes Zoe's hand in her own.

"Can you take Zoe back to the car while I talk to this detective?"

"I surely can." She winks at the EMT, who turns beet red.

I find the detective where he is waiting a few feet away.

"How did my daughter get here?"

"We were hoping you might tell us. Is that your car?" He gestures to the Subaru.

"It is, but Zoe doesn't even know how to drive. She just turned sixteen. She's supposed to be at home with her dad."

"We think maybe her friend did the driving."

"Her friend? What friend?" Then I remember Daniel's text. *She's out with a friend.*

"Mind coming with me?"

He turns on a heavy-duty flashlight and starts walking toward the beach. When he passes through the small crowd of people near the ambulance, they step aside for us.

"What exactly is going on?" I ask the back of his head, hustling to keep up, following the bouncing beam of light as the cement gives way to sand. He does not answer. I can hear the roar of the ocean as we walk down to the water, and the sour, salty smell hits me, making my guts churn. When I take my first step in the soft sand, my ankle turns, but I right myself quickly. As my eyes adjust, I make out a small gathering of people.

The detective stops short and puts his arm out the way a parent might in a car to protect her child from flying through the windshield. "Hold on," he says. Beyond him, a crouching photographer takes a photo—of what I can't see—a flash illuminating the beach like lightning.

"Detective, what is going on?"

He turns to face me. "Your daughter found a body on the beach. She called 9-1-1."

"What are you talking about? Whose body?"

"I'm going to ask you to try to identify a body. Can you do that for me?"

I'm trying to imagine why he thinks that I might be able to. Maybe it's a Washington Prep student, and he knows I work there. Ridiculous. He doesn't know me at all.

"All right. I'll try."

He nods, and I gird myself to look into a dead face. When I was a reporter, dead bodies were a regular part of the job. But that was a long time ago, when I was a different person. Not just younger but braver.

Motherhood has made me fragile. My whole body begins to shake, as under the light of the full moon, I come face-to-face with a girl, her wet hair splayed out like a mermaid's.

I gasp. I do recognize her.

"Oh god." I pause. "Her name is Emery Blake. She just graduated from the school where I work."

"And she's friends with your daughter?"

"No. They're in different grades. I don't think they even know each other." I don't add that my daughter is a socially awkward tenth grader, while Emery was one of the prettiest seniors at the school.

"Don't even know each other, huh?" His eyebrows shoot up. "When we got here, your daughter was hysterical, screaming that her best friend was dead."

CHAPTER 5

1994

Lies did not come easily to Nikki.

Not with her parents, at least, and certainly not the way they did to her classmates at Washington Prep. Her new classmates were so different from the kids she grew up with on Long Island. There was the obvious difference—she was the only Puerto Rican at Wash Prep, whereas back in Brentwood, it had felt like half the school was Puerto Rican. And there was the money thing—the way it never seemed to factor into any of the decisions the Wash Prep students made. Not about clothes, or eating out, or vacations or colleges.

But those were not surprises to her. She had been prepared to be one of only a handful of Hispanics at Wash Prep. (There were four, including her.) And it wasn't exactly a shock that the private school kids would be wealthier.

But what had taken Nikki aback was the disrespect the private school kids had for their parents. Not just normal attitude but a deep disdain. Like they really hated their parents.

Before her family moved to the D.C. area, Nikki had to do a report on her heroes for class. Nikki struggled between choosing her dad, who had just made detective at the Suffolk County Police Department, and her mom, who put herself through SUNY Stony Brook while working full-time. At least half of the kids in her school did the same—their moms and dads were their heroes. But at Wash Prep, kids acted like they were ashamed of their parents, which was crazy. Their parents were doctors and lawyers and ambassadors and even senators, but her friends said terrible things about them. And had no problem lying to them.

"Of course Shelby's parents will be there." Nikki didn't turn around to face her mother when delivering this whopper but directed it at the small duffel bag on the bed. Maybe lying without facing the person you were lying to was slightly less bad, like the idea of venial sin she had learned about in Catholic education. Venial sins were still sins, just not the kind you would burn in hell for.

"Maybe I should call them?" her mother asked. "Am I supposed to call? I feel like I should call."

"Don't call, Ma. Nobody does that." She felt a twinge of guilt. She knew her mother was self-conscious around the other private school parents, never sure if she was doing or saying the right thing, and Nikki was playing into those insecurities.

But she had to. She couldn't even imagine the conversation between her mom and Shelby's mom.

Oh sure, I'm letting my daughter and her friends stay at our beach house for a week, unsupervised, yes. There will be drinking and no doubt sex. These kids have to grow up sometime.

That was not her parents' perspective on things. Her parents had married right after high school. Her mother had never been with anyone but her dad.

"I just feel funny, sending you off like this."

"Well, don't. Everyone does it this way."

Nikki busied herself rearranging the clothes in the bag marked *Washington Prep Track & Field*. It was the team gift that year. Just big enough for a few days' worth of clothes. The string bikini she had bought surreptitiously with babysitting money did not take up much room, and she had it crumpled up inside a towel, just in case her mother should peek inside. Laid across the top was the high-necked one-piece she had no plans to wear.

"Hold on, let me get something." Her mom scurried out of the small room.

Never in a million years would they approve of her going to Beach Week. Hell, they would never even be able to wrap their heads around the concept. Her parents considered unsupervised teenagers a cohort to be pitied, because their parents obviously didn't care about them. As for drugs, her mother thought that smoking pot made you a druggie, that one hit could condemn you to the life of a loser.

She didn't get that you could smoke pot on the weekend and still play Division I lacrosse during the week. That the coke that these kids snorted actually helped them ace their AP courses and get into Yale.

Not that Nikki wanted to do drugs. It wasn't about that.

But she wanted to be like them, even if just for a week.

Wanted to just once taste entitlement. That sense that, even if you messed up—got stoned, drunk, crashed the car, hooked up with some random guy—there would be no permanent consequences.

Nikki wanted to wear that tiny bikini and drink—not just nurse a beer at a party, aware that she would have to navigate her way back from the mansions of northwest D.C. to her redbrick one-story house in Wheaton, and so had to keep her wits about her—but to get raging drunk, like Shelby or Whitney did, confident they could pass out on a couch, that their parents were out of town, and that no one would ever find out.

What was that freedom like?

To be free of the sense that you were a visitor in a world not your own and that your privileges could be revoked at any time? To be so sure that you belonged that you wore ripped jeans to chapel, like Whitney did? If Nikki wore ripped jeans, people would just think she was poor. Which she wasn't. But to these people, a middle-class Puerto Rican girl was the definition of poor.

Archer was different. He had it all, didn't seem the slightest bit uncomfortable being only one of a handful of Black kids at Washington Prep. Of course, his dad was Congressman Samuel Benoit, the first Black congressman from Louisiana since Reconstruction. He lived in a huge house on the Gold Coast, a section of northwest D.C. lined with Tudor mansions and historically home to the city's wealthiest and most prominent African Americans. Was that it? Did money trump race? Was there a point at which you were so rich that nothing else mattered? It didn't hurt that he was the captain of the basketball team and was going to Duke next year.

And that smile, the way it could totally disarm you.

Every time she tried to talk to him, she clammed up. The closest she ever came was when Liza, who knew about her crush and was also the yearbook editor, assigned her to get a quote from him for the school yearbook. But when she tracked Archer down, she became sweaty and nervous. And when he asked her what she was up to that weekend, all she could think of to say was: *studying.* Archer laughed. She'd made a fool of herself.

But Archer would be at Beach Week. Not at Shelby's beach house. She was pretty sure the boys were staying at their own house somewhere nearby, but still. There would be a lot of opportunities to see him.

"Here, bring these." Her mother was back, holding a blue-and-white cookie tin and beaming like her little brother, Cobo, did when he solved some complicated math problem. She was the unofficial baker and party planner where she worked in Congress, in the office of the resident commissioner of Puerto Rico.

She was one of the many women—Black, brown, and white—who made Washington, D.C. hum. Nikki saw them as they walked to the Metro in droves in the morning in their sensible outfits, white comfortable sneakers on their feet, while their low-heeled pumps stayed in their bags, and then up and down those crazy, height-defying Metro escalators that were always out of order.

They were the backbone of the United States government.

Nikki often thought of her mother, and these women, when she heard her Wash Prep classmates rail against lazy government workers. Did they have any idea what they were talking about, or were they just parroting their rich parents?

In her mother's world, a tin of chocolate crinkle cookies at Christmas and a sheet cake on your birthday was currency. Even after four years, she had no clue what these private school people were like. They belonged to a different species. Take Shelby's mom, a former Southern beauty queen who had never had a real job. Just last week, Nikki and Liza were at the Smythes' house, and Shelby's mom didn't even know her stove had a broiler.

"What the heck is a broiler even for?" she asked the maid.

Same at Whitney's house. They had a maid, a cook, and a gardener.

It was ironic that these Washington Prep moms put out a cookbook at the end of the year for charity. All the students were supposed to ask their mothers—not fathers, never fathers—to contribute family recipes. Nikki didn't tell her mom, but she found out about the project, anyway, and sent in a recipe for pollo guisado. Everyone oohed and aahed over it like it was the most delicious thing they'd ever tasted. *So exotic! So delightful!* When it was just a basic chicken stew.

Nikki cringed at the memory.

It was so subtle, but it was still there. That was the thing.

They were all nice to your face. It was almost worse than if they had said outright racist things. If their prejudice was so obvious everyone could read it like a neon sign. Then she could fight back and no one would tell her she was being oversensitive. The few friends Nikki had made from the neighborhood in Wheaton would ask her if the Wash Prep kids were stuck up, if they called her names, like in those teen movies. Nikki had to explain that no, it was worse, they were *nice.* Too nice.

Because they weren't threatened in the slightest.

They knew. They knew that even if she did go to Wash Prep

and made it to a good college—she had a scholarship to NYU in the fall—she was never going to take anything away from them.

Not their preppy boyfriends who played lacrosse or rowed crew. Not their huge houses in Spring Valley or their vacation homes in Vail and Nantucket. Not their anything. So they could afford to be nice. The way you were nice to a homeless person. That's how insignificant their kindness made her feel.

Not everyone, of course. Not Liza.

She was probably the only person Nikki would stay in touch with after high school. And maybe, hopefully, Archer.

"Liza's here!" her mother called from the other room. "I see her car."

The gulf was widening between herself and her mother, and she hated it. A tiny part of her wanted to go down to Liza and say screw this whole thing. It wasn't too late. She could stay home and sneak Cobo in to see *The Crow*. Then get black-and-white shakes at the Woodside Deli.

But then the front doorbell rang. She heard shuffling and Liza's chipper voice. "Hey, Mrs. Montes."

"Liza, sweetie. Come in!"

"No!" Nikki shouted and ran into the hallway, clutching the duffel bag. She ignored the hurt look on her mother's face and gave her a kiss. "We gotta go, Ma. Don't want to hit the bridge traffic."

She was halfway down the walkway when her mother called her back. "Nicole! You forgot!"

Nikki ran back up and grabbed the tin her mother was holding, knowing she would rather chuck the whole tin in the garbage than subject her mother's homemade cookies to the examination of her peers. "Remember to say please and thank you to Mr. and Mrs. Covington."

"I know, Ma."

"Remember, you're a guest in someone's house."

"I know."

"Call me at ten o'clock every night. So I know you're safe."

"I will." Her bag on her shoulder, cookie tin in hand, Nikki bounded down the path toward Liza, who was already in the driver's seat.

"Remember, ten o'clock," her mom called. "I love you."

"Love you, too."

When Nikki got in the car, Liza handed her a pair of sunglasses. "I'm Thelma, you're Louise."

"Okay, but let's not, like, die."

Liza laughed. "Yeah, let's skip that part. I'm actually shocked your parents let you come. I mean, since there won't be any grown-ups."

"Well, they don't exactly know."

"Really?" Liza's eyes widened. "So naughty. I love it. Are those your mom's cookies? Gimme one, will ya?" She peeled away from the curb and headed toward the Beltway.

Nikki passed Liza a cookie and took one for herself, taking comfort in the familiar sweet taste. As they pulled out of the quiet neighborhood and onto busy Georgia Avenue, Nikki tried to shake the residual sense of guilt hovering over her, like the one cloud threatening to ruin a picnic. It was just one lie, one little lie. And yes, maybe within that one lie were a thousand other lies nestled like Russian nesting dolls.

But she was eighteen now. She had played by all the rules. She had graduated and was headed to college in the fall.

How much harm could come from one little lie?

CHAPTER 6

LIZA

"Do you have Miss Blake's parents' contact information?" Detective Gaffney asked.

"No." I shake my head, still reeling from what he'd just said about Zoe. I may not know every detail about my daughter's life, but I'd know if she was best friends with this senior. Wouldn't I?

"No?" He looks up from the pad he's been scribbling in. "You don't know the parents of your daughter's best friend?"

"I didn't realize they were so close." The judgment stings, like a slap across the face. Later on, he'll tell others, *The mother didn't even know who her daughter's friends were.* I glance back at the lights in the parking lot, and in that split second, my mind scrambles to pull whatever information I have about Emery Blake. It's not much. She showed up this fall for her senior year, an oddity at a school where most students had been attending since they were little. What else did I know? She lived in Virginia, as about a quarter of the student body did. Another quarter lived in Maryland, and about half the kids at the school were from D.C. Her mother had passed recently.

I'd caught a glimpse of her father once, at school. The two of them were coming out of the main administration building together. She clearly inherited his height from him, but while Emery was fit, he was burly, sodden. He slumped, it seemed to me, not just from the extra weight but a palpable sense of sadness. His downward-cast eyes and stooped shoulders were a stark contrast to how Emery carried herself—shoulders back, head held high. Her father didn't even look up when he almost ran into another student outside the building. I chalked it up to grief over his wife's death the year before. Her death explained a certain aloofness about Emery, too, which seemed unusual for a girl her age.

I never once saw her with Zoe.

And Zoe never mentioned her to me.

But she had told this police officer they were friends.

Best friends.

It hurts way more than I want it to. My mom left us right before high school, and I always imagined that when Zoe got to this age, we would be so close. She would tell me everything, and I'd be her confidante. I was not going to repeat my mother's mistakes and be shut out from my daughter's life.

"And what school did you say they attended?" the detective asks.

"Washington Preparatory School. Most people just call it Washington Prep. It's a private school in D.C." I hate the way that sounds, aware that one year's tuition might equal his salary. *But we get a large discount,* I want to tell him. *I work there.* "What happened to her? Did she drown?" My voice cracks on that last word, my body hot and my head woozy. Twenty-eight years ago, the police came to a beach just up the road. Twenty-eight years ago, Shelby, Archer, and I—and dozens of other kids—ran up and down the beach, calling, *Nikki! Nikki!*

And now that same vast ocean has stolen another young girl's life.

"We don't know the exact cause of death, but it looks like she drowned. Pretty strong riptide tonight."

"She went swimming alone at night?"

"Looks that way, although we can't be sure. We tried to ask your daughter some questions, but she has not been cooperative."

I bristle. "She found a dead body, Detective."

"Nonetheless, we're going to need to get a statement from her."

"We're staying nearby, at the Stockley Creek Country Club." I note the corner of his mouth turn up slightly. We're *those* people, people who have second homes in private communities. "We can come to the police station first thing tomorrow morning."

He *tsk-tsks*. "Aww, I'm afraid that won't work for us, ma'am. We're going to need to get some kind of statement tonight."

The tears build behind my eyes. It's all too much. A young woman dead on the beach. Zoe out here when she was supposed to be with Daniel. The police. The stolen car. The alcohol is only making things worse. I want to take Zoe home and put her to bed, not expose her to a midnight grilling at a police station. "Look, Detective, my daughter was extremely upset. She was given a strong sedative and is barely coherent. Can't this wait until morning?"

"Ma'am, I have a dead girl on a beach, and I have a job to do." He offers a wry smile. "Don't worry. It won't take long—you and your daughter will be back at the country club before you know it."

Defeated, I trudge silently back up the beach with Gaffney at my heels and only the moon to light the way. Once we have crossed the parking lot to Shelby's gleaming SUV, Prentiss pops out of the back and rushes up to us.

"Hey. Zoe's in the back. She's passed out." Her eyes dart between the detective and me. I peer past Prentiss and get a peek of Zoe spread out on the back seat, covered by an old quilt that Shelby uses as a beach blanket. She looks so peaceful.

Detective Gaffney clears his throat and looks at me expectantly. "Ma'am, do you want to wake her up, or do you want me to do it?"

"I don't . . . I mean . . . ," I stutter, unsure of what to say. "Do we have to?"

"What's this?" Prentiss asks. I grit my teeth, willing her to go away.

"The police want a statement from Zoe," I tell her. "About what she saw tonight."

"Of course." Prentiss nods as if she knows what I'm referring to. Which she can't. "We can bring her by the police station for a full statement tomorrow morning. Right, Liza?"

I stare at Prentiss, unsure of what she is doing. "Of course," I say. "First thing, Monday morning."

"We'd really prefer to do this tonight," Detective Gaffney says, no longer able, or willing, to hide his irritation.

"I'm sorry, Detective? I didn't catch your name." Prentiss's voice manages to be both sweet and steely at the same time.

"Gaffney."

"Nice to meet you, Detective Gaffney. I'm Prentiss Crosby. I'll be representing the Takada family." She peers into her small white handbag and plucks out a card, which she proffers to him. "Zoe's not under arrest, is she?"

Gaffney coughs. "No. Of course not."

"Terrific. Then we'll be bringing her in tomorrow morning," Prentiss says brightly, with the enthusiasm of a young mom arranging a playdate. "How does nine o'clock sound?" She does not wait for an answer but turns and gently pushes me toward the back seat. "We should get Zoe home."

I allow myself to be guided into the car, turning back to see a flummoxed Detective Gaffney, mouth open, staring at the card in his hand. I empathize. I am not quite sure what just happened, either.

Once we've pulled out of the parking lot onto the road, Prentiss twists around in the front seat to face me. Zoe is fast asleep in my lap, and I stroke her hair as the car hums along the empty road back toward Dewey.

"Is it true a girl drowned? That's what one of the EMTs said." She doesn't wait for me to answer. "Young. That's what he said.

Maybe eighteen? Do you think she was a student down here from D.C.? Oh my god, I wonder if Olivia knows her."

"Drowned?" Shelby says in a high-pitched voice. "Who was it? Did they tell you, Liza? Not someone from Wash Prep."

"Actually, it was a Wash Prep grad." I take a deep breath. There's no point in not telling them. Everyone will know soon enough. "Do you two know Emery Blake?"

Prentiss sucks in her breath loudly. "I know her. She was new this year, right? Real tall? Long hair?"

"That's her." My insides churn. A wave of vertigo hits me, and I close my eyes and grip Zoe's shoulder to steady myself until it passes. Images of Emery's still face, her splayed hair, fill my head.

"How horrible," Shelby says. "That poor girl. She was so darn pretty. Do they know what happened?"

"I guess she went swimming." My voice is weak, and it takes effort to speak. "There was a riptide."

My words hang in the car. I don't say, *Just like Nikki.* Shelby stares straight ahead at the road. Is she concentrating hard because she's tipsy and it's late? Or is she thinking about Nikki? I don't see how she can't be. The sameness of the two deaths is inescapable. But I don't mention Nikki's name. I'm not sure why, but those are the rules. We don't talk about that night.

But I'm experiencing my friend's death all over again tonight.

"What's Zoe got to do with all this?" Prentiss asks. "She wasn't friends with Emery Blake."

I don't say anything.

"Look, Liza," she says, straining around the headrest to fix me with an intense stare. "I need to know everything if I'm going to protect Zoe in there tomorrow."

"You don't have to come. I can handle it."

"Ha." The laugh comes out as a sharp bark, like the kind uttered by a teeny white dog. "No offense, sweetie, but you have got to have a lawyer with you when you go in tomorrow."

"Zoe didn't do anything wrong."

She frowns. "You actually don't know that. And the last thing you want is for some hick beach cop to get Zoe in his sights. Anyway, never talk to the police without a lawyer. Don't you watch *Law & Order*?"

"You're probably right."

"I am. So what—did Zoe know Emery?"

I ignore the skepticism in Prentiss's voice. "Yes. According to the police, she told them Emery was her best friend."

Prentiss sucks in her cheeks, turning her mouth into an almost comical O shape. "Best friends? They weren't best friends, were they?" She seems almost offended.

"I don't know," I say in a hoarse whisper and point to Zoe.

"Did Daniel call you back yet?" Shelby asks, and I'm grateful for the intervention.

I take out my phone and peek at it. "Not yet. I'm going to kill him."

"Well, it is the middle of the night," she says.

"Please, don't make excuses for him. That means he went to bed without Zoe having come home." My voice rises with rage. "He didn't even notice she wasn't there."

Shelby sighs. "True."

We pull into the parking lot of the Corkboard and wait until Prentiss has safely retrieved her car before heading back to the house. In the back seat, I stroke Zoe's hair, staring out at the darkness, thinking about fathers. Zoe's and Emery's. One who didn't notice his daughter was even missing, and one who is about to receive the worst phone call of his life, if he hasn't already, his world transformed.

A few weeks after Nikki drowned, Washington Prep held a memorial in the school's chapel. It was packed with students, and the Montes family came. I remember how Nikki's mom looked like she had aged years in just a few weeks. Bags under her eyes, the joy of life sucked right out of her. At the end of the service, Mrs. Montes lost it and started yelling about how she wanted answers.

Nikki's dad ushered his wife out of the chapel, their young son trailing behind, head down, embarrassed by his mother's display of raw emotion. Most of the Wash Prep kids were slack-jawed, embarrassed into silence by this mother's raw pain.

But I get it now. If anything happened to Zoe, I'd go insane. I'd rip my clothes off my body, and I would never stop screaming.

We pull through the entrance of the Stockley Creek Country Club, and then it's a quick drive past the ninth hole toward the bay, to Shelby's parents' house, technically her house now since they basically handed over the keys a few years ago. The route is familiar, one I have taken countless times over the past thirty years, and I look forward to curling up in the pale blue bedroom overlooking the bay that I have come to think of as my home away from home.

Shelby parks and goes to open the front door while I begin to maneuver a semiconscious Zoe from the back seat. After propping the door open, Shelby comes back, and together we walk Zoe up the gravel drive. We're almost to the front steps when Zoe's body jerks and she mumbles something.

"What'd she say?" Shelby asks.

"Who knows? After the night she's been through, plus sedatives." We walk up the three front steps and through the open door. Zoe's eyes pop open.

"It's my fault, Mommy. I should have gone with her."

Shelby and I freeze; our eyes lock. "Gone where, hon?" I ask in a gentle tone. "To the lighthouse?"

"To meet that guy. I shouldn't've let her go alone."

"Meet who, Zoe?" Shelby asks in a gentle but prodding tone. "Who did Emery go to meet?"

But Zoe just closes her eyes. And just like that, she's out.

CHAPTER 7

ZOE

My eyes open, and for a fraction of a second, I don't remember.

Then it all comes rushing back. That moment after I got out of the Uber, but before I knew. Calling Emery's name into the wind. And then finding her on the beach, in her underwear. Dead.

My chest tightens, my lungs squeezed by some unseen hand. I sit upright in bed, gasping for breath. My mouth opens wide, but no air comes in. For a split second, I'm scared that I'm dying, that I will never be able to get a full breath. Then I cough, choking a bit, and soon I'm taking shallow gulps of air.

I'm alive. I'm still here, and Emery is not. Everything around me seems to mock this fundamental truth. That stupid lamp in the shape of a dolphin. The perfect white linen curtains. The mirror trimmed in whitewashed wood.

From below, a familiar laugh drifts up. Shelby. The sounds are like shards of glass on my psyche. What the hell is she laughing about? Emery is dead. Doesn't she know that?

No one should be laughing.

No one should be happy.

I lie back down, squeezing a pillow against my body. My mind replays the night before, starting with the moment Emery showed up unannounced at my dad's. I scan my memories for the exact moment when I should have acted differently, when

I could have prevented Emery's death. Like those Choose Your Own Adventure books my mom has saved from her childhood. You see a lion. Turn to page 60 if you approach it, turn to page 40 if you run away.

If only I could turn the page back to the right moment and make a different choice. But what is that moment? When Emery came to my dad's apartment? On the Metro up to my house? When she asked to take my mom's car?

Or was it at the party, when she told me she had to go meet someone, alone.

I have to go alone. But I'll be back, I swear.

Even then, I knew it was a bad idea for her to go alone. It didn't seem right, meeting in some desolate spot, away from where anyone could see.

Don't worry, Zoe. I got this.

A soft knock on the door. I roll over, pull up the blanket, and close my eyes. The door squeaks as it opens slowly.

"Honey? Zoe, you awake?" my mom asks in a voice barely above a whisper.

If I don't answer, maybe she'll go away, so I stay perfectly still. But she doesn't. I can hear her breathing. She won't leave until she knows I'm okay, that I'm alive, so I roll over to face her.

She's holding a mug. I can hear Walnut breathing behind her.

"C'mere, buddy." I pat the bed, and he jumps up and lies down beside me, squishing his big body against mine. The weekend my dad moved out, Mom and I went to a Lucky Dog Rescue adoption event. We were going to get a puppy, but as soon as I saw Walnut, I knew he was meant to be ours. My mom said it was crazy to adopt a ten-year-old golden retriever who's blind in one eye. But now it's impossible to imagine life without him.

"Half-caf, half-decaf." Her voice sounds fake cheery, like I'm a mental patient that might go off if she talks like a normal adult to me. I sit up and take the mug. It's a peace offering. My mom doesn't think teenagers should drink coffee.

She sits on the edge of my bed and reaches out to push the hair out of my eyes, but I duck out of the way. She's always trying to touch me these days. I know it's mean, but I just don't want her fussing over me like that. At least she doesn't make a comment. For years, my hair was long and black and straight, and she would brush it in the morning while saying how jealous she was of my straight, non-frizzy hair. Then last month, I cut it. Shaved on one side, long bangs hanging over my left eye. She hates it. Never fails to make a comment, or at least a face.

But not this morning. She just has this weird smile plastered on her face.

"What? Why are you smiling?"

"Nothing, honey. I just, I wanted to see how you were doing. That's all."

Without warning, the tears come, and this time, I can't seem to push them back where they came from. Soon they are gushing, and Mom's bent over me in some awkward hug. It's so uncomfortable, I want it to end, but at the same time, I don't want her to ever leave.

Then the eruption is over, and just as quickly, I stop crying. I pull away.

"I don't understand." I sniffle. "It doesn't make any sense. What happened to her? Why was she in the water?"

"I was kind of hoping you could tell me. I mean, Zoe, when did you decide you were coming out to the beach? Why didn't you contact me?"

I groan. Here come the questions. Rat-tat-tat. Like a machine gun. When she gets this way, she's not even really listening, just poking me with her questions like you'd prod a squirrel in the road with a stick to see if it's really dead.

I don't want to talk about how I broke her stupid rules. Doesn't she get it? None of that matters now. Not with Emery dead. A horrible thought hits me—where's my backpack? I had it with me at the beach, but it's not in the room. Did my mom grab it? Has she looked inside?

"Do you know where my phone is? And my backpack?" I ask, trying to hide the panic in my voice. If she suspects something, she is bound to go looking for it.

She clears her throat, disappointed. "Your backpack's downstairs, and your phone's in the kitchen. Charging."

"Oh. Okay." If she has looked inside, now would be the time she says something.

"Is there anything you want to tell me?" she asks.

We sit in silence like that for a minute. If only it were that easy. If only I could just start talking and not stop until she understood everything. It wasn't always this weird with us. I used to tell her everything. But she's not as good at listening anymore. She gets upset and angry so easily, and talks right past me. I know if I try to tell her what's been going on, she'll just focus on the rules I've broken, or the risks I've taken. She won't see the other stuff. After a few moments, she lets out one of those sharp sighs that are meant to be heard from across the room.

"So, honey, I know this stinks, but we need to go to the police station this morning. In fact, we have to leave in about twenty minutes. Prentiss has agreed to join us, so at least there will be a lawyer there."

"What? Why?" My heart starts to beat faster as I spin around. "Why do we need a lawyer?"

She looks at me, unblinking, and for a moment, I freak out. It's as if she has X-ray vision and can see through me, see everything I've been doing the past few months. Like she used to be able to when I was a kid. She'd just *know*. That I had stolen change from her purse, walked to the CVS in Friendship Heights and bought candy.

Will she forgive me for all the sneaking and lying? I brace myself, but all she does is give me that smile—the one where the corners of her mouth move but her eyes don't.

"Why? Maybe because you stole a car and ended up at a deserted beach, where a young woman drowned."

My jaw drops. "A car? My friend died, and you're upset about a car?" I know I'm yelling, but I can't seem to stop. "You don't get it. You don't get me. All you care about is your rules and what other people think." My mom winces as if I've slapped her. Good. I want her to hurt, like I'm hurting. "My friend died. Do you even care? My friend is dead."

The tears flow fast now, and I swipe at my runny nose with the back of my hand. But when she tries to touch my shoulder, I yank away. "Don't touch me."

"I'm sorry. I shouldn't have said that about the car. I mean, we do have to talk about it . . . but you're right. You lost your friend. And I'm so sorry. I know what it's like, Zoe, to lose a friend."

I hug my knees up to my chest and nod.

"When Nikki died, I didn't have anyone to process it with—"

"Oh my god, can you not?" I glare at her from the corner of my eye. "Can this just be about Emery? Can we not talk about Nikki? It's not the same thing."

She stands. "That's fair. I just wanted you to know that I'm here for you. And that I've been through something similar."

"I know. You've told me. Can you, like, leave, so I can get dressed now?"

Once she is gone, the ball of anger in my stomach melts into a hot wave of guilt. I don't want to be this way. I'm not trying to. A sob hiccups within me. Emery would understand. She was the only person I could talk to about this stuff. The only person who didn't make me want to scream and rip my own skin off my body.

And now she is gone.

And I'm completely alone.

CHAPTER 8

LIZA

The small room at the police station is incongruously dark and cold on this sunny June morning. Not too cold for Detective Gaffney, who sits across a table from Zoe and me in long sleeves and pants, but Prentiss, Zoe, and I are all dressed for the hot, muggy weather outside.

My phone buzzes, and I give Detective Gaffney an apologetic glance before switching it to silent mode. It has been on fire since about six this morning—texts from friends, other parents, even my boss, Geoff. Especially Geoff.

His first concern, registered at 6:10 a.m., was how this was going to make Washington Prep look. *It's all over social media*, he texted me. *How can we get a handle on this?*

We meant me. I don't just edit the alumni magazine. I do pretty much all the writing for the school. And Geoff wanted me to, in his words, *get out in front of this*. That meant writing a statement we could release today. Damage control.

I suppose it is understandable, even responsible, for him to worry about how Emery's death will reflect on Washington Prep, but it still bothers me.

"Let's continue, Zoe. You said you were at your dad's apartment in D.C. when you and Emery decided to go to the beach. To join your mother."

"Right," Zoe says. "We were meeting her there."

"That so?" Detective Gaffney looks at me. I nod, then quickly lift the large travel mug with the words *But first, coffee* written on it to my lips to hide the confusion that I'm sure is written across my face. When I asked Zoe last week if she wanted to join me at Shelby's, she said she couldn't think of anything worse than being stuck in a house with me and Shelby, watching us drink wine and talk about the good ol' days. Did she change her mind? Was she really coming to stay with me? Or did she sneak off to Beach Week with Emery to party, hoping that with the way things are with Daniel and me, we'd never find out?

But I don't say anything about my doubts. On the drive over, Prentiss told Zoe to tell the truth and then took me aside and told me to keep my mouth shut unless I was asked a direct question. "Don't contradict her. Don't add context. Don't provide any extra information, got it?" Her tone held the authority of a seasoned general heading into battle. "We're cooperating, but we're not going to help them build some kind of case against Zoe."

"What kind of case could they possibly build?"

Prentiss shrugged. "Underage drinking? Who knows. Then they use that as leverage to pull her into their investigation. Trust me. Short answers. Don't volunteer anything."

Detective Gaffney clears his throat. He looks the way I feel—like he did not get much sleep, either. The bags under his eyes are a lovely shade of violet. "So you two left D.C. for the shore around what time?" he asks.

Zoe looks up as if the answers are written on the popcorn ceiling. "I don't know. After dinner?"

"E-ZPass records say you crossed the bridge around 8:00 p.m. Does that sound right?"

"Well, I mean, if that's what it says."

"And did you drive directly to Dewey Beach?"

"Yeah. We were gonna go to the house where my mom is staying, but we stopped by a party first. Just to, like, say hi." Her voice is tentative. To the detective, it might sound like she is just an insecure teen, but to my ears, it sounds like she is trying this narrative out for the first time.

I can't tell if the cop is buying this. I try to steal a glance around Zoe at Prentiss, but all I can see is a curtain of blond hair and a tan shoulder.

"And this party, would that be at Parker Mallon's house?"

"Yes."

Parker Mallon was a senior, a good friend of Brody's, and a cocaptain of the lacrosse team. He was one of the Ledge Boys who got into trouble this past school year for rating the girls like a fantasy football league. There had been quite an uproar. He was exactly the kind of kid Zoe called a "prep-school douche."

What the hell was she doing there?

"Can you tell me what happened when you got to the party?"

She widens her eyes, all innocence. "I don't know. There were a lot of people. I kind of lost track of Emery."

What did Zoe say last night in her drugged stupor? That Emery was meeting someone? And she shouldn't have let her go?

"Did lighthouses have any kind of special significance for her?" the detective asks.

"What do you mean?"

"Oh, I'm just curious how she ended up there. Why at the lighthouse?"

Zoe shrugs. "I don't know."

"Was she planning on meeting anyone?" I asked gently.

She shoots me a look that could kill. "How would I know?"

Prentiss leans forward and glares at me. I shrink back into my seat. Message received. Last night, before the call from the police, I had been so relieved that my daughter was not one of the drunken revelers out on the streets of Dewey, but I had been wrong, so wrong.

"So, Zoe, tell me, how is it that you ended up at the Dewey Lighthouse?" Gaffney asks.

"Used my phone. Emery's on my Find My app."

I stifle a guffaw. The irony nearly kills me. She's tracking her friends, while her dad and I have no idea where she is.

"And how did you get to the lighthouse?"

"Called an Uber. It dropped me off, and I saw my mom's car. It took me awhile of looking around, but then I found her. Her body, I mean." She hiccups out a little sob, offering a peek behind the façade of teen insolence. I put my arm around her, and she leans into me ever so slightly.

"I'm sorry, Zoe, I know this is tough," Gaffney says in a flat tone that undermines his caring words. "Did you move her body at all?"

Zoe shakes her head. "I bent down to see if she was breathing. She wasn't. So I shook her by her shoulders, trying to get her to wake up. I yelled her name. I screamed it. But nothing happened. She didn't move." She pauses and bites her lip. I rub her back, trying to soothe her. It's clear talking about this is incredibly painful for her. "She was staring up at the sky, eyes wide open. Her skin was so cold. She had those little goose pimples everywhere." She shakes her head. "I don't want to think about it."

"That's okay, you're doing great, Zoe," Prentiss says.

"Did you see anyone else in the parking lot?" the detective asks.

"No."

"At the beach?"

"No, it was empty."

"And then what did you do?"

"I called 9-1-1."

"Okay, we're almost done." He pulls out a clear plastic bag of clothing. "Do you recognize these clothes?"

Prentiss places one manicured hand on the bag and pulls it across the table so Zoe can look at it. The bag holds a navy-blue shirt with the words *Penn State* written on it. We all watch her examine it with sorrowful eyes.

"Honey, are these Emery's?" Prentiss asks in a sweet voice.

Zoe nods and opens her eyes. "I mean, I think they are." Her voice hitches as if she is trying not to cry. "She wears that Penn State shirt a lot."

The detective clears his throat. "Just a few more questions. I know this is difficult. We found these folded up, near the base of the dunes, with her shoes. Did Emery seem upset last night?"

Zoe shifts in her seat. "No, not really."

The skin on the back of my neck tingles. Something is off about Zoe's response, but I can't put my finger on it. Maybe it is the grief of losing a friend, the shock of finding a dead body. It hits me that what happened last night will have ramifications for Zoe for a long time.

"Anything been bothering Emery lately?" Gaffney asks.

Zoe looks from me to the police. "I don't know. Normal stuff."

"Normal stuff? Did she seem depressed or talk about hurting herself?"

"No. She would never do anything like that." Her voice is emphatic as she looks to me in horror.

"And how long have you known Emery Blake?"

"Maybe, like, almost a year? We met last fall."

"What about her cell phone? You said you used it to track her, but we were unable to find one at the beach."

"Not sure." Zoe shrugs.

"Not sure?" the detective presses. "What does *not sure* mean, Zoe?"

"It means she's answered the question, Detective," Prentiss says. "Let's move on, shall we?"

Detective Gaffney turns his full attention on Prentiss, and they lock eyes across the table for a few brief moments. His deep-set eyes simmer with hostility, while Prentiss's are wide and bright, a small smile on her pink lips. *Who will break first?* I wonder. Then the detective looks down at the notepad in front of him and clears his throat. "Anything else you can tell us, Zoe, about last night?"

Zoe chews her lip and squints as if she is doing a math problem in her head in class. Finally, she shakes her head. "No. Nothing else."

"Okay. Officer Garcia is going to take you outside while I talk to your mom."

A young woman in uniform with a bun so tight it looks painful walks in and flashes Zoe a smile. "Come with me. We can get a snack."

Zoe stands up, and Prentiss scooches into the newly vacated seat. "Do you want me to stay?" she whispers in my ear. Yesterday, my answer to Prentiss would have been a resounding *no*. Maybe even a *hell no*. But today is different. She's levelheaded and tough and seems to instinctively know when the detective is pushing too hard. I nod.

We watch as Zoe shuffles out of the room with the officer, and my heart breaks a little. This is a giant mess. One that will take a long time to clean up. The discipline issue and her grief at losing her friend will both have to be addressed. I'll definitely be calling her old therapist to see what she thinks. Hell, I may call my old therapist. And Daniel will have to step up as well. This goes beyond getting busted at school for vaping. Although Zoe has been veering off track the last year or so, this is a sharp departure, a hard left turn. And getting her back on track is going to be the big project over the next few months. So much for the summer of Liza.

"I didn't want to say this in front of Zoe," Detective Gaffney starts, shuffling the papers in front of him. Prentiss reaches over and squeezes my hand.

"Go ahead," I say, steeling myself for whatever is to come.

"It's about Emery Blake's death." He's looking at me, pointedly ignoring Prentiss.

"All right." Every fiber of my being tenses as if I am about to experience a blow to my body.

"Emery Blake's drowning was not accidental."

CHAPTER 9

LIZA

"What do you mean, not accidental?"

"It looks like she drowned herself."

I stare at the detective, trying to make sense of his words. "Can people do that?"

"Yes, they can. Especially if they've been drinking or doing drugs. And initial tests indicate she was."

"But it could have been an accident, right? Like she was drunk and decided to go swimming? People do that all the time." People like me. People like Nikki. A ribbon of nausea uncurls in my gut.

"That's possible." He cocks his head to one side and pauses to show he is not dismissing what I'm suggesting. "But in Emery's case, we're sure it's suicide."

I wince at the word. "How can you be sure?"

"She left a note." Long pause. "She posted it on Instagram. Shortly before she went into the ocean, according to our time-line. It was along the lines of a *by the time you read this* sort of thing. That's how we know it was intentional and not a cry for help. It's not unusual for people to post suicide notes with hints about where they are, essentially pleading for intervention. But Emery did not do that."

I sink into my chair, trying to digest what he is saying. It was all planned out. Emery knew what she was doing, and she dragged my daughter into this. Anger bubbles inside me. And by posting her suicide note on Instagram, it is bound to generate the kind of white-hot heat that burns anyone connected to it. Like Zoe. "How did you find out about the post?"

"Her account is public." He glances up at the clock, which reads 9:30.

Prentiss and I exchange a wordless glance. We both know what this means. The news of Emery's death, and how she died, will ripple across the Washington Prep community by the end of the day. I sigh, the tiniest bit relieved that Zoe's phone is plugged in at Shelby's kitchen. At least that will buy me a little time. I'm going to have to break the news to her as soon as we leave the police station. She can't learn about this via a text message or, worse, through an Instagram post.

"Can't you stop it?" I know how old and out of touch that makes me sound. It's like Whac-A-Mole to try to stop a viral posting, like last fall, with the Ledge Boys' roster of girls. Every time the school caught a boy putting it up on social media, the administration would haul him in and order him to take it down. But it would show up the next day on some other kid's account. All we could do was wait for it to die down.

"It's complicated. We've alerted Instagram. We're confident they will take it down soon, but they can't really stop it from being reposted if people have screenshots."

I nod. I get it. I think about the many times I've yelled at Zoe to put down her phone, telling her that there was more to life than what was online. Shelby and I, all of our mom friends, we've had so many conversations about the futility of telling our girls to stop living online.

And now they are dying online, too.

I run my finger along the plastic, outlining the letters on the Penn State shirt inside. Was Emery planning to go to Penn State in the fall? It reminds me of Nikki and her purple NYU shirt. We had plans to stay in touch in New York, to meet halfway in Central Park to run. But on that night twenty-eight years ago, sitting in this very police station, drunk and weeping, I knew that we would never run together again. My father drove out from Washington as soon as I called him. He arrived at the station around 4:00 a.m. to find me sitting on the floor with dozens of other high school graduates—some from Washington Prep, some from other D.C. private schools, all of us cited for drinking under age.

A lot of details from that night are lost. But I can easily call up the deep shame that swamped me, how diminished I felt in my father's eyes. And then the pain of losing Nikki. It was still a shock that night—it had yet to turn into the aching grief that has stayed with me all these years. So when the tears sting my eyes now, I'm not sure which drowned girl I'm crying for. Prentiss takes a packet of tissues from her little bag and passes one to me. They're stiff and crisp, decorated with blue-and-white ginger jars.

More decorative than useful.

That's what I used to think about Prentiss, but maybe I was wrong.

"We'd appreciate your not saying anything to the press about this," Detective Gaffney says in an attempt at a gentle tone. "Until we release a statement. It's difficult to set the record straight after disinformation and rumor have taken hold."

"Of course. I have no intention of talking to the press." But my stomach churns at the thought of the phone calls that I know are coming, from reporters I regularly deal with. I have to keep Zoe out of the papers, to protect her. But I will have to do my job, too.

The detective grimaces. "Unfortunately, they have every intention of talking to you. And your daughter. Right now, there are two news vans and a handful of reporters in our front parking lot. A death during Beach Week is big news. Beautiful young girl." He shuffles the papers in front of him and closes the manila folder, signifying this meeting is over. "We have your car around back, ma'am. You can leave from there."

He stands up, pulls my car key from his pocket, and hands it to me. Prentiss and I follow him into the hallway, where Zoe is waiting with the officer.

"I'm parked out front," Prentiss says and gives me a big hug. "But I can go with you if you want."

I shake my head. "That's okay."

Prentiss turns to Zoe. "You hang in there, sweetie." She heads toward the front of the building, and Zoe and I follow the officer down the hallway in the opposite direction.

Outside, we find my car easily, and I have to stop myself from grilling her about last night. The list of things to discuss with Zoe is getting longer every hour, but the first thing I need to do is to tell her about Emery's suicide. Everything else will just have to wait.

I slow down as two white news vans, antennas on their roofs, come into view. A small podium has been set up in front of the police station. A press conference is coming. A handful of reporters stand huddled, chatting. Once upon a time, I was a reporter like them, chasing the sirens, waiting for the cops to give us some information I could use. As we pass the scene, headed toward the street, a man with dark hair breaks away from the crowd and begins walking to the entrance of the police station. I let out a little gasp.

"What?" Zoe asks.

"Nothing." But I peek in my rearview mirror as the man disappears inside. It was definitely the guy from the Corkboard last night. What is he doing here?

We drive on in an uncomfortable silence. Losing a friend is devastating enough, but finding Emery's body on the beach will make it all the more traumatic for Zoe. I know I won't ever forget seeing Emery like that. And now I have to add to Zoe's pain by telling her it was suicide.

As we drive past the turnoff to Stockley Creek Country Club,

I have a thought. "We could head up to Rehoboth," I suggest. "Stop by Pasqualini's and get a pastry?"

"Nah." She doesn't even turn from the window.

"You used to love their elephant ears. Remember when you couldn't say elephant and you'd call them *eleven ears*?"

My attempts at connection sound desperate even to me. Zoe continues to stare out the window, not bothering to answer. I long to reel her back in to me. But she stays stubbornly out of orbit. So I make the turn into the country club.

"Honey, do you want to talk? About anything. Last night. Emery. The police."

"No."

We pull into the driveway behind Shelby's BMW, and I put the car in park, but I don't cut the engine. Neither of us makes a move.

"Listen, Zoe, we need to discuss something."

Her eyes are wide when she turns her face to me, and suddenly I see all the Zoes she once was. Baby Zoe making smacking sounds with her lips; pursed-lipped Zoe, terrified of the escalator at three; serious Zoe asking me about heaven when my father died. I'm not prepared to deliver this news. But it's my job; no one else should do it. Certainly not the internet.

"I'm sorry to have to tell you this, but you're going to find out pretty soon. Emery didn't die swimming. Not exactly." I pause, but she is silent. "Emery took her own life. She died by suicide."

"Suicide?" A strange laugh bursts forth from her, then stops abruptly. "Why would you even say that? Is that what the police told you? They're lying."

"Honey, I know this is hard—" I reach out to touch her, and she recoils.

"No, Mom. Stop. Just tell me why you said that." Her voice is strained, wavering between fury and panic.

"Sweetie, Emery left a note."

"A note? I don't think so. I didn't see any note."

"On Instagram."

"On Instagram? Is this some kind of sick fucking joke?"

"Zoe, watch your language."

"Watch my language?" She throws open the door and bursts out. When she stops to glare at me, her face is a mask of pain, her mouth twisted and her eyes brimming with tears. "You are fucking unbelievable," she sniffles before slamming it and running into the house.

I force myself to exhale slowly. She's in pain, I tell myself, and her anger has nowhere else to go. It's a compliment that she's comfortable enough to express her anger with me. That's what the therapist I took her to last year said. It smelled like day-old fish then, and it doesn't smell any better now.

But it's all I've got to go on at the moment, so I'm clinging to it. It's impossible not to think of Nikki's pile of clothes. I was the one who found them, after all.

A rap on the window startles me. I look up and see Shelby leaning down, a concerned look on her face. I plaster on a wan smile and cut the engine.

"How did it go?" she asks me once I've gotten out of the car.

"Terrible. The police told me that it was suicide."

Shelby nods. "I know. Kinsey showed me the Insta post. Everyone is talking about it."

"That didn't take long."

"I did not know you could drown yourself. That is so awful." She puts her hand over her mouth and shakes her head in disbelief.

"It is awful. And it was so strange being back in that police station after all these years."

Shelby gives me a blank smile.

I'm taken aback. "Nikki. I'm talking about Nikki. And how we all had to go to the police station that night? I just kept thinking about that when they were talking about Emery. How strange this all feels, like there must be some cosmic meaning behind their two deaths, you know?"

"Very, very sad." Shelby frowns, but I can tell she is uncomfortable with this line of discussion.

"Sometimes I still get choked up about Nikki. It'll come on all of a sudden. Like if I hear a certain song on the radio. Or I see someone in an NYU shirt. It just still makes me so sad." I take a deep breath and exhale. "And now Zoe has to carry that same grief with her the rest of her life."

"How's Zoe holding up?"

"About as well as you would expect. She cussed me out." I don't tell her that I'm worried about suicide contagion—the increased risk of suicidal behavior simply because someone within one's family, or one's peer group, died by suicide.

"She's upset."

"It's more than that. It's like I don't even know her anymore. I mean, she is devastated by this loss, understandably, but I didn't even know they were friends. It's like she was hiding the friendship from me."

"Of course she's hiding things," she says. "She's a teenage girl."

"This whole coming out to Dewey with Emery is so sketchy. She used to tell me everything. More than I wanted to know. She used to follow me to the bathroom. Now I know nothing. She's pulled away from me."

"That's what they do, hon." Shelby rubs my arm. "They pull and pull until they're so taut like a rubber band, and just when you think they're going to snap, they come rushing back. Zoe'll come back. You did a good job with her; she'll come back."

"And until then?"

"Until then, there's wine and chocolate."

CHAPTER 10

ZOE

Suicide.

That was the last thing I was expecting my mom to say. The whole time we were driving back from the police station, my heart was thumping in my chest. I was so sure my mom knew I had lied to the police. She kept giving me these sidelong glances while we were there and letting out these little sighs.

I almost had a panic attack when I was being questioned. I mean, lying to your parents is one thing, but lying to the police is in a completely different category of bad. I think they might put people in jail for that.

When I answered that detective, it felt like a neon sign was blinking above my head: *Liar! Liar!*

And then we pulled up to the house, and Mom turned to me with that look on her face, and said, *Listen, Zoe, we need to discuss something.*

I was sure I was busted. I didn't expect her to say that thing about Emery. About suicide.

It feels like someone is screaming that one word inside my head as I push the front door open.

It's not true. I know it in my bones. It's all wrong—can't anyone but me see that?

Emery would never, ever do that. I never knew anyone who was so excited about the future. She would talk about it all the time. What college would be like, how she would learn how to make documentaries and expose powerful people who did bad things. She was on a mission, and nothing was going to stop her. There is no way she would randomly decide to kill herself. And post it on Instagram. It's so obviously not true, it's insulting.

I need to see this Instagram post for myself.

As soon as I step inside Shelby's house, everyone turns to me and stops speaking.

There's Kinsey, of course, and standing next to her are two other seniors, Olivia and Sophia, total dupes of Kinsey, in identical cutoff shorts and Vineyard Vines shirts.

I cringe as they envelop me like a swarm of bees, buzzing stupid, sweet words in my ear.

"Oh my god, Zoe!"

"You poor baby!"

"Are you okay?"

No, I want to scream at the top of my lungs. I'm dying inside. My best friend is dead.

This is more attention than Kinsey's paid to me in the last five years. She never liked me, even when we were kids. She was always *nice.* Girls like her are always *nice,* especially when grown-ups are around. But she was the queen of double-edged comments, those tiny little ones that rip at you like brambles. The kind where you don't even know that you've been pricked until later, when you pick out the thorn and you see the blood.

Shelby and my mom come inside. My mom just stands there, not saying a word, but Shelby comes right up to me.

"You hungry, sweetie?" She rubs my back.

"Not really," I say. My stomach is twisted into knots. I don't think I'll ever be hungry again. I don't want to be down here with everyone. I want my backpack and my phone, and to be alone in my room.

"We have muffins, cinnamon rolls, fruit salad." She waves her hand toward a spread of food on the kitchen island, like something you'd find at a fancy hotel.

"I think I just want to lie down," I say and grab my phone from where it is charging. I see my backpack slumped on a chair and pick it up, then head to the stairs.

"Let me make you a plate," Shelby says and begins piling food on one. Shelby is always pushing food on me whenever I come near her, although honestly I can't remember her ever putting a thing in her mouth the whole time I've known her. Besides wine, that is.

"Do you want me to come sit with you?" Kinsey asks, her voice syrupy sweet.

"That's okay."

"You sure?" she calls after me as I head upstairs. "We're here for you!"

"That was sweet," I hear Shelby say. I almost laugh out loud. I could tell Shelby a few things about her precious kids. Everyone knows Kinsey paid someone to basically write her Vanderbilt essay. And I'm not talking about the college coach Shelby hired; I'm talking about an actual kid at Washington Prep who charges like a thousand dollars to write college essays.

Not that Kinsey is the only one.

And the way Brody treats girls is borderline criminal. He pretty much ran the whole ranking thing last fall, although he got off scot-free. I wonder if Shelby has any clue what her kids are really like. Emery says she wouldn't even care.

Said.

Emery *said* that kids like that are the way they are because their mothers encourage them.

I remember how Kinsey stood up at school assembly last fall and complained that the Ledge Boys who were busted were being treated unfairly. That it was a bunch of pearl-clutchers making a big deal over nothing. *I'm in the league, and I'm not offended,* she said.

She didn't mention that her twin brother ran the league, which was super gross if you thought about it for five seconds, and that she was ranked number two. It was a total humblebrag. Everyone said only the ugly girls and the fat girls and the girls who weren't picked were upset about the league, which wasn't true at all.

Emery always said it was about entitlement. Being untouchable. That guys like that thought they could get away with anything, like that guy on the Supreme Court.

And then they grew up into assholes who *did* get away with anything. Just look at Archer Benoit.

That's why what Emery was doing was so important, she said. Holding men accountable.

Once inside the room, I shut the door for privacy and put a chair in front of it. It won't stop anyone from coming in, but it will slow them down.

The first thing I do is look for this so-called note on Instagram. It's not hard to find. It's been screenshotted and reposted a zillion times, and my feed is filled with it.

People are acting like they knew her, like they were her best friend. Even total strangers are posting it. Putting it in their stories with teardrop stickers. Disgusting. It's like when a Black person gets killed by a police officer, and everyone at my school runs to Instagram to show how much they *care* and how *wrong* it is. And then they move on. And it's back to glitter-bombed selfies with friends, or selfies in front of some cathedral in Tuscany— *look how fun and cool my life is!*—until the next outrage.

They'll all forget Emery. But not me.

I've lived with this pain for too long. I'm sorry to everyone who will be hurt by this, it's not my intention. Please forgive me, I just want to be with my mom. Xo, Emery.

Rage fills me. She didn't write this. It sounds nothing like her. I know how Emery felt about her mom's death. She was furious, not sad. I mean a little sad, but mostly angry. She used to always say that she wasn't going to waste her life like her mom did.

But if she didn't kill herself, then what did happen? And who wrote that post?

I toss my phone on my bed and grab my backpack. Has anyone looked inside it? This is the moment of truth. I unzip it and shove my hands inside. Immediately, I find the plastic envelope. I exhale. A pang of guilt stabs at me. I never did get that Band-Aid from Brody. A thought occurs to me: maybe I could get something of Kinsey's. She's right downstairs. I could yank out some hair. Okay, maybe not that, but I am going to get that sample. I still plan to send it in, like Emery wanted. Even though she's gone, I'm still going to follow through with what we started.

Then I reach deeper, and when my hand hits it, a wave of relief washes over me. I didn't just dream it. It's really there, and I feel better just touching it.

I pull out Emery's phone, and a light twinge of guilt about lying to the police ripples inside me.

But what do they need it for, anyway?

Her whole life was on this phone.

Everything.

The battery is almost out. In a few minutes, it will be dead. The only charger is downstairs, and I won't be able to charge it in front of everyone. I'll have to wait until I get back to D.C. to charge it.

I don't know who posted that message on her Instagram. I just know it wasn't Emery. Somehow I will prove that. And I don't know how this phone will help, but I'm sure that it will.

The password is her mother's birth date. That was Emery's password on everything. After unlocking the phone, I look through her texts. I see my own name, and next to it this cute photo Emery took of me last fall in Georgetown, outside Ladurée. Colorful pastries are visible behind me. I'll never forget that afternoon. It wasn't anything special, just us going in and out of all the shops, then getting macarons and coffee and walking down to the canal. We sat on the steps and pretended we were French. I swallow a lump in my throat, wondering how I can feel such happiness at the memory and grief at the same time.

I wipe away a tear that's formed in my eye and move on. It's not my own texts that I'm interested in. It's the last person who texted her before she died.

I scroll up until I find it.

It's from someone named Jericho.

Jericho. I don't know anyone by that name, but at the same time it is vaguely familiar. Where have I heard it before? I stare at the avatar with the letter *J* in the middle. No last name. No picture.

I'm at the lighthouse, Emery texted him at 10:20. *Where are you?*

And then his response, right after: *Turn around. I'm right behind you.*

CHAPTER 11

LIZA

"I'm hungry." In the passenger seat, Zoe is curled up cross-legged, scrolling through her phone. "Are we near the Crab Deck?"

"Not far," I say tentatively. "Are you using data?"

She scowls. "No. I'm playing a game."

We're approaching Kent Island, a little spit of land that lies at the eastern end of the Bay Bridge, dotted with waterfront condos and a few strip malls. We've been driving for almost two hours through flat farmland and towns with one stop sign. I've managed to keep my mouth shut and let her doze, even though I have a million questions. I know from past experience that if I come at her too hard, too fast, she'll clam up. And I can't risk that; I need answers.

"Can we stop? I'm starving."

My heart races at the thought of stopping. "We're really pressed for time, honey. I'm on deadline, and I need to get back home. Geoff wants me to get him a statement by four o'clock."

"We can do takeout. I'm so hungry, and I'm craving their crab cake sandwich. Please?"

I groan, but I find myself pulling into the large parking lot of the seafood restaurant, which overlooks the Chesapeake Bay. "In and out. I have to be home by two."

I relax a little. This is our ritual, after all. My own parents used to take me here when I was a kid, on our way back from our annual week at Ocean City. Daniel and I continued the tradition with Zoe after we moved to Washington and started spending a week each summer at Shelby and Todd's. I park the car and get out, grabbing Walnut's leash.

"You run in and order," I tell Zoe. "I'll take Walnut for a pee break."

Zoe rushes ahead while I help the lumbering Walnut out of the car. He's stiff from the ride. Walnut is a good boy and waits patiently for me to click his leash onto his collar. When Zoe is at her dad's and my house is empty, I have Walnut to fuss over. And there is something reassuring about his seventy-pound frame at the end of the bed at night. Not that I think he would protect me against an intruder, unless you can lick someone to death, but I like to hear him breathing.

And besides, when it seems like we have absolutely nothing in common, at least Zoe and I share a love for Walnut.

Outside the restaurant, a cluster of three women in pastel pants and visors waits for a table. I take a seat across from them on a wooden bench, trying to keep my breathing regular. Maybe we should have grabbed some fast food at a drive-through. Writing the statement for the school won't take long, but I can telepathically feel Geoff hovering.

In a few minutes, Zoe comes back out.

"What's the sitch?" I ask.

"They'll bring it out. About ten minutes. And just, no, don't say *sitch*." When she takes a seat beside me, one of the older women sitting across from us beams at us. "Mother-daughter lunch?" she asks.

I nod and fake a return smile before turning to Zoe.

"So can you tell me a little about Emery?" I want her to know that I care about what happened to her. That no matter what, I'm still her mom and I love her.

"Like what?"

"Like, how did you guys meet?"

"We went to the same school? It's not that big a deal, Mom. People meet."

"I know people meet." I ignore her brusque tone. It's masking her pain and grief, and I don't blame her one bit. It will take her awhile to process what she has experienced, finding her friend's body on the beach. It took me years to process Nikki's death, and it would have been so much worse if I had found her body. "I was just wondering *how* you two met. She was a senior, wasn't she?"

"So? You don't think a senior would want to be friends with me?"

"That's not what I'm saying." But that is what I'm saying, isn't it? I try a different tack. "You told the police officer that Emery was your best friend. You must have been close."

"She was the one person—" Her voice catches, and her eyes tear up. "The *only* person I could even stand at school. I hate the people there."

"Zoe, you don't mean that."

"I do mean it. Why do you say I don't mean it? You have no idea what it's like at that school, being one of, like, five Wasian girls. And the worst part is, you don't even care."

I flinch at the word *Wasian*, recalling the heated argument she had with Daniel, who coolly told her that she was technically *hafu*, the Japanese word for half. It had enraged her. *Don't tell me what I am, or what I can call myself,* she had screamed at him.

"I do care," I say. "You know that."

Zoe rolls her eyes. "Right."

"I know what it's like to not fit in. When I was at Washington Prep, I was the only Jewish girl in my grade."

"First of all, people can't tell you're Jewish from looking at you, can they? I mean, you can totally pretend you're not Jewish if you want. Besides, you're not even that Jewish."

I let out a short laugh. "Excuse me?"

"I mean, we only have a few Jewish things in our house, but

then we light the Hanukkah lights, and you're all like, *Oh, look, I'm Jewish*."

Her words sting. "It doesn't work that way, Zoe. I'm Jewish by birth, and no, I'm not the most observant Jew on the planet, but that doesn't make me *not even that Jewish*. By the way, you're Jewish, too. Because your mother is Jewish. Even if you never set foot in a synagogue. You understand that, right?" She looks out at the water, unwilling to meet my eye. If she doesn't understand, it is my fault.

"And Dad's even worse." She turns to me, eyes narrowed. "His whole thing about not using chopsticks. I mean, like, ever? It's like he's anti-Japanese."

"He's his own person, Zoe. A grown man who experienced a lot of racism as a kid in the seventies and eighties. Not using chopsticks doesn't make him any less Japanese American." It isn't often that I find myself coming to Daniel's defense, but I know he hates it when people make assumptions about him, and he often heads off those assumptions by adopting a completely contrary position. Like refusing ever to use chopsticks. "I would think you'd support his right to express his identity the way he wants."

But her face is turned away, and by the set of her jaw, I can tell she hasn't heard a word I just said.

"Are you listening to me, Zoe?"

"What?" She turns, fury in her eyes. "What do you want me to say?"

"Please keep your voice down."

"You're joking, right? *That's* what you're worried about?" Her shrill voice carries across the parking lot, silencing the women chatting on the bench across from us. The front door of the restaurant swings open, and a woman steps out with a large plastic bag.

"Takada?"

"My best friend is dead, and you're, like, lecturing me on how I should feel about being Wasian, or that I should keep my voice down. This is why I can't talk to you." She turns on her heel and stomps off toward the car, hands in fists at her side.

"Thank you." I take the bag from the waitress, unable to meet her eye. I can feel my cheeks burn red with shame. The same shame I felt when Zoe was a baby and cried for six hours straight on a flight to California. I sweated through my clothes, enduring the withering looks of the other passengers. What was the name of that shame? Failure as a mother.

As I walk to the car, I try to figure out how the conversation veered so off track. This happens to us more than I want to admit, often enough that I have to take some blame for it. My daughter stole my car and went drinking, and her friend drowned as a result. And somehow it all gets twisted around and I'm the bad guy. I need answers. Once I've settled Walnut in the back seat and am back behind the wheel, I try again.

"Zoe, first of all, I want to tell you that I am so sorry you lost your friend. And having to go to the police this morning. That must have been terribly upsetting."

"Thanks. I guess."

"But I need to understand how the night unfolded. Let's start with how my car ended up in Dewey." I hope the firmness of my tone indicates I won't be put off by theatrics.

She takes the plastic bag from me and pulls out a Styrofoam box. "What about it?" she asks, directing her gaze to the tartar sauce she is squeezing onto the crab cake.

I pull the car back onto Route 50 and head for the bridge. "Well, clearly you two stole it."

"We borrowed it."

"No. Borrowing is when you have permission. Stealing is when you take something that does not belong to you."

"So?"

"So?" I'm shocked by her nonchalance.

"Yeah, what's your point?" She takes a large bite of her sandwich. The fishy smell hits me, sending a wave of nausea through me. "If you're going to punish me, just punish me."

"Oh, believe me, I will punish you. But first, I'd like to know what you were thinking. Whose idea was it to take the car?"

"Oh my god, Mom. Just stop asking me so many questions and let me eat my lunch. Can you even do that?"

"Not okay," I say through gritted teeth, my body heat rising. "You don't get to talk to me that way, first of all. And second of all, do you have any idea how serious this all is? Because you're acting like I found you vaping behind the school again, Zoe. Only you lied to your father. You lied to me. We had no idea where you were!" My voice booms through the small space, but I make no effort to control it. All that anger is finally pouring out. "You could have gotten seriously hurt. You could have been killed. And you know what? A girl did. Emery Blake is dead, Zoe. That's a big deal."

The tiniest moment of silence is punctured by a loud wail, and Zoe begins to sob. "I know, Mommy. Don't you think I know she's dead?"

In an instant, my anger is replaced by concern swirled with guilt. What kind of mother yells at her daughter when she's just lost a close friend? I try to steady my own emotions, which go back and forth like a small vessel on a stormy sea. First, I lean toward going too easy on Zoe, then the winds blow and I veer into coldhearted disciplinarian territory. I need to find my balance.

"It's okay, honey." I reach across her and unlatch the glove compartment. "There are tissues in there."

"It's not okay. Don't say it's okay," she chokes out between sobs. "Can't you just let me be sad? Why do you have to try to make it better? Some things just suck."

I'm about to protest when a ringing in the car stops me. Geoff. If it were anyone else, I wouldn't answer. "I need to take this, honey. It's work," I tell Zoe, hoping that she'll understand she has to keep it down.

"Fine. Whatever."

"Are you back in D.C. yet, Liza?" Geoff's disembodied voice sounds panicked, and I don't blame him. This is his first year as head of Washington Prep, and it's been rocky. First, the Ledge Boys scandal in the fall, now this.

"I'm on my way now," I say as I get into the right lane that leads to the Beltway. Traffic is light, and I could be home by 1:30.

"The board is having an emergency meeting this afternoon, so I'm going to need the statement you're writing by four. That's the first order. Something like what we sent out in the fall."

I cringe, remembering that exercise in manipulating facts. How I longed to send something out that resembled the truth. *Attention parents: Some of your sons are grading girls based on their oral sex skills and willingness to do anal. Don't be alarmed.*

"Is this statement coming from the school or from you?" I ask.

He pauses. "From me. Warm, caring, nothing specific. Nothing about suicide."

Zoe rolls her eyes and lets out a harumph.

"So you know about that?"

"Know about it? It's all over social media. I've been fielding calls from parents, from press, from everyone. People are losing it."

"Fine. I will have something for you by four."

"At the latest. Earlier is better. I have to run it by our lawyers. And come in early tomorrow."

"I'm supposed to have coffee with Archer tomorrow morning. He's our cover story for the fall issue, remember? But I can reschedule."

Long pause. Geoff is salivating at the idea of Archer on the cover, the implicit promise being: send your child to Washington Prep and he'll be a nationally known cable personality when he grows up. It's also a rebuttal to accusations that Wash Prep is elitist and too white.

"No. Don't change it. Keep the meeting with Archer. But come into the office straight after." He hangs up, and I release a breath I did not even realize I was holding. He did not ask how I was doing, or how Zoe was doing, and that's because he doesn't know yet that Zoe is involved. That she's the one who found Emery. I take some comfort in this. If Geoff, with his tentacles deep in the school community, doesn't know, then maybe it can be kept quiet a little longer. It is the summer, after all. The whole thing might die down by the fall. But then I remember Kinsey and Olivia sobbing and texting in the kitchen this morning, and I know it is just a matter of time until everyone knows that Zoe is the one who found Emery's body.

Even if they aren't in school, they are all online.

And there are no secrets online.

CHAPTER 12

1994

"What's the Spanish word for *beer—cerveza*, right?"

"If you know, why are you asking me?" Nikki picked at a loose thread on her denim cutoff shorts. Chris de Groot was sitting a little too close to her on the back porch of Shelby's beach house, which overlooked the shimmering Rehoboth Bay. Dewey Beach, Delaware, was a thin, little town—*One mile long and three blocks wide,* Shelby had joked when they had arrived—really a spit of land bordered on one side by the Atlantic and by the bay on the other. But Shelby had assured them that her bay-side house was in walking distance of all the parties and all the ocean-side rentals.

Nikki turned her gaze away from Chris, to the left—she could just make out the unnaturally green expanse of the golf course, completely empty except for a landscaping crew. Directly in front of her, the less verdant lawn of the house rolled down to the bay, its perfection marred only by a small construction site containing a pile of concrete bricks. Shelby's parents were building a retaining wall at the edge of their property, but Shelby had said the workers would not be back until Monday.

Next to the construction mess lay Liza and Shelby in bikinis, shiny with baby oil. But where was Archer? There, she caught sight of him, with Todd, down at the private pier. A white speedboat bobbed alongside the dock in the sparkling blue water. The guys were teasing Whitney, pretending to push her in. Whitney was screaming, overplaying it as usual.

When Liza drove through the gatehouse by the sign saying *Stockley Creek Country Club*, Nikki knew the house would be fancy. But it still took her by surprise. Done completely in ivory and cream, as if the concept of dirt didn't even exist, the house looked like something from a glossy magazine. She felt nervous just tossing her tote bag in the room she was assigned to. Surely some tiny speck of dust would transfer onto the crisp, white bedding. The whole room, with its flowing white curtains, pale rugs, and whitewashed walls, seemed to jeer at her Old Navy outfit and her beat-up Nikes. It's like the room knew she didn't belong there.

Nikki couldn't help but contrast it to the only other beach house she had ever been to—her aunt and uncle's back on Long Island. Each summer, her family took their vacation back to Brentwood, where she had grown up, and stayed with them. The house was within earshot of the Southern Parkway and about a twenty-minute drive to the beach, but you would think it was oceanfront property from the way her aunt and uncle had decorated it. Almost every bare spot was covered in seashells and anchors, pictures of seahorses, and weathered wooden plaques with phrases written on them like *Happiness comes in waves* and *No worries, we're on beach time.*

"What about *bottle opener*?" Chris asked. "What's Spanish for *bottle opener*?"

Nikki peered at him out of the corner of her eye. She didn't want to look straight at him, both because it would encourage him and because Chris looked even more like a lumpy toad when he drank. It made him sweat, and red blotches appeared on his neck. It annoyed her that Chris always glommed onto her. She didn't want to be rude, but at the same time, she didn't want anyone, especially Archer, to think that she liked Chris.

"*El opener.*" Nikki took a small swig of her warm beer. She hated beer, but the only other alcohol they had was Zima, which she hated even more. It tasted like Scotch tape.

"Really?"

"No, not really." She rolled her eyes. "You're an idiot, Chris."

"How come you don't speak Spanish?"

"I don't know, Chris *the Great*. How come you don't speak Dutch?" Once, in history class when they were learning about how New York City used to be New Amsterdam, Chris had bragged that his ancestors—some of the first European settlers—had swindled New York from "the Indians," as Chris called them, on behalf of the Dutch West India Company. And that de Groot was Dutch for *the great*.

But one glance at him told her he didn't pick up her reference. He probably made comments like that all the time.

Nikki didn't want to be bitter. She tried hard to look at these rich white kids objectively, without judgment, like in that movie her social studies teacher had shown them about the white anthropologist who went into the Amazon and studied the Yanomami people. Anytime someone said something stupid to her, like asking when her parents came to America, and she had to explain that Puerto Rico was not a separate country and that anyone born there was an American citizen, she willed herself not to get mad but to make note of it coolly, like a scientist.

It's what she had done the past four years at Wash Prep—observe and learn. Her parents sent her there to get a good education, but she knew it was so much more than that. It was to learn how to be successful, and how to be comfortable around the rich. Because she would be both one day. Rich and successful.

And one of the most important rules of being rich was to act like nothing really bothered you. She was once with her friends at CVS when two girls from a nearby public school were making a fuss at the checkout, concerned that not all their coupons were going through. Whitney had rolled her eyes and muttered, "Poors."

Poors. It was a word she heard a lot at Washington Prep, used to describe basically anyone not like them. And a surefire way to behave like a *poor* was to get upset and lose your cool. Forget arguing over 10-percent-off coupons—getting vaguely offended about anything made you suspect.

One of the reasons Nikki liked Liza, felt so comfortable with her, was that she was one of the only people at Washington Prep who regularly stood up for what she believed in. Whether it was in class or with friends, she seemed to have no problem calling people out or telling someone who had made a racist joke, *You can't say that.*

Of course, they could say that, and they did say that, but Nikki appreciated Liza's attempts at least. It made her feel less alone.

A splash and a scream caught her attention, and she turned to see Todd pulling Whitney out of the water. She had fallen in, after all. Shelby had told them *do not go in the water.* That there were jellyfish in the bay or something.

Whitney ran up the lawn looking miserable.

"Heading to a wet T-shirt contest?" Chris called as she approached.

"Fuck off," Whitney said playfully and plopped down on a chair, wrapping herself in a towel.

Chris stood up, stretched, and headed down the grass toward Archer and Todd.

"He's like a different species from them," Whitney said.

Nikki nodded. Archer and Todd were like a photographic negative of each other—Archer dark and Todd golden, but both tall and broad-shouldered and, oh, those smiles. Todd had a wide grin that promised good times under sunny skies, whereas Archer had a way of half smiling as if he were thinking of a dirty joke, his eyes crinkling a little in a way that made her stomach go wonky. "Chris looks like a gorilla without the hair."

Whitney laughed. "He does. But be nice to him. This weekend is the anniversary of his mother's death."

"Oh?" Nikki felt bad right away. She wished that she could take back what she'd just said. She had heard there was some tragedy in Chris's past involving his mother. But she had never really considered how that affected Chris emotionally.

"Yeah. She died when he was ten. Drunk driver killed her on Dalecarlia Parkway. He doesn't show it, but it's really hard on him. And his dad is such a dick."

"I didn't know that."

"Uh-huh. He was the ambassador to Luxembourg in the eighties. But now he does some kind of consulting and he's gone, like, all the time. Chris lives basically alone."

"That's sad."

"It's, like, so sad? He lives with his housekeeper. And they're, like, best friends. Like, she's the one who knows everything about him. I mean, she's really nice and all, but I think it's lonely up in that huge house. That's why he's always having parties, you know. So he doesn't have to be by himself."

Nikki nodded. She had gone to one of Chris's famous parties at his enormous stone house on the edge of Rock Creek Park in Forest Hills. She went with Liza, but they both left when some girls from a public school up in Gaithersburg took off all their clothes and climbed into the hot tub in Chris's backyard.

The three guys ambled up the lawn and onto the porch. Todd plopped down next to Nikki on the bench while Archer took up a spot against the railing. If only Nikki could reverse their positions, like in chess. Swap them. The heat from Todd's leg against hers made her squirm. Todd was blond and dimpled and had an easy kind of charm. He and Shelby had been dating since forever, before she arrived at Washington Prep, but everyone knew he screwed around. Nikki didn't know how Shelby could stand it.

The guys started talking about college start dates—Chris was headed for Penn up in Philadelphia, while Archer and Todd were both headed to North Carolina—Archer to Duke and Todd to

UNC. They spoke in shorthand, half of which she didn't understand, punctuated by inside jokes and guffaws. She felt invisible. No one asked her where she was going or when her college started. Whitney laughed at everything they said, even though Nikki was pretty sure she didn't get the private jokes, either.

Just when she thought she might have disappeared into thin air without having realized it, Todd ran his fingers along her thigh. Nikki froze in place. Did anyone see that? The last thing she wanted to do was land in Todd's crosshairs. That would really piss off Shelby. She looked up to see Liza and Shelby approaching the deck, dragging towels behind them. Shelby was logy from the sun, but Liza's eyes were locked on her own. Nikki felt her face grow warm. Liza had seen what Todd had done.

The seven of them fell into easy banter about that night's plans and where the party was going to be. They all agreed to meet at a beachfront house off of Dagsworthy that Don Fraser's parents had rented for him and some friends. Shelby's parents' house sat on the bay side, but Dewey was so narrow that getting from the bay to the ocean was only a fifteen-minute walk.

"Maybe we can make a bonfire," Shelby suggested, but Todd shot her down, saying that was illegal. She stuck her tongue out at him.

"Don't forget it's my birthday," she said in a singsong voice.

"Not till tomorrow," Todd said.

"Technically, midnight."

Finally, the boys left, and the girls stood up to head inside. Liza held Nikki's arm, allowing Whitney and Shelby to go in ahead of them. "I call first shower!" Shelby yelled, the screen door slamming behind her.

"Hey, is something going on with you and Todd?"

"No. Not at all."

"I thought you liked Archer."

"I do."

"Listen, don't let Shelby see you flirting with Todd."

"I wasn't flirting, Liza. He just randomly touched me."

"Gross." Liza rolled her eyes. "I just don't want Shelby to flip out on you. She can be kind of crazy when it comes to Todd."

Nikki nodded. She had seen how Shelby's loyalty was unwavering and fierce, until it wasn't. She was like the sun on a cold winter's day—it could warm you and fool you into taking off your coat. But when that sun went behind a cloud, it got cold fast.

"I could not be less interested in Todd."

"Right. But that doesn't mean Todd isn't interested in you. I mean, there've been other girls . . ." Liza cocked her head to one side. She didn't have to name them—Heather, Lisa, Beth. They all knew who they were.

"I don't get it—why does she put up with that? She could do so much better."

Liza groaned. "Ugh. I know. But she thinks the sun rises and sets on him. You know she's going to Meredith College just so she can be near Chapel Hill, right? Even though she got into the Savannah College of Art and Design, which was, like, her dream school."

Nikki put a hand to her mouth. "What? How can her parents let her do that?"

Liza scoffed. "You kidding? They don't want her to be an artist. They don't even care if she gets a BA. The only letters they want attached to her name are *MRS*, if you get what I mean."

The front door swung open, and Shelby, wrapped in a towel, stuck her head out. "What are you bitches doing? It's time to get ready."

Nikki's throat caught. Had Shelby heard them? But Shelby exhibited not a hint of anger. Her freshly scrubbed face shone bright and eager. "Come on." She held the door for them. Inside, the girls took turns stepping into the steamy bathroom to shower and get ready. Although there were two more bathrooms in the house, they all buzzed around the one like bees in a hive. No one wanted to be alone. Finally, after outfits had been tried on, discarded, and then put back on, after lipstick had been applied and blotted, perfume dabbed strategically behind ears, the girls gathered downstairs in the living room.

"Hold on," Shelby said as they were getting their shoes on. She ran off to her room and came back moments later, hands behind her back. "I have something for you guys." She held out three little black boxes.

"You didn't have to get us something," Liza said, taking her box. "I mean, it's *your* birthday."

"Not until tomorrow," Whitney said from the couch. "Don't try to milk it."

Everyone ignored Whitney. Nikki had forgotten to bring anything for Shelby's birthday and felt a pang of guilt. They normally decorated each other's wood-paneled lockers for their birthdays, but the school year had just ended. What was she expected to do now? It's not like she could afford to buy anything Shelby would actually want.

"This one's for you. And this one's for you." Shelby handed boxes to Nikki and Whitney.

"What is it?" Whitney asked.

"Open it."

Nikki opened hers to find a gold chain nestled in light blue velvet. Attached to the chain was a pendant about the size of a dime. She peered closely. The small, gold circle was a miniature compass with the letters *N, E, W,* and *S* engraved on it. Next to the *N* was a tiny glittering diamond. A mixture of genuine gratitude and surprise filled her. "Thank you, Shelby. It's beautiful." She gave Shelby a long hug.

"Get it?" Shelby asked, scanning Nikki's face for approval. Nikki had not seen this side of Shelby before, eager for praise. "Each letter is for each of us. I designed them myself." She beamed as she described how the idea came to her.

"You did an amazing job," Liza said. "You could totally do this for a living."

"Who's *E*?" Whitney asked.

"Hello? It's me. Elizabeth?" Liza said.

"Oh yeah, right. I don't think of you as Elizabeth." Whitney nodded as if she were trying to piece it all together. Nikki caught Liza's eyes, and they both almost started laughing.

"Well, I love it," Nikki said, touched to be included in the gesture. Her place in this quartet had always seemed fragile, based entirely on her friendship with Liza, whom she had befriended on the first day of cross-country during the fall of her freshman year. She felt bad for the unkind thoughts she had occasionally harbored toward Shelby—that she was shallow, spoiled, frivolous. The winds of her opinion shifted, and at once, it was clear to Nikki why Liza liked Shelby so much. Beneath her party-girl exterior, she was a loyal and thoughtful friend.

Nikki felt warm inside. These were her friends. She would miss them so much next year.

"Is this real gold or gold-plated?" Whitney asked, squinting at her necklace.

"That's rude, Whitney," Liza said.

"I was only asking because I want to know if I can take it swimming. I love it, and I never want to take it off."

"It's real gold," Shelby said. "Fourteen karat. So yes, you can wear it in the water."

"Well, I'm never going to take it off," Nikki said, lifting up her hair and proffering her back to Liza.

"Never?" Liza latched the tiny clasp at the nape of her friend's neck.

"Well," Nikki said and turned around, "at least not during Beach Week."

"Me, either," Liza said.

"Me, either," Whitney and Shelby said.

"Hold on, let me get my camera." Liza ran to her room and came back with the small, silver device. She propped it up on a stack of cookbooks on the kitchen counter and fussed with it.

Once the timer was set and the red light was blinking, she hurried to rejoin the group.

"Hurry," Nikki called, making room between herself and Shelby.

The girls held frozen smiles, waiting, waiting, and for a moment—between the frenzy of primping and prepping for the night ahead—all four were still.

Then the camera emitted a tiny flash, and they were off.

CHAPTER 13

LIZA

After dropping Zoe at her dad's, I drive around Adams Morgan looking for a spot. A bit of luck—someone is pulling out in front of the Korean barbecue joint that was once Millie and Al's, a dive bar that was practically an institution when I was younger. Walnut sniffs at the curb, in doggie heaven, as I walk to Daniel's.

I let myself inside the nondescript door, tucked between two businesses, and Walnut and I climb the narrow stairs to Daniel's loft. I find him sitting at the industrial-looking, stainless steel kitchen island in the middle of the loft, staring at a laptop.

It's been two years since we separated, but there are moments when it still feels raw. Like now, when I could use a partner. It's not regret, exactly, more like a wound that keeps reopening just when I think it has healed. But I don't regret moving back to D.C. when my dad was diagnosed with multiple myeloma. We were living in New York City, and I immediately pulled Zoe out of second grade, quit my job, and moved home to take care of him. My brother was living in Israel at the time, and there was no one else who could do it. About six months later, Daniel found a job in Washington. And a year after that, Shelby helped me find my job at Washington Prep.

We never exactly decided that we were moving to D.C. permanently. Certainly not into the house I grew up in. But my dad lived for four more years, defying all expectations. Every day felt like we were getting away with something.

Maybe I was distracted—by my dad's illness, raising Zoe, and the demands of work—and that's why I didn't see how unhappy Daniel was.

I didn't want to see it.

But after Dad died, it became clear we had shifted from a couple in love to two individuals living under the same roof, co-parenting a child. We went along like that for years. Swept up by the day-to-day, yet moving further apart. At his job, he took any assignment that would let him travel. I ended up doing most of the parenting—the bedtimes, the meals, the doctors' appointments, the birthdays. And even when he was here, he wasn't.

And then one day, he told me he had been seeing someone else.

I knew we weren't happy, yet I was completely blinded by the betrayal.

He said he did it because his life had become an endless cycle of work, sleep, and household chores. But the affair was finished, and it was a wake-up call. He wanted to see if we could make things work.

The day he told me, I hired a lawyer. Once I knew he had cheated on me, it was like a switch had been flipped.

We were done.

Only, it hasn't been that simple. I question whether I did the right thing by blowing up my marriage. *He blew it up by cheating*, I try to tell myself. But that's not how Zoe sees it. And I wasn't anticipating just how hard it would be to be alone.

"Hey," I say. "Where did Zoe go?"

Daniel looks up and tilts his head toward a closed door in the back. "In her room." He frowns at Walnut. "He's not going to pee in here, is he?"

I roll my eyes. Daniel is not a dog person. "We need to talk. What happened last night? Where did Zoe say she was going?"

"Uh, let's see. Emery showed up here maybe five o'clock? And they left together. She said they were going to grab dinner, then spend the night at Emery's."

"And you didn't ask where that was, exactly? Or talk to her parents?"

He scoffs. "She's sixteen, Liza. And honestly, she spends so much time in her room, I was thrilled that she was actually leaving the apartment—and with a friend, no less. Obviously, I didn't know they were going to take your car and drive out to Dewey."

I decide to let it go and take a different tack. "Did Emery seem sad or depressed?"

"No. She seemed like a normal, happy person. I had zero clue." He gets up and stretches, his shirt riding up and exposing his six-pack. Instinctively, my stomach flutters. The worst is how well the divorce suits him. When Alan Plotz, the guidance counselor at Wash Prep, got divorced, he gained thirty pounds in one month and started wearing stained clothes to work. We had to have an intervention. But not Daniel. He's clearly been spending his free time at the gym, and he looks relaxed. He's like Benjamin Button, magically growing younger while the divorce has aged me. "Espresso? Wine?"

"No, thanks. It's not even three."

"Try this." He pulls a bulbous wineglass from a hanging rack. "Amazing Malbec. Paola brought it back from Argentina. Her family owns a vineyard there." He pours a glass and hands it to me. I don't bother to ask who Paola is. I used to ask about the women whose names he would casually drop in conversation, but I quickly learned there was little point, since as soon as I had memorized a few key facts about them, they would disappear from his life. I swish a mouthful of robust red grape. It is good.

"Nice, huh?" He takes a big sniff and smiles.

I look away, unable to give him the pleasure of liking his, or Paola's, wine. "I'm worried about Zoe. I think she's in trouble, Daniel. I'm scared this whole thing is going to make her pull away even more. And honestly, I'm upset that she's lying and sneaking around."

He gives me a half smile. "You mean, she's being a teenager?"

"Sneaking off to Beach Week is not typical behavior—not to me, at least. She could have gotten seriously hurt. And we would have had no idea where she was."

"But she didn't get hurt."

"Not the point, Daniel. The lying is a problem in and of itself. The going behind our backs. Playing us off each other. Not to mention that she stole my car."

"Stole? Isn't that a little extreme? Let's not criminalize normal teenage behavior."

"This isn't normal. Finding a dead body on the beach isn't normal. My god, Daniel—a girl died. Zoe was there. It could have been her."

"I didn't say that part was normal. That's just really bad luck. A tragedy. But she'll bounce back. Kids are resilient."

"This is not about resiliency. Aren't you concerned that your daughter lied to you? That she told you she was spending the night at her friend's house, then went to Beach Week instead? Fucking Beach Week, Daniel!" I take a deep breath. "Beach Week is three hours away. It's party central. Bad things can happen."

He nods. He knows what I am referring to. "All kids lie. It's developmentally normal." He takes a deep breath and exhales. "Look, Liza, you're upset. I get it. I'm upset, too. It's really, really sad and fucked up when someone young dies. Especially by suicide. But that doesn't make Zoe some kind of delinquent."

"I didn't say delinquent." I reach down and stroke Walnut's soft ears. I read that just petting a dog can lower your blood pressure. "But I think she's heading down the wrong path. Last year was a disaster. Cutting class, failing French. If she keeps it up, I think they're going to ask her to leave Washington Prep."

"And would that really be the worst thing in the world? To have to go to public school?"

I groan. Our never-ending argument about whether Zoe should be at Washington Prep at all. When she was in public school in New York, she struggled to learn to read in the large classes, disconnected. Where was Daniel then?

"Wash Prep isn't perfect, but she can't skate by there. She can't disappear in the crowd."

"Well, maybe she wants to."

I laugh. "I bet she does. But we as her parents have to stop her from doing that. We need to contact her therapist again."

"She refused to go, remember? That's why we stopped last year."

"But we could make her. We could bribe her or something."

"There's nothing wrong with her, Liza. You know, not everyone is cut out to be the captain of the track and field team and go to an Ivy League school. Doesn't make you a failure in life."

I blanch. "That's not fair. I just want what's best for her."

"No. You want her to follow in your footsteps. And she's reacting to that pressure."

"So this is all my fault."

"Nobody's saying that, Liza. Don't be such a victim. Just let Zoe be a teenager. She should get a say in her own education. She's her own person."

I decide to switch gears. I don't want to rehash this argument, and I know Daniel is more bark than bite. He won't actually make any effort to get Zoe into another school; he just likes to criticize. "Did you know this Emery girl?"

"I mean, I met her a few times. She was nice, sweet."

"I never met her." I try to keep my voice steady, but his words sting. "Zoe never even mentioned her to me."

"And why do you think that is, Liza?"

"I think it's because she knew I wouldn't approve, but I'm guessing you think it's because I'm too uptight."

"I'm just saying that maybe you could loosen your grip a little."

"Loosen my grip?" The words erupt from me, louder than I had intended. "She could have gone swimming with this girl, Daniel, on a dark beach in the middle of the night. Three hours away from where she was supposed to be. She could have drowned. Do you get that? And she lied! To you, to me."

"Calm down—"

"Don't tell me to calm down." I slap my palm on the counter, making a satisfying *thwack*. "I don't think you fully get it. We were at a police station this morning. A police station."

"I do get it," Daniel says, enunciating each word. "What do you think we should do?"

"Therapy. That's nonnegotiable. And a curfew. Every minute this summer has got to be accounted for. She has to earn back our trust."

To my surprise, he nods in assent. "What about her job?"

"I think she should go," I say without hesitation. Zoe is slated to work this summer at a coffee shop in downtown Bethesda. "She needs something to do during the day, and she made a commitment, so she should keep it."

"I agree," he says. "With all of it. I can drive her to the coffee shop in the mornings."

I'm taken aback. The plan was for Zoe to get there on her own somehow, a combination of bus and Metro. But I like this much better. "Good. Thank you."

The room is silent for a moment. I'm not sure what to do with this pent-up anxiety if Daniel is not offering any pushback. I'm not used to us being in agreement.

"Well, I'd better go," I say. "I need to get a presser out for Wash Prep by four."

"Of course," he says. "Duty calls."

I can't tell if he's being snide or genuine, and I don't have the mental bandwidth to figure it out. And now that we're not married, I realize, I don't have to. As I leave, I pause outside Zoe's closed door. I rap gently and open it a crack.

"What?" She sits upright on her bed, tucking her phone under the covers.

"Just wanted to say bye."

"Okay."

When it becomes painfully clear that this is all she is going to say, I shut the door and leave.

The car is scalding hot when we get in, and I lower the windows and blast the AC at the same time. Walnut hangs his head out the back, panting. As I pull the car out onto Eighteenth Street, I think about everything that has transpired since last night. Just forty-eight hours ago, I was packing for a few days at the beach with my best friend, to start "the summer of Liza." I was shedding responsibility, having fun. And now I'm in a swamp, knee-deep in murky water, mist shrouding me.

Driving back to my house, I realize that the one person who could help me cut through the confusion, Zoe, is the least willing to do so. I'm all alone in this. A wave of melancholy hits me, and I have to squeeze the bridge of my nose to stop from crying. Shelby doesn't know what it's like to be a single parent. My brother is all the way in California. And Daniel just makes me feel like I'm being neurotic and rigid. But Zoe is disappearing before my eyes.

An enormous willow oak near my house provides some shade to park under. I let Walnut out first, and he waits patiently at the curb as I gather my things. It's only Monday, but I am already exhausted. The whole week, in fact the whole summer, without Zoe stretches before me. A few years ago, when Zoe was small, I'd have killed for some alone time. Now I'm not sure how I will fill all the empty hours.

As I clean up the trash the girls left in the car—granola bar wrappers, an empty water bottle—the awfulness of it all overwhelms me. It's not one thing. It's not only Emery's death or that Zoe took my car and drove to Dewey. It's the lying, the sneaking. It's the entertained look Prentiss could barely hide on her face the entire time we were being questioned by the police. I'm sure her fingers are flying right now, texting her friends, posting

on D.C. Urban Moms. I shudder. This will be all over that forum. D.C. Urban Moms is a hugely popular anonymous forum
that's been around almost twenty years. Originally, it was moms
sharing pediatrician recommendations or venting about nanny
problems. But over the years, the site has expanded geograph-
ically, not just to the D.C. suburbs but around the country. It's
my number one guilty pleasure and time-waster. I usually spend
my lunch break at my desk eating a salad and reading posts like
"Would you send your *extremely* gifted five-year-old to public
school kindergarten?" and "Angry that my husband called our
nanny hot."

A Washington Prep scandal involving a suicide will be like
chum in the water.

My head begins to throb, signaling the beginning of a tension
headache. I need to clean out the car, take a Tylenol, and get to
work. I have less than two hours before I have to send in the
written statement to Geoff. As I am grabbing the detritus off
the car floor, the corner of a white cardboard box, tucked under
the front passenger seat, catches my eye. More garbage. Probably
a pizza box.

I pull it out. This is no pizza box. On the lid is a pretty rainbow made of different-size dots, above some lettering. It takes a
few seconds for the meaning of the words to register. And when
they do, a crack of pain shoots across my skull.

Discover Paternity Test—reveal his paternity without his even
knowing it!

CHAPTER 14

LIZA

Paternity test.

I sit at my kitchen table–slash–makeshift office, struggling to forget those words long enough to force myself to write the Washington Prep statement about Emery. My mind keeps wandering back to the little white box with the rainbow on it and its implications.

It has to belong to Emery. There's no way Zoe is having sex. I reach across the table and push the box under some papers, out of sight. I turn back to the computer screen. Geoff wants this by four. I have twenty-seven minutes to go. Walnut is curled up at my feet, and I dig my bare toes into his soft fur, trying to focus.

So far, the statement is bland, inadequate in face of the tragedy. It will be a balm to absolutely no one to know that "the Washington Prep community is grieving the loss of one of our own." There are no answers to be found in these anemic, bureaucratic lines, which resemble those that might be issued from any institution. Even if I were permitted to speak from the heart, what could I say about Emery? I didn't know her at all. She was one of about a hundred graduating seniors, externally no different from any other girl her age. The most remarkable thing about her short life is her death.

If I had been covering Emery's death back when I was a reporter, I'd have found some telling detail, some anecdote to flesh her out to readers. To bring her back to life through words, if only for a brief time.

When I first started working as a reporter after college, I was afraid to approach people who had lost loved ones. I worried about being seen as invasive or crass, my anxiety no doubt colored by TV and movie depictions of reporters hounding grieving families. But to my surprise, the opposite was usually true.

They needed me.

Not me specifically but someone in a semi-official capacity to witness what they were experiencing. And allowing those grieving to unburden themselves in front of me felt like a mitzvah, a sacred task. I often stayed long after I had what I needed for a story. The act transcended the automation of life, tying me to them in their suffering, binding us together.

Could I write something now that would jolt the Washington Prep community out of their quotidian life and bind us together? I doubt it. And even if I could, that's not my job. My job is to comfort and reassure.

The parents who read the magazine—mostly wealthy, busy, ambitious D.C. go-getters—want to be reassured that Emery's death is an aberration that will not derail their own children's paths to success. And the alumni?

I proofread what I have written once more and hit Send. It's a few minutes before four. I have never missed a deadline. But I don't feel good. I feel deflated. Guilt at having shirked some greater duty overtakes me. Beneath the table, Walnut shifts as if he's disappointed in me. I get up in the empty house, loneliness swamping me like a wave. I hate being alone. The house is so empty without Zoe. At times like this, I really miss my dad, and I think maybe I ought to sell the house. There are just too many memories—of him, my childhood, the early years with Daniel.

No one tells you this about divorce. It's emotional whiplash. Some days it seems like a great weight has been lifted off my shoulders and I have a new start on life. I'm at the beginning of a great adventure, and romance and travel await. Other days are like today, when a quiet panic settles over me like a low-grade fever. A fear that I'll be alone forever. The silent ticking of the clock. The long hours stretched out ahead of me. Whole weekends where no one notices if I've changed out of my pajamas or eaten anything besides cereal.

I wander through the kitchen aimlessly, trying to decide if I'm hungry. I have so many great memories of this kitchen. Standing at this counter with my dad in the evenings when he got home from work, eating takeout and laughing about something funny that happened to one of us. Or my brother coming home from college with some friends for Passover. We'd invite all kinds of random people to our seder, and Dad would let me drink wine. And I can still picture Zoe going through her baking stage in sixth grade. Almost every day would bring some new sugar-laden treat. We had so many cookies and brownies, I started bringing them into the office.

But now it's just me here.

It's too early for dinner, too hot for coffee or tea. I scoop some blackberry ice cream right out of the carton. Why not? That paternity test can't be Zoe's, I decide. She's not *that* much of a stranger to me, is she? No, it has to be Emery's. But who is the father? How frightening to be young and pregnant. I immediately think of Emery's own father; those broad shoulders already carry the weight of Emery's mother's death. Now his burden is even heavier. He's somewhere out there in Virginia. Did he know she was going to Beach Week? Perhaps he was like me, completely in the dark about what his daughter was up to.

I stop—spoon in midair. I've been muttering my thoughts aloud like a caricature of a lonely old lady. My phone buzzes, sending it skittering across the kitchen table. I reach for it—Shelby. I smile.

"You caught me eating Graeter's out of the carton."

"That bad, huh? How was the ride home? How's Zoe?"

"Not great." I toss my spoon into the sink and put the ice

cream back in the freezer. "When she wasn't ignoring me, she was yelling at me."

"I'm so sorry you're dealing with this, hon. Remember, she is grieving. And she's a teen. Tough combo."

"Oh, I know. It's the only thing that stops me from wringing her neck." I take the phone upstairs with me to my bedroom, where a basket of laundry is waiting to be sorted. I dump it out on my bed and begin separating the clothes. My flippant tone belies the deep ache I feel in my belly at the ongoing tension between Zoe and me. I want to be there for her, the way my mother was not for me. But the way I've always shown love—hugs and kisses, offers of ice cream, invitations to curl up on the couch to watch movies—are clunkers that drive her away.

"Everyone is talking about it," Shelby gushes, sounding out of breath.

"Are you back home?" I ask. "You sound like you're on your Peloton."

"Uh-huh. These last five pounds are killing me. Anyway, Kinsey and her friends are obsessed. They barely even knew Emery, but it's the closest thing to a real tragedy these kids have ever come to, and I think they're freaked out."

"I bet. I just sent a statement over to Geoff. You'll probably get an email in a few hours."

"Can you imagine all the parents when they get this? It's going to be insane, Liza. Just driving back from the beach, I had to shut the notifications off my phone because it was going nutso! I mean, this is truly the most insane thing ever."

"I can top it." I tell her about the DNA kit I found under the front seat of the car.

"Reveal paternity without his knowing it?" she repeats. "Holy cow. You don't think it's Zoe's, do you?"

"No." I stop folding the towel in my hands. "There's no way. Zoe? I'm not even sure Zoe is into boys. I mean, she shows zero interest. It's got to be Emery's."

"Oh my gosh, Emery was pregnant. And she didn't know who the father was?"

"Maybe. Or maybe she wanted proof. Like maybe he was denying it. Do you think that might be why she took her own life?"

"Damn, girl. This is a hot mess. What are you going to do?"

"Do?" I'm taken aback. "Nothing. Why, you think I should do something?"

"No. I mean, what can you do?"

We talk for a few minutes more, but when I hang up, I'm left with a sense of failure. *Do nothing.*

All of a sudden, the exhaustion from the past twenty-four hours hits. It's ridiculously early, too early for sleep, but suddenly I long for the comfort of my own bed. After I finish the laundry, I feed and walk the dog, and then change into PJs.

In bed, I try to read a Sue Grafton mystery. She's my comfort read—I've already gone through the alphabet with her, but this past year, I started over when I found myself unable to focus on anything denser. I'm at *F Is for Fugitive.* Even so, I find myself going over the same line without any of it sinking in. I put the book down and glance at Walnut dozing next to me. I realize what I can do. I can do what we never did for Nikki: I can write a real story that memorializes Emery. Not some corporate statement that has all the heart and soul wrung out of it, edited to make sure no one is offended. A real piece, like I used to write. And while I am at it, I'm going to find a way to mention Nikki. I'll keep the focus on Emery, but I'll get something meaningful in there.

Geoff won't like it. He'll say death is too dark for the alumni magazine. Not relevant.

But I'll insist. With Todd and Shelby on the board backing me, maybe even Archer, Geoff won't be able to stop me.

With a sudden burst of energy, I throw back the covers, alarming Walnut. I pad downstairs to the kitchen and grab a framed photo off the wall. I take it back to bed with me, where I examine it closely.

It's the four of us that first day at Beach Week, all those years ago. Heads touching, we four girls are standing in the kitchen of Shelby's beach house: Nikki, me, Shelby, and Whitney. I run my finger along the faces, stopping at Nikki's. She was friends with Shelby and Whitney, but mostly through me. There was no way she would have gone to Beach Week if it hadn't been for me.

I know her death is not my fault, but I feel responsible in a way.

That was Nikki's last night alive, and this is the last photo of her ever taken.

My stomach clenches. Twenty-eight years later, her loss feels even more poignant than it did at the time. Because at the age of forty-six, I now know what she missed out on. College, travel, falling in love, finding meaningful work. No marriage or children for Nikki, no grandchildren or nieces or nephews for her family. They also lost out on twenty-eight years of Christmases and birthdays, not to mention all the little moments that make up a life.

I wonder if there is a corresponding photo of Emery out there, from her last night. Then it occurs to me that if anyone would have it, Zoe would. They're best friends, after all. I reach for my laptop and drag it onto the bed.

It feels subversive, and it is—an invasion of privacy for which Zoe would kill me. Once in Zoe's cloud account, I browse through her photos. I find dozens of pictures of Emery. In fact, besides Zoe herself, Emery is basically the only other person in her universe.

My best friend.

How could they have been so close and I had no clue? I scroll down to the latest ones and find selfies of the two girls taken as they crossed the Bay Bridge last night, just as the sun was setting.

There's one of them on the Dewey strip, outside a crab shack. It's nighttime, and their faces are glowing from the neon. Zoe comes up to Emery's shoulder. They're so cute.

Looking at Emery, I search for a clue that she is so miserable that she will take her own life within hours. But the wind is whipping her long hair across her face, and all I can see is two happy teenagers, thrilled with a taste of freedom.

After a few awkward selfies of Zoe at a crowded party, I find a shot of her and Emery, cheek to cheek, grinning. I may not have known they were friends before last night, but this picture has *best friends* written all over it. It's right there in their young, sweet faces and wide smiles. Silliness, hope, private jokes, possibilities. Love.

It's probably the last picture of Emery before she died.

But it's the next one that takes my breath away. It's a close-up of Brody Smythe, thrusting forward a bandaged fist as if he is about to punch the camera. He has an arrogant scowl on his face, sneering at the viewer. I look closer. It's a screenshot from Instagram, taken at just before eleven last night. The caption reads: *Wipeout at Fountainhead. Worth it.*

I know Zoe is not a fan of Brody—or of Kinsey, for that matter. Some of her preferred epithets for the twins are: "prime examples of white privilege," "brain-dead prep-school zombies," and "why normal people hate rich people."

Last fall, when I asked her if she'd like to spend Thanksgiving at Shelby and Todd's, she mimed vomiting and said, *I'd rather pick my eyelashes out one by one.* It pains me that she won't make an effort with Brody and Kinsey. I get that they're not going to be best friends, but she's known them her whole life. They are like cousins. But everything is black and white with Zoe these days. You're in or you're out, hot or cold, love or hate.

Knowing her feelings about Brody, I have to wonder: Why is this the last photo in her camera roll? And is there any connection to the paternity test I found in the car?

CHAPTER 15

ZOE

My phone goes off at 5:15, and I slap at it until it shuts up. I'm supposed to be at Quartermaine Coffee in downtown Bethesda by 6:00 a.m. for my first day of work. When I applied for the job, for some reason I said I was a morning person and the early shift would be fine. The whole thing made more sense when I was going to be living with my mom up in AU Park this summer. That would have been a short bus ride up Wisconsin Avenue, or I could have taken the Metro.

My dad's place, though, is a lot farther from Bethesda. I could walk all the way to the Woodley Park station, but it would make the commute so long. Anyway, my father surprised me by telling me that he'd drive me.

I lie on my back, paralyzed by dread. I don't want to get up. My body weighs a million pounds, sinking into the mattress like concrete. I try to lift one leg, but it won't move. It feels like when I had the flu in fifth grade, an ache that reaches into every fiber and corner of my being.

I have to. I have to get up.

I drag myself to the bathroom. I don't want to look in the mirror. I take a towel and drape it over the medicine cabinet like how my mom covered all the mirrors when my grandfather died. I get it now. I don't want to see myself, and I don't want to see other people. I thought I might feel a little better today, but if anything, it's worse. Because I have to go on as if things are normal.

Dad barely says two words to me as we exit the apartment, and I am grateful. He doesn't pretend to be a morning person. He usually doesn't speak until he's had his coffee. I stand outside Tryst while he goes in to get his double espresso, which is absurd, because he is driving me to work at a coffee shop. But he says he can't wait the twenty minutes. Normally, I would give him a hard time, but I just don't care.

I turn my face to the morning sun. It's still early enough that the heat and humidity haven't turned the city streets rank. On weekend nights, this neighborhood gets crazy. People come from all over, spilling out of the bars, getting super drunk. It gets so crowded on Eighteenth Street that you can't even walk down the sidewalk, which reeks of beer and piss. But this early, the street is sad, empty of people as if a zombie apocalypse happened overnight, all the people zapped into thin air, leaving behind only their trash.

Dad comes back out with a danish and offers me a bite as we trudge up the hill toward Calvert Street, where the car is parked. He's too cheap to rent out a parking spot.

I take one tiny mouthful of the sweet apricot pastry, but I don't have much of an appetite.

"Hey," he says. "That all you want? That bad?"

"It's fine. Just not hungry."

"You should get a job at Tryst." He unlocks the passenger side for me and opens the door. "Then you can roll right out of bed and into work."

I give him a weak smile and climb in, tucking my backpack between my feet. It's a dark gray Fjällräven, and it basically holds my whole life. Including Emery's phone. Just knowing it's there makes moving through the world possible.

"I asked them," I say. "They're not hiring."

"Keep trying." He pops in a CD, and weird instrumental music fills the car, really soothing but also kind of spooky. My dad is the only person I know who still loves CDs. He claims to have more than two thousand, and I believe him. When he lived with us, Mom made him keep them in plastic bins in the basement. But when he moved, he had custom shelves built. They take up one wall in the living room. He even has an Excel spreadsheet where you can search based on genre, band, year, album, whatever.

"So what is this crap?" I ask.

"This *crap*, my dear, is Brian Eno, *Discreet Music*, 1975." We cross the bridge over Rock Creek and head up Connecticut Avenue. "Want to take a crack at the genre?"

This is a game we play. He puts on some random music and then tries to get me to identify things about it. "I don't know. Nursing home soundtrack?"

He laughs. "Close. It's called *ambient*."

I listen closely to the slow music. It makes me think of a cold, gray day on a beach. "It's weird, but I like it," I concede. "It's like what people in the seventies thought the future would be like. Like background music in a movie."

"Smart girl. That's exactly what it's meant to be—music for the backdrop of life."

We ride the rest of the way in silence. I stare out the window as we pass the National Zoo, letting the haunting notes wash over me, so glad that it's him and not Mom driving me. She would definitely ask me if I remembered all the fun we used to have at the zoo. She always does that, tries to remind me of how fun my childhood was, as if I'll remember and then snap out of my *mood* and magically transform into a teenager from a Disney TV show. Slightly sassy, but an all-around great girl! Or maybe she'd pepper me with questions about how I feel, and do I want to talk about Emery, and how can she help?

Dad's just Dad. He wants to talk about music and movies. That's pretty much it.

As we pass Gawler's Funeral Home, my stomach sinks. It's where my grandfather's funeral was held. I don't really remember much of it, only that there was a huge platter of butter cookies and I kept sneaking back for more. I remember being scared each time I took one, that someone would reprimand me, say, *That's enough*. But of course, no one was paying attention to me.

"I wonder if there will be a funeral for Emery," I say.

"I'm sure there will," my dad says.

"Like, if you're Jewish, you're supposed to be buried within twenty-four hours. But what if you're not? And how will I find out?" I screw my mouth up. The words coming out of it taste metallic and tinny. Do they sound as weird as they feel?

"You'll find out," he says. "Your mom will know."

I nod. He's probably right. But maybe not. Maybe her grandparents will have a funeral and not tell anyone. They were so strict and religious. They might do that. My heart starts racing. Dad doesn't get it. He always thinks things will just magically work out. But they don't. "I need to know. This is important to me. We have to find out!"

He glances at me and frowns. "We will, Zoe. You don't need to yell."

"I'm not yelling." Outside the car, the world rushes by in a blur. I want him to slow down. I want him to never get to Bethesda. Or better yet, keep going. "What if it's far away? How will I get there?"

"Your mom or I will drive you."

"But what if it's a workday—will you take off work?"

"Yes, Zoe. Even if it's a workday, we will drive you to the funeral."

Is that annoyance in his voice? Am I bothering him with my questions? They always say, *Come to us with anything. We're here for you. Whenever you need to talk.* But it isn't true. I don't blame him. He's just not like that. But it makes me so lonely.

Dad pulls up in front of Quartermaine and puts his blinkers on. It's a few minutes before 6:00.

"Look, sweetie." He shuts off the music and turns in the seat to face me. "You're going to the funeral. Even if it's in Nova Scotia, or Oklahoma, or Fiji. We will get you there, okay?"

"Fiji, huh?" I smile, but my eyes fill with tears. "I don't want to miss it. But at the same time, I also don't want to go."

"I can understand that. The funeral makes it real."

"Also, like, she was my *friend*. You know? And the funeral is going to be all these strangers—" A baby hiccup sob escapes me. "It sounds stupid, but I don't want to share her."

"That's not stupid. I totally get it. I remember when my cousin died in high school, Benji? I've told you about him. To me, he was this cool older-brother type, the guy who taught me how to do so many things. Like cliff jumping." He lets out a little laugh. "And then I remember after his death hearing all these people he went to school with talk about what a great student he was, and how he was in model UN, and it felt like I lost a little of him. Like maybe I didn't know him as much as I thought I did. It made me sadder."

I nod and wait for him to say more. To offer some advice, like my mom would. But he doesn't. We sit in silence for a moment. I watch the green digital numbers click to 6:01.

"Well, I'd better go," I say, wiping my eyes. "Work started a minute ago."

"Have a good first day," he says. "And don't get too jacked up on caffeine."

I get out and watch the car pull away. It's disappeared before I even enter the small shop. When I step inside, the rich scent of ground coffee envelops me like a warm hug. I can feel my shoulders drop a little. I used to come here all the time with Emery, and the smell reminds me of her, but not in a sad way. Not this time. These memories make me happy. Yonas is already there, behind the bar, polishing an immense metal espresso machine.

"Good morning, Zoe." He glances up and winks at me. He's one of those guys who seems to be able to grow hair everywhere—he has a massive mustache and bushy black eyebrows—except on top of his head. Yonas is why I have this job. Emery and I would get drinks and sit on the bench outside and just watch people. She would invent backstories for every single person that walked by, making me laugh so hard I thought I'd pee my pants.

Over time, we became friends with Yonas. Almost all the customers know him. He's kind of like a celebrity here, famous for making the best espressos and cappuccinos. He's older than my dad, moved here from Ethiopia, like, twenty years ago. He's the one who said I should apply for a summer job.

I take my spot behind the register like I was trained to. Next to me, the manager, Davida, is counting out my drawer.

"How are you this fine morning?" Yonas asks.

I look up at his smiling face but say nothing. Answering him would destroy me. Does he know about Emery? He doesn't seem to, but I can't bring it up. What if he asks questions? I don't want to talk about finding her body on the beach like that. How I shook her by her shoulders, trying to get her to wake up, yet knowing that she wouldn't. Her wide-open eyes staring up at the black sky. Her arms heavy and leaden as if filled with wet sand. Her skin so cold. I swallow hard. I open my mouth to say something to him, anything, but nothing happens. Not even one word escapes my throat. I shut my mouth again. I'm so afraid that the stitching keeping me together will burst open and that my insides will spill out of my skin onto the sticky floor of the coffee shop. Yonas cocks his head to one side, his dark eyes boring into me as if he knows all this.

"You can put your stuff in the back room," he says in such a soft voice that it is barely audible above the instrumental music playing in the background. "And while you're there, go ahead and grab an apron."

In the cool darkness of the back room, I find a folded navy apron next to boxes of lids and cups. I breathe in deeply. I just need to make it through the day. One day. Along the back wall stands a tall stack of cubbies, the kind we had in kindergarten, and I find a free one where I can store my backpack. Next to the cubbies is a handwritten sign: *Absolutely no cell phones at work!! Leave your phone here.*

Reluctantly, I place my phone in the cubby.

Back out front, the morning rush has started, and a line snakes out the door of the small shop. There's no time to think about anything. No time to dwell on Emery. Or what I could have done differently. Take the order. Punch it in the register, mark the cups, and pass them to Yonas. Tell people to swipe their cards or tap their phones. Take the order . . .

Just before ten, there's a lull, and that's when they walk in.

Olivia and Kinsey.

I don't realize at first who has entered the store, because I'm busy restocking lids. It's not until they're right in front of the cash register that I realize who they are.

"Zoe. Hi." Olivia's voice is the kind of sweet that makes me gag, like the gloopy white glaze on a cinnamon bun. She cocks her head to one side, so much highlighter on her cheeks and forehead that she looks like the Tin Man from *The Wizard of Oz*. It's not makeup for real life. It's makeup for Instagram.

I try to smile, but my mouth refuses, and I know it looks more like a grimace.

"I didn't know you were working here," Kinsey says in a sing-song voice. "That's so cute. Isn't it, Liv?"

"Totally. It's like that coffee shop on *Friends*. Remember when Rachel had to work there?"

I literally bite the inside of my cheek so that I don't say something awful. Like, *Why are you watching nineties shows? Are you that desperate to turn into your mothers?* I'm pretty sure telling customers to fuck off and die is a fireable offense.

"Do you guys want to order?"

Olivia makes pouty duck lips. They go back and forth about the merits of iced chai versus vanilla lattes like they're debating the best way to stop global warming. I'm waiting. Yonas is waiting. The customer behind them, a mom with a fussy baby, is waiting. Just when I think the mom behind them might smash their heads together, they decide on vanilla iced lattes. I tell Yonas, and he narrows his eyes ever so slightly. He has a not-so-secret contempt for adulterating coffee with flavored syrups.

I'm ringing them up when Kinsey says, "So are you going?"

"Going to what?" I motion for her to tap her Apple Pay.

"To Emery's funeral."

My whole body freezes. The small screen in front of me goes blurry as tears spring to my eyes. *Do not cry, not in front of them.* I can feel their eyes on me, waiting for me to implode.

"Oh my god, Zoe," Olivia says. "Are you okay?"

It takes all my focus to finish the transaction.

"Do you want a receipt?" My voice cracks. I have to ask. It's part of the job. Free coffee if I forget to give them one.

"Oh, you didn't know? Her funeral's the day after tomorrow." Kinsey gives me a sad, little, satisfied smile. "I'm so surprised. I thought you guys were such good friends."

CHAPTER 16

LIZA

Don't say anything to embarrass me.
  Why are you like that?
  Even the way you stand annoys me.
  Don't come in with me.
  Don't wait for me.
  Don't talk to me.
A collection of Zoe's greatest hits replays in my head on my way down to Capitol Hill to meet Archer. I've never felt further away from Zoe than I do right now. My chest aches when I think of how sad she must be about Emery and how she won't let me in. And then the panic creeps up on that sadness and overtakes it, as my mind goes back to the drinking, the lying, the paternity.

I pass my regular coffee shop on Massachusetts Avenue, which is in the same small shopping strip as Todd's latest restaurant, the Mill City Bar and Grill. It would have been so much more convenient for me to meet Archer up here, or even halfway between our two places, but he wanted to meet near the MSNBC offices, and I did not feel I could say no.

Up here, at the far western corner of Washington, D.C., "Mass Ave" divides the haves from the have-a-lots. My neighborhood, on the eastern side, is called AU Park, so named because it abuts

American University. Historically middle and upper-middle class, filled with government workers and academics, some of the houses on this side were made from mail-order kits. Mine is a "Westley" from Sears and Roebuck. But today, even the smallest homes in the neighborhood are running a cool million. If I hadn't inherited my father's house, I doubt I could afford to buy here now.

But the other side of Mass Ave is an entirely different story. Spring Valley is home to diplomats, politicians, and elite D.C. society, like the owners of the Washington Nationals. The rolling hills of the neighborhood boast large houses set back from the road on big lots and a bucolic privacy that belies the fact that it's technically in a city. It's where Shelby grew up and where she and Todd live now.

Traffic into downtown D.C. is not too bad, and before long, I am winding around Union Station onto F Street where I find a parking spot catty-corner from Ebenezers Coffeehouse. Archer lives on the eastern end of Stanton Park, smack-dab in the middle of Capitol Hill, and MSNBC's offices are a short walk away, tucked behind Union Station. Ebenezers Coffeehouse is about halfway between the two.

Inside the small shop, no seats are free, so I head back out to the brick patio to look around. Most of the wrought iron tables are occupied, and people have laptops or open textbooks in front of them, indicating little chance they will be moving in the next few hours. I hover near a guy with a sweep of blue bangs who seems to be finishing up. As soon as he gets up, I make a beeline for the table and throw my bag across the chair I'm not sitting in. No sign of Archer yet. I settle in to wait.

Archer is late, but he always is. I take the time to check my messages, bracing myself. As soon as I glance at my phone, I know that the pinging that started at six this morning has continued unabated. Everyone's sending me the same damn *Washington Post* story.

PREP SCHOOL STUDENT DROWNS AT BEACH WEEK

It might make me a relic, but I still get the newspaper delivered. It's not just because I used to be a reporter. I grew up in a
newspaper house. My father was a sports editor at *The Post* for
most of his career. Starting each morning by pulling the paper
from a plastic baggie is one of those little rituals that gives my
life meaning. I like the tactile feel of the paper as I eat my breakfast. I reach into my bag and pull out the Metro section. The article I'm looking for is above the fold, accompanied by a desolate
photo of the lighthouse, stark and solitary against a cloudy sky.
It's written by Indah Lubis. I've met Indah a few times. She's
new to the paper—smart, young, hungry. I don't yet have the
relationship with her that I had with her predecessor. But that
still does not explain why I didn't get a call from her.

*The drowning death of a Washington Prep student during
Beach Week has roiled the close-knit private school community.*

I suppress a bitter laugh. Roiled the school? That seems like
a bit of an exaggeration. School's not even in session. But Geoff
won't see this for what it is—sensationalism. He will be furious. Washington Prep is not just mentioned in the story, it's in
the lede. The board of trustees won't like it, either, and they'll
blame me. Maybe *blame* is too strong a word, but they will hold
me responsible. It's not my fault, of course. I can't control what
The Washington Post prints, but as the communications director,
I'm ultimately accountable. The board never wants to see Washington Prep in the news, unless it's a story about a student winning a competition or an alumnus who has just done something
spectacular, like get appointed to the Supreme Court.

It's a tall order to magically ensure that nothing negative
about Washington Prep ever appears in the news. Todd serves
on the board of trustees, so at least Shelby will have the inside

scoop on how they perceive I'm handling all this. I doubt they would fire me over this, but I'd still like to know which way the wind is blowing.

Teenagers who spend Beach Week at the Delaware shore are nicknamed "June bugs" because they descend on the towns like insects, wreaking havoc.

I skip down to the part about Emery.

"Emery was a radiant girl, just had her whole future ahead of her," said one Washington Prep mother who spoke on the condition of anonymity. "The world has lost a light. Not everyone is cut out for such a competitive school. I just wish she would have been able to get the help she needed."

The quote sickens me. It's all there—obliquely mentioning the suicide, blaming Emery for not being up to snuff, pretending to be close to Emery, and at the same time reminding everyone that Washington Prep is a top-notch school. The reporter should have called me instead of this anonymous mother.

And I know Geoff will also be wondering why I am not quoted in the story.

He'll want to know how this concerned mother spoke with Indah when I did not. The woman's choice of words was elliptical, with no explicit mention of suicide, but it's clear to anyone paying attention. And if you didn't figure out that Emery killed herself from the quote, the reporter kindly added the phone number and website address of the National Suicide Prevention Lifeline at the bottom of the story.

I fold the paper back up and shove it into my bag.

When I started as a reporter, newspapers still regularly mentioned suicide in articles. Now, newspapers do not, unless the victim is famous or it is somehow newsworthy—for example, if the act was committed in a public place. The change resulted from raised awareness that press coverage might trigger suicide contagion and copycat behavior. But whether *The Washington Post* uses the word or not, every student at Washington Prep, and probably every private school kid in the D.C. area, knows it was suicide. And all those kids, especially the ones already suffering from depression, are now a bit more vulnerable.

Including, of course, Zoe.

The mood around me shifts ever so slightly, and I look up, knowing instinctively that Archer has walked onto the patio. He makes his way to me, seemingly oblivious to the turned heads and whispers. Or maybe he's just used to it.

"Let me grab an espresso," he says. "You need anything?"

"Define *need*."

He laughs. "I take that as a yes."

"Make it a double. Please."

I watch through the plate glass window as Archer chats with the woman in line ahead of him. She flips her hair and grins. I can see she is clearly charmed by him, even from where I sit. When it is his turn at the counter, he makes the barista throw her head back and laugh. I wonder what it is like to go through life winning everyone over like that. In a few moments, Archer returns outside with our coffees and takes the seat across from me.

"How you holding up?" he asks. "How's Zoe? Poor kid."

I wince. "So you heard."

"Well, Shelby told Todd . . . You get the idea." His dark brown eyes lock with mine with such intensity, it is like they are peering into my soul. He has that same gift that people described Bill Clinton as having. Apparently, even Clinton's enemies were mesmerized by his charisma. "There are no secrets with our friends."

"I figured," I say.

"It's pretty messed up, Liza. Both that it happened and that Zoe found her. She must be really shaken up."

"She is. And honestly, so am I." I pause to take a sip of my coffee. "I mean, it's déjà vu."

He frowns. "How do you mean?"

I blink hard. "I mean Nikki Montes. She drowned at Beach Week, too. You didn't think of that?"

He nods slowly as if he's just putting the two events together. "That's right."

"It's the first thing I thought of." I chalk up his reaction to some misguided machismo, an unwillingness to show vulnerability. And Nikki is a vulnerable spot for all of us, isn't she? "Truth is, I've been thinking a lot about Nikki lately."

"Really?" Archer furrows his brow. "Like what?"

I sigh. "Like did we do enough for her? As her friends? I feel like we just let her go."

"What could we do, Liza? She drowned."

"I don't know. We just moved on with our lives so quickly. I didn't stay in touch with her family. And I feel really guilty about that. I know she had a younger brother. I met her parents a bunch of times. But I just moved on with my life."

"Your feelings are understandable, but we were eighteen. There was nothing we could do."

"Maybe. I don't know. I don't have any answers." I used to think of grief as a temporary visitor, like an owl that flew in through the chimney and sits ominously on your bookshelf. One day, it would be gone. One day, I won't have to tiptoe into the living room with trepidation, afraid of spooking it. But now I know better. Ever since my father died. Grief never leaves; you simply learn to live in the same house with it.

And now Zoe has her own permanent houseguest, who will travel with her wherever she goes—to college and beyond. It's not just Emery's death she'll have to deal with but those searing images of finding a dead body on the beach. I shudder.

"You okay?" Archer asks. "You sound like you feel guilty."

"Do I?" I ask, startled. "I can't explain why, but I have this sense of unfilled obligation to Nikki."

Something flickers across his face. Something I have never seen in Archer. Doubt? Pain? It's like the mask of self-confidence has dropped for the briefest moment, revealing a vulnerable human riddled with the same insecurities and doubts as the rest of us. And just like that, it's gone. "And are you going to do something about it?"

"Actually, yes." I smile widely. "I was thinking of doing an article about Emery . . ."

"Go on."

"And, well, the alumni magazine has never run anything about Nikki. I checked. Nowadays, if a current student dies, we do a page for them. Two years ago when Piper Bogardus died of leukemia, we did a lovely little tribute to her. But the magazine never did that for Nikki. So I thought I could do a little piece about her when I write the piece on Emery."

Archer shifts in his seat. "You really want to get into all that?"

"Just a small portion of the larger story. Maybe a sidebar. Nothing major."

"Does Geoff know?" His tone is pointed, the one he uses to grill oily members of Congress.

I squirm in my seat. "Actually, I was hoping you could help. We both know that if *you* happened to mention it was a good idea . . ."

He laughs. I don't have to say anything more. A positive word from him would make this article happen. There's nothing more valuable to a private school than having successful alumni, and Geoff seems particularly in awe of celebrity. Unlike his predecessor, the stodgy Dr. Kales, Geoff seems to relish the social aspect of being the head of the school, never missing a chance to rub elbows with the more prominent parents and alumni. I've seen his calendar, which is filled with lunches, cocktail parties,

and galas. Dr. Kales belonged to a different time, when ostenta-
tious displays of money were considered tacky. He thought himself a steward of young scholars, not a glad-hander. It might be
why the endowment suffered under him, and he was pushed out.

Under Geoff's short reign, the endowment has swelled to almost fifty million, and we've hired an anthropologist in residence, established a teaching kitchen, and the athletic fields have
undergone a total renovation.

Archer glances at his watch. "While I'd like nothing more
than to chill with you the whole day . . ."

I nod and pull out my notebook and pen. I may no longer be
a newspaper reporter, but I still love my little spiral-bound note-
books. "I have most of what I need for my article about you, but
I do have a few follow-up questions."

We spend the next fifteen minutes talking about how amazing Archer is and how he owes it all to Washington Prep. He
knows exactly what I need, and he delivers line after line. Back
in the old days, at newspapers, we used to say, *So-and-so gives
good quote*. Well, Archer gives good quote and then some. Almost all his lines could be pull quotes, those large-font bolded
lines that grab your eye in a story. He was a walking PR machine
for himself, for the school, for whatever he wanted to promote.
I wonder, not for the first time, what it was like to date him.
Did he ever let down his guard?

I'm putting away my things when I notice him staring at me
with narrowed eyes. I stop what I'm doing. "What is it?"

"Listen, is everything okay with Zoe? I mean, besides everything that happened at Beach Week."

"*Besides* her friend dying?" I try not to bristle. "I mean, I guess
she's fine. Why?"

"I don't want to overstep my bounds."

"Well, the past two years have been tough on her. You know,
splitting time between Daniel and me."

"And it's tough on you, I bet."

"Yes, but it's different for kids." Archer is one of the few people I know who made it into his forties with no children in tow. He can cluck sympathetically when Todd, Shelby, and I talk about how exhausting parenting is, but at the end of the day, he retreats to the silence of his luxury condo, carved out of the former bell tower of a Gothic nineteenth-century church overlooking Stanton Park and complete with ten-foot-tall stained-glass windows.

"I wasn't going to bring this up, but . . ." His voice trails off.

"But what?"

"It's just, I'd want someone to tell me if it were my kid."

I roll my eyes. "Tell me what, Archer?"

He pulls out his phone. "Remember the last Kentucky Derby party at my house?"

"Of course." Every spring, Archer holds a party in his condo, the guest list a who's who of the D.C. media elite, carrying on a tradition started by his father. In high school, we'd all get dressed up and go to the Benoits' lavish derby-watching party at their home. We'd sneak mint juleps and hide out in Archer's room.

"Remember how Zoe showed up?" he asked.

"I remember. She wanted my keys. She locked herself out." Was he upset that a sullen teenager had crashed his party?

"Uh-huh. Well, I have security cameras. Upstairs."

"All right." I cock my head. That is odd. Why would he have security cameras inside his home? But before I can ask, he turns his phone to me.

"And one of them caught this."

He taps the phone, and I watch as a video begins to play—black-and-white grainy footage of a long, empty hallway.

"That's my bedroom." He points to a closed door at the end of the hall.

"I don't understand."

"Just wait."

We sit in silence for a painful few moments. Finally, a door opens and a figure emerges, head down. Shutting the door, the figure turns, head tilted up, face caught by the camera.

My stomach does a little flip as Zoe's face looks up at the camera for a second. It's like she can see me watching her. But she clearly does not see the camera. She glances both ways and then looks down. It's unclear what she is doing, until I realize she is fidgeting with something in her hand. But what?

She starts down the hallway, but not before she stuffs the object into her pocket, momentarily exposing it to the camera. I can hear myself suck in my breath when I see what it is.

A plastic baggie stamped with a rainbow made of dots.

The same rainbow as on the paternity test I found.

CHAPTER 17

1994

An Ace of Base song blasted through the house on Dagsworthy, the bass so loud that the empty cans of Milwaukee's Best vibrated on the kitchen table. Shelby and Whitney danced in front of the sliding doors that were open to a deck looking out over the dark Atlantic. At the round kitchen table, Nikki stood behind Archer. Everyone watched reverently as Don Fraser, whose parents had rented the house, poured beer into the eight shot glasses lined up in front of Archer.

Nikki was trying to figure out the rules of the game, which all the guys seemed to know instinctively. All she had gleaned so far was that they called it "Evel Knievel."

Archer took the quarter he had been holding and bounced it on the table, sending it flying over the glasses closest to him and into the one at the end. Everyone at the table groaned while he pumped his fist in the air.

"Yes!" He handed out the glasses to several of the guys at the table. Nikki couldn't help noticing that the guys were playing while the girls behind them were clapping like cheerleaders. At what point, she wondered, do girls get to do the interesting stuff? Maybe college.

Across the room, an old-fashioned cuckoo clock, the kind with carved, wooden pine cones, chimed the time. Nine thirty. Her parents were expecting her phone call at ten. God knows what they might do if she didn't check in. She could picture her wild-eyed mom waking her father and insisting he call Shelby's parents or, worse, the Dewey police. Nikki shuddered at the thought of the embarrassing depths to which her family might drag her.

She went in search of a phone in a quiet part of the house, but no luck. Maybe Don would know. But when she located him, he was busy guzzling beer from one end of a tube while Whitney sat on his lap, arm held high, holding in the air the other end of the tube, which had a funnel attached to it. Quick glances into both upstairs bedrooms told her they were occupied with couples. That left only the phone in the kitchen. Nikki stood at the edge of the room and surveyed the scene. There had to be at least fifty people crammed in here. Todd let out a loud "Damn!" as a quarter clanked off the rim of a shot glass and fell onto the table. The crowd chanted, "Drink! Drink!"

Damn it. What was she going to do?

Nikki pushed her way over to the counter where Shelby and Liza were hanging out.

"There you are." Liza threw an arm around her, smelling of beer. "My New York buddy. We are going to have so much fun."

Nikki leaned on her friend's shoulder and inhaled her strawberry-scented shampoo. She and Liza were the same. Not just because they both were kind of outsiders at Washington Prep but because they were outsiders in real life, too. Once, she was complaining to Liza that most of her Salvadoran and Honduran neighbors automatically assumed she was Central American, too. "They act like I'm the one who's weird because I don't know some Salvadoran singer. Why would I? Because I'm Hispanic? I can't wait to move to New York and be around other Nuyoricans."

And Liza had gotten it. She said she felt so awkward when she went to her dad's colleague's house for a Passover seder. It was all in Hebrew, and she didn't know a word of it. She said everyone was scowling at her.

"I felt like such a fake Jew," Liza had said. "And then I go back to school, and I have to explain to everyone what matzah is."

Nikki planted a kiss on Liza's frizzy hair.

"Eww, stop. You're making me jealous. And it's my birthday, you know. So you're supposed to be nice to me. It's the law." Shelby threw a crumpled napkin at them. "I'm totally gonna come visit. I want to see *Beauty and the Beast*."

"The movie?" Liza asked.

"No. The Broadway show. I heard it's amazing."

Liza wrinkled her nose. "Umm, maybe. As in, probably not. So no. I'm not gonna do that."

"Why not?"

"'Cause I have taste?"

Nikki guffawed. She had been thinking the same thing but would never have said that.

"Bitch, don't be such a snob. Your idea of fun is to go watch someone fill out the *New York Times* crossword puzzle."

Liza laughed. "Touché."

"Wait, what?" Shelby pushed around the cases of beer stacked on the counter. "No more Zima?" She stuck out her lower lip in an exaggerated pout.

"Just drink beer like everybody else." Whitney came up behind her and grabbed a can.

"No way." Shelby made a face of pure horror, and everyone cracked up. Nikki felt sorry for her. She'd seen Shelby scribbling the caloric intake of every morsel that passed her lips into her hot-pink Filofax.

"I need more Zima. We have to go back to the house and get some," Shelby said.

"Aww, hell no," Whitney said, her eyes flitting toward Don. "I think I'm gonna hook up with Don tonight."

"You totally should," Liza said. "Just use a condom."

"Okay, *Mom*." Whitney rolled her eyes.

"C'mon, guys, come with me?" Shelby wheedled. "I don't want to go alone."

Nikki saw her opportunity. She could offer to go get more Zima from Shelby's house, where she could call her parents in privacy.

"I'll do it." Nikki straightened up. She was already picturing herself in Shelby's living room. She wouldn't even have to lie to her parents about where she was, not technically. She *would* be at Shelby's house when she made the call. It was genius.

"Really?" Shelby looked surprised. "You'll come with me?"

"Actually, I'll go by myself." She didn't want anyone to witness her checking in with her parents.

"What?" Shelby scrunched up her nose. She had one of those little noses, the kind that belonged on baby dolls. "You don't have to do that."

"I don't mind. It's your birthday."

"Stop. It's not for another two hours."

Whitney whooped and then belched. "Don't be milking it, Covington. You're still seventeen for now."

"Aww, our little baby." Liza leaned in and gave Shelby a kiss on the cheek. "I'll go with you, Nikki. I don't mind. Anyway, you can't carry a cooler by yourself."

"Really, it's fine. I'll be fine." Nikki sounded a little too strident, and she worried they would become suspicious. It was so obvious she didn't want them with her. She forced a laugh. "Guys, it's fine. I can carry some Zima a few blocks by myself. It's not that far. I'll use the red wagon. The one in the backyard?" She had seen the Radio Flyer sitting there, near the concrete bricks for the new wall.

She waited for the pushback, but a Snoop Dogg song came on, and Whitney squealed and dragged Liza into the middle of the kitchen to dance.

"The key to the house is inside the little frog," Shelby said. "You sure?"

Nikki nodded and left before any of them could change their minds.

Outside, the night air was thick and muggy, but it felt so good to be free. Maybe she was an introvert, after all. She had taken the Myers-Briggs personality test one afternoon at the Tenley-town library with Liza, just for fun. Liza had been excited by the results. *We're both introverts. That's why we get along.* But Nikki had bristled at the label, protesting that she wasn't shy.

"It's not about being shy," Liza had said. "It's about having to recharge your batteries by being alone."

Well, Nikki thought, maybe Liza was right. She'd been with other people since the moment she left Wheaton this morning, and it felt like a relief to get a little break from the nonstop chattering. As she walked toward the bright lights of the businesses and bars on Route 1, she touched the pendant hanging on her neck. It was a sweet gesture on Shelby's part, she thought. Un-expected. Not to mention four of these would not be cheap. But she was back to doubting that she'd ever hang out with Shelby again—or Whitney, for that matter. Maybe at reunions or par-ties over Christmas break, but that was about it. Liza was an-other story. College would be a whole new chapter for her.

She stopped short when she got to Route 1, surprised to see the street was packed with people eating pizza, laughing, and just hanging out. To her left, a cop straddled a bicycle in front of three teenage boys who were sitting in a line on the curb, feet in the gutter. It looked as if the officer was writing them tickets for having open containers of alcohol.

Nikki went over the route back to Shelby's house in her mind. Across Route 1, then through the neighborhood streets to a cut-through that led to a small park. Beyond the park was the coun-try club entrance.

From there, it was simple. Shelby's house was the third on the right. Only, it was dark now, and it was positively pitch-black across the street, where she was headed. She was starting to regret volunteering to do this. Not to mention that on the way back, she'd have to pull a wagon through this intersection to get the Zima back to the party. The risk of getting caught with all that alcohol made her nervous. There were cops everywhere. Was it okay as long as the bottles were unopened? She wasn't sure. Alternatively, she could go south a few blocks where there was less action, but it would mean a much longer walk and most of it in the dark.

The dark. It figured into so many of the cautionary tales that her dad, a Montgomery County police detective, told at the dinner table. Stories of high school parties that raged like out-of-control wildfires in places like Bethesda or Potomac. He spoke of faux-château mansions that looked like Barbie's DreamHouse come to life, with acres of sprawling green lawns. Her mother's shock was a renewable resource when it came to these stories. Each one caught her off guard and disgusted her anew. Much the way a child thrills to a terrifying fairy tale about monsters, her mother relished these tellings of alcohol poisonings, date rapes, and DUIs. The most shocking detail of all was how the parents were often at home, that they even bought the alcohol, and then were hostile to the police when they showed up.

Her father and mother would trade gasps and horrified looks at the idea of parents corrupting their own children, not to mention disrespecting the authorities once they were exposed.

If only they knew what Nikki had witnessed firsthand over the past four years, they would have shipped her off to an all-girls' Catholic school.

There was no way she would survive getting busted for pulling a red wagon full of alcohol. She didn't have the kind of parents who would laugh it off as a rite of passage. Unlike Liza's dad, who let her sip his beer during the baseball game or have wine at Passover, her own parents strictly forbade any underage drinking.

Suddenly, someone tapped her, interrupting her thoughts. Nikki jumped. She turned to see a man beside her in a baseball cap, holding a bottle. It took less than a second to register the face: it was her track coach from Washington Prep.

"Oh, hey," she said. "I didn't recognize you . . ."

"Without my whistle?" He laughed.

"No, it's just here, in Dewey. Like out of school—"

"Relax, I'm just teasing you."

A lot of the girls at school had crushes on him or at least pretended to. Nikki could see why. He was younger than the other teachers and coaches, not just years-wise but also in the way he acted. He listened to Dave Matthews, cracked jokes at practice, treated the students more like equals. Rumor had it he even went to some house parties and bought beer for seniors on the track team, but Nikki didn't believe that.

"What are you doing here?" she asked.

He thrust his chin toward the Corkboard, where the crowd was spilling outside onto the sidewalk. "With friends. My parents have a beach house in Bethany Beach. What about you? Beach Week?"

"Yeah." Bethany Beach was about fifteen minutes south of here. From what she had gleaned, it was more family-oriented, with fewer dive bars and less binge drinking. She wondered if he was going to lecture her about drinking, but he held his beer out.

"Want a sip?"

She looked around to see if any police were watching. A little voice inside her screamed, *Danger!* but she took a swig, anyway. That's what you did when guys offered you a drink. You didn't say no. As soon as the alcohol hit her gut, her insides churned, and she felt like she needed a bathroom. "That tastes a lot different from the beer I usually drink."

"What beer you guys drinking back there?"

"Umm, Milwaukee's Best?"

"Ah, the Beast. Brings back memories." He looked at the bottle. "Yeah, Sam Adams is a slight upgrade. So where are you going by yourself? Shouldn't you be with friends?"

She hesitated, wondering if she could tell him the truth. "I'm on a Zima run."

He made a face. "Zima? Really? Aww, man."

She giggled. "It's not for me. It's for Whitney. And Shelby."

He grinned. "Aha. Shelby Covington of the administration building Covingtons."

Everyone knew about the Covingtons. And not just because the name was on the largest building on campus. Shelby's three older brothers—all popular athletes—had swaggered through the halls of Wash Prep. Her father and uncles had, too, as well as her grandfather. "So where is this Zima stash?"

Nikki jutted her chin toward the darkness across the street. "Shelby's house. It's in the country club. We're all staying there." She cringed a little at her response. She wasn't sure why she had added the country club part. That made her sound dumb, like she thought it was a big deal. But he didn't seem to notice.

"Nice. And how do you plan to transport your contraband?"

"I think there's a wagon I can use?" She winced at her own intonation. She hated the way she always sounded like she was asking a question, even when she was sure of herself.

He laughed. "How much Zima we talking?"

"Like two cases, maybe three?"

"All right, tell you what. In exchange for getting to use a non-disgusting bathroom, I'll help you with your Zima mission."

"What makes you think our bathroom is non-disgusting?"

"Hmm. Something tells me the Covington lavatory is a step above the Corkboard's."

She smiled, but her mind was racing. His being there would interfere with the privacy she needed to call her parents. On the other hand, she could use the help carrying the Zima. Plus, she would feel safer if he came with her. She knew the odds were low of a serial killer waiting in the trees to jump out and rape and murder her, but the thought of poking around in the dark still terrified her.

"Okay," she said, and together, they crossed the street. "Thanks, Coach."

He grinned. "C'mon. Call me Geoff."

CHAPTER 18

LIZA

I stare at Archer's phone, unwilling to lift my eyes to meet his. I'm afraid of what I will see in his face and what he will see in mine. The rhythmic whoosh of my own heartbeat fills my ears, drowning out the chatter around us. After a few moments, he pulls the phone back and clears his throat.

"It's not that big a deal. I just thought you should know."

"What did she take?" Keeping my tone neutral takes every fiber of my being. I hope I sound concerned and curious, rather than revealing the panic swelling within me.

"I don't know," he says. "Nothing was missing."

"I'm so sorry, Archer."

"Oh, uhhh . . ." He waves away my apology, visibly uncomfortable.

"You don't, by any chance, keep pot or any other, uh, substances like that in your bedroom, do you?"

He shakes his head.

"Painkillers? Vicodin?"

He grins. "Nope. Strictly a bourbon-and-beer guy. Look, maybe she was just using my bathroom."

"Maybe." Neither of us believes it.

"There is a guest bath downstairs, but maybe it was occupied . . ." His voice trails off. Neither of us knows what to say. He flashes that megawatt smile. "Look, I'm not trying to bust Zoe or anything. Lord knows I did worse when I was in high school. I mean, you could probably tell some tales on me."

"All of us," I say weakly.

"I just . . . I'm worried about her. It would be awful for her to become tangled up in the criminal justice system."

My mouth drops open. I stare at Archer in disbelief. Did he really just say that? A young woman stops by our table and stands over us, oozing a sickly sweet perfume, a several-thousand-dollar Gucci bag hanging off her wrist. "Hi, you're Archer Benoit, right? I freaking love you. I watch you at the gym every day. Can I get a selfie?"

As Archer stands, I seize the moment to gather my things and make a quick exit. I have to get out of here before he realizes how upset I am.

Work, I mouth, grateful he is occupied and can't say anything more about Zoe.

Archer turns away from the camera long enough to flash me a smile.

I sit inside my car on F Street, trying to get my bearings. It is just after nine o'clock, and I've already sweated through my shirt—my bra is sticking uncomfortably to my skin. I position the vents toward me and blast the AC. What the hell is going on? Did I just watch a video of my daughter sneaking a DNA sample from Archer? And what was with his remark about the criminal justice system? Tossing that little hand grenade into the conversation does not seem like an accident. Any parent would freak out. *But he's not a parent,* I tell myself. Maybe he doesn't realize how scary those words are.

I stare at my phone, debating whether I should call Zoe. I can't bring myself to interrupt her first day at work. She probably doesn't have time to talk, anyway. But the questions keep stacking up—this damn paternity test. First, Brody's bandages, and now Archer. Just what the hell is going on?

As soon as I am back on Massachusetts Avenue heading toward work, Daniel calls.

"Yo." He sounds sleepy. I picture him in his empty apartment, splayed out on the sofa, dozing. I'm jealous, to be honest. "I have a thing today." He yawns loudly. I can picture him stretching like a cat. I banish the image of Daniel's six-pack from my mind. "Do you want to pick Zoe up from work?"

"Yeah, sure." With my flex hours, I can leave early if need be. It will be the perfect chance to talk to her face-to-face. " Listen. I just had coffee with Archer. He told me something rather disturbing."

"Let me guess. They're moving him to a Thursday morning slot."

"Ha ha. He has footage of Zoe leaving his room. She took something." I don't mention the paternity test. I want to hear from Zoe before I bring that up.

"What footage?"

"Apparently, he has security cameras all over his house."

"Well, that's creepy. Is that even legal?"

"Not the point. The point is he has footage of our daughter entering his bedroom—his bedroom, Daniel—and leaving with something she's shoved into her pocket."

"What was it?"

"Can't tell." Not completely a lie. I know what I think it is. At least from what I could see. But now in the car, I can't swear to it. Maybe my mind was playing tricks on me. It could have been a plain old Ziploc baggie.

"Is he missing anything?"

"Not that he knows."

"So . . a guest, the daughter of a guest, comes to one of his parties, and she wanders upstairs. That's not a crime."

"This is not about what can be proven in a court of law. You're not taking this seriously."

"Taking what seriously, exactly? So she was snooping a little. Teens do that. Nothing was missing. Maybe it was a tissue she shoved in her pocket. Maybe it was her lip balm. Christ, Liza, tell me you didn't confront her about this."

"No," I say, annoyed. "Not yet."

"She's having a rough enough time of it. Her friend just died. By suicide." A silence follows, and for a moment, I wonder if we've been disconnected. But then I hear the distant wail of an ambulance coming through his end. Daniel clears his throat. "Listen, when you pick her up today, don't go yelling at her, Liza. Just listen to her. Can you do that? Just listen?"

After I hang up, I realize begrudgingly that he might have a point and that calling her would have been disastrous. As much as I hate to admit it, Daniel might be better at parenting a teen than I am. I was a great parent of a baby and a toddler. I saw all the dangers, childproofed everything. I made sure she learned to swim, I scheduled her vaccines and wellness visits, I taught her about stranger danger. But no one informed me that what had worked so well during Zoe's younger years would backfire in spectacular fashion once she became a teen.

I remember what her therapist said last summer, right after Daniel and I told her about the split. Dr. Weiss told us to *hide the talking in an ice cream cone.* She meant, don't speak in anger, don't deliver a lecture, but wait until everyone's in a good mood, and dole out your thoughts while doing something fun.

That's what I'll do with Zoe this afternoon. I just pray she is in a good mood when I pick her up.

Because I need answers.

You could be forgiven, upon driving by the wrought iron gates of Washington Prep, for thinking that you were passing a country club. The school, founded in 1850, sits tucked away on several acres off Foxhall Road. The only tell that the tree-lined drive leads to a school is a large crest on the gates with the school's motto beneath: *Veritas vos liberabit.*

The truth will set you free.

From the moment I stepped onto this campus for a school tour in sixth grade, I fell in love with the place. I had just finished reading *Pride and Prejudice* for the second time, a gift from my father for my eleventh birthday, and I remember how the small stone chapel with the climbing roses struck me as exactly what the Hunsford Parsonage might look like.

Thirty years later, cresting the rolling green hill and taking in the old stone buildings is still an escape from the chaos of the modern world, a step back into a gentler and serener time. Of course, the sound of hundreds of shouting, laughing students can shatter that sensation, but not in the early summer, when the campus enjoys a rare lull between the end of school and the beginning of the summer offerings.

I park my car in the small lot by the Covington building. I gave Zoe the option of taking any summer class she wanted here—squash, coding, Chinese immersion, but she sniffed at every class in the catalog and said she'd rather get a job.

Fine, I said, so sure she would never actually get one. I've watched the kids in Zoe's generation struggle with things that came easily to mine—getting a driver's license, applying for jobs, talking to strangers, navigating public transport.

But she surprised me.

Covington's heavy oak doors open to reveal a grand foyer with two Chesterfield sofas flanked by potted ferns too tall to fit in ordinary rooms. Oil portraits of white, stern-faced men stare down from their perches on the wall. *Do you think you're good enough?* they seem to ask potential applicants. There is talk of replacing one or two with a woman or a person of color, but it never moves beyond talk.

I walk by Shelby's great-great-grandfather Prescott Covington on the way to my office. He might be a good candidate to be taken down. He helped found the school thanks to a fortune made from a peanut plantation in North Carolina.

The whole school, like so many others in the nation, was built with the profits of slavery. Georgetown University made news a few years ago for creating a fund to pay reparations to the descendants of 272 enslaved people sold by the college. Last year, I suggested to Geoff that I write a story for the alumni magazine tracing Wash Prep's history with slavery.

He nixed it.

Someday there will have to be a reckoning.

"Thank god you're here. The phone is ringing nonstop, and I don't know how to use the hold thingy."

Two years out of college, sweet and scatterbrained, Wei Wei jumps when the phone rings and can't figure out the copier.

"I'll handle the phones," I tell Wei Wei as I walk into my office.

"Everyone is calling about that *Washington Post* story," she says, following me. "And it's all over Insta and Snap, and people are, like, yelling at me."

"I'll take care of it." I sit in my chair, dropping my bag at my feet.

"Thank you, thank you." She shoots me a grateful look but doesn't leave.

"Is there anything else?"

"So is it true we're putting Archer Benoit on the fall cover?"

All sweetness and light, Wei Wei sounds like a child asking about Santa. But I sense an undercurrent.

"Yes. I just met with him, actually."

"Uh-huh. It's just that . . ." She twirls a lock of hair around one finger and looks past me out the window. "I don't know, but didn't he sexually harass a makeup artist at MSNBC?"

I force myself to smile. It's true that around the time that #MeToo really exploded, a story began circulating about Archer. He denied it vehemently, but for a few weeks, it looked as if the accusation might gain traction and do some real damage.

"That's never been verified." Inwardly, I cringe at my lawyer-like answer.

"Right." Wei Wei drags out the word. "But, like, isn't it true that when she went public, people started trashing her? Like using her past against her? Drug use, a DUI, a restraining order against her from an ex-boyfriend. I mean, isn't that why she didn't pursue it?"

Her words sting a bit. At the time, everyone who knew Archer, including me, tried to help. The whole Wash Prep community rallied around him—alumni and parents spoke on his behalf to the press, and the board invited Archer as their keynote speaker on Career Day, publicly throwing the school's support behind him.

"I see what you mean, but all those things about his accuser were true."

"Yeah, totally, but wasn't it kind of an organized campaign to discredit her? Wasn't there another woman, from college or something, that said he assaulted her?"

"Wow, you're really up on all this." Even though I did not like the way in which this woman's complaints—and her character—were trashed, I was relieved for Archer when the whole thing went away.

"Yeah, there's a whole article about it on Vice. I mean, doesn't that make you uncomfortable as a woman? A mother of a daughter?"

For a moment, I am stunned. I would never have spoken this way to my boss when I was her age. Then I take a deep breath and respond as calmly as I can.

"Look, I've known Archer for more than thirty years, and I have never seen anything that would suggest he was predatory. Not that I know everything he's ever done behind closed doors, but he is my friend, and I believed him when he told me it didn't happen. And, I might add, nothing was ever proven. Not in criminal or civil court. And in this country, you are presumed innocent until proven guilty." I flip open my agenda on my desk to signify that this conversation is over.

From the corner of my eye, I see her slink away. A few moments later, she's back again hovering in the doorway like a hummingbird.

"Yes, Wei Wei?" It's impossible to keep the exasperation out of my voice.

"Oh, I forgot to tell you. Geoffrey wants to see you in his office."

I wait a moment before grabbing a yellow legal pad and standing up. Maybe I've just gotten old, but it seems nuts to me that Wei Wei would lecture me in my office while forgetting to tell me that the head of school wanted to see me.

I march to Geoff's office, located at the opposite end of the building, my footsteps echoing on the marble floors. At the entrance to his office, I knock and wait. Geoff spins around in his leather swivel chair. He's on the phone, looking like a little boy playing at being grown-up in his daddy's office, floppy haircut and all. He has the look of a long-distance runner—tanned and ropey. I'm guessing he thinks the New Balance sneakers beneath his chinos keep him looking hip.

I'd have laughed in high school if you had said my former track coach would one day be the head of school. We all would have. About a year after we graduated, he left under a cloud of suspicion—fraternizing with students, buying them alcohol, that sort of thing. So when Dr. Kales announced his retirement two years ago and Geoff resurfaced seemingly out of nowhere, I was surprised.

The school board chose him over a woman in her mid-fifties who had been an administrator at one of the oldest boarding schools in New England for ten years. In contrast, Geoff had floated from school to school, moving farther west with each short tenure. It looked like a pattern of trying to outrun a bad reputation. He had landed in New Mexico at a small boarding school for troubled teens, which had been cited for child endangerment. Geoff, of course, was not implicated. But that whiff of scandal would have derailed another candidate's chances.

Geoff holds up his right hand, fingers splayed, the universal message for *five minutes*.

I nod and wander back into the hallway. Five minutes will probably mean ten. Not enough time to go back to my desk and get any work done. Instead, I find myself backtracking halfway and stopping at the records room—a dark, dusty, oversize closet, really. I yank open the door, and a wave of moldy air assaults my senses, burning my nose and stinging my eyes. I switch on the light and take it all in—the tan metal filing cabinets lining the walls, the bankers' boxes filled with god knows what. Everything is online now, but anything before 1999 is still here. Chatter about digitizing all the old files gets ignored in favor of sexier to-do items like a yoga instructor or a robotics lab.

I find the cabinet that holds the *M–Z* files and flick through it until I find *Nicole Montes*.

Emery and Nikki. Nikki and Emery. The two girls, and their deaths, feel linked. *Girls*. If Nikki were still alive, she'd be forty-five years old. She might have graying hair or laugh lines or other signs of having survived this far. But her death captured her like a butterfly in resin. Never to age or grow. Always a girl.

But if they are linked, is it only to me? I have a connection to both, but will anyone else care? I need to make Geoff see that writing about both of them is in the school's best interest.

I know this idea, like anything that casts the slightest shadow over the school, will meet with resistance. But I will find a way. I won't give up the way I have in the past.

As I search through the filing cabinet, the article I want to write takes shape in the back of my mind like a physical object that I can't quite make out. Two promising lives cut short. Young women on the verge of adulthood. Of course, Emery will be the main focus. I don't want to downplay her death just to ameliorate my own guilt. I mentally tick off what I have to do in regard to Emery. I'll need to reach out to her father—the school should have an address—and some of her teachers. Even though she'd only been here a year, surely she made an impression on at least one of them. I'll also find any other friends who might help flesh out who she was.

As for Nikki, that will be tougher. I have no idea if her family is still in the D.C. area. I remember her dad was a police officer in Montgomery County, Maryland, just outside D.C. But I can't remember his first name. I can't remember her mother's name, either. Started with an *A*—something unusual. I locate the file and pull it out.

Next to her father's name, the words *Deceased 2012* are written. My heart sinks for reasons I am not entirely sure of. I keep reading until I find her mother's name.

Awilda García Montes.

Of course. Awilda. The name loosens something in my brain, and a slew of memories cascade down like pulling out that one item on a high shelf that sends them all tumbling. The time Awilda arrived home from work as I was dropping Nikki off after track practice. It was a warm spring evening, and we all stood outside their house talking. Nikki and I gently teased her about how she wanted to get inside so she could watch *Nash Bridges*. She had a crush on Don Johnson.

Someone has stuck a note on the inside of the file folder. Written on the note in big red letters is: DO NOT CONTACT.

CHAPTER 19

LIZA

"What are you doing in here?"

The man's voice startles me. I turn toward it, dropping the file and scattering papers everywhere.

"Geoff. Oh my gosh, you scared me." My voice is breathy, and I feel silly at how frightened I appear.

Geoff bends down and scoops up the loose papers. "Nothing to be scared of, Liza. It's just me. Please. Come join me." He turns on his heel, and I watch him leave with the file tucked under his arm.

I take a moment to gather myself and for my heart rate to return to normal. That was weird. Why didn't he just text me if he wanted me? He's never been easy to read. Sometimes he's overly friendly so that I let down my guard. But as soon as I feel comfortable, he tightens up, becomes officious, authoritarian. It's exhausting working for him, wondering in what mood I'll find him.

As I walk after him down the corridor, I wonder why he snatched Nikki's file like that. Did he mean to take it, or did he just pick it up because it fell on the floor? I tell myself not to read into things. I can't deny that seeing Emery's body on the beach has shaken me to the core. It is as though a heavy cloud has descended over me, shading everything. I remind myself that it is ten times worse for Zoe and to try to be patient with her.

In Geoff's office, I take a seat in one of the two leather club chairs facing his desk, making a note of Nikki's file sitting on top of a stack of papers. What does he want with it?

"We need a plan. How are we going to handle the whole Emery Blake situation?" Geoff doesn't wait for any response from me. "The first thing we have to deal with is *The Washington Post*. Did they reach out to you before they went to print?"

"Unfortunately, no." I exhale, hoping that shows I'm equally frustrated, and look around the room. It is almost exactly the same as when Dr. Kales was here. The same blue-and-white Staffordshire ceramic dogs flank the same oil painting of a vase of daffodils above the nonworking fireplace. I doubt this is because Geoff has the same taste as Kales did. More likely, he doesn't have his own at all or the confidence to insist on changes. Maybe on some level, he knows he won't last long as head of school and sees little point in redecorating.

"This Indah woman," he says, rolling her name in his mouth like it is a sour candy, "called the school and left a message, but of course the offices were closed. I've already called the editor and had a word with him. But the damage is done. That's not the worst—there's a blog post on the Parenting section of the *Post* website this morning about how irresponsible Washington Prep parents are—*What kind of parents let their children go to Beach Week* type of thing. Not good."

He pushes some papers across the wide mahogany desk. I take them—printouts of the blog column he was referring to. "Go ahead. Read it out loud."

I clear my throat and begin to read. "Emery Blake was not the first Washington Prep student to drown at Beach Week. Twenty-eight years ago, Nicole Montes, also a Washington Prep student, met her watery death during Beach Week. How many Washington Prep students have to die before parents and administrators ban this so-called tradition?" I look up. "At least they didn't mention that it was suicide."

"I guess that detail does not fit with their narrative of blaming Washington Prep."

I bite the inside of my cheek to stop from saying something I will regret. I wonder how I will get through this meeting without revealing how distasteful I find his reaction to Emery's death. "I think that was sensitive of them."

"Well, I think her suicide is relevant. This was a disturbed young lady. It really had nothing to do with Beach Week or with Washington Prep, yet we're being blamed. I mean, she graduated. She doesn't even go here anymore. We need to get the suicide into the paper so people know she was entirely responsible for her own death. You were a reporter, Liza. How can we do that?"

My mouth seems to be sealed shut. I'm galled by his insensitivity. I shift in my seat. With effort and focus, I answer as calmly as I can. "There was a brief allusion to suicide in today's *Post* story."

"Allusion? I don't want an allusion. I want a sledgehammer."

"The media won't report on suicide unless it has some news value—like it's a public person or happened in a public place."

"Well, this was in a public place. It was at a state lighthouse, for god's sake. Can't get more public than that."

"Geoff, surely you understand that it might not be in the best interest—"

"I think people deserve to know that she was unbalanced," he says, cutting me off. "That's the story. Not that she was a Washington Prep student. We need to change the narrative. You need to call Indah and make sure she knows about the suicide."

"She knows." My voice is quavering with anger. My hands clench and unclench in my lap. "If it makes you happy, it's all over Instagram and Snapchat. Everyone is talking about her suicide there."

I am sure my sharp tone will get a rebuke from him, but instead, it elicits a smile.

"Good, good. Are there other venues we can use to get this information into the public sphere? You know, ones adults use?"

"Adults use Instagram and Snapchat."

He scoffs. "Really, Liza. I'm not sure the average Washington Prep parent is active on Snapchat. What about D.C. Urban Moms?"

I want to laugh—the idea is so absurd—but it's clear he is not joking. "Are you suggesting that your head of communications start a whisper campaign on a parenting board?"

"Have any better ideas?"

"Actually, I do have one. Tackle it head-on."

"Meaning what, exactly?"

"I think what we do now is listen," I say slowly, giving myself time to come up with something that might calm him down. "Really make it obvious we care. We can put something out to that effect, that we're listening, and then maybe you could host some kind of town hall meeting later this summer for students and parents. Not to solve anything but just let people express themselves. Then we go from there. Just don't make any promises right now."

He scrunches up his nose and shakes his head. "Don't like it. Those town hall types of things can get derailed fast. Did you hear about that school board meeting in Virginia? Totally derailed by this one activist. I don't think we can take that chance."

"Okay, how about a listening session in the fall? With counselors. Students can meet in small groups and discuss how they're feeling about what happened."

"Maybe." He makes a face. "Work on that. It sounds like a bit of a HIPAA nightmare. God, I just pray this will all blow over by the fall." His voice is tinged with hope, and I don't have the heart to point out that it is just as likely this will pick up steam and become a major issue next year. "All right, write up a proposal for these *listening sessions* just in case. And let's hope we never have to use it."

"Yes, of course." His lack of concern for his students' well-being has almost stunned me into silence, but it's now or never.

I point to the file on his desk. "You know, we've never written about Nicole Montes."

"Yeah, I meant to ask—what were you doing with this file?"

"It's been almost exactly twenty-eight years since she drowned, and with Emery's death, I think now might be the perfect opportunity to do a small piece."

He recoils, appalled. "Your response to this nightmare is to dig up *another* death associated with Washington Prep? You'll have to excuse me if I don't see how that's helping."

"We'll appear that we're sensitive to these tragedies," I say calmly, with as little emotion as possible. "There's no hiding from uncomfortable realities anymore. Not in this day and age with social media. You have to get out in front of things, go on the record."

"So that's why you were rummaging around the records room? Doing research on Nicole Montes?"

"I've got to tell you that people are asking me why we've never covered Nikki's death." I lower my voice. "Was it because she was Latina?" I let the question hang in the air, unanswered. Geoff is exquisitely sensitive to bad press, and I hope this will do the trick. "We don't want that to be the next *Washington Post* headline."

Geoff draws his palms together as in prayer and taps his chin. "I can't help but feel this is fueling the fire, not putting it out."

"It's all in the way we handle it, Geoff." I hope that the sentiment, delivered in a gentle tone just above a whisper, will soothe him.

"Sorry, Liza, this is an alumni magazine for a fairly conservative audience. I realize you got your start as a police reporter, but no one wants to read an investigative piece that delves into race and class and death over their morning cappuccino."

"Of course not." I keep my voice neutral, but his complete rejection of the idea stings.

"Washington Prep is a color-blind institution, and our alumni don't want to see the divisions in our society reflected here."

"Right." I wonder what Zoe would have to say about that.

"Anyway, I'm sure you have your hands full with next year's capital campaign."

I grit my teeth and nod. Just like that, the story is killed. Geoff, like everyone employed at the school, is terrified of the parents—high-powered men and women who think nothing of reaming out a Latin teacher the same way they do the gardeners who tend their perfect lawns. I have also been on the receiving end of vitriolic phone calls and bruising emails over the tiniest perceived slights in the alumni magazine.

"Now, tell me the Archer Benoit profile is coming along."

"Almost done," I say with forced cheer.

"Finally, some good news."

I stand up, anger simmering in me. I'm almost out the door when he calls my name. I step back inside, and he motions for me to shut the door. I do so, but remain standing. The school has an official open-door policy.

"Tell me, Liza, how is Zoe holding up? I know she's the one who found Emery."

I wince. "You heard that she found Emery?"

"You know how tight-knit this community is. Can't keep a secret."

"She's all right. She's in shock."

"Understandable." I'm half expecting him to say, *Do you need some time?* But he doesn't. Instead, he says, "I'm concerned about some of the things she's been saying on social media. I understand she is in a state, but other kids are picking up on her posts and reposting. What's that saying? A lie can travel halfway 'round the world before the truth can get out the door."

I blink hard, my throat constricting. What lies is he talking about? First, Archer this morning, now this. Everywhere I turn, people are warning me about my daughter. I plaster a smile on my face. "Of course. I'll talk to her."

"Good. I appreciate that."

His phone rings, and he reaches to pick it up, giving me a small nod to let me know I'm dismissed.

On my way back to my desk, I pause in the cool, dark hallway to scroll through my phone to Instagram. When Zoe first got the app in eighth grade, one of the conditions was that she let me follow her. I've never commented on or liked anything she's posted. Maybe she's forgotten I'm one of her six hundred followers, which seems like a lot for a girl who says she hates people and has no friends.

Who are these people?

I find her latest post, a picture of Emery inside a car, my car, the setting sun glinting off her hair as they cross the Bay Bridge. It's from that batch of photos I was looking at last night, taken that last day.

But it's the caption that sends a shiver straight through me.

RIP Emery Blake—police say she killed herself, but I know she was MURDERED and I WILL prove it!!!

The post has four hundred likes.

CHAPTER 20

ZOE

"Poor Zoe! Oh my gosh. You're upset," Olivia says.

"We thought you knew." Kinsey makes a pouty face, and for a second, it's like I'm staring at Shelby.

"Everybody knows about the funeral." Olivia's typing into her phone as she says this. Dropping this bombshell on me at work has already bored her.

"A whole bunch of us from Wash Prep are going, if you need a ride," Kinsey says.

My feet are cemented to the sticky linoleum floor. I wish the ground would open up and swallow me whole. I know I'm bright red—the heat rising from my face. They've won. Whatever I thought I could muster against these two, I don't have enough of it. Not without Emery. Without her, I'm lost.

Literally, a loser.

"I don't need a ride." The words barely make it past my lips in a mumble. I *do* need a ride. I'll have to ask my parents. And while the thought of my mom taking me to Emery's funeral makes me cringe, I'd rather die than get in a car with Kinsey and Olivia.

Mercifully, Davida appears and sends me to the storage room for more lids. I find them easily enough in a large cardboard box, but I don't head right back. I stall, hoping Olivia and Kinsey will leave. I pull my backpack down from the cubby and take out my phone. Details of Emery's funeral are not hard to find. It's all over Instagram, sandwiched between close-ups of açai bowls and ads for the perfect plunge bra. Everyone is reposting and liking. I'm being buried alive. Every heart emoji and candle and pair of hands clasped in prayer is like another little handful of dirt tossed on me. It's like being hollowed out on the inside with a grapefruit spoon to see people Emery despised taking ownership of her in death.

I finally get a half-hour lunch break at eleven. I grab my backpack and a bagel from the pastry case and head outside. It's humid and gross in the sun, and downtown Bethesda is packed with moms pushing strollers and people in corporate clothes on their lunch breaks. I cross the street and head down the Capital Crescent Trail, which is a hike-and-bike path built over an old railway track. After a few minutes, I find a bench along the trail in the shade of some tall trees.

I pull out Emery's phone. A part of me feels guilty, that I ought to give it to her grandparents or her father. But I can't. Just the thought of not having it makes me panic. I turn it over in my hand, happy to have something of hers, something she touched a hundred times a day. I don't know what I'm looking for, exactly, but I know there is something out there that is going to help me make sense of all this.

Girls like Olivia and Kinsey have claimed Emery in death, but what they have is an illusion. A pretty girl. A wide smile. Good grades. I had the real thing: her friendship. And I'm the one who is going to figure out what really happened to her.

I scroll through her texts again, looking for something in those simple words that I didn't see before.

Turn around. I'm right behind you.

It was the last thing she read. He was there. Whoever this Jericho is, he was the last person to see her alive. I click on his info again, as if some new details about him have magically appeared overnight. But there is nothing more than his name and number. I hesitate for a moment, looking up as a red-faced guy jogs past, panting and sweaty. This Jericho could be who killed her. Pushed her into the ocean and drowned her. He could have sent that fake suicide note to Insta. It wouldn't be hard to do. Hell, I could post one right now.

Or he could have seen what really happened.

Hey, I text. *You there?*

I stare at the phone. Nothing. An elderly couple walks by arm in arm. They're dressed for cold weather in matching cardigans. The woman smiles at me, and I can't help but return the smile. It's crazy to me that such love and sweetness exist in the same universe that killed Emery.

Emery's phone is silent. No response. I don't know what I thought would happen. That Jericho would be waiting by the phone and text back immediately?

I try one more time. *My name is Zoe. I'm Emery's best friend. I need to talk to you. I need to find out what happened to Emery. I think you were the last person to see her alive.* Then I pause. *What do you think the police would say?*

I know it's dramatic, but I need to make an impression. My hands are shaking when I hit Send. A ripple of adrenaline shoots through me. The mention of the police has to get his attention.

My break is almost over. I return the phone to my backpack, sling it over my shoulder, and start walking. At the crosswalk, I hear a faint ping. It takes me a moment to realize it's coming from my own backpack. My whole body is vibrating when I stop outside Quartermaine to pull it out.

I'm so nervous, I almost drop the phone.

The notification on the front screen tells me there is a new text message. I swallow hard and unlock the phone. The text is short, but it sends me stumbling back into the glass window of the coffee shop.

Stop asking questions, the text reads. *Look what happened to Emery.*

CHAPTER 21

LIZA

"I'll be working from home the rest of the day," I tell Wei Wei before heading out. No one really keeps tabs on my flex hours. Besides Zoe's tuition discount, it's the other reason that I'd never quit this job. Not until Zoe graduates from high school, at least.

As I head out of the building, I swing by Geoff's office to pick up the Montes file. He's not there, so I grab it off his desk and hurry out. I need to pick up Zoe by two, and I don't want to get stuck in traffic. In Washington, rush hour starts early.

Downtown Bethesda is packed as usual. When I was growing up, there wasn't much here. But in the past fifteen years, boutiques and restaurants have sprung up everywhere. There are always tons of kids and teenagers wandering around. I pull up to wait outside Sugarfina, a candy store where a small box of alcohol-themed gummies will set you back close to ten bucks. A pair of girls walk by giggling and leaning into each other as they pass. A pang shoots through me. Zoe lost her best friend. Whether I knew about the friendship or not, it must be excruciating for her.

They say that comparison is the thief of joy, but I can't help it. I've been doing it since Zoe was born. *Why isn't she walking yet? Or speaking? Why can't she read? These other pre-K kids can read.* These days, I find myself wondering, *Why isn't she happy? Why doesn't she have more friends?* It's exhausting, and I do it to myself.

Zoe comes out of Quartermaine, her face blank until she sees me and her eyes narrow. Not her happy look. She runs across the street and gets in.

"Where's Dad?" she asks by way of greeting. "I'm staying at Dad's."

I grimace. "Yes, I know. I'll drive you there. I just thought maybe we could hang out a little." I breathe in through my nostrils, hold it, let it out. I try again in a softer tone. "How are you? How was your first day?"

"Fine."

This isn't going well. The conventional wisdom is to approach sensitive topics when the other person is in a good mood, but I can't recall the last time I saw Zoe in a good mood, and this afternoon certainly is not that time. But I'm determined.

"Want to stop and grab an ice cream?"

Zoe twists her face into a mask of horror. "Do I want to do *what*?"

Teenagers have the most exquisitely attuned bullshit detectors, but I plow on. "An ice cream. Or we could go to the Little Red Fox and get a pastry."

"No, thanks."

I refrain from telling her how much she used to love their pie. "Well, how about bubble tea? Sarah's is on the way to your dad's." Not entirely true, but I'm willing to make a detour.

She tilts her head, a small smile appearing. My heart flutters. It's crazy that my own daughter makes me this nervous, this eager for her approval. "Yeah, I guess we could get bubble tea."

Elation. Instead of turning left toward D.C. at the intersection with River Road, I turn right toward Sarah's. It'll add a good twenty minutes to the drive home, but I know how much she loves her bubble tea. We park the car in the tiny, cramped lot next to a black SUV with diplomatic plates. It wasn't too long ago that Zoe and I would point out these pale blue plates to each other and then come up with crazy backstories about the drivers, trying to guess which countries they hailed from. But I don't say a word.

At Sarah's, Zoe orders us pomegranate white bubble teas with popping mango bubbles, while I try to ignore the siren call of the ice cream in the glass case. I'd much prefer a salted caramel cone with hot fudge syrup, but I make like I love slurping slimy little balls through a straw.

We take our drinks and find a bench in the shade outside.

"So listen, Emery's funeral? It's the day after tomorrow." She doesn't look at me when she says this. "Can you drive me? It's all the way out in Virginia."

"Of course." I try not to show how pleased I am to be asked.

"I mean, the whole school will be there, which is kind of nice, but also kind of gross."

I will myself to stay still, as if I've come across a wild creature and any movement might frighten her away. I wait for her to elaborate.

"I guess I could get a ride with someone." Her voice is quiet, tentative. "But I don't want to get stuck in a car with who knows."

"Happy to take you." Questions bubble up inside me. I want to blurt them all out. What's behind the video from Archer's house? What about the paternity test? Does she truly believe that Emery was murdered? I don't know which is most important, and I may only have one shot. What should I prioritize?

"Zoe, can I ask you something? I found something in my car yesterday when I got back from Dewey."

"Okay." She drags the word out, on guard.

"It was a box for a paternity test."

This statement is met with silence. Finally, she cocks one eyebrow. "And?"

I have to give it to her, she has chutzpah. I'm trying to imagine if my own father had confronted me with a paternity test when I was that age. I'd have melted at his feet like a crayon before a flame.

"*And* is there something you want to tell me?"

She takes a long slurp of her bubble tea. "Not really."

"I'm just going to ask you bluntly. Zoe, are you pregnant?"

Her mouth opens wide, and she blinks at me twice. Then she guffaws. "Oh my god, you're serious, aren't you?"

"Just answer me."

"Could you know me any less? It's insane."

"So you're not pregnant."

"No, Mom. I'm not pregnant."

"Then what's with the DNA test? Was it Emery's?"

"Yes, it was Emery's, if you have to know."

"Does this have something to do with Brody?"

She looks me right in the eye as her shoulders rise a fraction of an inch. That small movement baffles me. Is she refusing to answer me, or is she saying that she has no knowledge of what I'm talking about?

"Brody Smythe?" she asks.

"Yes, honey. Brody Smythe. What other Brody would I mean?"

Her eyes widen ever so slightly, but otherwise, her face does not betray even the slightest hint of emotion. No anger, no fear, nothing. She would make a great poker player.

"I saw you had a screenshot of him in your photos, Zoe. It was the last picture in your photos. Can you explain that to me?"

Instantly, her eyes snap into focus, and she scowls. "Oh my god. You're spying on me. That is so creepy."

"Did Emery think . . . Is Brody the father?"

She laughs dismissively. "You have no idea what you're talking about."

"So tell me. I'm all ears."

Silence.

"I need to know what's going on. I have a right."

"No, you don't. You don't have a right to know everything. I have a right to privacy, and as long as I'm not breaking the law—"

"You mean like stealing? Is stealing breaking the law?"

"What does that mean?"

"I saw a video of you upstairs at Archer's house. What did you take?"

"Wow, you have really been, like, super-duper checking up on me, haven't you? Do you have time for anything else? Like maybe your own life?"

Ouch. I ignore it. "I didn't go looking for this. Archer brought the video to my attention."

She scoffs. "I bet he did."

"What's that supposed to mean?"

"Remember, like, two years ago, when all those women came out and accused Archer of sexually harassing them?"

"Of course I remember." I don't add that this is the second time I've had to discuss this in one day. "And it was *one* woman, not *all those* women."

"And you all were like, *No, not our precious Archer.*"

"That's not what happened, Zoe."

"It totally is. It was like"—she flutters her hands in the air and continues in a falsetto—"*Oh, #MeToo. Believe all women, blah blah blah.* Until one of your friends gets accused. Then it was all: slut, liar, druggie."

"That is not accurate." The words come out shrill, louder than I intended. A man locking up his bike turns to look at me. I glare at him until he skulks away. "You're changing the subject. I don't want to talk about Archer; I want to talk about you."

She stands up, tosses her cup in the garbage, and walks to the car.

When I was a young mother and Zoe a sweet little toddler, I was appalled when I saw teenagers behaving this way. Clearly, I thought, these were the products of bad parenting. I just knew that my own little girl would never act like that. Younger me had no clue.

I watch Zoe climb into the passenger seat of the car, leaving the door open. I take a small measure of satisfaction knowing how hot the leather seats are and how stuffy it must be inside the car. So I take my time. I'm going to finish this sickly sweet, five-dollar drink.

I riffle through my bag for something to distract me for a few minutes. I pull out Nikki's file and open it in my lap. There's a piece of paper tucked in the front that was not there before. It has the Wash Prep logo on it, and I immediately recognize Wei Wei's handwriting.

Chris de Groot called twice. Says it's URGENT.

Next to that is today's date.

I stare at the words. I hadn't thought about Chris de Groot in years, and here he is, popping up on my radar twice in one week. First, Archer and Todd visiting him out at the shore, and now he's calling Geoff? What could possibly be urgent?

And why would this note be tucked into Nikki's file?

A car horn jolts me out of my thoughts, and I look up to see Zoe leaning across the front seat. She motions for me to hurry up. I tuck the file back into my bag and head to the car.

I can only extinguish one fire at a time.

CHAPTER 22

1994

No streetlamps lit their way once Nikki and Coach Estes left the bright parking lot outside the Corkboard. The road they were walking down felt even narrower than it really was, thanks to overgrown beach grass that was almost as tall as she was.

Her skin prickled walking beside him, suddenly aware of how strange it was to be walking in the dark with her coach. During the past two years, on varsity track, she had spent plenty of time with Coach Estes, as well as the assistant coach, but it had always been in a school setting. And in daylight.

Of course, she and Liza and other athletes had sometimes crammed into his Jeep to drive back to Washington from tournaments in places like Havre de Grace, arriving back well into the night. But never alone. Away from the brick red of the track and the gothic stone buildings of Washington Prep, he was simply a man.

A strange man, walking beside her in the dark.

"So Boston, huh?"

"New York, actually. NYU." She remembered she had told people Boston College was her first choice, but she only applied there to please her mother. That it was a Catholic school gave her mom a great sense of comfort, as if Nikki would be personally protected by priests and tucked into bed at night by nuns. She didn't tell her mom that half the kids at BC weren't Catholic and 100 percent were partying. Meanwhile, she secretly applied to her first choice, NYU, and prayed that if she did get in, her mother would be swayed by the fact that New York was closer to D.C. and that Nikki would be living near relatives.

To her surprise, it worked.

"Yeah? You going to run track there?" He was weaving a little as he walked, and she wondered if he was drunk. Every once in a while, his shoulder would brush against hers, forcing her farther into the street.

"Maybe. I don't want anything to interfere with my studies. So we'll see." She waited for him to ask what she would major in. That's what grown-ups always asked. Other kids hated this. But Nikki liked it. She was going to be a lawyer—a DA, specifically—and she was going to prosecute people who hurt people, like child molesters and rapists. Sort of like her dad, only she wouldn't have to carry a gun. She would use her words, her *smarts,* to make the world a safer place. It was Mr. Gold who had planted this seed in her head junior year, over dinner at Liza's house. *There's more than one way to fight evil,* he had said.

But Coach Estes didn't ask.

They passed the sign that read *Stockley Creek Country Club* in large green script, and Shelby's house came into view. Nikki started to relax.

"I know the steeple coach at NYU," he said.

"Oh yeah?" The 2k steeplechase was her best event.

"Yeah. You should keep at it," he said. "You have the body for it."

"Uh-huh."

"No, really. You have long, strong legs. Perfect for hurdles. Not a lot of fat. Small breasts."

In the darkness, her face burned. Was he just being factual? Was he like her cousin Tommy, who said the most inappropriate things to people without realizing the effect he had on them? *You've gained a lot of weight,* he once said to her mom. Or, *You're not as good an artist as your sister,* he told one of their cousins. No one got upset when Tommy said these things. *That's just Tommy,* they said.

"You have a beautiful body," he went on. "Exactly my type."

His words lit up the skin on the back of her neck like a bolt of lightning. They were at the edge of Shelby's driveway now. And this time, there was no mistaking his intent. This wasn't Tommy territory. This was something dangerous, like a snake slithering through the grass and you weren't sure if you really saw it or it was just your imagination. But if you were right, it could strike you down.

Nikki walked ahead of him, toward the back of the house, determined to find that red wagon, load it, and then send him on his way. It was wrong what was happening, she was sure of it now. Coaches weren't supposed to talk this way to students. But then, she realized, *I'm not a student anymore. I'm eighteen. I've graduated. So does he think that makes it okay?*

The backyard was dark. Thanks to a bit of moonlight coming through the clouds, she could barely make out the pier and the bay at the bottom of the lawn. Nikki hummed an Arrested Development song under her breath as she edged toward the wagon-like shape with caution. She knew that half-hidden in the overgrown weeds lay piles of excavated earth, concrete bricks, and other debris from the wall construction.

Coach Estes appeared beside her just as she yanked the wagon from the vines that had woven their way through the wheels.

"All right, thanks for walking me back."

"I'll help you load it up," he said.

"It's okay. I don't mind." Inside, she was panicking. He wasn't going to leave.

"C'mon. I don't mind. Those cases are heavy."

"I guess." What could she do? Argue with him? He was right.

"Anyway, you promised me a clean bathroom." He chuckled, and a chill ran down her spine. She was hoping he had forgotten.

She didn't want to let him inside, to be alone with him. Could she tell him no? If Liza or Shelby were here, Nikki would have the guts to tell him to pee in the bushes. So why was she so meek all of a sudden? Because he was her coach. And for the past two years, she had done everything he had asked without questioning—fast legs, A skips, repeat miles. She had gathered with her teammates in a semicircle around him like sunflowers turned toward the light, looking for guidance. She had listened with all her being as he whispered, his hand on her shoulder, a few last-minute words of advice before a race.

Pulling the wagon behind her, Nikki slunk to the front door, praying for some kind of divine intervention in the next few minutes. But nothing happened. She retrieved the hidden key from a small, wrought iron frog on the top step. After unlocking the door, she replaced it.

"The old spare key in the frog, eh?"

She didn't like that he had seen that and made a mental note to tell Shelby that she should move the key later. She couldn't very well do it in front of him.

Inside, she flipped on the lights and blanched. Girlie things—makeup, bikini tops, hairbrushes—were strewn everywhere. She had forgotten how they had left the place in their frenzy to get ready for the night. She could hear his breathing, and all she could think was that her coach was staring at her and her friends' private things. She felt that she was betraying them.

Nikki went to the refrigerator.

"Here, let me help," Coach Estes said. She passed three cases to him, and he carried them to the living room, stacking them by the front door. After they were done, he let out a long groan and stretched. "Where's the bathroom?"

She gestured down the hall, realizing too late that Whitney's bra and underwear, which she had been wearing when she fell into the bay, were hanging to dry from the shower rod. Her face flushed at the thought of him being in there with them. Would seeing them put sex on his brain? And trigger something un-controllable, like a wolf smelling blood? That was the way her parents talked about men. As if they had hidden switches that might be flipped at the sight of cleavage or upper thigh.

She was always quick to mock their old-fashioned views, so why was her heart racing?

Now that he was inside the house, she couldn't call her parents. She couldn't risk Coach Estes coming out and saying something loud enough that they would hear that there was a man with her.

At ten o'clock at night.

Ten o'clock, in her parents' world, was when you curled up on the sofa in your pajamas to watch TV. It wasn't for doing a liquor run. And it certainly wasn't for hanging out with your track coach alone.

The toilet flushed, and a moment later, he came out, still pull-ing up his pants. She could see his checked boxer shorts. Nikki looked away, embarrassed. She walked to the door.

"Guess we should head back." She decided she would start back with him and then say she forgot something. He would go on without her, and she could come back and make her phone call.

He started toward the door. For a moment, it seemed every-thing was going to be fine: she would lock the door behind them, and they would be on their way with the wagon of Zima. But suddenly, he was touching her, brushing a strand of hair off her face, rubbing her arm. "You'll have guys falling all over you at college. You a virgin?"

She didn't know how to answer this. The answer was yes, but she didn't want to tell him anything about her personal life, let alone her sex life. She wiggled free and stood a few inches away, hemmed in by the cases of Zima. "Should we take these out-side?"

He grinned. "Sure." But instead of grabbing a case, he pushed his body against hers. She was slammed into the wall. The light switch pressed into her back. He mashed his mouth against hers, reeking of beer. Nikki twisted her head to one side, cheek against the wall.

"Oh, you want to play that game."

"I'm not playing any game."

"C'mon," he cooed into her ear. "You invite me here, back to an empty house." Nikki brought up her knee sharply until she felt a satisfying thud of knee against flesh. He backed up, doubled over, clutching his groin. "You fucking cunt," he gasped. "Jesus, that fucking hurt."

He looked up, rage contorting his face. Still doubled over, he reached one arm out to grab her, but Nikki jumped out of the way. She ran to the bathroom, then slammed and locked the door behind her.

A few moments later came the knocking. "Nikki, c'mon, no hard feelings."

She stood still on the other side of the door, one hand on the cool porcelain sink.

"Come out, come out, wherever you are," he sang. When she didn't answer, he slammed his fist on the door. "Goddamn it, Nikki! Open the door."

Heart pounding, she stared at the small brass doorknob as it swiveled back and forth.

"Fucking cock tease!" he shouted. She winced at his anger, even though there was a door separating them. She ran to the window at the far end of the small bathroom. Octagonally shaped, there was no way to open it. She banged on it, pleading with it. "Please, please." A small sob escaped her. Even if she smashed it, she would not fit through.

The doorknob went still, but only for a second. Then came a boom that Nikki felt all the way into her bones, making the door shake on its hinges. There was nowhere to go. Her heart crawled up into her mouth. She would vomit her own heart, she was sure, but when she coughed, nothing came out.

Another slam, and the door quaked. Nikki could picture him hurling himself at the door. She curled up behind the toilet, by the wall. She hugged her legs close to her chest, trying to make herself as small as possible. Her whole body was shaking, and she buried her face in her knees. She thought of her mom and dad, her little brother. She should have stayed home. She shouldn't have lied. This was divine punishment. The tears welled in her eyes.

The door shook again.

Tighter, tighter, smaller, smaller. Could she make herself so small that she could hide, unseen?

Please, God, she murmured, *I'll be good from now on.* The familiar prayer poured out of her without any thought. *Dios te salve, María. Llena eres de gracia: el Señor es contigo.*

And then, all was quiet.

CHAPTER 23

LIZA

Running late, be there in ten.

I let out a groan. Walnut's ears perk up, and he lifts his head, his brown eyes imploring.

"Do you want me to go meet Shelby for a drink?" I ask him. "Or stay home with you and eat black raspberry chocolate chip ice cream?"

Wednesday flew by without my getting a chance to take a deep breath or do any real work. I didn't even have time to eat the lunch I'd brought with me to work. I'd spent the day fielding calls from press, not just in the Washington area but nationally. Monitoring our social media was also a big time suck. I don't know why Wash Prep needs a Twitter presence, or Instagram, but managing, responding, and reporting comments took up most of my day.

Which is why my computer is open now, catching up on the work I've neglected. Thank god all was quiet on the Zoe front and Daniel was able to get her to and from work.

I search Walnut's rheumy eyes for guidance. "Well, drinks with Shel or ice cream with you?" He lays his chin flat on the floor.

As if reading my mind, Shelby texts, *You can't stay home with the dog every night.*

That's it. She's right, and I'm fried. I shut down my computer.

I can take this job too seriously sometimes. But unlike Shelby and Todd, I can't actually afford the tuition. Zoe doesn't get it. She thinks I'm obsessed with grades and getting into a top college, but it's so much more than that. By attending Washington Prep, she has crossed an invisible threshold into a world that looks like the one regular people inhabit but actually operates quite differently. The people that populate this world will have as much impact on her future as anything she herself does. Every year that you attend a school like Wash Prep, a thousand tiny, invisible strands are spun, creating a beautiful web. Only this web isn't meant to trap you; it's meant to serve as a net should you fall. If it's strong enough, you'll barely notice your descent—in fact, you'll bounce back even higher than before. Geoff is a case in point.

I recognize how unfair it is, that simply by going to Washington Prep she will get internships, job offers, recommendations from prominent people that she wouldn't otherwise get. Her classmates will invite her to their summer homes, and their parents will gladly open doors for her.

So many well-deserving kids will not have this.

But I still want that web of security for her.

I change my clothes, swipe on a little lip gloss, and just before I head out, call Awilda Montes one more time. This is my third call today. Like before, the phone rings and rings until finally an old-fashioned answering machine picks up, and a woman's quavering voice directs me to leave my name and number and to wait for the beep. Is it even Awilda? I don't know.

I hang up this time. I don't want to leave more than one message in a day.

Five minutes later, I park my car in the lot behind the Mill City Bar and Grill, affectionately known as MILF City for its ability to attract age-defying, middle-aged women. It opened last fall, the latest venture from Todd's restaurant group. Todd spent his twenties partying in Georgetown, getting fired from one job his dad procured for him after another. He jokes that he got into the bar and restaurant business after his dad said, "Too bad you can't get paid to hang out at bars all night."

Well, Todd is getting paid, all right. He and his business partner own several high-end eateries in D.C. and the surrounding suburbs of Maryland and Virginia. Todd is at Mill City almost every night, so Shelby is, too. Even on a Tuesday.

And I go to keep Shelby company. Archer stops by when he can, and there's always a rotating cast of Washington Prep alumni, D.C. power brokers, and private school parents who live in nearby Spring Valley.

The hostess smiles at me as I enter the cavernous room, directing me toward the tall tables near the bar, where Shelby usually sits. The signature dish is pulled pork brushed with a spice-and-vinegar mixture and served with coleslaw and potato salad. But the most popular dishes, at least with women, are the various salads named for private Southern schools—the Auburn, the Sewanee, the Clemson.

With twenty-foot ceilings, the restaurant tries to emulate the look of an old mill. In fact, a plaque on the wall tells waiting patrons that the restaurant is built with "oak from abandoned barns of the Old Dominion" and the tables are "hewn from sweet gum trees harvested from a single source in South Carolina." Lots of Southern pride, but zero Confederate flags. It's the new South minus the old South.

The place is packed, and I have to push through the crowd to get to Shelby. In a town where pleated khaki pants count as cutting-edge fashion, MILF City bucks the trend. The women here are decked out in cleavage-baring, brightly colored tops and white jeans, teetering on nude platform heels, the bags dangling from their wrists costing more than the average American's monthly mortgage. Washington was once a serious place, the home of the navy pantsuit and pearl studs, with dignity and gravitas trumping hotness.

But the city has changed a lot since I was growing up. There's a lot more money floating around, and I'd bank that there's not a gray hair in sight tonight.

"Hey, girl." Shelby lays a kiss on both sides of my face. I can smell the alcohol on her. It's only seven fifteen, but she's clearly started without me.

"Ordered you a frosé about twenty minutes ago," she says. Frosé is Mill City's specialty: rosé wine blended with liquor and ice.

I look around. "Where is it?"

"I drank it." She lets out a whoop. "What? It was melting, and it gets yucky when it melts. I did you a favor." She grabs a waitress walking by. "Hey, sweetie, can you get us two more frosés?"

"Sure thing, Mrs. Smythe."

"I hate the way she says that," Shelby whispers to me. "Makes me feel so old, like Todd's mom. Notice Carly's skirt? Short enough?" She tilts her head toward the hostess who'd greeted me. Sometimes Shelby gets like this. Jealous, insecure. I chalk it up to what happened when Brody and Kinsey were babies and Todd opened his first restaurant. He was gone from morning until night, and Shelby's attempts to recapture his attention all failed—flirting with her tennis pro, dressing in skimpier and skimpier outfits, drinking. Then she learned he was sleeping with the restaurant's decorator. It was a fling; he was sorry. But she took the twins and decamped to Bald Head Island, where her family has a house. She spent the whole summer there. I listened to her talk about what a bastard Todd was, how he didn't appreciate her after all she had done for him. She talked about divorce, about going back to school for art or design. She even sent me real estate listings. She'd had enough.

Then Todd came down at the end of the summer for a week, and they all came back as a happy family, with Shelby sporting a diamond Cartier necklace. She never mentioned divorce again.

I learned my lesson. Whatever drama these two get into, they're married for life.

"Everything okay with you?" I ask.

"Who, me?" She lets out a sharp laugh. "Couldn't be better. I mean, no one appreciates all the damn sacrifices I make for them, but what else is new? You think Todd could do all this"—she motions toward the crowd—"without me taking care of everything else? And I mean *everything*."

"There's no way," I agree.

She nods vigorously. "Damn right there's no way. If I had put half the effort into being a jewelry designer or an interior decorator that I've put into being the perfect wife and mother . . ." Her voice trails off.

I reach out and squeeze her hand. Regrets, self-doubt—it hits you hard in your forties. You take a close look at your life and wonder, *What the hell happened?*

"Enough about me. How's Zoe holding up? Poor thing."

"Not good. I'm worried about her. It's clear that this whole Emery thing has devastated her, but she won't talk to me. She gets mad at everything I say."

"Kinsey's the same way, little wench. Girls. They're awful, aren't they? Thank god for my little man. I mean, without Brody, I would go nuts. I think God sent me Brody so I could survive Kinsey in one piece." She lets out a sharp laugh. "I mean, don't get me wrong, I love her to bits."

A little bubble of discomfort wells in me. I want to ask Shelby what she thinks of the photo of Brody's bandaged hand and its possible connection to the paternity test. But how do you ask your best friend if she thinks her son knocked up a dead girl? We've seen each other through our darkest hours—burying parents, postpartum depression, breast cancer scares. But something is holding me back. This isn't just about me; it involves our children. I toy with how I should phrase my concern, but before I can say anything, Shelby lets out a hoot.

"I mean, Zoe's posts. Girl, you must be going out of your mind."

"You saw those, huh?"

"Everybody's seen 'em, Liza. They have hundreds of likes." She swallows the last of her frosé and passes her glass to the waitress in exchange for the two fresh drinks. "Truth bomb?"

"Go ahead," I say cautiously. *Truth bomb* is a dumb code word we made up in high school to ask permission to quasi-insult each other. As in: *Truth bomb, Whitney? You can't pull off that shade of green.* The idea was that agreeing to a truth bomb meant you couldn't get mad at what the person said. The nickname was spot-on. Like a bomb, it usually left the target shattered.

"Does Zoe really think Emery was murdered?" Shelby asks. "'Cause that has me worried about the mental state of our girl."

"Me, too. I think she's having trouble processing that her friend could take her own life. It doesn't seem like there were any signs. Maybe it's just easier right now for her to believe she was murdered."

"It's all Kinsey and her friends can talk about." She wrinkles up her nose in disgust. "Not to mention the moms."

My back stiffens. "What do you mean?"

"Just, you know. The usual crap. You might want to tell her to cool it a little."

"Ha. Trust me, I'm trying." *The usual crap.* When it comes to the school's moms, that can be pretty brutal.

"I know, sweetie." She rubs my knee and then suddenly straightens up, a huge smile breaking out on her face. "Hey, Bonnie!" Shelby sings out. I turn to see Bonnie Campbell, a toothy blonde who makes Shelby look like an earth mama. She's one of D.C.'s primo crisis management experts, the woman who keeps your little dalliance with two escorts off the front page. For every elected official in Washington, there are a hundred individuals who make their living off them—consulting, doing PR, throwing events, and managing scandals. Even more if you count all the journalists and pundits who provide the color commentary.

"Are y'all coming to the Courage Cup Charity Gala?" Bonnie stares at us with large blue eyes framed by such thick eyelash extensions I can only imagine the Herculean effort it must take for her to blink.

"What's that one for again?" Shelby asks. "Kids in Guatemala who need Vineyard Vines hoodies?"

"Oh, Shelby, you are hysterical." She looks at me with a *what are we going to do with this one* grimace. "You know that we expose inner-city kids to polo."

"You expose them to polio?" Shelby hollers. "That's not very nice." I stifle a giggle. Shelby can get downright seditious when she drinks.

"Not polio, Shel, *polo*." She manages to say this through her giant clenched teeth. "Every summer, Dana Houser and I bring one dozen kids from some of D.C.'s worst neighborhoods"—she leans in and continues sotto voce, "really, really, terrible slums," then straightens back up—"and we go out to Middleburg, Virginia, and teach them the basics of polo. The Housers generously host it at Tippen Farm. You've been there, right?"

Shelby makes a face. "A farm? No."

"Oh, it's so much more than a farm. Dwight and I were out there this spring with Bob and Sally Sparling." She pauses for a fraction of a second to allow it to register that she's been spending time with the attorney general and his wife. "Anyway, the kids get to stay for a real polo match. Would you believe that some of these kids"—she bites her bottom lip, pausing for dramatic effect—"have never even ridden a horse? It's so sad."

"That is sad. Bonnie, you know Liza, right?"

Bonnie turns to me and shakes her head, a sorrowful look on her face. "Hi. Nice to meet you."

"Actually, we have met." I take one of her tiny, cold hands in mine, as fragile as a bundle of icicles. I try not to squeeze too hard. "My daughter, Zoe, was in French with your son last year."

"You don't know Liza?" Shelby practically shouts. "Everyone knows Liza. Liza, this is Bonnie Campbell, and this is Liza Gold, my oldest and dearest friend. And, of course, she works at Wash Prep."

Bonnie's mouth drops open in a comical fashion. "Oh. My. God. Your daughter is the one who found Emery Blake, right?"

I tilt my head slightly and say nothing, hoping my silence will nip this conversation in the bud.

Bonnie leans in to our table really close and fixes me with her doll-like eyes. "Is it true the two of them had a suicide pact?"

CHAPTER 24

LIZA

"Jesus, can you believe her?" Shelby's voice is halfway between a whisper and a scream. "If her table beeper hadn't gone off, I'd have kicked her ass. You okay? Do you want to leave?"

I bring my glass to my lips and take a long, sweet sip. "No. I'm fine."

"I mean, do you think that's true? What she said?"

"Actually, no. Zoe doesn't even believe Emery died by suicide, so I'm pretty sure they didn't have a pact. It's just more the idea that these women are gossiping about this kind of stuff. Mental health is a serious issue. We're not talking about who got into Princeton or which student made the best promposal."

"I will check D.C. Urban Moms and all the message boards and make sure no one is saying a damn thing about our Zoe."

"Thank you. I really can't stand that woman."

"I know, right? Such a *pick-me* girl. Total name-dropper. The Sparlings! The Housers! And does anyone really think that's what those poor kids need? To learn about polo? As if. I mean, I live in a bubble, but at least I know I live in a bubble." Shelby throws back her drink. "She has a logo of her girls, Liza. It's a pale pink silhouette of two girls, and under it, it says, *Spencer and Mallory's mom.* She signs all her emails with it."

"So you're not going to her gala?"

She looks at me like I'm nuts. "Of course I'm going. I saw the most gorgeous Miu Miu dress, and I need an excuse to buy it. You should come with me. Todd will be working that night, and I hate going to these things alone."

"No way."

"C'mon, Liza. We can get drunk and make snarky comments." She raises one eyebrow. "And they usually have pretty good apps."

"How can you stand those things?"

"I can't. But I have to go. Did you know Bonnie and Dwight made the cover of the *Washingtonian*? D.C.'s hottest couple on the charity circuit or some bullshit like that. Bitch, please. That should have been Todd and me."

I laugh, but it makes me sad that she feels this way. She has it all—the rich husband, the gorgeous house, the launched kiddos. So why is she still so obsessed with belonging to "society" in D.C.? She panics if there's a ladies' luncheon, inauguration ball, or fundraiser that she's not invited to. I blame her parents. With all their connections, they could have helped her pursue her own dreams. Instead, all she ever got was pressure to become a perfect mom and wife. I have a vivid memory of Shelby's mom in her ubiquitous tennis whites in their kitchen as Shelby showed off her sketchbook full of drawings. Her mother offered a tight smile and said in that sweet Southern accent, "They're pretty, but no man ever married a girl 'cause she knew how to draw. Now, if you put half as much effort into losing that baby fat as you did into your art, you'd have the boys busting down your door."

"How's the dynamic duo doing?" Todd pulls up a chair, and Shelby leans in to give him a big smooch. He puts a plate of food on the table.

"Latest app. We're testing it out this weekend. Everything is sourced from Virginia. Black figs from a farm near Warrenton, wrapped in paper-thin slices of Smithfield ham."

I pop one in my mouth. It's delicious—the sweetness of the fig is tempered by the salty ham. I give him a thumbs-up, and he gets a goofy grin on his face.

"Good, right? Drizzled with a reduced nectarine vinegar from Vinegar Works in Shipman. I worried that it might end up being too sweet, but the vinegar retains its tang."

In high school, I'd never have predicted Todd would become a foodie. Back then, he was an archetypal preppy kid. He looked like he could have sprung to life from the pages of a J.Crew catalog— floppy blond hair, blue eyes, wide grin, lacrosse stick in hand.

But then he grew up, as we all did. And now he's an expert on different kinds of vinegar. Age trimmed away his all-American softness, hardening his blurry lines—crinkles around his eyes, a smattering of silver in his hair. On a woman, those characteristics would make her look old, worn-out, but on him, they convey a sexy ruggedness he never had when younger. His white teeth and perpetual tan don't hurt, either. He gets a lot of female attention, and I can see why Shelby gets jealous.

"Did you ever manage to hook up with Chris de Groot the other night?" I ask.

He shakes his head. "Nope. He flaked. Not surprised. He probably got drunk and passed out somewhere."

"Apparently, he's been trying to reach Geoff at work. Something urgent, which I find kind of weird. I mean, he's wanted nothing to do with the school since he graduated, right?"

"That is weird," Todd says. "What did the messages say?"

"They didn't. But he never returns my calls. Why is he calling Geoff? Are they friends or something?"

Todd frowns. "Not that I know of. I've only seen Chris, what, a half dozen times since we graduated? I mean, he's almost impossible to get ahold of. He never shows up at reunions or anything he's invited to."

"I wonder what he wants." Shelby bites down on her lower lip, a gleam in her eye.

A waitress with a face full of freckles stops at our table. "Sorry to interrupt, Mr. Smythe. I mean, Todd. But there's a guy at the bar who says you're supposed to meet him."

He grins at her. "I'll be right there."

He stands up, gives Shelby a kiss, and then turns to me. "Hey, Liza, listen. My mom is going to Italy for the summer, which means her apartment is just sitting empty in New York. If you and Zoe, or just you, ever want to use it, let me know. It's in a great neighborhood, a few blocks from the Guggenheim and Central Park."

"Thanks, Todd. That's really generous."

"Well, I remember how much Zoe loved going to Carnegie Hall with the school chorus a few years ago. Thought it might cheer her up, or at least take her mind off things. Sometimes a change in scenery is just what the doctor ordered."

Shelby flags down the waitress to order some food and another round of drinks. I tell her I've had my share and watch as she orders drink number five.

"Too much," I say.

"Oh, shut up, you." Shelby winks at me. As I look at her, warmth spreading over me, I suddenly feel like everything is going to be okay. Everyone is looking out for Zoe—Daniel, Archer, Todd, Shelby. Even if they don't always communicate it how I'd like, the love is there. They're showing it in a hundred different little ways. Daniel driving Zoe to work in Bethesda even though it's a pain in the ass. Shelby monitoring the message boards, checking up on me. Archer showing me that video. And now Todd offering his mom's apartment because he is worried about us. And isn't that what love is? It's not being perfect; it's showing up and trying. I'm finally feeling a little better.

Or maybe it's just all those frosés.

Driving back to my house, I'm filled with a strange energy to do something. I'm not tired, and the thought of my empty house is utterly unappealing. My dad called this *shpilkes,* the Yiddish word for ants in your pants.

I think of the answering machine I left the message on. It was

Awilda's voice, wasn't it? Or did I just want it to be so badly? As I approach the turnoff for my street, I keep going straight on Western Avenue, past Wisconsin Avenue, and then past Chevy Chase Circle. Without even really deciding, I find myself going the back way to Wheaton, taking Beach Drive past Meadowbrook Park and ending up on East-West Highway. At this time of night, it's questionable whether the shortcut saved me any time, but it's ingrained in me. One of my father's greatest joys was teaching me all the secret ins and outs of the D.C. area. The little back ways that could shave just a few minutes off an afternoon drive and mean the difference between being stuck in traffic and getting home in time for dinner.

Soon I'm turning up Grubb Road, waves of nostalgia washing over me. All those weekends my dad and I spent at the Parkway Deli after my mom left and my brother went to college. *Not half bad* is what he'd say every time he bit into the latkes. He was born and raised in New York and only moved to Washington in 1972 to work at *The Washington Post*. One of his favorite hobbies was unfavorably comparing D.C. food to New York food.

Pizza? Inedible.

Bagels? What bagels? You call these hockey pucks *bagels*?

But the deli's latkes were a solid *metza-metz*, which was a compliment in his book.

I choke back the emotions as I drive through a neighborhood of small, redbrick homes. I haven't been back here since, well, since the day I picked Nikki up to take her to Beach Week. I'm surprised how it all comes back to me. Her block hasn't changed much at all. I pull up in front of her old house and sit.

The grass is overgrown, and several newspapers, their bright plastic bags faded from the sun, litter the concrete walkway. When Nikki lived here, I remember annuals always lined the walkway—mums in the fall, pansies in the spring. Bright zinnias the last time I was here. We were so young and naive back then. Bad things happened to other people, not us. I wish Nikki were still alive. I'd give anything just to see how she turned out, what she ended up doing with her life. My chest tightens, and a sob escapes me. No. I don't want to cry. I can't.

I glance at the dashboard. It's after ten. Even if someone did live here, it's too late to knock on the door. Then a light goes on in the living room. A dark figure passes in front of the curtained windows. Someone is home. Someone is awake.

Without even thinking things through, I cut the engine and get out. My heart starts beating faster. I know I should turn around and go home, but the urge to see Awilda is so strong. To talk to someone who knew Nikki, who loved her. It's why it is so important that Zoe goes to Emery's funeral and has a chance to experience some kind of resolution. Not that anything gets resolved, exactly, but she will at least see a public acknowledgment of Emery's death and all the people it is affecting. Solitude makes grieving even more miserable.

I need to apologize to Awilda. It's been sitting deep inside me for twenty-eight years, but I can't hold it any longer. A part of me knows this is so selfish, to barge in on her like this. I promise myself I'll play it cool, read her reaction. If it looks like I'm upsetting her, I'll leave.

Of course, for all I know, Nikki's parents moved out a long time ago.

My nerves are on high alert as I take the concrete steps to the front door two by two. I'm at the door, ringing the buzzer. *Thump, thump, thump.* My heart beats wildly. This is crazy, but it feels right.

As the door creaks open, I prepare myself to face the mother of the friend I lost so long ago. I need to see forgiveness in her face, but I prepare myself for the opposite.

The door opens wide, and before me stands a familiar face. But it is not Awilda in front of me.

It's that guy from the Corkboard and the Dewey police station. "Hi, Liza. I've been wondering if you'd show up."

CHAPTER 25

ZOE

Dad is out with Paola, trying some new tapas place on H Street. They invited me, but I could tell by the frozen smile on Paola's face that she was begging the gods I'd say no.

So I did.

The apartment is too quiet without Dad playing some weird music. The only noises are street sounds drifting up from below, but they sound far away, muffled by the glass. I peer out the window, watching some guys whoop it up outside a bar. Desperate for some noise, I put on *Dance Moms* on my laptop, just to hear the sound of their bickering. The night stretches out before me, and I know I'm not going to be able to sleep.

As soon as Dad drove me back to the apartment, I went into my room and burst out crying. I didn't mean to. It's not even that anything had happened at work. Olivia and Kinsey didn't come in like they did yesterday. It was more like I had been holding all my feelings in all day.

Still, a heavy sadness weighed me down, like I was wearing a heavy cloak. I thought about Emery telling me that, when she was sad, she would spin her Wheel of Joy. And it wasn't some imaginary thing; she actually made one. It was small and looked like the wheel on *Wheel of Fortune*. Different pieces had different memories on them. I remember one pie piece was a memory of her dad. Her parents separated when she was really little, and she didn't see him that often. He struggled with alcohol and drugs, she said, like her mom, and he was absent from her life for months at a time. But when he came back, he would always take her to Trader Joe's for a balloon. One time, he was taking her back home and the balloon slipped away and disappeared into the sky, and he popped her right into the car and drove her back for a new one. She didn't see him a lot, but she knew he loved her.

I made a list of good moments and gave it to Emery so she could make a wheel for me. But she never got around to it. And after work this afternoon, I thought about how now she never would, and then I just lost it. And then I fell asleep. I always do after a big cry, when my eyes get so swollen and heavy that I can't keep them open anymore.

Now I'm going to be exhausted for the funeral tomorrow, because I won't be able to sleep tonight. My stomach does little flips thinking about it, seeing all those Wash Prep students and parents. I have no idea what to expect. Will it be super religious, like her grandparents are? Will they ask people to come up and speak, or is that arranged in advance? I have so much I could say, but there is no way I can get up in front of a bunch of people. But I have to go. I have to say goodbye.

I rummage through the clothes in my closet, trying to decide what would be good for a funeral. The only funeral I've been to was my grandpa's when I was ten. It's kind of a blurred memory. The part I really remember is back at the house, helping Mom set up the house for shiva, covering the mirrors and bringing chairs into the living room.

I google what to wear to a funeral. Pictures of hot women in slinky black dresses fill the screen, like funeral porn. No, thanks. I throw my phone down. I kind of want to call my mom and ask her. She would definitely know. But if I ask her to help me find an outfit, I know she's going to start grilling me again. I'm still angry about yesterday. Acting all nice, taking me to get bubble tea so she could interrogate me. Talking about me with Archer. Archer of all people. Who is he to judge anyone?

I get up off my bed and look in my closet. It's been years since I've worn a dress. I don't think I even own one. Or if I do, it's tucked away in a storage box somewhere. I flick through my clothes. Jeans. Shorts. I find a plain black tank top, and a black skirt I wore to the Christmas concert at school. It's short—I wore it with black tights—but it'll do. I try on the dress shoes I wore last year. They pinch my feet, making me wince. The only other black shoes I have are my Doc Martens and my Converse.

I settle on my Doc Martens. At least they're not sneakers. I lay them on the floor, under the chair where I've put my clothes. It's like an invisible girl is slumping in the chair or she was sitting there and was vaporized. I'm like that. The invisible girl.

But Emery saw me.

I remember the first time we met at school. I was sitting on the orange, carpeted steps just inside the front door of the main building, where everyone hangs out when it's too cold or rainy to be outside. I was sitting in my usual spot on the top step, which is level with the second floor of the building, with my back against the wall. I had my head down and didn't see her coming. Even if I had, I wouldn't have thought she was coming to talk to me.

Not that I knew who she was. School had just started, and it was her first year, but she just wasn't the type of person to talk to me. Emery looked like one of those girls that was on the cover of some cheesy YA rom-com. Long, wavy hair, thin, the kind of pretty where you knew she just rolled out of bed, like she was kind of annoyed with her looks. Not like Olivia and Kinsey. Girls like that are as fake as the sea glass you can buy at Ocean City, where they take shards of blue and green glass and tumble them through a machine until they're completely smooth.

I'll never forget it, because she was practically on top of me when I looked up. I had pulled my legs back because I thought

I was in her way, but she didn't pass me. She sat down and gave me a sort of sad half smile. "You're Zoe, right?"

I lie across my bed, holding Emery's phone in my hand, just the way she held it a million times. I'm not dumb—I know it's not some magical connection to her. But I like getting lost in it, if only for a little while. Reading her texts, looking at her photos and videos. I almost forget that she's gone. I know it won't last forever. It can't, can it?

I roll onto my back and stare at the ceiling. I knew what Emery was doing, sort of.

"I want to help," I said to her the first time she told me what she was working on.

"Some of these people might be friends of your mom," Emery had said. "Are you okay with that?"

Yes, I told her. Yes. It was more than okay. I was ready to see the truth around me. I could help. I had access to people like Archer.

Something happened at Beach Week, she told me, back when my mom and her friends had just graduated from high school. And she wasn't talking about my mom's friend Nikki, who drowned. She was talking about something else—a rape. Emery wouldn't tell me the details, said she had sworn confidentiality to the woman. But that she wanted to be like Michelle McNamara, the woman who chased down the Golden State Killer: fearless. It was a major project for her. She was always looking things up and stepping away to make private phone calls. Emery showed me things about Archer. Not just what was in the newspaper but other things. Things maybe my mom didn't even know.

Like that article on Medium. And yes, I know anyone can post on the website, I'm not clueless, but when I read it, it just felt true, deep in my gut. You can't lie about pain like that. The writer said she had gone to Duke with Archer, and they got drunk one night. He walked her home and forced her to do oral. Then there was that woman on Twitter who had worked with him at a news station in North Carolina when he was first starting out. She said he was always making jokes, pushing the limit, touching her in weird ways.

I took screenshots. I tried to show them to my mom, but she dismissed them without even reading them.

"You can't believe everything you read on the internet," she said.

"Just because it's not in *The Washington Post* doesn't make it a lie."

"Look, honey, if it were true, real journalists would be reporting it."

It made me crazy. She didn't understand that things were different now, that we didn't need to wait for the "real" journalists to report things. We could report them ourselves on Twitter, on Instagram, on TikTok.

My phone pings. It's a text from Jericho. The little hairs on my arm stand up. I hadn't expected to hear from them after that message the other day telling me to back off.

I told u 2 stop digging
now yr mom is involved
no beueno

My stomach tightens like before I have to throw up. My mom? How could she be involved with this? She doesn't even believe what I've been trying to tell her. I wonder what she might have done.

Who are you? I type. *What do you mean about my mom?*

Three dots appear, and my heart races while I wait, holding my breath.

she's nosing around.
and if she gets hurt its yr fault.

CHAPTER 26

LIZA

On the front stoop of Nikki's childhood home, I look straight at the man in the doorway. He is wearing a tight, black T-shirt and has a day's growth on his face. He looks as if he's been expecting me.

"You don't remember me?"

Looking at him up close, I realize that I've seen this man before. And I don't mean last week in Dewey; I mean before that. Way before that. He wasn't a man then but a boy. A boy in an ill-fitting suit at the Washington Prep chapel. "Of course I do. You're Nikki's little brother, Cobo."

"Nobody calls me Cobo anymore. People call me Jacob." His words are measured, but an underlying hostility comes through. "So are you coming in or what? I know you didn't drive all the way out here from Spring Valley to learn my given name."

"AU Park."

"Huh?"

"Not Spring Valley. AU Park."

"Oh, right." He steps back, allowing me to come inside. "Huge difference."

The front door opens directly into the small living room, just like I remembered. In fact, it looks much like it did the last time I was here. Same blue velvet couch, and two matching floral chairs, one with a crucifix hanging above it. The room emits a museum-like quality. It's not dusty but forlorn. As if no one lives here.

"So are you following me?" I ask.

He lets out a throaty laugh. "You showed up at my house, remember?" Then he smiles, a deep dimple forming on one side of his face. "You're the one harassing my family."

"I'm not harassing—"

"You keep calling my mom's phone. You don't think we have caller ID?"

"I wasn't sure if she was getting the messages."

"Well, she's not." He walks over to a small table by the sofa and picks up a beer. "You want something?"

I shake my head. "No, thanks."

He sits down on one end of the sofa next to a patchwork teddy bear, and I sit in one of the chairs. "I had to put her in a home a few months ago. The Parkinson's got so bad."

"I'm so sorry to hear that."

He looks up, something flickering in his eyes, his face softening slightly. "Sure you don't want a beer or something? Coffee?"

"Water would be good, actually."

He gets up, and I hear him rummage around in the kitchen. In a few moments, he's back with a glass of water. "Sorry it took so long."

He hands me the glass, and I can tell he's a little nervous having me here.

"So why are you calling my mom, Liza?" he says when he sits down.

"Well, I'm writing a piece about Nikki, actually. For the Washington Prep alumni magazine."

"Why?" His tone is cutting, and the word slices right through me.

I'm taken aback. "To remember her."

"So now you want to remember," he spits out. "Funny, none of you could remember a damn thing when it happened."

His anger reminds me of his mother's rage at Nikki's memorial service. I remember how strange it was to be back on campus only a few weeks after we had all graduated. That day was the end of the chapter we called our childhood. I remember the joy I felt throwing my cap into the air with everyone else. We thought it was a forever goodbye, and then a few weeks later, we were all back for a different kind of goodbye.

"I don't know what you mean by that."

"You don't, huh? Let me ask, where is this coming from? This renewed interest in my sister. Is it because Emery Blake is dead? Is this a *trend* piece, Liza?" His voice drips with disdain.

"You know about Emery Blake?"

"Why wouldn't I? It's in the paper. So sad when a pretty white girl dies. Such a tragedy."

"It is a tragedy," I reply, raising my voice. "It was a tragedy when Nikki died, too. I loved her, you know. She was my best friend."

"That right? Funny, we never saw you again after that summer."

"I know. And I apologize. I should have stayed in touch. I didn't know how to handle it. I was just a kid."

"All these years. You all just went on with your lives like nothing happened."

"That's not true. I think about her all the time."

"Me, too," he says quietly, picking at the label of his beer bottle. "Me, too."

He sighs and his shoulders sink. It's like watching the air leave a balloon. "It ruined my family," he whispers. "We were never the same. My dad stopped talking. He started working later and later and just never spoke again, at least not at home. I mean, I'm sure that's an exaggeration, but that's what it felt like. It was like he couldn't risk loving me, risk getting hurt that way again. My mom changed, too, but in the opposite way. She became a nervous woman, jumping at the slightest sound. She worried about me constantly. She went to see psychics, and when I say *see* them, I mean she spent thousands of dollars trying to figure out what happened to Nikki." Cobo clears his throat and looks me in the eye. "Tell you what. I'll help you with your story about Nikki, and you can help me with the story I'm working on."

"What are you writing?"

"A book, half–true crime, half-memoir, about a Latina girl who drowned at Beach Week almost thirty years ago," he says, bravado in his voice. "And how no one from her fancy private school gave a shit. And now I'm working on a chapter about how another girl, from the same damn school, also drowns at Beach Week. Funny coincidence, huh?" He meets my gaze and holds it, challenging me.

"You're writing about Nikki and Emery?" I ask. "And your angle is how terribly Washington Prep handles it all?"

"No angle, but there's a twist. Everyone wants a twist these days, you know?"

"And what's the twist?"

"The twist is that it wasn't an accidental drowning."

"No, it wasn't. It was suicide."

"I wasn't talking about Emery."

My eyes widen. "You can't mean Nikki."

"But I do."

"She drowned. It was an accident. I was there." This was as true to me as the fact that the sun would rise in the east tomorrow. "We were at the party, drinking. Then we decided to go swimming. I know—bad idea. We were all on the beach. We took off our clothes and went in the water. Not just us girls but the guys, too." It was exhilarating, swimming in the surf under the moonlight, the boys teasing us about sharks. It was glorious, until it wasn't. "But Nikki never came out of the ocean. I'm the one who found her pile of clothes on the sand."

"They never found her body, you know. Never washed up on the shore anywhere. Don't you think that's weird?" He doesn't wait for me to answer. "My mom was convinced she was alive somewhere out there." He laughs and gives me a sad smile, his earlier anger seeping away before my eyes. It's too hard to sustain anger like that. "Like maybe some crazy thing happened with the mob. Like Nikki witnessed a crime and had to fake her own death. It made my dad crazy, all her theories. She couldn't let go of the maybes without a body. Maybe Nikki had amnesia, had washed up on the shore and was in some hospital. My mom would study the tide charts, go down to the shore regularly and talk to the fishermen. Where did Nikki go? When she was well, my mom took my sister's dental records and drove as far up north as Maine and as far south as Georgia looking for Nikki. Missing dead girls. Unclaimed bodies. But when my dad died of a heart attack about eight years ago, she lost her spirit. The Parkinson's came on so fast. It was like she couldn't keep it together without him around." He wipes at his eyes, and I have to bite my lip to stop from crying.

He picks up the teddy bear beside him and rubs its purple head. "My mom made this, you know," he says softly. "Out of Nikki's clothes, her favorite things." He rubs a finger over the belly. "Her track shorts, her favorite sundress, and of course that damn purple NYU shirt that she pretty much lived in. She gave me the bear when I went to college so I would have a piece of my sister with me." His voice cracks. "I was the only guy in my dorm with a teddy bear, but I didn't care."

I sniffle loudly.

He looks up at me and grins. "Whoa," he says. "That was a lot, right?"

"I'm so sorry your family went through all that. And I'm so sorry I did not stay in touch. Your mom was one of the warmest people I knew."

He smiles. "Thank you for saying that. Sorry if I kind of yelled at you."

I stand up. "May I use your bathroom?"

He points down the hall. Once inside, I blow my nose and

stare at myself in the mirror. I'm glad I came and that I stayed until his anger melted, revealing what was really there—so much pain. I reapply some lip gloss, telling myself it's because my lips are chapped, not because I'm trying to look nice.

I step out into the hallway and walk back toward the light of the living room, but as I pass an open door, something catches my eye. Papers on a wall. I push the door open slightly. It's a bedroom that's been transformed into some kind of workroom. Bankers' boxes sit stacked against the wall, and the small bed is buried under piles of paper.

Pinned on the wall is a photograph of Emery.

And below that, one of Zoe.

"Listen, I can explain."

I turn to face Cobo in the hallway. "What the hell is this? Why do you have a picture of my daughter on your wall?"

He opens his mouth to answer, but I speak first. "Never mind. I don't want to hear it. Stay away from my daughter. I'm warning you."

I push past him, my head throbbing. What was I thinking? I don't know this man at all. He was in Dewey when Emery died. He has a picture of Zoe. My gut is telling me I've made a mistake. I need to get out.

I'm halfway out the front door when he calls to me. "It's not me you have to worry about, Liza. Don't you get it?"

"Meaning what?" I spin around, taking one step back so I'm firmly outside, on the front porch. I'm freaked out, but at the same time drawn to him. I want to hear what he has to say.

"That night, when my sister died. You guys reported her missing, drowned, a little after midnight?"

"I don't know. That sounds right. But it was twenty-eight years ago." I jiggle my car keys in my hand, ready to bolt.

"That's what the police report says." He says this with the certainty of someone who has that report on his nightstand and reads it every night before bed.

"All right. Then that's what must have happened."

"The thing is, Nikki called our house that night. She was real upset. She wanted to talk to my dad. Wanted me to wake him up. So I knew it was serious."

I frown. I don't like hearing this, even twenty-eight years later. My picture of that night is set. Nikki spent her last night on earth having fun with her friends. She was happy. Was she upset when she went into the water that night? Is that what he's implying? My stomach roils. I don't want there to be more to the story.

"I don't know anything about it, Cobo, or Jacob, or whatever your name is."

"Just listen." His brown eyes plead with me. "The weird part is where the call came from—1050 Egret Lane. That's Shelby's house, isn't it?"

"So?" I'm scared of what he might tell me, but at the same time overcome with the desire to know, no matter how ugly the truth is.

"Well, if Nikki made that call from Shelby's house at midnight, tell me, Liza, how was it that she was drowning in the ocean *at the exact same time*?"

CHAPTER 27

1994

Nikki tiptoed to the bathroom door. She pressed her ear flat to the wood, straining to listen. But all she could hear was the *whoosh whoosh* of blood pounding through her head. Her mind played tricks on her—was that his heart beating or hers? His breath or her own?

Minutes passed that felt like hours. She stepped back from the door and waited for a counterreaction on his part. Silence. But still she did not open the door, lest he spring upon her as soon as she let down her guard like some horror movie apparition that rises from the dead. How long she waited like that was hard to tell—seconds, minutes, hours. A warm buzzing of shame began to spread across her skin.

How did she get herself into this situation? She was so street-smart, not like the other girls at Washington Prep. The ones who didn't know how to take a bus or were scared of the Metro. And she was smarter than the girls she read about in the paper or saw on the news, or the ones her dad told her about. The ones who made poor choices. Who walks home alone at night? Who gets a ride from a stranger?

Those stories confirmed her belief that terrible things happened when you were dumb and let your guard down. But she wasn't dumb, and she didn't plan on ever being dumb.

So how did she end up quivering in the bathroom of a friend's house, all alone?

When enough time had passed and only the slight scraping of a tree limb against the window could be heard, Nikki unlocked the bathroom door. With wild eyes, she took in the empty living room and focused on the front door, wide open to the inky night sky. She raced to it and locked it, slipping on the chain even though she knew it was useless.

Then she remembered the spare key and flung open the front door, only to find the frog on its side, belly empty.

The spare key gone.

Nikki swallowed hard and shut the door again. She was sure she had put the key back. It could mean only one thing: Geoff had taken it. How was she going to explain this to Shelby? That because of her, someone now had a key to her parents' beach house? And how was she going to feel safe sleeping here tonight?

She looked up at the big clock on the kitchen wall. Only twenty-five minutes had passed since she'd left the party. It had felt like hours. It was almost ten after ten. Her parents would be waiting, concerned. She took the phone off the wall and dialed her home number.

"How's it going?" her mom answered in a singsong voice. She sounded happy, but distracted. Not anxious at all. Canned television laughter filled the background. She launched into a funny story about their elderly neighbor, but Nikki interrupted her.

"Is Daddy there?"

"No, he ran out to the store. Why? What's going on?"

"Nothing's going on."

"What's wrong, Nikki? You not having fun?"

"I'm fine, Ma."

"The house nice? Tell me about it."

Nikki turned toward the large living room and began describing it in detail. She told her mother about how everything was white, that the house was at the edge of a golf course, and the private dock on the bay.

"Wow, sounds so fancy. You being good? Helping out around the house? Making your bed, picking up after yourself?"

"Ma, it's been less than one day."

"All right. Just remember you're a guest in someone else's house."

"I remember." *I want to come home,* she longed to say. *I don't want to be here anymore.* But she couldn't say the words. It's not that her parents wouldn't come get her. It's that they would. And doing so would activate a chain of events that could not be undone. They would see that no parents had been supervising, and they'd grill her during the three-hour drive home. She would break, confessing everything. There would be discussions, a punishment, and then endless hurt looks and sighs and recriminations. It would color the entire summer, her last summer before leaving for college. No, she had to power through. Tomorrow would be fun. The plan was to spend the whole day at the beach. She could wear her bikini.

"We're going to the beach tomorrow," she told her mom.

"Sounds fun, honey. Call me tomorrow. I love you."

"Love you, too, Ma."

"Cobo, put that down." Her mother's voice was distant and small, already reabsorbed into the domestic drama of home. And then the line was dead.

Nikki sighed. She went outside, looked around but did not see anyone, and stacked the Zima in the red wagon. The entire time she was pulling the wagon, she was afraid. That it might tip over, dumping the Zima onto the street. That Geoff might be waiting in the bushes to pop out at her. That the police would stop her. She swore that when she got back, she'd find her friends and stick to them for the rest of the night.

She was more than ready for the fun part to start.

The walk back was uneventful, and when she emerged in the

parking lot on Route 1, the bright lights of the businesses stunned her. She crossed a block down from the Corkboard, where all the action was. A girl was vomiting into the bushes as her friend talked to a cop. Nikki slipped by totally unnoticed. Once she reached the beach side of Route 1, it was only a short walk to the party.

She pulled the wagon toward a group huddled near the path that led down to the beach. They were laughing and chatting, and Nikki's dark mood began to lift.

"What up, Nick?"

She recognized the voice immediately. "Hey."

Archer stepped out of the shadows and threw his arm around her. She let herself be pulled into him, enjoying his warm grip on her shoulder. She loved how he made her feel so little.

"Where you been?"

Nikki shrugged in the darkness, hoping that he couldn't see her cheeks redden. She had thought about this moment so many times after that embarrassing yearbook interview. Her second chance. In her mind, she was flirty but cool, kind of sassy and aloof, too. Not one of those girls who just giggled at every stupid thing. But all that imagined confidence failed to appear. Where were her clever lines now? All she could think of was that he had noticed she had been gone.

"I had to go get Zima. For Shelby."

He laughed. "No shit. She had you go all the way back to her place just to get Zima?"

Nikki laughed, too, a little guilty about the portrait she was painting of Shelby. After all, Shelby hadn't made her do it; she had volunteered. "I didn't mind. The police didn't even notice."

Together, they unloaded the alcohol in the kitchen, which was now almost empty of people.

"Everyone's down at the beach," Archer said as if reading her mind. He handed her a Zima and hoisted one of the cases over his shoulder. "C'mon."

She didn't want to drink it, but since he had given it to her, she opened it and took a sip. He smiled, and a lovely warmth spread across her body. Together, they walked down toward the ocean, where the sound of surf mixed with laughter and shouts. Happy. *This is what happy feels like,* she thought. A guy you liked, a moonlit night, the salty air. It was perfect.

"So how'd you even end up at Wash Prep?" Archer asked as he led them toward a scrum of activity.

Nikki took a swig of the Zima—it wasn't quite as terrible as she'd remembered it being—and shrugged. "It's kind of crazy. We moved down here from New York when I was in eighth grade, and then my first year at my new school, a gun went off in some guy's locker. No one was hurt, but my mom flipped out."

"My mother would have, too."

"She immediately began looking at private schools. And this lawyer where she works, in Congress," Nikki said, proud of her mom, "told her about Wash Prep. He was on the board or something."

"Cool. My mother is on the board, too."

"Yeah?" She wanted to ask him about that. How long his family had been rich. If he felt weird being one of the only Black kids at school. It didn't seem like it felt weird for him, but she didn't feel like she ought to pry. Not yet. Maybe when they knew each other better.

"Yeah, my mom says that as soon as my dad got elected to Congress, she researched two things—the top interior designer in Washington and the best schools in D.C."

"Oh yeah?" She didn't tell him how much of a long shot her application had been. Her family's dining room table had been transformed into command central for getting into the school. How her mother became obsessed with the idea; how together, as a family, they had filled out the application. The month of anxiety of waiting to see if she got in. The gratitude for the little nudge from that lawyer at her mom's work. *That's the way these people do things,* her mom had said. *They help each other out.*

"Well, it's a great school," she added. She regretted it as soon as it came out of her mouth.

"So how's that Zima? Worth the trip?"

She grinned. "It's actually pretty decent. It's like Sprite with a kick. Has a little zest to it, you know?"

"A little zest?" he teased. He dropped the case of Zima next to a pile of jackets and rummaged in a red cooler until he found a beer. "You sound way too sober."

"Yeah?" Maybe that was the problem. Maybe the only way to really enjoy a night like this was to drink. A lot. "Maybe so."

"C'mon, Nick," Archer said, offering her a beer as well. "Drink this. We need to get you wasted."

CHAPTER 28

LIZA

The black dress I wore to my father's funeral pulls across my back, refusing to be zipped. It shouldn't come as a surprise that I'm not the same size I was six years ago, yet it's a tiny defeat I wish I didn't have to deal with this morning.

I want to look pulled together at Emery's funeral. Vain, yes, but I will be facing not just parents from the school but my boss as well.

I take one last look in the mirror before I take off the dress. I never really liked it. Even at the time, I thought the long sleeves and high neck made me look matronly, and now that I'm in my forties, the effect is even stronger. The color also emphasizes the dark circles under my eyes. I didn't sleep well, ruminating about what Cobo said. Every time I shut my eyes, I'd see that wall with Zoe's picture on it.

I have thought about that night at Beach Week so many times that it has become impossible for me to discern whether I'm remembering what actually happened or whether I'm remembering a memory of what happened. As I lay awake last night listening to Walnut's gentle snoring, I tried to turn my mind into a blank canvas, inviting hidden images and memories I had tucked away to surface and reveal themselves. But that same damn movie reel kept replaying.

Splashing in the water. Shelby yelling about her birthday.

Nikki skittering at the edge of the ocean, and me calling for her to come on in. Bodies disappearing in the gentle surf and popping up under the moonlight.

How long were we in the water? It is impossible to say. We didn't have cell phones then. No one was taking pictures or videos, time-stamping our lives with geolocations. We went in right around midnight, of that I'm sure. We were celebrating Shelby's birthday.

I toss the dress into a bag I have in the hallway for donations and go to my closet. I opt for some stretchy black pants and a white tank top. But I look like a cater-waiter, so I trade it out for a black tank and grab a blazer while I'm at it. All three items are slightly different shades of black, a sartorial offense that would have horrified my younger self.

My phone rings as I'm putting on my makeup, and I see it's my brother, Aaron, calling me back.

"Finally," I say and slip in my earbuds so I can talk and get ready at the same time. "I called you Monday, and now it's Thursday."

"What's going on? You sounded upset."

I fill him in on what's happened—Zoe sneaking out, Emery's death. Growing up, my brother and I weren't close. He's four years older, and by the time I hit high school, he was heading to college. But the summer between my sophomore and junior years of college, we were both living back home in D.C. and finally became good friends. We just don't get the opportunity to talk that much, since we're both working parents, and the time difference with California adds another layer of difficulty.

"Poor Zoe. Losing a friend to suicide is scary stuff."

"I know."

"Is she talking to anyone?"

I know he means a professional. He was the one who urged me to get Zoe into counseling right around the time of the separation. "No. She quit her therapist last year. I'm going to see if she'll go back, but I doubt it. She's so angry these days. She hates Washington Prep. She's really struggling at school. She feels alienated because she is one of the few Asian kids."

"I'm happy to speak to her if she'd like." Aaron is a rabbi at a very reform shul in Berkeley—his husband teaches at the law school—and counseling is a big part of his work. "I may not know exactly what she is going through, but I can relate a little. It wasn't easy being gay and Jewish at Washington Prep."

"I didn't know you had a hard time. I mean, I know it *was* the nineties—" Homophobia was as ubiquitous in the nineties as baby doll dresses paired with combat boots. But I've never heard Aaron say anything specific about Wash Prep.

He lets out a soft laugh, and I can picture his face, the same almost-black eyes as our dad's, the wide grin of our mom's. "Well, it wasn't like that movie *School Ties.* No one ostracized me. It was subtle. And sometimes not so subtle. Like, my senior year, AP history. We learned about how in Germany, during the Third Reich, all newborn Jewish children had to be named Israel if it was a boy, or Sarah if it was a girl."

"I didn't know that."

"And adult Jews were forced to change their names if their original names were deemed not Jewish enough. All the men became Israel, and all the women Sarah. Well, Mr. Duffy called me Israel for the rest of the year. So did a lot of the students."

I gasp. "I'm so sorry. I don't think you ever told me that."

"They would say it in a joking, teasing way. I don't think they were trying to be malicious."

"Still. That's awful. Nothing like that ever happened to me at school."

There is an awkward silence. "What about that senior year dinner? The one held at the Capital Crescent Country Club?"

The memory comes flooding back. The spring of my senior year, we heard that the Capital Crescent Country Club would be inviting the graduating class at Washington Prep to a formal dinner. Everyone was excited. Shelby and I talked about what dresses we would wear, how we would do our hair. I was looking forward to it. But when the time came, I did not get an invitation. Neither did Archer. Or Nikki. We figured out pretty easily that none of the nonwhites and non-Christians had been invited.

"Oh my god, I totally forgot about that," I say. "But that wasn't the school's fault. That was the country club."

"You're splitting hairs. It's the same people." He sighs. "The point is, I'm happy to talk to her if she would like. No pressure at all."

"I'll tell her. She might actually agree to that."

The call with Aaron leaves me with mixed emotions. I'm always happy to talk to him, and I appreciate his offer, but what he was saying about Washington Prep bothers me. It's as though everybody but me thinks the school is a bastion of prejudice. I'd never heard Archer say anything about feeling uncomfortable or discriminated against. But then again, I never specifically asked him, either.

I take one last look in the mirror and groan. I look like a color-blind accountant at a failing company. I sort through my jewelry box. Then I see it: the small gold disk on a delicate gold chain. It's the necklace Shelby gave us all at Beach Week. I take it out and run my finger along the tiny diamond next to the *E*.

It feels right somehow.

I manage to score one of the diagonal paying spots along Eighteenth Street, right in front of Daniel's building. I'm fifteen minutes early to pick up Zoe, and I have no desire to kill time in Daniel's apartment. Instead, I grab an iced coffee from Tryst. None of their overstuffed chairs are free, so I decide to walk around the block with my coffee, pop in my earbuds, and call Shelby.

"Hey, girl, you haven't been on D.C. Urban Moms today, have you?" she asks as soon as she answers.

"No, why?" Despite its parenting focus, the site is still ground zero for any Washington-related gossip.

"Just a lot of trash-talking about Emery," Shelby explains.

"I'll check it out." I sidestep a young guy who is staring at his phone and almost barrels right into me.

"No, don't. Trust me, you do not need to read this. I just wanted to give you a heads-up and let you know I have already reached out to the administrators and told them to take it down."

"Why, what are they saying?"

"There are references to Zoe. Not by name," she quickly adds. "But anyone who is familiar with what's going on would recognize . . ."

I stop short. "What are they saying, Shelby?" I toss my coffee cup in the trash and pull up the website on my phone.

"Liza, I'm telling you, stay away from D.C. Urban Moms. I'm dealing with it, okay?"

"Fine." But the site is already loaded. I squint at the tiny type on my phone, trying to find any mention of my daughter.

"Good. Now call me after the funeral. I'm dying to hear how it goes." She coughs. "Sorry, poor choice of words. I wish I could go with you, but I promised my mother I'd take her to some gardening thing at the club." Shelby's parents were on the board of the Capital Crescent Country Club. For her wedding, they gifted Shelby and Todd a membership—which, if I'm right, ran about $80,000 just for the initiation fee.

I start scrolling through the forum to find the offending post. I know I shouldn't. It will be ugly. It always is. There's something about the anonymous nature of the forum that allows posters to transform from respectable moms and career women into fire hoses of vitriol. Private school parents are called racist elitists. Public school parents are losers who don't prioritize their children. Sometimes when I see the women of D.C. in the wild—at the gym, the coffee shop, school events—I wonder if these are the same women who log on to their MacBooks at night to spew poison on D.C. Urban Moms and rip other women to shreds.

I find a thread titled "Wash Prep student kills herself."

Very troubled girl. Mother was mentally ill, too. Runs in the family.

My daughter went to school with her. She was unstable.

I'm a little dizzy reading this. But then it turns even uglier.

Everyone knew she was into drugs. Her mother OD'd last year. Apple doesn't fall far from the tree.

I scroll to page 2.

Her friend, the one who found her, is a known druggie, too.

Yup, Total head case.

My face burns red. I resist the urge to throw the phone on the ground and stomp on it. Instead, I shove the phone in my pocket and turn toward Daniel's building.

I need to get Zoe and get on the road, even though what I want to do is write a lengthy screed right then and there on the street in Adams Morgan. Outside Daniel's apartment, I pause to look at my phone again. I can't help it. It really is an addiction, but I have to know what they're saying about Zoe.

Have you seen what her friend's been posting on Insta? She's to-tally unhinged.

Not surprised at all, writes the next poster. *My daughter was friends with her when they were younger. Total mess. Busted for drugs last year. Messed-up homelife.*

Fury infuses my whole body. Last fall, Zoe got caught vaping marijuana after school. She swore it was her first time, that she barely knew the boy who had passed her the pen. That she was simply curious. We punished her, but I had no clue everyone at school knew. Although I am not surprised. I clomp up the stairs to Daniel's, eyes glued to my phone. These women are pecking away at their keyboards like turkey vultures feeding on an animal carcass. I could rip them apart with my bare hands.

But it's the next post that takes my breath away.

Don't be surprised if her friend is the next one to off herself.

CHAPTER 29

LIZA

Daniel clucks his tongue when I tell him what's going on with D.C. Urban Moms. He's in a T-shirt eating a late breakfast, looking sleepy and sexy with his hair hanging in his eyes.

"That's it?" I glance at Zoe's shut bedroom door and add in a hiss, "This is your daughter we're talking about."

"This is why Shelby didn't want you reading those posts. You get so upset." He shovels a forkful of Spam into his mouth. "Hungry? Want some?"

"No, thanks." I shudder at his plate of white rice, scrambled eggs, and bright pink meat. Spam is one aspect of his child-hood in Hawaii that I was never interested in sharing with him. "What about the posts? Why aren't you more upset?"

"I'm upset. It's awful," Daniel says. "But I can't do anything about what a bunch of strangers say on the internet. I can only control what I do." He blows gently on his coffee. "They don't know her, Liza. We do. And Zoe is having a tough time, but she's a good kid. She's going to work, she's coming home and not going out every night. No drugs, no drinking that I can see. Have some faith in her."

I pause and let what he said sink in, trying to absorb some of his unflappable attitude. "Okay."

We both turn when Zoe walks out of her room, and it takes all my strength not to comment on what she is wearing. She's dressed for a day at a skate park, not a funeral, in a short, black skirt, Doc Martens, and a tank top.

I shoot Daniel a look. Can't he do any parenting? But he's assiduously avoiding my gaze.

Zoe stops abruptly, halfway to the kitchen. "What?"

"I didn't say anything." But she knows. She's so good at reading me.

"Mom, you're looking at me."

"I'm not." I avert my eyes, settling on a framed movie poster Daniel has hung near the bathroom door. The poster, in black and white, is for Jim Jarmusch's cult movie *Coffee and Cigarettes*. I remember when Daniel showed it to me in college. I hated it, but it felt like a test, so I pretended to love it.

"So. Let's go."

I turn back to Zoe. "Do you want to brush your hair?"

"I did."

"Oh. I see. Do you have a sweater or a jacket?"

"Mom, it's like eighty degrees outside. We're not going to the Arctic."

"No, but where we're going might be air-conditioned."

Zoe rolls her eyes.

"Just bring it, Zoe. You never know when a sweater will come in handy."

She lets out a little grunt but grabs a sweater and follows me downstairs. I can tell she is right behind me by the thumping of her clunky shoes.

As we drive through D.C. toward the bridge that will take us to Virginia, I steal glances at my daughter as if I can discover in her profile whether there is any truth to what those people are posting on D.C. Urban Moms.

Is this the profile of a girl struggling as she evolves into womanhood or of a child on the edge of an abyss? Or just a teenager addicted to her phone?

"Sweetie, you want to put that away for a minute?"

"Huh?" She looks up. "What's up?"

"I spoke to Uncle Aaron this morning," I say.

"Cool." She smiles. She likes Aaron. Everyone does. He was always that guy who was friends with all kinds of people, who never lost his temper or was sarcastic. He has a way of getting her to relax.

"I told him about what happened. With Emery." Her reaction is so subtle, I wonder if I'm imagining it. A slight tensing of her posture, a hardening of her jaw. "He wanted to let you know that he is always there if you want to talk."

"Maybe."

I try not to smile. A maybe is more than I had hope for.

"Or, if you'd like, we could call that therapist again. What's her name? Sherry?"

Zoe swivels her head to stare at me. "No. No more Sherry. She is so cheesy. Remember the coloring-book thing?" She faux shudders. "I'd so much rather talk to Uncle Aaron."

"Got it." I'm happy. That was a reasonable exchange. Confidence surges in me, so I try some more conversation. "You know, my mom hated driving into Virginia when I was a kid," I say as we enter McLean. "To her, it was the South with a capital S. She acted like Confederate soldiers would be waiting for her on the other side."

"I know. You told me," she says, turning back to her phone. "She had never even left New York City until she moved here."

"Uh-huh, that's right. Total New Yorker." I ignore the slightly irritated tone, the fact that she can't look away from her phone for more than two minutes. "When I had playdates with students who lived in Virginia, it was always my dad who picked me up and dropped me off. Truth is, I didn't come out here that much. Whitney was my only close friend in McLean, and she never wanted to hang out at her house, and I didn't blame her. Her parents were really religious. As in no drinking, no cursing, no makeup. It was a beautiful house, huge—I think it was based on Monticello—but it was no fun to visit. You know, we should go to Monticello this summer; that would be fun."

I pause, expecting her to scoff at my idea, but Zoe's head is pressed against the glass, mouth open, napping.

Riding in a moving car has always had that effect on her. When she was a baby and wouldn't sleep at night, I'd bundle her into my 1995 Toyota Corolla and do a circuit—drive up First Avenue to the Upper East Side, and then take Park all the way back down. If I timed it right, I'd hit all the green lights, cruising alongside yellow cabs and an occasional bus.

We pull into the parking lot of the Liberty Church in Mc-Lean, which backs up to a large graveyard, bordered in the distance by woods.

The lot is packed with luxury cars—mostly SUVs made by Mercedes, BMW, and Porsche, a few with diplomatic plates. I count five black Cadillac Escalades scattered around the lot, all with government plates signifying five people important enough to need a security detail—a member of Congress, a cabinet member. The only spot I can find is at the end, half on gravel and half on the patchy grass under the shade of a towering oak. I'm glad to see so many cars. I went to a handful of ill-attended funerals as a reporter, and there is nothing more depressing.

Zoe stirs. "Ugh, I'm starving. Can we get something to eat?"

"Well, the service is going to start in a few minutes. There will be food at the reception after."

"I'm dying."

I rummage through my bag and pull out a granola bar and some bison jerky.

"Jerky? Seriously, Mom? Who carries around jerky?"

"So eat the granola bar."

She screws up her face but takes it, anyway. Before we get out, I grab the cardigan off the seat and pass it to her.

"It might be cold in there."

I don't tell her that she ought to cover her shoulders in church. I learned that lesson the hard way my first fall at Washington Prep, at an evening Vespers concert when an officious English teacher laid her own sweater over my shoulders without saying a word, just a glare. Afterward, she held me back. "I don't know the rules of synagogue, Elizabeth, but in church, one covers one's shoulders."

Humph. Turns out, I do have a few more of those incidents than I wanted to admit.

Right before we enter the white clapboard chapel, I see a local news van with a satellite dish on top enter the parking lot. Of course. This is an event. *Beautiful prep school girl dies.* Zoe reaches out and takes my hand. My heart skips a beat, and we hurry inside. Right away, the smells hit me—that chemical air-conditioning scent, the musty old hymnals, the redolent white lilies that crowd the altar. We find spots in a pew toward the back. An elderly couple I don't know sits at one end. But filling the rows before me is a who's who of Washington Prep, a room full of praying mantises, their spouses, and their children. The murmurs and light chatter, the air kisses—they could be at a fundraiser. Standing in the shadows, hands clasped in front of them, are men in dark suits, coils in their ears. Secret Service.

I keep my eyes fixed on the altar ahead, resisting the urge to look around, lest I accidentally make eye contact. I don't trust myself right now. I'm still buzzing with anger about the posts on D.C. Urban Moms. I shrink in my seat a little as Prentiss, in a skintight black dress that manages to skate the line between risqué and conservative, passes by.

"Do you see that? They're already posting on Instagram." Zoe nudges me with her elbow and shows me her phone. A selfie of Olivia and Kinsey in front of the lilies fills the screen. *So sad,* the caption reads, *no words.* And then about a dozen hashtags, including #tragic, #tooyoung, and #RIPemery.

I look toward the front, but I don't see either Olivia or Kinsey. What I do see is a dark green casket up near the altar, the lid raised to reveal white quilting.

"It's so gross." Zoe's head is cast downward and her thumb is scrolling, scrolling.

"If it upsets you, why not put your phone away?"

She ignores me. When a minister in a long, white robe steps up to the podium, I nudge Zoe, and she puts her phone down. The room settles into a respectful silence as he begins.

"We are gathered here to say our farewells to Emily Blake and to commit her into the hands of God—"

I glance at Zoe, whose mouth is wide open. I take her hand in mine to let her know that I get it, but every time the priest says *Emily*, I wince a little. I can only imagine what Zoe is feeling.

The rest of the service blurs together. A sermon, several hymns, the audience rising and sitting several times, small Bibles or hymnals dutifully held open in our hands. The pastor offers communion, and Zoe and I sit patiently while most people line up to receive it. At the conclusion of the Lord's Prayer, I am sure the funeral is over, but then someone steps up to the podium. Emery's dad. I can sense his discomfort from all the way back here. He is hunched, visibly sweating. The room is hushed, waiting perhaps to see an eruption of grief.

But he is composed as he stares down at the paper in front of him, refusing to show these people his face. He clears his throat and in a wobbly voice begins to read. "This is 'Loss,' by Winifred Letts."

> *In losing you I lost my sun and moon,*
> *And all the stars that blessed my lonely night.*
> *I lost the hope of Spring, the joy of June,*
> *The Autumn's peace, the Winter's firelight.*
> *I lost the zest of living—*

Beside me, Zoe lets out a little sob, and I wrap my arm around her. When the short poem is over, her father simply walks away. It takes a moment to realize the funeral is over. People stand, and lines begin to form in the aisles to view the body. A gruesome exercise that I'd be happy to forgo.

"You don't have to go up there if you don't want to," I whisper to Zoe.

"I want to." She takes her place in the back of the line. I do the same.

This is what it means to be the mother of a teenager. To follow her into uncomfortable territory. You spend those first years leading—leading them into the water, into school, onto the playground, telling them to trust you—but at some point, the roles switch. It's subtle at first, but then clear. She's leading the charge into the unknown future. If I want to be a part of her life, I need to follow.

The sleek wood of the green casket glows in the sunlight that streams through the windows. My stomach clenches with dread as we inch nearer. I don't want to see Emery's corpse again. Once was enough. And I'm worried about Zoe. I send waves of invisible love toward her.

Finally, we're next. Ahead of me, Zoe leans forward, closer than the other mourners did when it was their turn. For a moment, I'm scared she's going to do something dramatic, but she doesn't. She pulls back and looks at me, eyes narrowed.

"What is it?" I whisper, but she doesn't answer. She turns and follows the crowd streaming toward the exit.

I steel myself as I pass the open casket, but I needn't. Emery looks like a wax doll of herself, with none of the disarray or fear that I saw in her dead face on the beach. I'm about to step forward when something catches my eye. A glint of gold.

I stop and take a closer look. Circling Emery's neck is a chain, and hanging at the end is a small, gold compass. My head swims.

It's exactly like the one I'm wearing.

Only the diamond on hers is next to the *W.*

CHAPTER 30

ZOE

Outside the church, I break away from the crowd, the sobs coming so fast I can't stop them. People mill around the parking lot in small groups, chatting like we are at a soccer game.

Soon pallbearers, Emery's casket hoisted upon their shoulders, descend the steps. They march toward the graveyard, and people fall in line after them. I recognize Emery's father as one of the men carrying the casket, but I don't know who the other three are.

I follow at a distance. Everyone heads toward a blue canopy in the center of the graveyard. I can't spot my mom in the crowd, but I don't dive in to look for her. I don't want to talk to anyone. A woman nearby lets out a sharp laugh. It feels like a slap on my cheek. I fall back even farther, my hands balled into fists. As I walk down the rows of headstones, tears blur my vision.

Everyone tries to cram under the blue tent, but it's not big enough, so people spill out of it. Olivia, Kinsey, and other students from Washington Prep stand on the side of the tent in clusters, heads bowed, not in reverence but better to look at their phones. I want to scream at them.

Instead, I walk to the far side where it is less crowded.

I can't see the pastor, or the casket, from where I am on this side. But that's okay, I don't want to watch the casket lowered into the ground. Seeing Emery lying in the church was bad enough. She looked like a grotesque version of herself. Same long hair, same nose and lips. But the thing that made her Emery was gone. Her soul.

"Receive the Lord's blessing," the pastor says, his voice carrying to where I am.

It's all so wrong, her being buried here, behind this church she didn't care about, watched over by a pastor who doesn't even know her name. I wipe my eyes with my sweater and pray I don't start bawling. Ever since Emery died, I've had these crying fits that overtake me, and then just as quickly, they're gone, like a summer thunderstorm.

"The Lord bless you and watch over you."

The graveyard is even bigger than it looked from the parking lot. I feel sick thinking about all the bodies buried beneath. These are the people Emery will be with for eternity. I take a step farther away from the tent to look at the headstone that will be closest to her.

Whitney Bascombe Blake
April 17, 1979—January 5, 2021
Beloved daughter and mother, she has finally found peace with God.

I frown. Whitney Bascombe Blake? Whitney Bascombe is my mom's friend from high school. My brain swims. And she has Emery's last name. I look at the year she died—last year. I think of the compass necklace, just like my mom's, that Emery was wearing. The diamond was on the *W*.

"The Lord make his face shine upon you and be gracious to you."

Whitney was Emery's mother.

My face gets hot. The ground feels unsteady beneath me. Can that be? Does it add up? And if it's true, why didn't Emery ever tell me that? I remember how whenever she came to my house, she would stare at that damn Beach Week photo hanging on the wall.

I feel so stupid. The memory of me explaining who everyone

was and what happened to Nikki fills me with shame. Shame at having been so clueless, at not being worthy enough of her truth.

"The Lord look kindly on you and give you peace."

My whole body aches with the thought that she kept this from me. *Lied to me.* Did she think she couldn't trust me? Was she using me?

No. I shake that thought away. We were friends. Real friends. I thought we told each other everything. I feel sick to my stomach. I back away from the crowd even farther until I find refuge behind a large weeping willow. I sink to the ground among the gnarled roots.

"There you are. You okay?"

I look up to see my mom bending down beside me. She found me, after all. I nod and try to answer, but no words come out. My mouth is dry. I am not okay. Emery's face, cool and lifeless. Whitney, grinning in that photo from Beach Week.

My mom settles among the roots beside me. I wait for her to say something, like *This is a nice spot,* or *Where's your cardigan?* or something mom-ish, but she's silent, her eyes sort of glazed over.

"Whitney was Emery's mother," she says in a far-off voice. She's touching her necklace, the same one that was around Emery's neck.

"Yeah. It looks that way." I point toward the grave marker. "That's her grave over there. She died early last year."

"Aha. I see. And did you know that, Zoe?" She doesn't sound mad. She sounds tired. "That Whitney was her mom?"

I shake my head. "No. She never told me. I just found out. Just now."

"How could you not know? I mean, didn't you ever talk about her mom?"

"Not really. I mean, I knew she died last year, but it's not like Emery wanted to talk about it all the time."

"And she never told you her mom's name?"

"Mom! Stop it, okay, just stop it!" Tears spring to my eyes.

"She didn't tell me. I mean, maybe she said her mom's name was Whitney at some point, but I never made the connection. Not until I saw the necklace and the gravestone."

"I just find it so odd, that's all."

"So what's your point? That you don't think we were really friends? Because you can be friends with someone and not tell them every little thing, you know."

"I know. You're right. I didn't mean it that way. I'm just shocked, is all."

"Yeah, well . . . me, too." I sniff.

We both look up and watch the crowd disperse. Soon all that is left is an open grave with a casket beside it.

"Are they just going to leave it like that?" I ask.

My mom shakes her head and stands up, brushing dirt off her pants. "They'll lower it later on and bury it."

I shudder at the thought of Emery lying under all that dirt.

"C'mon, honey, let's catch up to everyone." She holds out a hand to me. "That is, if you still want to go to the reception."

"I do." I take her hand and let her pull me up. We pause by Whitney's grave as we walk out.

"I wish I had some flowers," my mom says.

"We can come back. Bring flowers for them both."

She gives me a squeeze. "That's a good idea. Let's do that."

We turn to walk back through the cemetery the way we came when a very small headstone, just beyond Whitney's, catches my eye. I can make out the name *Bascombe*, but that's all.

"Hold on. What's that?" I ask, pulling my mom over. The headstone is shiny, and the reflecting sun makes the faint carving difficult to read. Together, we step closer to better read the words.

Henry Bascombe
March 19–March 23, 1995
Beloved son of Whitney Bascombe. Too pure for this world.

CHAPTER 31

LIZA

My vision blurs as I stare at the words on the headstone.

Not only is Whitney dead but she had a son. I do the math quickly. If her baby was born in March of 1995, it means that Whitney got pregnant the summer after we graduated. A wave of nausea rises within me, and my body starts to sway.

"Mom, are you okay?" Zoe asks, grasping my arm.

I try to smile, but my face feels frozen. My whole body tingles like it's going numb. Something is squeezing my chest, making it hard to breathe. Zoe passes me an open bottle of water, and I take a swig.

"Thanks." I choke out the word.

Whitney's dead.

She had a baby boy.

The words echo in my brain. I can see Whitney, staring out from that photograph hanging in my house—the one of all of us at Beach Week.

And then there were two.

"We should go, Mom. We're the last ones here."

"Of course." It feels like this all adds up to something important, but what? A week ago, my past was just that: past. Over. Settled. And now it is unraveling before my eyes. First, Nikki's brother and his take on her death, and now Whitney. What is going on?

Back at the car, I climb into the driver's seat, but I'm on automatic pilot. My head is spinning. I am in the same emotional turmoil as Zoe, but I need to keep it together. Our car is one of the few left in the lot. I toss my jacket into the back seat. Although it was parked in shade, it's sweltering inside the vehicle. I blast the air and wait for Zoe to buckle.

A few cars pull out of the lot and turn right. I follow them. I plan to follow the caravan to the reception. I think I saw the address written on the back of the funeral program. If I get separated from the other cars, I can always ask Zoe to punch it in to Google Maps. I grip the wheel tightly and focus on the procession of vehicles snaking down the winding road, but my mind keeps drifting back to Whitney.

Our friendship was like a sore that would not heal. The morning after Nikki drowned, Whitney was gone. No note, no goodbye, just gone. As soon as we got back to D.C., both Shelby and I tried to find her, but her parents said she was spending the summer in South Carolina with her grandparents and wouldn't be back. That was news to me. Whitney was supposed to lifeguard at the McLean Country Club.

Somehow I got her grandparents' number. I called and left messages, patiently spelling out my name and leaving my phone number each time, but I never heard from her. When she didn't show up for the memorial service the school had for Nikki, both Shelby and I were pissed off. During my college years in New York, I tried half-heartedly to locate her. She had been accepted to the College of Charleston, but I had heard she never went. The summer before my senior year in college, she joined me and a group of friends at the Brickskeller near Dupont Circle in D.C. I remember being surprised that she'd actually showed up. She was high on something, agitated, and couldn't carry on a conversation. That was the last time I saw her in person.

I did reach out to her after Zoe was born, during one of those long, lonely nights in New York nursing a newborn, scouring

Facebook for some human connection. I found her there. Her page featured pictures of her drinking and hanging out with different guys. We exchanged a few bland messages, and she liked a few photos of mine. I abandoned Facebook after a while. I reached out again a few years later when my father died, but she never responded. And that was it. I talked about it with Shelby at the time. We chalked it up to hard partying, different paths taken in life.

I always held on to the hope that we would reconnect and that Whitney would find happiness and stability one day.

I blink back tears. I won't cry in front of Zoe. I won't make her take care of me. I follow the train of cars as they turn off the main road onto a narrow lane, trees and hedges creating impenetrable walls on either side, shielding the houses from view.

"It's like the country out here," Zoe says, looking out the window. "No sidewalks. You can't even see the houses."

The caravan slows down and turns into a driveway whose entrance is flanked by two tall, brick columns. My heart thumps. I know where we are. As the car creeps up the long, wooded driveway, I shiver. It's been twenty-eight years, but I swear nothing has changed. Soon enough, the enormous brick house, its white portico supported by four thick columns, comes into view. I look for parking along the wide, circular driveway, going slowly up the side that abuts a large pond. This is Whitney's parents' house. My breathing is jagged, and I need a cold drink, but the thought of going into that house terrifies me. I wedge the car between two others and put it in park. Just one moment to collect myself.

"This is a mansion," Zoe says in a soft voice.

"Yes, it is. You've never been here?"

Zoe turns to me. "No. I knew she lived in Virginia with her grandparents, but she never wanted to hang out there. She said she hated it there."

"I've been here. Back in high school."

"Really?"

"Yup." Whitney was an only child, a late-in-life miracle, she said her mom called her. Twenty years of childlessness for Whitney's mother had been filled with decorating, charity, and church. At the age of forty-two, she gave birth to Whitney. But while they had room for Whitney physically, they never seemed to make room for her in their hearts. I remember how the house reminded me of the historic homes we used to visit on field trips. Antiques and oil paintings, drapes on floor-to-ceiling windows, and gold-leaved, leather-bound books on library shelves. No children's art stuck to the fridge with magnets, no field hockey gear left out in the hallway. No signs of family life.

Before getting out of the car, I pull down the mirror and reapply lipstick. Not pink gloss, but a fire-engine red. It's my armor—the redder it is, the stronger I feel. Zoe turns as a group of kids her age walks by. They're so close that I can hear them murmur, though I can't make out the words.

"Shouldn't we go?" she asks.

We get out and approach the wide front porch together, but as soon as we start up the steps, Zoe turns to me and says, "No offense, but can you not come in with me?"

I pause to let her walk through the immense front door alone.

Once in the foyer, a young woman dressed in a white shirt and black pants offers me a lemonade in a crystal goblet. I pray there is harder stuff somewhere in the house, but if I know Whitney's parents, there won't be.

Zoe has disappeared, so I follow the hum of conversation into the large living room, where people are congregating. Solemn classical music plays softly in the background while groups of people stand speaking in hushed voices, like the most subdued cocktail party ever. From a corner of the room, Prentiss catches my eye and gives me a little wave. Two other blond women in al- most identical black sleeveless dresses, their sinewy, tanned arms clutching wineglasses, turn and stare at me.

I pivot, get a glimpse of the buffet table, and make a beeline.

When in doubt, eat. I cross back through the foyer into the dining room, where a gleaming table, easily big enough for twelve, is laden with platters of finger food.

I recall a few dinners here with Whitney and her parents. Silent affairs that seemed to drag on forever. Speak only when spoken to, don't ask for food—wait to be offered, ask permission to be excused. I remember being in awe of the fact that she had one servant who cooked all the food and another who served it.

I'm piling fresh strawberries on my plate when I sense someone watching me. I look up to see Geoff in a stiff, dark suit. When I glance down, I see he is wearing navy-blue New Balances. I'm embarrassed for him.

"Oh. Hello, Geoff."

"Liza." He plucks a shrimp kebab from a display. "Beautiful service. Good turnout. She was clearly beloved."

"Yes, it was lovely."

"Remember when I said the other day that you should not write the Nicole Montes story, that it might be stepping on toes?"

I blink hard. "Um, yes."

"It looks as if some toes have been stepped on. *Stomped* might be a better word." He presses his lips together so hard they are losing color.

"I don't know why that would be. I haven't done anything." I think back over the last forty-eight hours. The only person I tried to contact was Awilda, and she's in a nursing home. And I doubt Cobo Montes would call Geoff to complain. "Can you tell me who complained?"

He dismisses this with a short shake of the head. "I'm afraid I'm not at liberty."

"Geoff, I haven't done a thing. I swear." I clear my throat. "But I think I should. Did you know that Emery was Whitney Bascombe's daughter?"

He does not look surprised.

"So you knew."

"What the hell does that have to do with anything?"

"A lot, I think. I mean, she was the daughter of a Wash Prep alum. And her mother, who recently died, was friends with Nikki, too. We can't just ignore all this."

"We can, and we will. I don't know what the hell you think you're going to accomplish by digging this all up, Liza, but I would strongly advise that you stick to your job." He leans in close enough that I can smell his lemony aftershave. "You know, Liza," he says in the kind of quiet, sweet tone that people use with small children, "you'll catch more flies with honey than with vinegar."

"I didn't realize I was in the fly-catching business."

He straightens up, offering a rigid smile. "Boss Babe may be a fun slogan, but you can take it too far. There's such a thing as being too assertive. You need to tone it down before someone gets hurt."

With that, he pivots and walks out of the room. I watch him go, my mouth hanging open. He just threatened me, I am sure of it. But I couldn't specify how, exactly. One thing is clear: he does not want me or anyone looking into Nikki's death. Which only makes me want to more.

A woman across the table from me whispers to her companion, "Well, he looks nervous. I mean, I can't blame him. I heard he was sleeping with the dead girl."

"No. That can't be right," the other woman says.

I keep my eyes on the asparagus salad but train my ears in their direction.

"That's what the scuttlebutt is," the first woman says. "And you know, apparently, she wasn't the first student."

"I don't believe it. I've never seen anything like that at Wash Prep."

"I didn't say it happened at Washington Prep."

CHAPTER 32

ZOE

Standing in the doorway of the living room, I feel like I'm watching a play. All these people are playing the parts of grieving friends, but really they're just here to gossip and hang out. I can't see Emery's dad anywhere, and he would stick out, he's so tall. But I don't blame him for not wanting to be here.

An older woman, whose silver hair is swept up so it looks like a crown, sits on the sofa holding hands with a younger woman. I can tell this is Emery's grandmother just by looking at her. Emery used to say her grandmother sat as if she had a metal rod for a spine. And that's exactly how this woman is sitting. Even in her grief, her head is held high.

"Zoe? You okay?" I turn to see Kinsey standing there. "I was calling your name."

"I'm fine." But I am not fine. I'm wobbly, and the doorframe I am leaning on is holding me up. Should I tell her that my insides feel like jelly, and every laugh, every voice in this house feels like an ice pick stabbing my heart?

"That was so sad," Kinsey says, her eyebrows forming an upside-down V shape. "It's literally tragic. I still can't believe it."

I stare at Kinsey. It's disturbing how much she looks like Shelby, almost identical to some of the old photos my mom has of her from high school. It reminds me of a novel I read in English class about this guy who had a portrait of himself that would age, while he never grew older. I wonder if it bothers Shelby to have a younger, prettier version of herself in the house.

"We're so worried about you, Z."

I wince. That's a nickname my mom uses sometimes, but no one else. I pick at a loose thread hanging off the hem of my shirt, just to have something to do. *She'll get bored of this,* I tell myself, *and move on. Just hang in there.*

"We just don't want you to, you know . . ." She presses her lips together as if she can't bring herself to finish her sentence. That's fine with me.

"I should go. My mom's waiting."

She lays one hand on my arm, so gently that it barely registers.

"I know you think you were helping Emery with her thing," she whispers. "And, like, that's really sweet. But I think it would be smart to just let her whole little project die with her."

I want to pull away from her, but my legs won't move. I'm frozen in place.

"You're in over your head, Zoe." Her breath is warm and sweet. "I'm saying this as a friend. Just let it go. I'd hate to see you get hurt. Your mom would be so, so sad."

Finally, I stumble past her into the foyer, dizzy and disoriented. The voices from the living room ricochet in my skull, overlaid by Kinsey's warning. *Die with her.* I run up the wide staircase in search of quiet.

The landing on the second floor is as big as my living room, big enough to have a sofa and a bookcase. At the end of the hall, I find the room I am sure is Emery's. It has the same old-fashioned antiques as the rest of the house, but as soon as I see the poster on the wall for the movie *Diva,* I know it's Emery's.

She would always tell me how great that movie was, and I would joke, *I'm not watching a movie all in French. It's bad enough I have to take it at school.* Now I wish I had seen it so we could have talked about it together.

I shut the door behind me, and a calmness starts to come

over me. It's quiet. I'm alone. And I am in her space. The bed is covered by a white bedspread edged with tiny, white balls, and for some reason, this makes me really happy. That she had such a pretty place to sleep. A small, blue teddy bear sits propped up on the pillows. There are little bits of Emery everywhere.

A tennis racket in the corner.

A bulletin board with photos, including one of Emery and me.

I smile, remembering when we took it. It's one of those old-fashioned photo-booth pictures that come in a strip. It's from the annual Flower Mart at the National Cathedral. We spent the day eating greasy food and trying on hats and dresses at all the vendors. I bought my mom a little lavender plant. I walk over, take the photo down, and slip it into my backpack. No one else will want it.

Next to her bed is a table stacked with books and journals. I recognize her sketchbook and sit down as I flip through it. It's like a record of her year in Washington. Sketches of this huge maple tree at school that turns bright red in the fall, the big snow we had in February, the cherry blossoms at the Tidal Basin in spring. When I get to the last page, I freeze. It's a circle divided into sections. Above it, in beautiful script, Emery has written *Zoe's Wheel of Joy*.

My throat catches, and tears sting my eyes. It's all there—everything on the list that I gave her. Half the sections have been painted. She didn't have a chance to finish. I tear the page out and squeeze my eyes tightly to stop from crying. I'm so sick of crying. In a few moments, the sensation passes.

I wish I could talk to her one more time. One more conversation. I'd be willing to let her go if I could have that.

I lie down on her bed, running my hand over the nubby bedspread. How many times did she lie here thinking, plotting, planning? She told me so much. But she also kept so much secret. That her mom was Whitney, my mom's friend. That she had a brother and was trying to find his father.

I roll over and look at the drawing. Getting coffee with Emery at Quartermaine is sandwiched in between going to a Nats game on the Fourth of July with my dad and visiting Ojiichan and Obaachan in Hawaii and eating yomogi mochi for the first time.

No matter what, I know she loved me. Even if she kept secrets from me. Both things can be true at the same time.

I sit up and place the sketchbook back on the table, when I notice another book. A thick paperback by Chris de Groot, the kind you get at the airport. I pick it up and flip it over to the back, which is just one huge photo of the author looking off in the distance, scowling. My mom always complains that women don't get to scowl; they don't get to *not* smile. She hates it when strangers tell her to smile.

Well, Chris de Groot has no problem with that. In fact, he looks pissed off, like he was in the middle of a nice walk in the woods when some asshole photographer jumped out and took his picture.

I vaguely remember him from when I was a kid. He was just one of those grown-ups I'd see every now and then at parties my parents brought me to. And I've heard my mom talk about him. We have all his books, although I don't think my mom has read any of them. I turn to look at the front cover.

Intense Gravity.

Under the huge, gold letters is a shadowy figure running at full speed. And below that, in smaller letters is:

A Kurt Jericho thriller.

A chill runs through me. I sit straight up and take out Emery's phone from my backpack. It can't be a coincidence. Chris de Groot was at Beach Week in 1994, alongside Archer and Todd. Emery said he had been impossible to reach.

But maybe she did find him.

I take her phone out of my backpack and open up her texts. My fingers are fat and clumsy as I scroll to the last text from "Jericho."

Turn around. I'm right behind you.

I look at the book again. It has to be him, using his character's name.

My whole body buzzes. I reread the texts that I sent, and then his warning.

Stop asking questions. Look what happened to Emery.

But maybe there is another way to interpret his words. What if they are not a threat but a warning? I'm not sure which version is right. But I know I need to talk to him. I need to know what happened that night.

I scroll up to the first text in the chain. It's from early April, and it's from him.

Do not call me at that phone number again. If u want to reach out to me, text me on this one. List me under Jericho in ur contacts.

My body is vibrating. It *has* to be de Groot. The date of the first text he sent was April 9. I go to Emery's calls and scroll through. There are only a few. Like me, she doesn't make or get many calls on her phone. There's nothing on April 9. But on April 6, 7, and 8, she made three outgoing calls to a D.C. phone number with no contact listed.

Each call lasted less than ten seconds.

Long enough to get voice mail and leave a short message.

I stare at the phone number. This could be the person who knows what happened to Emery. Or he might be the person who was responsible for her death. I don't know what to do. I'm light-headed. I can't just ignore what I've figured out. I play out in my mind what would happen if I told my mom everything. The scenario unspools in my imagination. She would flip out.

Would she go to the police? She didn't believe me before that Emery hadn't killed herself. Would she believe me now? I think about what Emery would do, what she *did* do. She would be brave. My whole body tenses. I know what I'm going to do. I'll be careful, of course. I'm not stupid. But the need to find out is so strong. I dial the D.C. number, just as she did in early April. The phone rings and rings, with no voice mail picking up. Finally I hear a click, and I wait for a recorded voice to tell me to leave my message.

Instead, a man clears his throat. "Hello?"

I swallow hard. "Hi. Is this Chris de Groot?"

"Speaking."

"This is Zoe Takada, Liza Gold's daughter? We met when I was little?" I wait for a response, for some kind of resistance, but nothing comes. "Anyway, Emery Blake was my best friend. I'm at her funeral now, in fact, and I have her phone." I am about to tell him that I know he saw her the night she died, that I have proof they were texting. But I don't get a chance.

"I'm guessing you're calling about the paternity test, aren't you?"

CHAPTER 33

LIZA

A large potted plant, the type you might find in a nineteenth-century conservatory, serves as cover while I sip a glass of lemonade and munch on finger sandwiches. Not surprisingly, there is no alcohol at this thing, only various beverages served in vessels normally used for alcohol—highballs, wineglasses, goblets—clearly provided by the caterers.

I could use a drink. And someone to talk to. Gossip is marbled through the Washington Prep community like fat on a New York strip steak, but still—Geoff and a student? I don't believe for a minute he was involved with Emery. But him being inappropriate with a student at another school has that ring of truth. And if parents know about it, how did he ever get this job?

"Hi, Liza."

A little yelp escapes me, and I spin around. "Hi, Jacob."

"Please, call me Cobo."

"I thought no one called you that anymore."

"Yeah, I just said that last night. Not sure why." He smiles, and that dimple shows up. I have to remind myself that he has crossed a serious boundary, pinning a picture of Zoe to his wall. I survey the large room. Zoe is nowhere to be found.

"What are you doing here?" I ask curtly.

"Same thing as you. Paying respects to someone who died."

"Okay. Well . . ." I'm not sure what to say to him.

"Look, I want to apologize about last night. I get how freaked out you must have felt seeing your daughter's photo on the wall. I'm not a stalker or a serial killer. I'm just trying to find out what happened to my sister. And somehow Emery and Zoe are involved."

He sounds sincere, and I want to believe him. I decide to extend a little bit of trust. "Did you know Emery?"

He nods. "Yes. I met her a few times over the years."

A mom I know from orchestra catches my eye from across the room and gives me a small smile. She starts walking toward me, so I motion for Cobo to follow me into another room. We wind our way through the house until we come to a bright room with a sunroof, filled with plants. Once we're inside, I shut the french doors and take a seat at one end of a white wicker sofa with thick coral cushions. Cobo sits across from me in a matching chair.

"You need to tell me what is going on. I want to know everything," I say as soon as I'm settled. "I just figured out that Emery was Whitney's daughter. Did you know that?"

His face betrays no emotion as he lets out a low whistle, and I realize he did know. "You just figured that out, huh?"

"I saw the gravestone at the cemetery. I had no idea . . ."

"She died last year, overdosed. According to Emery, she had been trying to stay clean and had been doing a pretty good job for a while. But when they had those hearings for that judge? The one who assaulted a girl in high school in the eighties?"

I nod. It was all over the news—the gut-wrenching testimony of the now-grown woman, the aggressive posturing of the judge, the end result of nothing happening.

"Well, that triggered something in her, according to Emery. She became obsessed with the hearings, in fact, and told Emery she had her own story she planned to share."

"What story? Was it about her being pregnant?"

He ignores my question. "It started to consume her life. She lost her job because all she was doing was this project. And she started using again."

"Heroin?"

"No. Cocaine. It was laced with fentanyl."

I rest my forehead against my hand and close my eyes. It's too much for me to process. Knowing that Whitney suffered so much feels like another thing to grieve, along with her death. I wish I had known. I wish I had stayed in touch with her better than I did.

"I still don't understand how all the pieces fit together. Did Emery tell you all this?"

"Not just Emery but Whitney, too. Over the years, we've seen each other a few times. Trying to reconstruct that night at Beach Week. Figure out what happened to Nikki. Whitney wasn't exactly in a great place. Not a reliable source, if you will, but she wanted someone to talk to. She was really angry about Washington Prep. After Whitney died, Emery came to me. She had been living in Pennsylvania, but after her mom's death, she moved in here with her grandparents. Her dad, well, he's not exactly in the picture, from what I gathered. She wanted to know some things about her mom. She was after the truth, and she knew I was, too."

"How did she know about you?"

"I guess Whitney must have told her about me. Anyway, Emery said if I helped her, in exchange, she would share anything she learned about Nikki. She said that now that she was living in D.C., she could find things out. I told her no, of course. She was a teenager, not a private detective. I told her I didn't want her help, but she didn't listen to me. She was really stubborn."

"Does this have something to do with the baby, the one who died? From the dates on the marker, it seems he was conceived right around Beach Week."

He looks startled. "You really have no idea what happened that night, do you? I mean, I used to think everyone from Washington Prep was in on the cover-up, but I don't know, Liza. I think you genuinely have no idea what your friends did."

"What are you talking about?"

"I'm talking about Whitney and her baby. She was raped. At Beach Week."

CHAPTER 34

1994

The laughter was contagious.

First, Liza fell on the sand, laughing so hard she was gasping, then Nikki joined her, doubled over, beer shooting out of her nose. What was so funny? Nikki could barely follow the story Shelby was telling about one of her older brothers and a rooster he was trying to catch. In the middle of Shelby's story, some guy—was his name Brett?—showed up and interrupted them, just started talking about nothing, and Shelby started pulling all these funny faces behind his back.

The party had migrated outside. All earlier cautions about open containers and keeping a low profile had been abandoned. Nikki felt it, too, all her earlier concerns fluttering away in the ocean breeze. Now she got why people drank.

"It's midnight!" Liza yelled, her legs splayed out in front of her in the sand. "You are officially eighteen!"

Shelby let out a whoop as she leaned into Nikki, and the girls sank down, a tangle of bare legs. They rocked back and forth, laughing, drunk, the cold sand squishing beneath their bare toes.

"Where the hell is Whitney?" Liza asked, looking up and down the beach. Clusters of kids dotted the dark expanse of sand. A girl did cartwheels down to the shoreline. Beyond her, a few guys were diving in and out of the surf, laughing.

"No clue." Shelby pulled off her T-shirt and tossed it behind her. Then she stood up, wiggling out of her shorts. "I want to go swimming." Without waiting for a response, she ran down to the water's edge in her underwear.

"What about sharks?" Nikki asked. But Liza was already stripping down to her bra and panties, too. Nikki watched as Liza bounded down to the water, letting out a little scream when the waves hit her.

Woozy from the alcohol, Nikki stood and walked toward the ocean, stopping when the cold water lapped at her ankles. It sent a shiver through her whole body. Too cold. She couldn't see Shelby. She must have dived under. Liza was a few feet ahead of her, the surf up to her hips. She turned, grinning, her hands wrapped around her midsection. "C'mon."

"I need to pee!" Nikki shouted.

"Just pee in the water."

Shelby surfaced a few yards away and bobbed in the surf. "C'mon, losers. It's my birthday—you have to do what I say."

Nikki stood there, her hands on the snap of her jean shorts. Behind her, several girls shed their clothes and then rushed past her into the water. She was being left behind.

And yet she didn't move. She had to pee really badly now, but she had never been able to go in the ocean. When she was little, her mom had to drag her across the hot sand, back to the parking lot and the nasty public restrooms. And tonight was not going to be her first time, not with all these people around.

She climbed back up the sandy embankment, past a pile of clothes, and broke into a jog back to the party house. She would zip into the house, use the bathroom, and be back before anyone really noticed. More people were heading down to the water. Nikki picked up her pace. She didn't want to miss the fun.

The house was mostly empty. A couple lay on the sofa in the living room, making out, and Don Fraser and a few guys were sitting around the kitchen table playing cards. Nikki waved hi to Don and made a quick trip to the bathroom. She was back out the door before she even snapped up her jean shorts. Excitement propelled her back down to the beach, where she jogged past a group of guys. For a brief moment, she thought it might be Archer and Todd, and she prepared herself, sucking in her stomach and throwing her shoulders back. She had gotten separated from them after everyone showed up at the beach. Her heart raced as she imagined herself with Archer, swimming in the moonlight. She would get Todd to come, too, and that would make Shelby happy. She touched the small gold compass at the base of her throat.

But it wasn't them, just a group of boys that she didn't recognize. She continued on. As she was walking by the dunes, something caught her eye.

She stopped short, sensing a creature nearby. Was it a raccoon? Back home in the D.C. suburbs, it wasn't unusual to encounter the glowing eyes of a raccoon at night, especially before trash day. Did raccoons even live at the beach? No, this was some other kind of animal, bigger than a raccoon, writhing in the dark, moaning, its mane splayed. An injured deer, maybe? But deer didn't have manes. She had heard of wild horses at the beach, but that was farther south, in Assateague. One step closer and those swampy, illogical thoughts were quickly displaced by the knowledge that it was not a mane she was looking at but hair.

Belonging to a girl.

And not just any girl, but Whitney, her shirt pushed up around her neck, revealing her bra.

Nikki rushed to her side and squatted down. "Are you okay?"

Whitney let out a whimpering groan. "Gonna be sick."

Nikki leaned back on her haunches and tried to hold Whitney's hair out of the way while her friend vomited. Whitney was obviously drunk. Nikki would help her out of the dunes, get her some water. She'd be all right.

But something white caught Nikki's eye. A piece of cloth. She picked up a thin piece of driftwood and stretched out her hand, poking at the cloth, trying to bring it closer.

And once she did, she realized she was looking at a pair of girl's underpants.

CHAPTER 35

ZOE

"I'm talking about Whitney and her baby. She was raped. At Beach Week."

I gasp, shifting forward so I can better hear what the dude is saying to my mom. In doing so, I make a noise knocking a wooden duck off of a side table. I scramble to pick it up, but when I look up, they are all staring at me.

"Sorry," I say weakly.

"Zoe." My mom stands up. "How long have you been standing there?"

I turn, rush back out of the room, and weave my way through the crowd toward the foyer. I can feel everyone staring at me, but all I can think is: *Why did it take me so long to figure all this out? I'm an idiot.*

In the back of the foyer is a small window seat under the stairs. I sit down there, trying to slow my racing heart. The thoughts march mercilessly through my brain like soldiers in lockstep.

Rape. Dead baby. DNA. Paternity.

Both things are true. Henry wasn't just Whitney's baby. He was the product of rape. By one of my mom's friends.

And Emery was trying to find out which one.

"Honey, talk to me."

I look up and see my mom's worried face inches from mine.

Her face is scrunched up, making those two lines she calls her elevens between her eyebrows.

"Did you know that one of your friends raped Emery's mom?" I blurt out. "Did you know it when it happened?"

She glances behind her. That one little movement ignites my anger.

"What are you looking for? Answer me, Mom."

She draws in her breath, her mouth pinched tightly. "No, Zoe, I did not know about her assault until five minutes ago. This was the first I heard of it. And we don't know who was responsible."

"Yes, we do," I say. "It was Archer, or Chris de Groot." I study her face for some flicker of acknowledgment, but there is none.

"Honey, what are you talking about? I was there at Beach Week. There were hundreds of kids from several different schools. It could have been anybody."

"That's not what Emery believed."

She sighs heavily as if I were some dumb, naive kid who believed everything she read on the internet. "Honey, Emery was upset, understandably, about what happened to her mother. And maybe some of that clouded her judgment. She doesn't know who assaulted her mother."

"She was trying to find out. She told me she was solving an assault from Beach Week—"

"Wait, she told you what?"

"Yeah, that someone from Beach Week had been raped years ago, and she was going to bring that person to justice. She just didn't tell me it was her own mom."

"Well, who did you think it was?"

"I don't know! I didn't ask, okay? I was just trying to help her do the right thing. And now, I learn today that it was her mom who was raped. Probably by one of your friends. And whoever did it got scared because she was going to prove it. There's a paternity test out there, you know, to compare the samples to."

The look of shock on my mother's face emboldens me.

"Yeah, that's right," I continue. "And I think whoever did that to Emery's mom killed Emery to keep her quiet. And they made it look like a suicide."

My mom lets out a nervous laugh.

"Are you laughing at me?" The fury within me makes my head hot, as if it might blow.

"No, honey. I'm not laughing at you. I understand how upset you are. I do."

"This isn't about me being upset." Beyond my mom, two girls I know have stopped in the foyer and are staring in our direction. As soon as they see me glaring at them, they turn away. "It's not that crazy. Look at Harvey Weinstein. He hired ex-Mossad agents to stalk his victims."

"You can't seriously be comparing Todd or Archer to Harvey Weinstein. You've known these guys your whole life. Honey, these are some of the kindest, most generous people I know."

"So? Ted Bundy volunteered at a suicide hotline."

"Ted Bundy? Where do you get this stuff? Look, I think Emery was troubled. And I don't blame her one bit—"

I raise my hand to stop her from talking. "Emery wasn't crazy."

"I didn't say she was crazy. But, Zoe, do you think it was a coincidence that Emery became friends with you?"

I flinch. I know what she's getting at. It's nothing I haven't already thought about. "No. It's not a coincidence."

"She targeted you, Zoe."

"She didn't target me, Mom. She's not the predator."

"Keep your voice down," she hisses, crossing her arms over her chest. "She used you to get access to Archer. Am I right?"

"She didn't use me! Stop saying that." I stand up, furious. "You don't get it. I chose to help her. She was my best friend. She got me. She was the only person who has ever understood me."

"For the last time, lower your voice, please. People are nearby."

I turn my head. More people are in the foyer now. They are standing there silently, trying to pretend they are not listening to us fight. "I don't care." I hold my arms out and let them flop by my sides. It feels good. I need to get out of here. I need air.

"I don't want a scene, Zoe. This is a funeral."

"Why are you so obsessed with what these people think?" I'm yelling now, aware that the foyer has gone completely silent. Good. Let them hear what I have to say. "Your friend was raped, her daughter was murdered, and all you can think about is your image."

My mother's jaw drops open. It satisfies me to see real hurt on her face. I grab my backpack and start to walk away.

"Where are you going?" she calls.

"Away from you."

Once through the open front door, I stomp down the wooden steps and then break into a run down the tree-lined driveway. I gulp in the humid air, my boots pounding my heartbeat out on the ground. When I reach the road, I stop and put my hands on my knees. I'm panting, lungs on fire.

Slowly, I begin walking down the road in the direction we came from. At least, I think it's the direction we came from. I didn't really think this through. My mouth is parched, and I need water. If I don't come to a store soon, I'll order an Uber. I want to go to Georgetown, to Chris de Groot's. I have to get my hands on that test.

And Chris said he would give it to me.

But I don't want to go there alone. It could be a trap. The two urges battle within me—to rush after the truth or to withdraw to the safety of my dad's.

Still, I keep walking, hoping an answer will come to me. The last thing I want is for my mom to pull up in her car.

The hedges are so overgrown that I have to walk on the white line that runs along the edge of the street to avoid getting scratched by branches. I don't even notice there's a car behind me until it zips by and stops, blocking my way. The little hairs on the back of my neck tingle as I'm forced to walk in the street to go around the humming car. As I pass, the driver rolls down his window and calls out for me.

Inside me, a voice screams, *This is how girls get abducted. This is the moment my parents have warned me about my whole life.*

It feels like a prophecy coming true.

But when I turn and recognize his face, the panic lifts. I giggle as the fear melts into embarrassment.

"You scared me."

He smiles at me. "You okay, Zoe?"

I nod, heart still racing.

"Good," he says. "Need a ride?"

CHAPTER 36

LIZA

Shock. Embarrassment. Worry.

The emotions swirl and crest inside me. I stare at the open door that Zoe just ran through.

Around me, the silence in the room is physical, a heavy quiet of more than a dozen people holding their breaths, using all their self-control not to stare. The only sound is the thin strain of violin music floating through the air.

My feet are glued to the floor.

"You look like you need this."

"Huh?" I look up, startled, to see Prentiss holding out a drink.

"Sorry it's not stronger."

I take the glass and gulp down the sweet, fizzy concoction.

"I've been meaning to reach out to you. I spoke to the police in Dewey."

"You did? Why?"

"Just tying up some loose ends. They told me the autopsy showed no signs of foul play. I mean obviously, or they wouldn't have allowed this funeral. But maybe that can bring Zoe some solace. I know she thinks maybe Emery's death was suspicious. Anyway, perhaps this will give her some comfort?"

"Thank you, Prentiss." And I mean it. But right now, my focus is finding my daughter.

I hand her the glass and walk out into the blinding sunshine.

Standing on the wide porch, I scan for Zoe, but I see no sign of her. There's a swimming pool on the property, if I remember correctly. Maybe she went there. I wander around in the heat in my all-black outfit, soaking in my own sweat, but I see not another living soul. The tennis court is empty, too. I come back to the circular drive in front of the house. She might be at the bottom of the long driveway by now, even farther if she jogged. And once she hits the main road, who knows which direction she'll take. It's a winding lane with no sidewalks, and Zoe is upset, not thinking clearly. It would be all too easy for a car speeding around a corner not to see her.

Someone has parked up against the front bumper of my car, leaving not even an inch of space. I get in and start the engine. I put the car in reverse and give it a smidge of gas, but I instantly feel resistance from behind. I'm parked in on both sides. I'm not getting this car out of here. I slam my palms on the steering wheel, a small sob escaping my throat.

Why are you so obsessed with what these people think?

Zoe's words ring in my mind. *Obsessed.* Am I? I don't think so. But I do care what people think. Washington Prep was my life growing up. When my brother left for college, my mom left, too, to find herself. It's taken me years to trust her, to forgive her. Even now, she feels like an acquaintance, not family.

But I found my family at Washington Prep. Lifelong friends, teachers who cared about me, coaches who pushed me, people who cheered me on. I can't imagine what my life would be like without that school.

As hard as I've tried to get Zoe to feel that same connection, it's never taken root.

A knock on my window startles me, and I look up to see Cobo standing there. I lower the window.

"What?"

"C'mon." He jerks his head. "I'll give you a ride. We'll find her."

At the end of the driveway, we turn right onto the road. As we drive, I hold my breath and stare intently out the window, searching for a figure in black. There is not a soul on the road. When we reach Georgetown Pike, Cobo pulls over. "What do you want to do?"

"Maybe she went the other way."

"We'll go back." There is no conviction in his voice, and I'm not optimistic, either. He makes a U-turn and drives back the way we came, passing the entrance to Whitney's old house. My stomach clenches, waves of nausea grip me. Sitting in my lap, my phone offers no help at all. My calls to Zoe go straight to voice mail.

"I don't get it. Where did she go?" The country lane that looked so bucolic when we drove down it earlier now feels ominous, the wall of brush intimidating, as if hiding secrets behind the lush greenery.

"Did you check her location?"

I curse myself for not having thought of that right away. When I see her avatar moving slowly on Georgetown Pike, I exhale.

Where are you? I text.

This time, she responds immediately.

Got a ride to Dad's.

"That was Zoe," I say. "She must have called an Uber." My newfound relief turns to anger. "I can't keep doing this. It's a roller coaster. I don't know if I can take it any longer."

Cobo pulls into a small shopping center and parks the car. "You need a cup of coffee." He gets out without waiting for my response. I follow him into the McLean Family Restaurant, an old-school diner, because it's the easiest thing to do right now, and honestly, it feels good to let someone else be in charge. I know I can't go back to the Bascombe house and face everyone there.

Inside, we find a booth at the back. I slide onto the hard plastic seat, still feeling stunned. An older guy with a bad comb-over shuffles around from behind a long counter to our table. Cobo orders two coffees and a piece of baklava, which arrive in moments. Cobo picks up one of the forks and breaks off a piece of the pastry.

"Not too bad," he says after a bite, and he pushes the plate at me.

"I feel like my brain is on fire," I say and take a teeny bite. It is sweet and flaky. "You know what Zoe said before she ran out? She thinks it was Archer that raped Whitney. And then killed Emery. Can you believe that?"

"Maybe," Cobo starts in a tentative voice, "you don't have to believe it. You just have to allow for its possibility, right?"

"I honestly can't. Rape and murder? I've known these guys my whole life. Archer is vegetarian because he won't eat anything he isn't willing to kill. And I'm supposed to believe he raped our friend and then twenty-eight years later murdered a teenage girl to cover it up?" I bring my cup to my lips and breathe in the warm scent of coffee. "Please."

But Cobo just looks at me, unsmiling. He doesn't agree the notion is preposterous or laugh it off. I squirm in my seat.

"What, you think it's possible?"

"Actually, yes. I believed Whitney. She said she was raped. And I have no reason to doubt her."

"And who did she say raped her?"

"She didn't know, Liza. She told me she remembered practically nothing about that night. But she did remember waking up with bruises on her inner thighs, on her neck, and a bite mark on her breast." His words are like nails firing from a nail gun, pinning me to my seat.

I wince. "That's horrible."

"Yeah. It is."

"And you think one of my friends is responsible?"

He shrugs noncommittally.

"I can't even picture when this rape would have happened," I say. "We were only at the beach one night. We left the day after Nikki drowned. When could a rape even take place?" My words sound like excuses even to my ears. My heart speeds up. How long does it take to rape someone? Was I really watching Whitney that whole evening? Of course not. I drop my fork. "I need to talk to Shelby. Ask her if she remembers anything."

"You want to ask Shelby if one of your friends is a rapist?"

"No." I feel pinned by his direct gaze. "Not exactly. But what if it was one of those gray situations?" I feel slightly queasy even saying the words. His eyebrows shoot up. "You know, where everyone's drunk? Consent—it wasn't such a big thing in the nineties."

"That's putting it mildly. Back then, the concept of being too drunk to consent to sex did not exist," Cobo says.

"I just can't believe that Whitney never told me. All those years, we were in touch on and off. I knew she was struggling, but I had no idea anything like this had happened. Why wouldn't she tell me?"

"Seriously, Liza? Do you know anything about trauma? Even though she was the victim, she probably felt ashamed."

"Of course. But I was one of her best friends." But even as I say it, I know it is not true. We were in the same social group in high school. We hung out; we partied. But we were never that close, not the way I was with Shelby and Nikki. I didn't really know what was going on with her, and she obviously did not feel close enough to me to tell me what had happened to her.

"You were also good friends with her rapist."

"We don't know that for sure," I say, indignant. "There were tons of guys there that night, and not just from Washington Prep. There were Landon guys, Georgetown Prep guys." I put my elbows on the table and hold my head. It's pounding. I need Tylenol. I need sleep. I need to know what happened that night, but at the same time, I'm scared of what I might find out. "Look," I peer up at Cobo, "I know you think this is all somehow wrapped up with what happened to Nikki. But I was thinking about what you said. About the phone call? You must have the time wrong. There's just no way. I was the one who found her clothes, Cobo."

"It was a Saturday night, and on Saturday nights, I'd pretend to go to sleep and then get up right before midnight and put the TV in the living room on real low and watch *USA Up All Night* with Gilbert Gottfried. Remember that guy?"

I smile and nod. Gottfried was a comic with an annoying voice who was everywhere in the nineties—on *Conan, Saturday Night Live*, guest starring on TV shows.

"I remember everything about that night," Cobo says as he absentmindedly runs one finger around the rim of his coffee cup. "The movie was *Friday the 13th, Part VIII*, if you can believe it. *Jason Takes Manhattan*. I was so psyched. Every show had an intro with Gilbert Gottfried before the movie started. So the movie never started right at midnight. And I remember so clearly that the movie had just started when the phone rang. I was annoyed because—remember, this was the old days—you couldn't pause anything. So I knew it was after midnight, but not way after. Maybe twelve fifteen? Twelve twenty?"

I twirl the fork in my hand, trying to channel my discomfort as I listen to him talk.

"It was Nikki. She was upset, and she wanted me to wake up my parents. My dad, specifically." Cobo laughs. "I don't know if you ever met my dad—"

"No. But he was a detective, right?"

"Montgomery County Police, major crimes. He was not the kind of guy you woke up in the middle of the night unless it was serious. And I should have known it was." His voice grows solemn. "But I was just a kid, and I was pissed that I was missing my movie. So I told her no, and then she hung up. I went back to watching the movie. I thought if it was important, she would call back, but she never did. I didn't think that would be the last time I ever spoke to her." His voice cracks, and he pauses, not moving. He looks up at me and gives me a sweet smile. "Sorry."

"It's okay," I say and reach across the table to give his hand a squeeze.

"You have no idea how many times I've replayed that night in my head. She was in some kind of trouble, and I didn't help."

"It wasn't your fault. You were a kid."

"But that's why I need to find out what really happened. I can't let it go, you see? And I know it was after midnight when she called, Liza. I know it. So she could not have drowned at midnight."

My world is spinning, and I feel faint. Something has cracked open inside me, revealing an ugliness I can't look away from. In a hoarse whisper, I say, "I believe you."

He looks at me and sniffles a little.

"Hey," I say. "I know you don't owe me anything, Cobo. But I was wondering if I could ask you for something."

"What is it?"

"I was wondering if you would let me give you a hug."

Silently, we both stand and wrap our arms around each other in the aisle of the diner. His body is solid and comforting. I lay my cheek on the sleek material of his suited shoulder and let the tears come. For Nikki, for Zoe. For all of us.

CHAPTER 37

ZOE

"Where to?"

"Umm, Georgetown?" Chris de Groot was waiting for me at his house on O Street. *Big yellow house,* he had said. *Can't miss it.*

"At your service." Mr. Estes nods, and I sink into the soft leather seat. The car is immaculate—no wrappers or crumpled-up napkins. No dog hair, like in our Subaru. I lean back and try to focus on the eighties song playing softly. It's the one about red balloons, and it makes me think of my mom and how much she loves this song. If she were in the car, she'd crank it up and sing really loudly. A sharp pang hits my chest. I feel bad about yelling at her.

"That was pretty upsetting, how that pastor kept referring to Emery as *Emily.*" He doesn't look at me when he says this, just stares straight ahead at the road.

"I know. I mean, that's your one job. Get the person's name right."

He doesn't respond, and I worry that I sound too angry. I wonder if he expects me to talk, ask him questions, stuff like that. But we're not in school, I remind myself, and I'm not in trouble. Still, I don't love being around grown-ups by myself. I never know how to act or what to say. Instead, I stare out the window. We're crossing the Key Bridge into D.C., and I can see the spires of Georgetown University on the left. I wonder if my mom is looking for me. I reach down and unzip my backpack. I'll just text her, let her know I got a ride home.

He glances over at me, frowning. I know he hates cell phones.

"I'm just telling my mom I got a ride home." I type a quick message and then slip my phone back into my backpack.

"Good idea. Liza worries about you."

I can't help but laugh a little. "That's true, Mr. Estes."

"Oooh." He grimaces. "That sounds way too formal. How about outside of school you call me Geoff."

I nod, but I don't think I'll be able to do it.

"Your mom's a good person. She always wants to do the right thing. Not everyone is like that."

"I know." I feel chastened. I know my mom is a good person. I know her better than anyone. But it doesn't make it any easier to live with her.

"You seem to be the same way, Zoe. Interested in doing the right thing."

I wait for him to continue, but he doesn't. We drive along listening to music for a while. He unknots the tie at his neck, keeping one hand on the wheel, and then tosses it into the back seat.

"Hate those damn things."

"Neckties?"

He laughs. "I mean funerals. But I'm not a fan of neckties, either. You were very close to Emery, weren't you?"

"Yes. She was my best friend."

"I'm sorry for your loss. I knew her mother, Whitney. I tried to help her over the years, you know. A lot of people did. But in the end, none of us could save her."

I don't know what to say to this, so I curl my legs up under me and stare out at the city streets.

Then he asks, "You don't believe Emery died by suicide, do you?"

The question jolts me out of my thoughts. "Pardon?" Washington Prep students always say *pardon*, never *what*.

"I saw on your Instagram that you think something bad happened to Emery. Is that right?"

"Yes. Actually." It feels weird that an adult is looking at my Insta and actually taking me seriously. Especially the head of school. I'm just so used to seeing Mr. Estes leading morning meeting and speaking at Wednesday chapel. I haven't had that many one-on-one conversations with him, although everyone seems to like him. He's a lot less uptight than the old head, Dr. Kales.

He nods. "Emery was trying to find out who the father of Whitney's baby was, right? She was asking a lot of questions, poking around?"

I nod, surprised. "How did you know that?"

"Well, as head of school, you hear things," he says. "But like I said earlier, I knew Whitney. And I knew Emery, too. I suspected she was working on something. She came to me to get Chris de Groot's contact info. Told me it was for some project about publishing."

"She did? Did you give it to her?"

"I couldn't really do that. But I did pass along her info to him, along with a message that Whitney's daughter was trying to reach out to him."

"My mom didn't know. That Emery was Whitney's daughter. I didn't even know until today."

"That's understandable. Emery herself never mentioned it to me. I'm not sure she necessarily wanted anyone making the connection. I figured it out when her father enrolled her and put her grandparents' names down as an emergency contact. I recognized the Bascombe name and the address. But we never discussed it. I was trying to protect her privacy."

"Then how did you know about what she was working on?"

"I pieced it together. From what I had heard from Whitney about the circumstances of Henry's birth. Little things I heard from your mom about what you two have been up to. Trying to get DNA from Archer, for example."

"She told you that?"

"Sure. Your mother and I are quite close, Zoe. She didn't think there was anything to it, but I do. I get it. I was there back then, as a coach, you know, when everyone was in high school."

"So you know what happened at Beach Week in '94."

He nods. "I doubt you'll ever be able to figure it all out, though. There's no DNA to match these samples to, right?"

"Actually, there is. There was a paternity test done at Henry's birth. And Chris de Groot claims he has it."

He turns and narrows his eyes at me. "Really?" He laughs, a kind of raspy noise that sounds more like a cough. "Well, that's a surprise. Anyway, getting ahold of Chris de Groot is no easy feat. I'm sure Emery tried, but I doubt she had any luck."

"Actually, she did. They were texting the night she died, in fact. He used a fake name, but I figured it out." A little balloon of pride swells within me. "It wasn't that hard to do."

"Impressed. You're smart. So they were texting that night? Do the police know this?"

I shake my head. "No. I just figured it all out today. I called him and left a message that if he didn't call me, I would go to the police."

"You should, anyway."

"I will." My voice is confident, but until just that moment, it hadn't really occurred to me to call the police. Now it seems obvious.

"What does your mom say about all this?"

I roll my eyes. "She doesn't believe it. She won't really listen to me. It's like she can't imagine any of her friends ever doing anything wrong. She thinks it's, like, all some misunderstanding or that there's a *reasonable explanation*."

The car bounces along the cobbled streets of Georgetown. My chest tightens as if a giant hand is squeezing it. I want to see Chris de Groot, but I'm scared. What if he's lying and there is no test? What if he is the one who hurt Emery?

"So where to? A friend's?"

I take a deep breath. Maybe he can help me. Mr. Estes seems to believe me. "Actually, I'm meeting Chris de Groot."

He doesn't look at me or act surprised. "That makes sense. He lives around here, doesn't he?"

"Yeah. He said he would give me the paternity test. He said I could test the samples we've been collecting against it, and we would know for sure."

"You sound hesitant."

"I don't know if I can trust him."

He chews on his lower lip. "Any way I could talk you out of doing this? Drive you to your dad's or mom's instead? Tell you to forget all about it?"

I swallow the hard lump in my throat. "No. There's no way. I'm going."

"Then I guess I'd better go in with you."

CHAPTER 38

LIZA

"Did you ever tell the police?" I ask Cobo once we're back in his car. "About the phone call at midnight?"

He gives me a knowing look. "Liza. The police didn't want anything to do with what happened to Nikki. Even my dad couldn't get any traction with it, and he was a detective. The police out there wanted it to be an accident, and so it was. You know there was pressure from the beginning to make this go away."

"From who? The other kids' parents?"

"From the parents. From your school." He turns the engine on but makes no move to leave the parking lot. "It was like, 'We're sorry a brown girl died, but we don't want to ruin these bright young white people's lives. We don't want Washington Prep dragged through the mud.'"

"You think Nikki's death would have been handled differently if she were white? I mean, I guess I see what you're saying, but—"

"But what?"

"I'm embarrassed to say I never even thought about that."

His eyes widen. "You ever heard of the Freeway Phantom?"

I shake my head. "Is that a serial killer?"

He nods. "Killed six Black girls in D.C. and Prince George's County in the early seventies. Abducted, raped, and killed them, then dumped them by the side of the freeway. The police never took it seriously." He spreads his hands out in front of him. "Liza, if you saw the notes from that case, read about the things the police did, the things they said to the families, you would be horrified. It's not like in the movies, with concerned detectives rushing to find the bad guy. They treated the families with suspicion and the victims like degenerates. Said it was their own fault, basically. It's still unsolved. They've closed the investigation, and they actually purged the evidence." He nods vigorously. "Yes, *purged* is the word they used. Can you believe it? Six dead girls, and the investigation is closed. You think that would happen with six dead white girls from northwest D.C.? Or Chevy Chase? The youngest victim was ten years old."

His anger is like a crashing wave, and I brace myself to allow it to break over me. It's hard, but I resist the urge to argue that there has to be a logical explanation. Instead, I sit with the discomfort. For a few moments, we stay like that, both staring straight ahead at the entrance to a dry cleaner.

"I'm sorry," I say finally, turning to look at his profile. He won't meet my eye.

"You know what? The same thing happened with Nikki. Same damn thing." He steals a glance at me. "They tried to smear her, make it look like she was troubled, like her disappearance was her own fault. They said she was into drugs."

"Nikki didn't do drugs."

"I know that."

"Who said that she did?" The idea infuriates me. "Nobody ever asked me about drugs, and I was her closest friend. I'd have known."

"Your classmates, that's who. Told the cops she was a drug user, that she had gotten high that night."

I shift in the small car seat so my body is turned toward him. "Who told them that, Cobo? What are their names?"

He shrugs. "Don't know. I have my suspicions. The police made my mother cry with this shit. It tortured her that people

were saying these things about her baby girl. People in the neighborhood, at our church, they would whisper when we walked by."

"That's horrible. I had no idea."

He puts the car into reverse and begins backing out. "There's
no way Shelby Covington's death would have been treated that
way."

I bite my tongue. I can't disagree.

"They also came after me." We're out of the parking lot now,
on the road that will take us back to the Bascombe house, to my
car.

"Who came after you?"

"Your friends, that's who. When I got to college, around
2001, 2002, I couldn't stop thinking about my sister. How her
death destroyed my family. I wasn't like my mom, who wouldn't
accept that she was really dead. You know, 'cause we never found
the body. I wasn't like that. I believed she had died. I knew she
wouldn't be out there and not contact us, torturing us like that."
He clears his throat and lets out a sad little laugh. "I mean, to
be honest? Yes, sometimes I would see a girl from the back and
think it was Nikki. I'd be so sure. But only in that moment. I was
convinced, I still am, that something happened to her at Beach
Week and that someone knows where her body is. I became obsessed with the idea that I could find out the truth about what
happened. Anyway, I started a blog—remember blogs?—called
The Nikki Project."

"I never knew about it."

He shrugs. "Wasn't exactly popular. I posted pictures of her,
a bio, little stories, asking if anybody knew anything. And you
know what? I got a bunch of anonymous tips. Most of them
useless, but not all . . ."

"What did they say?"

"Maybe they were just messing with me, but one guy, or girl,
reached out to me. They said that Nikki was dead, but that she

didn't drown, that it didn't go down the way everyone said it did. This person, they were anonymous, said to look at the police file. That the truth was in there. Well, I tried. I reached out to the police, and they sent me the file. It was so thin. All it had was two pieces of paper—the incident report and a list of people who had given statements, like you. That was it. When I asked where was the rest, they said they had *misplaced* it." He takes one hand off the steering wheel and makes air quotes when he says the word *misplaced*. "And then, boom, I got a cease and desist from a lawyer."

"Whose lawyer?"

"Archer Benoit's."

Silence fills the car. I'm stunned, confused. "Archer's?"

"His lawyer sent a letter to my mom's house, scared the crap out of her."

"Why would he do that?" I'm genuinely shocked.

He shrugs. "You tell me. All I was writing on the blog was that he was there the night Nikki disappeared. And that I had reached out to him, and he never responded. Which is all true. And that was enough for him—or his family—to sic their lawyers on me and my mom. And then the dean at my college called me in and told me to drop it. Said he had received some phone calls from some important people. That I was attracting the wrong kind of attention to the college."

"You're kidding."

"Nope. And my mom, she freaked out. She begged me to drop it. 'I don't want to lose you, too,' she said. So I backed off. Until last year, when I moved back from Atlanta to care for her. Being back in D.C., it really brought up all those feelings again. And when Emery showed up, asking all kinds of questions, I felt like it was a sign from God or something."

He slows down to take the turn onto the Bascombes' driveway. Soon we will be parting ways, and this thought sends a little jolt to my stomach. I realize that I want to keep talking to him.

"I get why you have a picture of Emery on your wall, but why do you have a picture of Zoe?"

"I'm sorry about that." He shoots me a glance. "I know that freaked you out. But Zoe was with Emery the night she died. When Emery first moved to Washington, she got in touch with me. She told me about her plan. Apparently, her mom told her that when she had Henry, she took a paternity test but never learned the results. When Henry died a few days after his birth, Whitney didn't want to know the results of the test. So Emery was on a mission to collect a bunch of DNA and compare it to the test results. If she could ever find them. It seemed crazy to me, but I understand that when you are grieving, sometimes you need to do something, have a mission, to keep yourself going. But then Emery called me last week, told me she was going out to Dewey to meet with someone who knew what really happened. Someone who was there twenty-eight years ago. She wouldn't tell me who. I told her not to go. Said it was way too dangerous. I couldn't get her to tell me who. Archer? Todd? Chris? So I told her I would be in Dewey, and she could call me if she needed help. I would come right away."

The house is in sight now, and I can see a couple standing on the porch as if they're waiting. But the driveway has emptied out, with only a handful of cars still here.

"And also, to be honest, I wanted to know who she was meeting," Cobo says. "I thought they might have some answers for me, too. That's why I was out in Dewey."

"You think Zoe knows something about that night?"

"Maybe. She might not even know that she knows it."

"How come you never reached out to me over the years? I was Nikki's closest friend."

"I would have eventually, but you were not a top priority." He pulls into the empty spot behind my car.

"Thanks a lot."

He grins. "You gave the police a statement."

"I remember."

"My top priority was the people who refused to talk to the police."

"Who refused?"

He paused. "You sure you want to go there?"

"Yeah, I'm a grown-up. I think I can handle it."

"Everybody but you refused."

My stomach lurches. "Everybody?"

"Archer. Whitney. Shelby. Todd. Chris de Groot. Not one of them would talk to the police." He sighs. "I think the police might have pushed harder if Washington Prep hadn't stepped in."

"Stepped in how?"

"Nothing official. But when that teacher vouched for them, said he was with them, that kind of shut the whole investigation down."

"Which teacher?" A hot sensation starts to spread across my chest.

"Geoff Estes."

ZOE

"Go on, ring the bell," Mr. Estes urges.

The large yellow house in front of us juts out a bit farther onto the sidewalk than its O Street neighbors, like the bully of the block. I take a tentative step onto the worn stone stoop. My whole body trembles, but I can hear Mr. Estes breathing behind me, and I tell myself it's going to be okay. He won't let anything bad happen.

Twice I ring the bell, but no one comes. I cup my hands and peer through the glass door. It's dark inside, and I can't make out much. A table with an urn on it. A tall mirror. I am about to turn away when a figure passes into the light, and the front door swings inward.

"Are you Zoe?" the man before me asks in a gruff voice. He sounds like my dad when he first wakes up. I wonder if I have woken him.

"Yeah. Hi."

He grumbles something I can't understand and then steps back to make room. As I enter the cool, dark foyer, Mr. Estes pushes past me.

"Geoff. What the hell are you doing here?" Chris de Groot barks. The three of us stand in the foyer, hemmed in by a round table piled high with mail.

Mr. Estes shuts the door behind him. "I thought I'd join Zoe."

The two men stand on either side of me in silence. My skin starts to prickle. Something is off, but I can't tell what. Mr. Estes's face is blank, unreadable. Chris de Groot has that same annoyed look he had in the photo on the back of his book. Only his face is redder and puffier.

"All right. Let's talk in the living room." Chris pushes past us, and we follow him. He reminds me of a bear, lumbering and ungraceful. In the living room, he gestures for us to sit, and I take a seat on the edge of a worn velvet couch while Mr. Estes sits across from me. But Chris de Groot stays standing.

My stomach churns. This was a bad idea. But I don't know how to get out of it. Can I just stand up and leave? I tuck my hands under my thighs and dig my nails into my skin as if causing myself pain will somehow ward off disaster. A dumb superstition, like when I was little and I'd flush ice cubes down the toilet and wear my pajamas inside out because I thought that would cause a snow day.

"I've been calling you, Geoff." Chris rocks back and forth on his heels, his arms crossed over his wide chest. "Haven't been returning my calls."

"Apologies, but I'm here now. Let's talk." Mr. Estes spreads his arms out as if this is his office and not someone else's house. I look around, and my heart sinks. This is not the house of a normal person. Piles of books and newspapers cover every surface. Empty coffee cups and plates balance on chairs, on the mantel. The air is damp and smells like dirty socks. I look to Mr. Estes, but his face shows no concern. *Focus,* I tell myself, *you're here for Emery.*

"Too late. I've made up my mind. I'm not going to lie anymore. I don't care if it lands me in prison."

The word *prison* sends a current of electricity through me. Chris looks deranged, like a wild man. But Mr. Estes chuckles as if this is all a joke. "Let's slow down, Chris. Let's think about this. We don't want to ring a bell that can't be unrung."

Chris slams his fist down on a pile of books, sending a wine-glass toppling to the floor, where it smashes to bits. "The bell has been rung. It's too fucking late. The bell was rung twenty-eight years ago." His voice is like thunder, filling the room. I pull my legs closer together, terrified.

Mr. Estes gets up. "If you want to ruin your life, that's your own business. Drink yourself to death for all I care. But I won't let you drag everyone else down with you."

"You brownnosing bastard. Are you trying to protect Washington Prep, or your own ass?" He lunges at Mr. Estes, knocking over a stack of files. "When does it end? I'll tell you—*now*. I can't live with the guilt. I don't care who else gets hurt. I'm willing to pay. I *want* to pay."

"Don't be stupid."

"Stupid is getting up day after day, putting one foot in front of the other, all the while hiding from who I really am. Stupid is pretending that night never happened and that I could outrun what I had done. I'm not running anymore."

What does he mean, pretending that night never happened? Which one? Last Sunday, with Emery, or twenty-eight years ago with Whitney? All the potential answers terrify me. My whole body shakes. I want out of this overstuffed house with these two men. I need air. I can't breathe.

"Where's this test, Chris? Does it really exist? Is that a piece of fiction, too?"

"Fuck off." He taps his shirt pocket. "It's here. It exists."

My eyes go to where he is tapping, but I see nothing. Just a pocket on his pink oxford shirt.

Mr. Estes holds out his hand and takes a step closer. "Show me. Let me see for myself."

My eyes dart around the room. Maybe this is my chance to run. But they are blocking the way to the front door. And I don't want to run deeper into this crazy house. I'll text my mom; she'll come get me. I pull my backpack around to my front and pull out my phone. She'll come for me. I know she will drop anything if I need her. My hands tremble as I type. The phone slips onto the floor with a clank and skitters away.

"Shit." I fall to my knees and chase after it. I am about to reach it when a foot stomps down, pinning the phone to the floor.

"What are you doing, Zoe?" I look up to see Chris glowering at me. He sways a little like a tall pine tree in the wind. "Who are you calling?"

I swallow the lumps in my throat. "Nobody."

He swoops down and takes the phone. Then he pulls me as if I am as light as a rag doll. I am only a few inches from him. Liquor and sweat peel off his body in waves every time he moves.

"Let her go," Mr. Estes says.

Chris releases me. I back up against the carved wood staircase, my eyes flitting from Chris to my backpack still on the couch.

"I'm not going to hurt her." Chris sounds petulant, on the verge of erupting into anger. "What the hell're you doing here, anyway? I didn't invite you. When I needed you, you wouldn't take my calls. Why are you here at all?"

"Zoe came for the paternity test," Mr. Estes says. "And if it really exists, I'm here to make sure she gets it."

Chris lets out a howl of a laugh that makes my whole body quiver. I scooch up the first few steps. I shouldn't have gotten in the car with Mr. Estes. I shouldn't have come here. I choke back a small sob.

"You mean you're here to make sure that *you* get it. You think I'm stupid?" Chris barrels toward Mr. Estes. "This is my house, not Washington Prep. You're not the boss here, and you'll do exactly what the fuck I tell you to do." Every few words, he jabs a finger into Mr. Estes's chest. "Now get out."

He grabs hold of Mr. Estes's neck and forces his head forward, but he resists. Mr. Estes may be smaller and wirier, but he's strong. The two men lock arms on each other's shoulders like crazy dance partners. They crash toward me, and I scurry up a few stairs to get out of the way. I have no phone. And my backpack, which holds Emery's, is on the couch, out of reach. When Chris pins Mr. Estes near the edge of the stairs, I climb farther, as if the spindly banister can protect me. My head is pounding as if all the blood in my body has rushed into it before it explodes like a volcano. I watch as Mr. Estes, his face turning purple, grabs a large vase and smashes it against Chris's head. *Thunk*. It doesn't break. Chris wobbles, touching his head. When he pulls his hand back, it's covered in blood.

I scream and then clamp my hand over my mouth. But they don't look up. Chris lets out a guttural roar and charges Mr. Estes. I run through the upstairs hallway, which is clogged with boxes and books and white trash bags. I weave through the mess as fast as I can until I find an open door.

Inside, I slam it and sink to the floor. Crashing sounds and loud grunts rise up from below. I want to go home. *It's too late for that, Zoe.* I squeeze my knees closer to my chest. It's so musty in here, I can see dust motes floating in the air.

I squeeze my eyes tightly. My breath comes in short bursts. I feel dizzy. I'm going to pass out. I'm going to die here.

No.

I force myself to open my eyes. I won't give up. I stand and push my way through the boxes and garbage bags to the window. It looks out on the back alley. I don't know what I will do if I open it, but I have to try. I push against the frame with all my strength, but it is painted shut.

I swivel my head around. There has to be something that can break a window in this cluttered room. I find it on the dresser: a metal statue of a hunting dog. Wrapping my hand in my cardigan, I turn my head away and smash the glass. It cracks easily. Carefully, I use the dog statue to knock out what's left of the windowpane. When it is clear, I stick my head out. I am high up. The brick alley below me is lined with garbage cans. Not a person in sight.

Too high to jump.

"Hello!" I yell. "Somebody, please!"

But my voice just evaporates into the sticky air of the alley.

And no one knows I am here.

CHAPTER 40

LIZA

As soon as I get home, I leash up Walnut, then head back out on foot in the direction of Spring Valley. I need to see Shelby, and the dog needs a walk. Thoughts swirl through my mind as we wind our way through the quiet streets. The late-afternoon heat is oppressive, and at the small shopping center, I decide to pop into Compass Coffee for a cold brew. I tie Walnut up on the Pup Deck and go inside, where Julie the barista greets me.

"Hey, you're all dressed up," she says.

I look down and realize I'm still wearing my black shirt and pants. "I was at a funeral."

"That's so sad." Julie frowns, her sweet face immediately registering sorrow. She's about twenty, and she represents a hope I have for Zoe—that she will pass through the storm of her teenage years and come out one day on the other side as cheerful as Julie is. "Somebody close to you?"

"Not really. She went to school with my daughter."

Julie's mouth drops open. "Not that girl who died at Beach Week?"

I press my lips together and give her a little nod.

"Oh my gosh. It's so sad. She used to come in here, you know."

My head snaps up. "In here? Really?" Emery lived in McLean. Although Wash Prep is only a few miles from here, it isn't convenient to the school if you don't have a car. And it could hardly be considered a hangout for teens.

"Uh-huh. I remembered after I saw her picture in the paper. She was super tall, right? And had that long, long hair. She came in with your friend. What's her name? The blond, really bubbly one?"

"Shelby," I blurt out.

"Right. Shelby. I think of her as *half-caf skinny latte*."

Behind me, a man coughs, and I step aside to wait for my cold-brew iced coffee, my legs feeling leaden. I don't like this. I can't fathom why in the world Shelby would have been meeting with Emery.

And why she wouldn't mention it to me.

The walk to Shelby's is uphill, and by the time we get there, both Walnut and I are panting. We pause at the curb so I can catch my breath. Shelby's house resembles a European stone manse with twin topiary boxwoods flanking a double wooden door. But inside, it is completely modern, with a two-story foyer, ten-foot ceilings, three fireplaces, a media room, and an indoor lap pool. Shelby jokingly refers to it as "the Compound." She even had an intercom installed because her kids couldn't hear her calling them for dinner all the way from the kitchen.

Shelby answers the door, a little unsteady in her heels, dressed in a body-hugging white dress. She clearly had a few drinks at the club.

"Hey, girl," she says. "Hey, Walnut! Who's a good boy?" Shelby wobbles over to Walnut and scratches his ears. "I just got home. Come inside; I need a glass of wine. I mean, six hours at the club with my mother? I need the whole damn bottle."

"Tell me you never met Emery Blake at Compass Coffee."

Shelby straightens up, startled. "Whoa, what?"

"Tell me that didn't happen, Shel." I know I sound strident, but I'm on the verge of freaking out. "Because you would have told me if it had, right?"

Shelby bites her lower lip. "You'd better come inside."

I follow her into the gleaming white kitchen and sit at the large Carrera marble island. Shelby gets a bowl of water for Walnut. "Here you go, boy."

"Tell me what's going on, Shelby." I tap my foot. Walnut slops at the water greedily, spilling it all over the floor.

Shelby grabs a bottle from the custom wine fridge. "Thirsty? Rosé okay?"

"I don't really care."

Shelby pours us each a glass of pale pink wine. I tap my fingers, anxious for her to start explaining.

"So Emery reached out to me awhile ago and asked if I could hook her up with Chris de Groot." She reaches over the island and grabs a hand towel, then tosses it on the floor near Walnut's water bowl as if it is going to magically mop the water up by itself like in *Beauty and the Beast*.

"You never told me that."

She does not respond.

"And you didn't think that was weird?"

"No, not at the time." She places the bottle next to a ginger jar filled with white calla lilies. I don't think I've ever been in a Washington home that did not have at least one blue-and-white ginger jar. "Now I think it's weird. But she said she was doing her senior-year internship. The only thing I thought was odd was that she was sort of late to the game. Most seniors have their spring internships set up in January. At least, Kinsey and Brody did."

"All right. Go on." It makes sense so far. The senior spring internship is a big deal at Wash Prep. All alumni with connections are expected to step in and help students secure high-profile placements.

"She said she wanted to do it in book publicity and marketing. She was interested in meeting a bestselling author. Someone told her about Chris de Groot and that I might be able to help." Shelby takes a swig of wine. "So I agreed to meet her."

"Did you know that Whitney died last year?"

"What?" Shelby sucks in her breath. "Where did you hear that? I had no idea. How did she die?"

"Sounds like it had something to do with drugs."

"Oh my gosh, poor Whitney. I mean, I knew she had her struggles . . ." Her voice trails off. "I'm so sad to hear that. Did you find that out at the funeral? Did someone tell you? I mean, how did that even come up?"

"Emery was Whitney's daughter. I found out today, at the funeral. It was open casket, and Emery was wearing Whitney's necklace." I touch the small gold compass around my own neck. "Then I saw the grave marker."

"Wait, what? Whitney was Emery's mom? Are you sure?"

"One hundred percent. The reception was at Whitney's parents' house. Remember that place?"

She nods slightly. "Holy shit."

"Exactly. When I saw that necklace around Emery's neck, it was as if the breath had been sucked out of me."

"Oh, honey."

I blink hard to keep back the tears. "It's dumb to be so upset. I haven't—sorry, *hadn't*—talked to Whitney in years, but learning she was dead, all these feelings came whooshing back at me."

"I get it. Did Zoe know Whitney was Emery's mother?"

"She says she didn't know until today," I say. "And don't I feel like the world's most clueless mom."

"No, don't say that. Kids are so good at keeping secrets. I'm lucky if Kinsey comes out of her LED-lit cave to grunt at me some nights. Who knows what they're doing?"

"So you had no clue, either?" I ask.

"None. Emery didn't say anything about Whitney when I met with her. At all. I mean, she and Whitney have different last names, *Blake* and *Bascombe*." She sighs. "I truly thought she was just a regular ol' Wash Prep student, so I gave her what contact info I had on Chris. I told her she had a better shot of getting Stephen King to respond to her, but whatever. That's it. End of story. I swear."

Shelby's explanations click into place, but I am still uneasy. I feel like I'm inside the Second Glance photo in *The Washington Post Magazine*. Everything looks the same as in the first photo, but something's off. Something is missing.

"You still have the necklace," she says with a sad smile. "I have mine somewhere. I just never wear it. It seems so sad."

"There's more," I say. "Whitney was assaulted. At Beach Week." I watch Shelby's eyes widen in disbelief. "And she got pregnant."

"What?" Shelby straightens up. "What are you talking about, Liza?"

"I'm talking about the fact that Whitney got pregnant at Beach Week and had a little boy named Henry. And no one knows who the father is."

"How did you learn all this?"

I fill her in on what happened today, how I saw the headstone, my conversation with Cobo about how he had met with Whitney over the years.

"Who's Cobo?"

"Nikki's younger brother. I went to Nikki's old house last night, and he was there. He's been researching and investigating what happened to Nikki all these years."

"And he says Whitney told him she was raped? And you believe him?"

"I do. Did you have any idea something like that happened? Because I don't remember anything like that."

"I don't remember anything like that, either. Of course, you know, with Nikki . . ."

I nod. I know what she means. Nikki's death was the darkest of storm clouds, obliterating all light. I have a hard time remembering anything else from that night. So much is a blur.

"I feel terrible for her," Shelby says. "I wish she had told us when it happened. Why do you think she didn't?"

I shrug. "Who knows? Shame? Fear?" What I don't say is what Cobo had brought up earlier, that Whitney did not say anything because it was one of our friends who hurt her.

"You know, it sort of makes sense in retrospect." Shelby lets out a long sigh. "How Whitney just disappeared? When Nikki died that night, we all kind of freaked out in our own ways. It was so horrible." Her voice catches, but I keep my mouth shut. She so rarely talks about Nikki, I am eager to hear what else she has to say. "I remember this kind of panicky feeling that whole summer," Shelby says. "Like sometimes I would forget she had died, and then I'd realize it and feel like the world was closing in on me. I couldn't be alone. I had to be with Todd or someone all the time. When I was alone, the bad thoughts came. But you were the opposite. You were never around that summer, remember? You were always running,"

I nod. Running became an escape for me. I ran in the mornings, and I ran in the evenings. I could not sit still with my grief.

"I mean, when did Whit move here, eighth grade? We were all friends for so long, and then she just leaves and doesn't come back to D.C.? At the time, I thought she was reacting to Nikki's drowning. But then later, I realized there was something else going on."

I frown, her words taking me by surprise. "Like what? You never told me that."

"Yeah, I did. In college. Remember?" She tucks her chin under and looks me directly in the eye. "I saw Whitney over spring break my freshman year, and she was totally drugged up. And I asked you, do you think they were doing drugs at the beach, she and Nikki, the night Nikki died, and is that maybe why Whit took off? Maybe she felt guilty or something, or thought people would blame her for what happened to Nikki."

Wisps of this conversation come back to me. "Now that you're describing it, I vaguely remember this theory of yours. I think I put it aside because it was so far-fetched."

"You were all: 'No way. Nikki never did any drugs. Not even pot.' You were kind of offended."

I nod, remembering now. "Well, that's because Nikki never did drugs. Did you tell the police that Nikki did drugs?"

She scowls. "No. I barely even talked to them."

"Yeah, about that. Cobo told me that no one from Washington Prep cooperated with the police that night. Is that true?"

Shelby hangs her head. "It's true. Daddy got a lawyer for me and told me not to talk."

"But why, Shel? Why not help the police?"

"I don't know. I was eighteen. Barely. I just did what I was told to do. I guess Daddy was afraid of a scandal."

Her answer sickens me. *Daddy was afraid of a scandal.* My own father insisted I do everything to help the police. Not that I didn't want to. "I just can't believe your parents told you not to cooperate. And that you never told me."

"What do you want me to say?" she says, her voice rising. "I did what they told me to do. Would I do things differently now as a forty-six-year-old woman? Yeah, I would. But you can't go back and redo things, Liza. The past is in the past."

"You're right," I say, but I have my doubts. What did Shakespeare say? What's past is prologue. But I drop it. I have other questions I need answered. "Another thing Cobo told me was that Geoff vouched for the guys. Whatever that means."

"Wow, this Cobo guy sure is a chatty Cathy."

I ignore her sarcasm. "Did you know Geoff Estes was at Beach Week? Don't you think that's kind of weird? He was the track coach and a PE teacher back then. What's he doing hanging out with a bunch of teenagers?"

My phone pings, and I take it out. "It's Daniel." I frown when I see the message. *Call me.*

"What's wrong?"

I hold up my finger to quiet her while I call him back. I put the phone on speaker and lay it on the island counter, my heart beating wildly.

He answers after the first ring. "Hey. When are you dropping off Zoe?"

"What do you mean? Didn't she come home yet?"

"She's not with you? You guys aren't in Georgetown?" Daniel, usually so calm, sounds agitated.

Panic grips my chest. I grab the phone, stand up, and start pacing. "What are you talking about, Daniel? Why do you think we're in Georgetown?"

"Well, the app thing says she's somewhere in Georgetown. Where are you?" The concern in his voice is unmistakable.

"I'm with Shelby. At her house. Zoe told me she got a ride home to your place from the funeral." I circle the kitchen island as I talk, then pivot and walk back to Shelby, who is staring at me intently. "I had no idea she wasn't going right to your place."

"Who did she get a ride with?"

My chest tightens. He's asking reasonable questions, but I have no answers, and it's freaking me out. I just assumed she got an Uber or a ride with a friend when she left the funeral. Why didn't I check again? Why didn't I make sure she got to Adams Morgan?

"I don't know, Daniel. Did you call her?"

"Straight to voice mail. She hasn't moved from this spot in the last twenty minutes. Who lives in Georgetown? Let me see if I can get an exact address. Hold on." After a few seconds, he says, "Looks like O Street."

Fear grips me. I stumble back, trying to push down the waves of panic breaking over me.

I slip my shoes on and head toward the door. "I'm on my way," I tell Daniel. "I know exactly where she is."

Chris de Groot lives on O Street.

CHAPTER 41

ZOE

Silence.

I've lost track of time. My throat is dry, and I have to pee.

Yet I still don't move. The room is hot now, thanks to the broken window. I'm exhausted, ready to surrender.

I'm not brave like Emery. I can't do this. I don't want to do this. I want to be home, at my house, the one I grew up in. I want to curl up in my bed.

Footsteps on the stairs send a jolt of adrenaline through me. I hold my breath and stay very still. I want to be invisible. Then the footsteps pause. The doorbell is ringing. I choke out a little sob of relief. Someone is here.

The footsteps retreat. I stand up and crack open the door. Shelby's high voice rings through the house. "Zoe! You up there?"

I throw the door open and run down the stairs. At the bottom, I land in my mom's arms. I push myself into her as far as I can as if I can meld with her. "Mommy." Snot mixes with tears, but I don't care. Walnut presses his body hard against my shins as if he is trying to get in on the hug. I drop to the floor at my mom's feet and bury my face in his soft scruff.

"It's okay, baby," my mom says as she strokes my hair.

"What the hell is going on here, Chris?" Shelby asks.

I pull back from Walnut and see Shelby across the room. In a white dress, with her hair blown out, she looks out of place.

She's bent down beside Mr. Estes, who's lying on the floor, not moving. I see blood trickling from his forehead onto the floor and gag a little.

"We need to call an ambulance," Shelby says, standing up and dusting herself off. "Now."

"No." Chris shakes his head. "I can't let you do that. Not yet."

"You don't have a choice, buddy." Shelby straightens up, but she's still tiny compared to him. I notice she has no cell phone or bag on her. Not even shoes. "Liza, where's your phone?"

"Let's all just calm down, okay?" my mom says.

"Calm down? Liza, Geoff is hurt. Zoe was locked upstairs." Her words run together. I can tell she's been drinking, but her anger makes me feel safer. Shelby is a force of nature. "We need to call the police. Now give me your damn phone."

I glance at the couch where my backpack is, but Chris stands in my way. I turn to look at my mom, whose wide eyes flit from Chris back to Shelby. "Hold on, Shel," she says. "Let's just take a moment. Talk it through?"

I don't know why she's acting so weird. But then I follow her gaze to Chris's arm hanging by his side. He's holding a gun. I gasp, and my mom squeezes my hand hard.

"Can't let you do that, Shelby," Chris says. "You're not in charge anymore."

"Shut up, Chris."

He raises his right hand, and she laughs. "What're you gonna do?" Shelby puts her hands on her hips and lifts her head high. "You gonna shoot us all?"

My mom lets out a nervous laugh. "Nobody's shooting anybody."

"Let's go," Chris says and wraps one beefy hand around Shelby's arm.

She tries to wiggle free. "Get your damn hands off me."

But he easily half drags her across the room to a closet door. He opens it up and pushes her inside.

"You, too." He points the gun at me.

"Don't point that at her, Chris," my mom says.

"I'm not going to hurt her. I don't want to hurt anyone. But I need you to come with me, Liza. And I can't have anyone calling the police." He steps forward and grabs my hand. "C'mon, Zoe."

"Mom?" I call out, but he pushes me into the dark closet. Shelby grabs my hand.

"It's going to be okay, honey," my mom says. "I promise."

Shelby pulls me close to her in the small, dark space that reeks of mothballs. "I'm here," she whispers. "We'll be okay."

"Mom!" I get one last glimpse of her face, twisted with fear, before Chris steps forward, blocking my view. He shuts the closet door, and all goes black.

Then we hear the click of a lock.

CHAPTER 42

LIZA

The car hurtles forward on the Beltway into the coming darkness of night. Beside me, Chris grips the steering wheel, sweat pouring down his face, soaking his shirt. The gun he was waving around back at his house now sits wedged between his legs, near his crotch.

I eye it, but there's no way I can grab it without him stopping me. Instead, I stay frozen, trying to play nice. "Please, Chris, can we call someone to let Zoe and Shelby out?"

"Shut up, just be quiet. I need to focus."

He leans forward, squinting at the numerous signs, and then veers the car abruptly to the right onto the exit for Route 50. Behind us, cars honk.

"Go to hell!" Chris yells.

The car is a total mess. To make room for my feet, I had to kick aside some papers and empty cups. A quick look at the back seat tells me it's in much worse shape. You can't even see the leather, which is piled with papers and books and some crumpled clothes at one end.

"Are we going to Shelby's?" I ask gently. I saw a true crime show where a woman had managed to talk her kidnapper into letting her go by being kind and listening. It's worth a try. "Please, Chris, talk to me."

"Do you think about that night, Liza?"

I pause. "I do."

"I think about it all the time. I didn't use to. Right after it happened, I pushed away all memories and thoughts. I didn't want to feel the responsibility for Nikki's death or for what happened to Whitney. It wasn't hard at first. I started drinking and writing, my two loves. And they have kept me very busy over the years. They did a good job of keeping the darkness away. And as long as I avoided anyone at Washington Prep, I could pretend it all never happened."

"I always wondered why we never saw you."

He smirks. "And I always wondered how you could continue to spend time with each other. How the collective guilt didn't destroy you all."

Signs for the Bay Bridge appear. We must be going out to Dewey. "Explain that to me. I'm serious. What collective guilt?"

"Let's talk about Whitney," Chris says. "Whitney Bascombe did not have it easy. To outsiders, it may have seemed she had everything—money, parents, a nice home."

It sounds like he is narrating a movie trailer. I wonder if he has practiced this little speech.

"I certainly did not understand it back then. I was a self-absorbed prick. I couldn't see two inches beyond my own face. We thought . . . well, what did we think? That she was a party girl. Fun. Fast. Up for anything. A slut. You're not supposed to say that word anymore. But back then, that's how we saw the world—good girls and fast girls. Not bad girls. We all liked Whitney. It wasn't that we didn't like her." He takes a swig from the metal water bottle nestled in the cupholder between us. As he does so, the car swerves into the oncoming lane. Someone blares their horn, and my stomach plummets until our car rights itself.

"What's in the bottle, Chris?"

"Pappy Van Winkle."

"I can drive, you know, wherever we are going. If you want to pull over. I don't mind."

He snorts. "I think I've got this, Liza. I've been drinking and driving for years; it's not a problem for me."

That does not reassure me.

"Where was I? Whitney the slut. Whitney the party girl. We stayed in touch, you know, off and on. Some years more off than on, but she knew she could always call me. I was there in the hospital when Henry was born."

Stunned, I wait for him to continue.

"I offered to let her put my name on the birth certificate, so he would have a father, but she refused. But I insisted on a paternity test. She didn't see the point, but I told her, *Real money could be involved.* It was the type of thing my father would have said, and I remember feeling very grown-up and wise when I said it. She could not have cared less, especially once little Henry died later that week. But I kept that damn test. All these years."

"I'm sorry, I just can't wrap my mind around this. I didn't even know Whitney was pregnant. And you were hanging out with her? I had no idea you two were so close."

"We weren't. That's the thing." He laughs viciously. "Her real friends had abandoned her."

"That's not fair—"

"Shut up, Liza. Just shut up." He takes his eyes off the road and glares at me with such hatred, it feels like I have ice in my veins. "No one wants to hear you talk. This is my story, get it?"

I nod.

He exhales. "Where was I? Oh right, I bumped into her quite by accident up in the Philadelphia area that fall. She had moved out of D.C. to stay with some relatives. Couldn't be seen pregnant at eighteen in Washington. They frown on that kind of thing at the Capital Crescent Country Club. I went to Penn, if you recall. It was not a good first year for me. I was miserable, lost, guilt-stricken, at sea. When I saw Whitney, she was clearly pregnant and did not want to discuss it. I didn't push her. Neither of us had friends. We were two losers. We glommed onto each other.

And then I went home for the summer, and when I came back sophomore year, I didn't get in touch right away. Eventually, I called her relatives. They said she moved out and left no forwarding number. She just disappeared."

His story resonates in some corners of my mind but shocks me, too. A sodden sense of guilt engulfs me as we pass through the tollbooth onto the Chesapeake Bay Bridge. I didn't track Whitney down when she clearly needed a friend. The lanes on the bridge are narrow, the cars right next to ours, and the drop to the water below is about a million miles. When I was a kid, a tractor trailer rear-ended a woman's car while she was driving on the bridge, sending her plunging into the bay. She managed to kick through a shattered window and swim to safety. For years after, I kept my eyes shut tightly until we had crossed. I grip the armrest as Chris veers a little too close to the car in the next lane.

"You're scaring me."

"I cross this bridge several times a month," he says, irritated. "I know what I'm doing."

"Where are we going, Chris?" I ask. "What is it you want to show me? Just tell me."

"Answers. The truth. That's what you claim to want, right? Well, you are about to get them. But it's a high price, I warn you."

I don't know what he means, exactly, but by the hostility in his voice, I know it's not good.

"When Emery showed up, asking questions last fall, I tried to stonewall her. But she was so insistent. She knew about the paternity test. Whitney must have told her. She was determined. Still, I thought she would go away if I ignored her. But then—" His voice catches, and I wonder if he is going to cry. He grimaces, nostrils flaring as if he is a man possessed. We've reached the highest point of the bridge, and the Chesapeake Bay lies spread out on either side, dotted with white sails and sprinkled with shards of the last of the evening sun. But I don't look for longer than a second. "I don't want to talk about it." He slams his fist on the wheel as if he is arguing with some invisible person. "No more. Now is the time for action, not talking. Enough talking."

We barrel forward in silence across the Eastern Shore. Past strip malls, fast-food joints, a gun store, a Dollar General, and through the fields of knee-high corn that will be towering by the end of the summer. We drive so fast, I am sure we will be pulled over or take a sharp turn and end up in a ditch. It isn't until we see a sign for Dewey that I exhale fully and dare speak again.

"Where are we going? To the lighthouse where Emery died? Shelby's parents' house? Your place on Fenwick Island?" The not-knowing gnaws at me like a dog's teeth scraping a bone. He ignores me, his eyes fixed straight ahead. Terror courses through me. He's unstable, guilt-ridden, and drunk. There's no telling what he has planned.

When he turns toward the Stockley Creek Country Club, I realize we are going to Shelby's.

"What's at Shelby's, Chris?"

He ignores me as we drive through the gates. My heart starts beating wildly. My mind is blank. Chris starts shaking. He's more agitated than since we started driving. He brings the car to an abrupt stop on the driveway. Landscaping lights illuminate the grounds. A few burn inside. I pray someone is here.

He hurries out of the car, comes around to my side, and opens the door. "Get out." He grips the gun at his side, arm shaking.

I don't move.

"Now, Liza." He waves the gun, wild-eyed, hair matted to his wet forehead. He looks like a madman. When I don't move, he yanks me out of the car, his meaty hand tight around my forearm. "Hurry. They're going to be coming soon."

"You're hurting me," I say as he drags me across the backyard, past the patio and down to the water. Who is coming soon? Todd? Brody? The police? My throat tightens, making it hard to breathe. I feel like someone is squeezing my throat into a pin-hole. But at the same time, I allow myself to be pulled along, curiosity compelling me.

At the edge of the water, next to the dock, Chris pauses. "It's our fault. And we need to pay. All of us."

"What do you mean?" The words barely squeak out my throat. Every fiber in my body is sizzling, on high alert. *Danger, danger.* Whatever he says, I won't go into that water with him. I'm terrified I might not come out. I try to dig my heels into the dirt as he drags me down into the cool water, but I'm no match for him. Farther and farther we go, the water rising to my shins, then my knees. With every step, my feet sink into the muddy bottom. "Stop!" I cry and try to pry his beefy fingers off my arm.

"I know she's here. I know she is. They can't have moved her."

"Who are you talking about?" But a yawning void has opened in the center of my body. Deep inside, I know who he means. *Nikki.*

He looks around wildly, slack-jawed. "Killed Nikki because she *knew*. Saw what happened to Whitney. Had to die."

My mind struggles to piece together these fragmented sentences as he pulls me closer to the dock. He slaps the gun on top of it without loosening his grip on me. "Come on, are you going to help me or what?"

"I don't know what you want me to do." I eye the gun. Chris stands between me and the dock.

He takes out his phone, turns on the flashlight, and passes it to my free hand. The small beam of light dances on the black water beneath the dock. "Lower," he says.

I try to hold the light steady as Chris squats under the dock, pulling me closer.

"Down here." I aim the light over his shoulder. I am terrified but riveted. The secret beneath the dock draws me toward it. Chris holds his nose and then disappears under the water. In a moment, he emerges sputtering.

"Damn, damn," Chris says. "These damn cinder blocks." He takes an exaggerated gulp of air and disappears under the water again, this time letting go of my arm. I could turn and run. I could grab the gun and go. But I don't. I'm desperate to know what's under there. I have to know.

Chris emerges again, hair plastered against his face, coughing.

"Hold it right there." The voice comes from the lawn above. A bright light washes over the dock. I turn, but all I can see is a blinding light. I cover my eyes.

"That you, Liza? You okay?"

I nod.

"It's Todd. Get out of the water."

I start to slosh through the water when Chris pulls me back by my shirt.

"Wait," he says. "Look."

"Let her go!" Todd shouts.

I turn toward Chris and aim the phone's flashlight at his outstretched hand.

"I said let her go!" Todd shouts again. A loud crack explodes in my ears. A gunshot. Chris lets go of me as a guttural noise escapes him. He looks stunned as he touches a red stain spreading across the chest of his wet shirt.

He reaches his other hand out toward me and unfurls his fingers.

The light catches on the pale sticks in his grasp.

It takes about half a second to realize I'm looking at the bones of a human hand.

CHAPTER 43

LIZA

"Is it Nikki Montes?" I ask.

"Won't know until we test the remains."

I wince at Detective Gaffney's choice of words. When I think of my friend, she is fully alive, black hair whipping around her face as we drive out to Beach Week in my dad's car, belting the lyrics to the Cranberries' "Dreams" out of tune. *Remains* is such a clinical word. It belongs in a laboratory. But of course, after twenty-eight years in brackish water, there would not be much of an identifiable body.

"We need to be able to get in contact with you. You still have that female lawyer?"

I cringe. He means Prentiss. "Yup."

"Are you staying here or heading back to D.C. tonight?"

"I'm spending the night here." I tilt my chin at Shelby's house behind me. I'm too tired to return to Washington tonight. The adrenaline that carried me this afternoon has abandoned my body, leaving in its wake a deep fatigue. I would curl up on the grass under the moonlight and sleep for hours if I weren't so cold.

Zoe, I know, is safe at her dad's. Daniel went to Chris's house, where he found her and Shelby in the closet. Then he called 9–1–1. Geoff Estes was taken to the hospital, unconscious but alive. After questioning from the police, Daniel took Zoe back to his apartment, and Shelby drove Walnut out here.

They are inside now. Todd is down at the station making a statement. The detective who drove him said he would be back that night.

Once Gaffney is done with me, he shuts his notebook and tucks it into the back of his pants. I wonder how much thought he will give this whole episode once he leaves here. Will he be able to push it out of his mind. Is it all in a day's work?

There will be no such compartmentalizing for me. No shutting this night away in a notebook and shoving it into a dark pocket. Cobo was right all along.

Nikki was murdered. And it was one of us. It was Chris de Groot all along.

A sob racks my body, and I feel like I might pass out. I need to get inside, too. But the backyard is still crawling with officers and technicians. Somehow I feel obligated to stay outside until they leave, like a host at a party praying her guests will finally go home.

Stupid. I don't need to be here. Or do I? My mind is cloudy. This feels like a dream, but it's unfolding in front of me. How many summer afternoons have I walked across that dock to watch the sunset with a drink in my hand? Or taken my morning coffee out there? The thought that Nikki lay under that dock while I stood on top nauseates me. As bile rises in the back of my throat, I scurry past a woman unwinding a roll of police tape and into the house.

After a long, hot shower, I change into a Bethany Books T-shirt and a pair of worn out joggers I find in a dresser drawer. My own clothes reek of brackish water and will need to be washed. But first I sit on the bed and stare at my phone. I want desperately to talk to Zoe face-to-face, to see how she is holding up, but it is late. Instead, I call Daniel. When he answers, I pepper him with questions.

"How is Zoe processing all this? Does she seem okay?"

"She seems tired," Daniel says. "Kind of stunned. I heated up some leftover sukiyaki." It's Zoe's favorite comfort food, a Japanese beef stew served over rice. "Now she's in bed—oh, wait, here she is." He pulls the phone away, and I hear murmuring.

"Mommy? Is that you?"

"Zoe, hi. I figured you'd be asleep by now."

"I'm going to bed soon. Are you okay? I was so scared for you."

"I'm fine. Don't worry about me. You must have been terrified," I say. "In that closet?"

"Shelby was there. And Walnut was on the outside. He kept scratching at the door and whimpering. I felt so bad for him."

"He's a sweetie." Walnut's ears perk up.

"I miss him," Zoe says. "Is it okay if I sleep at the house tomorrow, when you get back? Just for a couple of nights."

"Of course," I say a bit too eagerly. "Stay as long as you like."

"It's just that I miss Walnut."

I pet Walnut in silence. For a moment, neither of us speaks.

"I knew you'd come, Mommy. When I was at Chris's."

I open my mouth to respond, but nothing comes out. The utterance of a single word will dislodge a dam holding back a torrent of tears.

"Well, good night," she says. "Give Walnut a hug for me."

"Will do. I love you," I say, sniffling a little.

"Love you, too."

Tucking my dirty clothes into a ball under my arm, I head down to the laundry room. I move on autopilot, adding detergent, starting the washing machine. When I walk back into the kitchen, Todd and Archer are standing by the counter, talking in low voices.

"Archer, hey," I say, letting him give me a hug. "When did you get here?"

"I came as soon as I could. How is Zoe doing? Is she all right?"

"As well as can be expected. She's exhausted. I think it will all hit her in the upcoming days." A shiver runs through me. "To think that monster had my baby girl trapped in his house. And then when he forced Shelby and Zoe into the closet . . . Leaving them was one of the hardest things I've ever done. But at least it was me he took and not Zoe."

Archer nods. "What a nightmare."

I turn to Todd. He looks more haggard than I have ever seen him. "They let you go, huh?"

He smiles weakly. "For now."

"I'm so grateful you were there," I say, reaching around his neck to hug him. His back is damp from sweat. We hug for a few seconds. I can't find the right words to express my appreciation for what he did. All I can come up with is "Thank you."

Shelby appears from the pantry, holding a bottle. Her face is red, eyes puffy, and her blond hair in a messy bun. "Bourbon. It's all I could find."

"That'll work." Archer takes four glasses down from the cabinet and fills them generously. We stand at the counter under the harsh light, sipping our bourbon. As if reading my mind, Archer hits the dimmer, lowering the lights.

"How did it go at the station?" Archer asks Todd.

Todd gives us a rundown of what happened. He was asked to describe what he saw when he came to the house, and when he retells the part about finding me and Chris in the water, next to the dock, he gives me a sidelong glance before continuing.

"It's okay," I say.

"I freaked out. I thought he was trying to hurt you. I mean, Shel called, told me Chris had kidnapped you. That he had a gun. When I get to the house, there's Chris dragging you under the dock. I didn't plan on shooting him." He bites his lower lip and looks down at the floor. "He went for the gun."

"What did the police say?" Archer asks.

"They just asked me a bunch of questions and took my statement." He lifts the glass to his mouth, and I can see his hands are shaking. Shelby sidles up next to him and wraps her arms around his torso. He wraps one arm around her. "They let me go home. I've called a lawyer, but hopefully there won't be any charges."

"Charges!" Shelby spits. "You saved Liza's life. Chris is a murderer. And poor Nikki under my dock all these years." Tears fill her eyes. "I can't wrap my mind around it. It's so awful."

"Same here." I take a swig of the bourbon and make a face. It burns my throat. It feels more like a punishment than a treat, but I keep drinking. I want to get to where Shelby is. Halfway to passed out. "All those summers we hung out here, not knowing."

"Ugh." Shelby shudders. "Poor Nikki. Her poor family."

"Did you have any idea about Chris?" I look at Archer when I say this. He shakes his head, but he doesn't meet my eye.

"Nothing? No clue?" I turn to Todd. "What about you?"

Todd gives a little shake of his head.

"I don't even understand how this happened. Do you guys? Nikki went swimming with us, didn't she? How did she end up back at the house? Why was Chris with her?"

It's lightning fast, but Archer and Todd exchange a glance. So brief that if I hadn't been staring at Archer, I'd have missed it. Shelby is examining her nails, oblivious. But I saw it. And I know Archer. He is the king of eye contact. He's stared down accused murderers and powerful politicians. But he won't face me.

"Archer," I say, "you need to tell me everything you remember about that night. Even if it's uncomfortable. Even if it makes you look bad. I don't care. I have to know what happened to Nikki."

He doesn't answer.

"Did you know that Emery was Whitney's daughter?"

"Emery? You mean the girl who drowned a few days ago?" He straightens up. "What? No. How did you figure that out?"

I tell him and Todd about what I learned at the funeral, all of it, starting with seeing the necklace around Emery's neck. "Help me understand what happened that night," I continue. "Chris assaulted Whitney? And Nikki saw it and was going to report it, so he killed her? Is that what happened?"

"We don't know, Liza." Todd's voice is surprisingly harsh.

"Do we have to do this tonight?" Shelby asks. "Can't we just have a moment where we're happy that everyone is safe and sound?"

The combination of the day's events and the bourbon is muddling my mind. I pull out a stool and sit. I'm so confused. I don't understand how they can't want answers, too. Is it only because Zoe is my daughter that I care?

Archer pulls out the stool next to me and sits down.

"I don't know what happened with Chris and Nikki. That's the truth." He shoots Todd a look.

I examine his face. I've known Archer forever. Seen him grow from a gangly, cocky teenager to a confident, successful media star. But I also know the ways in which people lie. The half-truths they tell themselves to make them feel better about the bullshit. When I was a reporter, I really honed my bullshit detector. I witnessed the "leaky faucet" approach plenty of times while interviewing folks. People who didn't want to come right out and tell you the whole truth, because it made them look bad, so they let out one little drop as a test. To see how you'd react. Then another little drop.

And that's when I realize that I know what happened. As sickening as it is, it fits.

"But you did know what happened with Whitney and Chris, right? You knew Chris attacked Whitney." The question of others being involved and of the paternity test skulks at the murky edges of my mind, inviting closer examination. But I push those thoughts back into the darkness. I need Archer and Todd to first fill in the blanks of that night.

Archer buries his head in his hands.

"Liza, please," Shelby begs, sniffling. "Please. I can't handle it."

"I just want to know the truth," I say. "I think I deserve that from you guys. Did you know that Chris assaulted Whitney at Beach Week?"

The room is silent, and I wonder if I have pushed too far. After more than thirty years, it seems that I might finally have discovered the limits of friendship. I can't believe this is happening. Todd and Archer know something, but that's not the part that's eating through my stomach like acid. It's that they're hiding it from me.

Todd clears his throat and straightens up. "Well, the truth is we kind of knew, but we didn't know." His voice has returned to normal, low and measured, without any of the hostility from a few minutes ago. I sit perfectly still, eager to catch every word. "And we didn't bother to find out exactly what happened, because honestly, we didn't really care what happened with Whitney and Chris." He looks up at each of us as if daring us to challenge him on this assertion. I make my face a neutral mask. There will be a time for judgment, but now I want the truth. "That's the truth. I'm sorry to say it, but we didn't really care."

"Is that your take, too?" I ask Archer. I look at his face to see how Todd's words have hit him, but he's a pro. I can't read anything in his perfectly symmetrical features. "That you kind of knew, but you didn't really care?"

His eyes flit to me, and he holds my gaze a few seconds. Then he nods. "When Nikki drowned—"

"Died," I interrupt. "She was killed. Nikki didn't drown."

"All right," he says. "When she was killed, that eclipsed everything." He takes a deep breath. "Do you hate me?"

"Of course not." I don't have to think about my answer. "I don't hate you. I'm just, I don't know . . ." What am I feeling? Disappointed. Disgusted. Sad.

Maybe on some level, I saw this coming, starting at the graveyard, seeing those dates on little Henry's headstone. Then when Cobo said Whitney had been raped at Beach Week. Deep inside, I suspected it was someone from Washington Prep. But realizing that my friends knew all these years and never said anything has unmoored me.

Shelby tops off all our glasses with the bourbon, and everyone but me lifts their glass. I can't. For the first time in as long as I can remember, I don't want to be a part of this group.

"It doesn't make sense," Shelby says in a dreamy voice. Her eyes are unfocused. She is ten minutes from blacking out, I'm sure. "Nikki was in the water with us." I don't blame her for changing the subject. It's easier for her to talk about Nikki than the fact that her husband knew about a rape and did nothing. But no one responds to her comment.

"You doing okay with all this, Liza?" Archer asks.

I extend a smile, a temporary measure, putting our friendship on a ventilator. I doubt it can breathe on its own, and I'm not prepared to pull the plug tonight. "I'm tired. I'm going to bed."

They all wish me good night, and I wonder if they can see in my face the turmoil I'm experiencing.

As I climb the stairs, I think about Archer's question. Do I hate him?

I don't. I feel numb toward all of them. When the shock of today wears off, I'm afraid of what will be left. At the top of the stairs, I pause outside my bedroom. It's the one I always stay in when I come here, the same room I've been using for thirty years. And I know this is the last time I will go to sleep in this house.

From below, I hear murmurs. Are they talking about me? Whispers, secrets, in-jokes—they are the stuff of long-term friendships and tight bonds. Like tiny gossamer threads, each one is breakable, but collectively they are powerful enough to bind people together in a cocoon.

In the past, I might have strained to hear what they were saying. But now I don't care. I open the door. I'm outside of the cocoon now.

There is no getting back in.

CHAPTER 44

1994

Nikki had to get Whitney someplace safe. She was clearly incapable of doing it on her own. The only resource Nikki had was her moral indignation, and she felt it ignite like a flame, reaching every filament in her body and making her taller and stronger than she was.

She pulled a whimpering Whitney to her feet and grabbed Whitney's panties, which were lying in the sand. It disgusted Nikki to touch them, but she managed to shove them in the pocket of Whitney's skirt. This was not the time to be squeamish.

"C'mon," she encouraged Whitney, who was a bit shorter than she was, but stockier. As Whitney leaned on her with her full body weight, Nikki felt she might collapse. It was a balancing act, pushing Whitney forward enough so they could keep moving, but not so far away that Whitney simply toppled over into the sand.

Whitney moaned and swayed, and Nikki feared for a moment that she would not be able to pull this off. She didn't know exactly what had happened to Whitney, but her mind was already filling in the blanks with the worst possible scenario.

Drunk Whitney.

In the sand.

Skirt pulled up.

Underwear a few feet away.

It was a pitiful sight, and she wanted Whitney to rally, to show some strength, but Whitney just kept mewing like a little kitten.

"Let's go, Whit." She made her voice stern, like her mother's when she and Cobo were taking too long in a store. "One foot in front of the other." She marched her from the dunes toward the rickety wooden walkway that led to the street. She'd seen her uncle Dom get drunk, seen her dad help him *walk it off*. Maybe that would work with Whitney. Get the blood moving, and she would sober up.

She was so focused on her and Whitney's feet that she didn't see them standing there until she was practically upon them. The boys were backlit, their features hidden like silhouetted trees in a moonlit forest. As Nikki and Whitney approached them, they did not move a muscle or make a sound.

That's odd, Nikki thought. And then she realized that the reason these boys were not acting surprised at the sight of Whitney was that they knew.

They knew what had happened to her, and they could see Nikki was helping her. And now they were blocking the path. On either side of the wooden planks stood flimsy fencing that protected the dunes. There was no way she could go around them, so she stopped. She was panting, yet she stared them down. She did not flinch or look away, and in a steady voice from the center of her being, she said, "Move."

As a child, she had seen her mother do this at a Long Island grocery store one icy winter evening. A man was crossing the deserted parking lot as they loaded their groceries into the car. Nikki couldn't remember what he'd said, only the white-hot fear that gripped her. Awilda had stepped in front of her to shield her. Her tiny mother drew herself up, commanded the stranger to stay back, and ordered Nikki into the car. It worked. As they drove home in trembling silence, Nikki knew they had averted something terrible. If she had any doubts, they were erased when they pulled into the driveway and her mother turned to the back seat to say, "Do not tell your daddy about this."

"Where you guys going?" one of the boys asked. She recognized the voice. Todd Smythe. He tried to sound casual, but Nikki saw right through him.

"Get out of our way, Todd."

"Hey, Nikki. Relax." It was Archer who said that. "Where are you taking her?"

"I'm taking her back to Shelby's house," Nikki said. "Although she probably needs to go to a hospital."

"Whoa, whoa, whoa." Archer laughed, waving his hands in front of him like they were kidding around in study hall or something. As if his megawatt smile could transform reality. "She doesn't need a hospital. She's just drunk. She'll be fine tomorrow."

"Get out of my way, or I'll scream." Her heart galloped as she spoke. Would they call her bluff? She looked over her shoulder at the ocean, where the sound of laughter could barely be heard above the crash of the surf. Everyone was swimming. No one was here to help.

"Why you being so dramatic?" Todd asked.

"Everybody just calm down," Chris said. "Whit had too much to drink. We found her throwing up."

"Oh, please," Nikki spat. "You don't expect me to believe that, do you?"

"Believe what you want. It's true. Right, guys?" Chris turned to his friends, who grunted in assent.

"I know what you guys did. I'm not dumb."

"Nikki." Todd used her name as a warning. He didn't need to say anything else.

"I'm not afraid of you," she said. "If my father were here, he'd beat the shit out of you and then arrest you. He locks up guys like you every day."

Archer stepped back, and she saw her chance. No one said a

word or tried to stop her as she and Whitney stumbled by. It was slow going, getting to the street. She trudged forward, not daring to look back, her heart beating like a little creature trapped in a cage. Whitney smelled like beer and cigarettes, and her long curly hair kept falling in Nikki's face. She managed to get Whitney across Route 1 without attracting any attention. Or maybe the sight was just so common in Dewey during Beach Week that no one paid them any mind.

Nikki paused on the other side of the road to catch her breath. She had a ways more to go to get back to Shelby's. She muttered a curse. This was not how she had hoped this night would go. But what choice did she have?

She plunged into the darkness with Whitney. Somehow they made it through the park and onto the lane that led to the country club and Shelby's house. They were so close. She could picture it. This time, when she called, she'd ask for her dad, even if it meant waking him up. It's what he would want her to do. The thought of how proud he would be of her spurred her on.

Whitney, who was mumbling incoherently, stumbled and stopped short.

"Let's go," Nikki said, her voice devoid of kindness. Then she felt bad and told herself to reach deeper. Whitney needed her.

"C'mon, Whit," she said sweetly. "Just a little more." She yanked at her friend, trying to get a better grip on her. In twisting her body around, she caught a glimpse of something behind them in the brush, hidden in the shadows about thirty yards back. An animal, maybe? No, too big. A person. A shudder ran through her.

"Who's there?" Nikki yelled.

There was only silence. Nikki stared at the darkness, willing the creature to make itself seen. In front of her was the lighted sign for the Stockley Creek Country Club. It was only a matter of minutes.

She began walking again, dragging Whitney along.

There was no choice but to keep going.

CHAPTER 45

LIZA

The morning light wakes me. The room has sheer curtains, unlike my blackout shades back in D.C. A glance at my phone tells me it's not even six. I groan and roll over, but I can't fall back asleep. Everything comes rushing back to me, and even though I'm exhausted, I drag myself out of bed.

Everyone else in the house is still asleep. Walnut follows me down the stairs and into the laundry room, where I quickly change into the clothes I was wearing yesterday. In the kitchen, I leave a note. *Picking up muffins for breakfast.*

After walking a few minutes, I feel lighter, less encumbered by everything that has happened. The most important thing is that Zoe is safe. I hope she can put this all behind her. I think about what Prentiss told me at the funeral, that there was nothing to indicate Emery did not drown on her own accord. No broken bones in the neck, or anywhere else, no bruises, nothing to indicate a struggle. With Chris dead, I wonder if we will ever know the truth of what happened that night at the lighthouse.

Walnut and I walk toward the ocean, cutting through the park and continuing until we reach Route 1, the same path that I've taken countless times. It's the way we walked on that first and only night at Beach Week, to get from Shelby's house to the party. And it's probably the route that Nikki walked later that night, but in reverse. I am guessing that she was killed on Shelby's property, and not somewhere else and then moved. But the police will have to determine that for sure. How did it go down? Maybe Nikki went back to the house and saw Chris assaulting Whitney or something like that. Then she called home.

But then what?

How did she end up under Shelby's dock for twenty-eight years?

Was there a confrontation with Chris? Did he go berserk when she called her dad? Walnut and I walk all the way down to the beach access, where I pause to let him smell the base of a sign that reads *No Dogs Allowed*. In the distance, I can see a man running with a small dog close at his heels. Walnut would love to run, too, but I don't want to break any rules.

To my left sits the house Don Fraser rented that night so long ago. Weathered and run-down, with warped brown siding, it's clearly still a party house. A young guy in cargo shorts and a grungy, gray T-shirt steps onto the back deck. I watch as he stretches and then pulls an e-cigarette from his pocket. He could be anywhere from sixteen to twenty-five. I've become terrible at guessing ages.

I yank at Walnut's collar and pull him back to the road.

Chris is dead; he's joined Whitney and Nikki. With him died the last chance to find out exactly what happened that night. Those three were the only ones who could tell us what transpired. It's deeply unsatisfying to me. In a way, I wish Todd hadn't killed Chris.

But I will have to live with uncertainty. So will Cobo. We have some answers, but we may never know, for example, why Nikki headed back to the house at all.

This is the way my brain works. Never content with the obvious answer. Always probing. It's what made me a good cops reporter, but also what makes it miserable to live inside my head. It's why I pushed for the ugly truth I learned last night. That Archer and Todd knew all along.

Not just suspected but *knew* that Whitney had been raped.

I tie Walnut up outside Baked in Dewey, where I buy an assortment of cinnamon buns and muffins. As I'm walking back to Shelby's house, my phone rings. It takes a little maneuvering with the leash and pastry bag, but I answer it in time.

"I'm here in Dewey," Cobo says, sounding slightly out of breath. He tells me everything that has happened in the last twelve hours. The call from the Delaware State Police. The identification made through dental records that Cobo has had at the ready for more than a decade. "It's not the first time I've emailed them somewhere; it's just the first time I've gotten a match. What about you and Zoe? Are you guys okay? All I heard was that Chris de Groot is dead."

"We're fine now." I give him the short version of what happened after we parted yesterday. "I'll give you more details when I see you."

"I'm so sorry, Liza. That sounds really frightening."

"What about you? How are you holding up?"

"I'm tired, for one. Didn't sleep last night. Running on caffeine. I've thought about this day for so long, and now it's here." He exhales loudly. "It feels like a strange dream. There's a weird sense of relief, that at least it's over. I can give Nikki a proper burial. I can tell my mom. I can move on. But at the same time, I feel kind of empty."

"That sounds normal. As much as you can prepare for it, it's still a shock."

"I just can't believe my sister was *murdered*. They say her skull was fractured. All those years, I kept asking the police, *Where's the body?* And they just blew me off."

"I'm so sorry, Cobo."

"And now I'll never really know what happened. Because Chris de Groot is dead."

"Funny, I was just thinking the same thing before you called. I need to tell you something." I fill him in on last night's conversation and what I learned. A light-headedness hits me. I've crossed a line, spilling secrets to someone outside our foursome. They would view it as a betrayal, but I don't care. They betrayed me first.

"Where were you when you spoke to them?" His voice is stiff; he's clearly upset.

"Shelby's. We all stayed over last night." There is a long pause. My stomach does a little flip. Have I said something wrong? "Hello? You there?"

"I just don't see how you can still even talk to them, much less be in the same room."

"Because I wanted answers. And Todd is the one who saved me." As I pass through the entrance to the country club, an older woman power walks by, pumping her fists determinedly. We exchange nods. "Look, I know that we wouldn't be in this situation if they had come forward twenty-eight years ago. If they had told the police about Chris. I think it's horrible."

"Oh, Liza." He sounds so sad.

"What?"

"You still don't get it, do you?"

I stop short. I'm so close to Shelby's, but I want to wrap up this conversation before I go inside. "Get what? I hate when you do that. Just say what you want to say."

He laughs. "Do I do that a lot?"

"Yes!" His laughter makes me smile. "So, please, tell me what it means, Cobo. I'm too tired to play detective."

"Geoff vouched for all three of them. Not just Chris. All three."

"Right. We knew that already."

"If you were writing this story, would you be satisfied with this ending?" He pauses. "Ask Archer and Todd about the DNA tests, Liza. Tell them you're still going to run them against Henry Bascombe's DNA, and see what they say."

LIZA

"I made coffee. Want some?" Shelby, still in pajamas, is holding a coffeepot in midair when I come into the kitchen through the back sliding door.

"Sure." I put the bag of pastries on the counter and unhook Walnut's leash.

"Oooh, what's in the bag?" Archer appears in the doorway, rolling his head from side to side, clearly having just woken up.

"Muffins," I say. "Where's Todd?"

"Shower. Why? What's up?" Shelby hands me the mug, and I flash a tight smile. I want everyone here when I do this. Not Zoe, of course. I bring the coffee to my face and breathe in the steam. My father used to say there were two things in this world that smelled better than they tasted—coffee and pipe tobacco. My skin is tingly as I take a sip, and a dull ache has settled into my chest. It's preemptive grief. I'm about to change our friendship. But I need to know the truth.

After a few minutes, Todd comes in wearing shorts and a tee, his blond hair wet and slicked back, looking like a relaxed beach bum, not a man who took another person's life last night. I'd be a wreck, but he gives me a smile and heads straight to a seat where Shelby has poured him a coffee and placed a blueberry muffin on a plate.

Terrible things happen—girls get raped, kidnapped, they

drown—and Todd will continue to sail through life, opening restaurants, playing golf at his country club, being served breakfast by his loyal wife. I realize that I had never wanted to believe that he and Archer were involved. That they could be so close to someone else's pain without it taking a visual toll on them. But I was wrong.

It's time for me to break the silence. "I need you guys to tell me the truth. The whole truth."

Everyone stops what they're doing and looks at me.

"Okay," Archer says slowly. "About what?"

"Liza, what are you doing?" Shelby asks. "Do we have to do this first thing in the morning? We're trying to eat breakfast."

"Shelby, just let the guys talk, okay?" My tone is firm. "Don't answer for them. Don't make excuses for them."

"What is that supposed to mean?"

I ignore her and turn to Archer. "Geoff Estes. Explain to me how he fits into all this. Why did he vouch for you back in 1994? What does that even mean?"

Archer and Todd turn and hold each other's gaze. I grip my coffee mug. I'm on the verge of learning something, yet I'm not sure I'm ready to hear it.

"Answer me. Please just answer me." They're silent, and neither will look at me. "Archer? You have to tell me."

"I don't know if I can," he mumbles into his coffee.

"Well, I don't know if we can be friends if you don't."

Shelby gasps. "Liza, you don't mean that."

"I'm going to run the DNA," I say. "I have both of yours. You know that, right? Emery and Zoe collected it. And I have the baby's. They kept it at the hospital." I wait to see if anyone will challenge this lie, but no one moves a muscle. "His name was Henry. What are the odds Chris is Henry's father? One in three, right?"

A choking sound, a wheeze of incredulity, escapes from Shelby. "What are you saying?"

Before I can answer, Archer clears his throat and sits up. "That sounds about right. We don't know who the father is." Archer looks at me and then at Shelby. "Because we all had sex with Whitney."

Shelby seems to collapse a little, her shoulders dropping as if she's been sucker punched.

"You mean you all raped her," I say, trying to keep the emotion out of my voice.

"No, no, no. It wasn't rape," Todd says. "We were drunk—all of us."

I look over at him, trying to read his face, but there's nothing there. He looks like a human, with a square jaw and bright blue eyes, but I can't sense any humanity.

"Are you saying it was consensual?" I ask. "The three of you and her?"

"We were kids. What did we know about consent?" Todd slaps his hand on the counter. "We were drunk, and Whitney was into it. That's the truth, Liza. *She wanted to.*"

I recoil at his outburst, taking a step back. At the same time, adrenaline pumps through my body. I feel like I'm talking to strangers. "Todd, you have an eighteen-year-old daughter. Do you think Kinsey would be *into it*? Fucking three guys at once?"

"Liza!" Shelby shouts, and I turn to her. She is glaring at me, lips pursed. I almost laugh at the absurdity. The suggestion that her daughter might hypothetically have sex with three guys is worse than knowing this about her husband.

When I look at Archer, he is examining his hands. "Do you feel that way, too?" I ask him.

"It was a mistake," he says quietly. "It shouldn't have happened."

"And so what did happen?"

"Does it matter?" Todd asks, barely concealing his anger. "Haven't we all been through enough?"

"It matters to me," I say.

"We were drunk. We had sex. It was twenty-eight years ago," Todd says curtly. He seems almost aggrieved that I dare ask him about this. "I don't remember the details. We were kids."

"And after? How does Nikki get involved?"

"Nikki walked Whitney back to Shelby's," Archer says. "Whitney was super drunk."

"And what, Chris followed her?"

He shrugs. "I guess Chris must have followed her back there. Until last night, I swear I didn't know." Archer looks me in the eye. I want so badly to believe him. "Nikki said she was going to put Whitney to bed. That was it. We were drunk, Liza. We didn't think it was a big deal at the time. We went swimming right after that."

"Did Nikki know what you guys had done? With Whitney?"

He drops his head. "Uh, it's possible."

"So I guess it was pretty convenient for you guys that Nikki disappeared."

"That's a fucked-up thing to say, Liza," Archer says.

"This is a pretty fucked-up situation. Look at Whitney, at what happened to her. She was raped. She lost a baby. You could argue that's what started her using. A case could be made that what happened that night killed her, too."

"Liza, c'mon." He spreads his hands across the counter in a pleading gesture, and all I can think of is all the women those hands have touched—women like Whitney and the makeup artist that accused him. How many of those touches were wanted?

"We made a terrible mistake," he said. "But that doesn't make us murderers."

"And Geoff? How did he get involved?"

"A few days later, Whitney's parents contacted the school. And the school contacted my parents. And Todd's. And then it was just, I don't know, sorted out. It just disappeared."

"Because Geoff vouched for you guys. What did he do, provide an alibi? Say you were with him?"

"I guess." His sheepish and juvenile tone grates on me.

"You guess? Yes or no?"

"Yes. He did."

"Why would he do that? You guys didn't run track. Money? Is that it? Is that what he got in exchange for lying?"

Archer won't look at me, but he doesn't deny my accusation.

"What else did Geoff get? A career boost? He got to be head-master?"

"Something like that. We've helped finance his lifestyle a little. Call it a stipend," Todd says. "Being a coach and a PE teacher is not exactly a lucrative career."

"This is all so disgusting."

"We get it, Liza," Todd says, his tone sharp, his chin jutting forward. "We're not perfect like you. We were assholes. We got too drunk and maybe pushed a girl past her limits of what she might do when she was sober. But we're not criminals. We're not rapists in the bushes grabbing random strangers and violating them."

"I think that's the problem," I say, my voice rising, all the frustration I've felt this last week rushing out of me. "All these years, you still don't think you really did anything wrong." I look to Shelby for accord, but what I see in her eyes is a mix of fear and rage. Is that anger directed at her husband or at me? And who is she afraid of? What I don't see from her is surprise.

"You knew." The words slip out in a whisper.

Shelby shakes her head feverishly. But her eyes tell me the truth. I know her too well.

"I can't believe you knew what they did." My voice is steady, but my guts are clenched and cramping. "All these years, and you never said anything."

"They're not bad people, Liza. These are *our* people. We're talking about Archer. About Todd. It could happen to any guy." Her tone is imploring, her eyes wide and beseeching. "You don't have a son, but I do. I worry about him all the time."

"You worry that Brody is going to assault someone?"

"Don't say it like that. Kids get drunk. They do stupid things. I worry he's going to make a mistake that haunts him for the rest of his life or get accused of something he didn't really do. Think of Zoe and all the mistakes she's made. You think their lives should be ruined forever? What about Whitney? Doesn't she have any responsibility in this? C'mon, Liza. You remember what she was like."

I shake my head in disbelief. "And Kinsey? You think something like this could never happen to her?"

Shelby brushes away the question. "Kinsey's not dumb. She can take care of herself."

"What does *dumb* have to do with it, Shelby? Is that why you think Whitney was raped?" My voice is barely a whisper. My whole head and neck aches from the struggle not to scream. "Because she was *dumb*?" I take a step back. "I'm done. I'm going to pack my things, and then I'm leaving. Give me your keys." I hold my hand out. "I need your car to get back, and then I'll drop it off later."

"I can drive you," Archer says. "I'm going back."

"Keys." I thrust my hand at Shelby. I'm a little surprised when she grabs them from the bowl behind her and presses them into my palm. As she does so, she squeezes my hand, not letting it go.

"Liza, you have to forgive me." Her voice is so soft that I can barely make out the words. "I'm so sorry."

"You lied to me," I say, grabbing the keys and pulling my hand back. "I trusted you. And now I don't."

CHAPTER 47

1994

For a split second, when Nikki pushed open the unlocked front door at Shelby's house, she half expected Geoff to be waiting there. He had taken the key, after all, and she had been forced to leave the door unlocked. But no, the house was as empty as she'd left it. She dragged Whitney inside and locked the door.

With one final burst of energy, Nikki pulled Whitney up the stairs into one of the bedrooms, the one with a glass lamp filled with seashells, and lay her on the bed. Whitney looked in her direction with lidded eyes, but Nikki couldn't tell if she was looking at her or just spacing out.

"Do you need anything? Like water?"

Whitney shook her head in a tiny, almost imperceptible motion. Nikki knelt beside her. She did not know Whitney well. The only times they hung out were in a group, with Liza. She had honestly never given the girl much thought. If anything, she had dismissed her as being spoiled and lazy. Whitney wasn't someone who took grades seriously. She had plans to attend the College of Charleston, where her dad had some pull. She would joke about how her Cs didn't matter because she was a Bascombe.

But curled up before her was not the Whitney that Nikki knew. Another girl had taken her place. Someone hurt and raw, her mascara streaking from the corners of her eyes. There was a vulnerability in her face that Nikki had never seen before. And when she looked closely, she could see an ugly, reddish welt on her neck.

Nikki stroked her hair. "I'll be right downstairs, 'kay?"

Whitney frowned, her lower lip trembling. "When are you coming back?" she asked. "I don't know why they did it. Why me?"

"Shhhhh," Nikki said. She couldn't think of a decent answer.

Whitney rolled over, turning toward the wall, as if satisfied with Nikki's nonanswer. Nikki stood up. The only thing she could do for her now, she told herself, was to call her dad. He would know what to do.

Walking down the stairs, she paused when she heard a scratching outside the front door. Her body instantly grew hot. Someone was there. Her heart raced, and she waited for the door to swing open.

But it didn't.

The wind, she told herself, only half believing it. Nikki scurried into the kitchen, where the phone was. It was a fat, white, cordless thing attached to the wall. She removed the receiver and walked through to the dining room, where large sliding glass doors overlooked the backyard, the dock, and the bay.

She punched in her home number as she stared out into the dark night. It was hard to believe that only a few hours ago, they were all here in the sunshine, Whitney running by them all in her wet clothes. This whole trip was a terrible idea.

The line at her parents' end began to ring. She could picture their old-fashioned phone—avocado green, with a rotary dial—on a nightstand next to her parents' bed.

"Answer," she hissed desperately, and just then, the phone clicked.

"Yo." Her little brother's voice sounded sleepy and annoyed. Relief flooded her.

"Wake up Dad."

"What? Who is this?"

"It's Nikki. Who do you think it is? Now go wake up Dad."

"Yeah, right. You crazy? Hey, call back later. My movie just started."

"Cobo, don't be such a little shit. Just get him."

"I'm a shit? Did you just call me a shit?" Then a click. The phone went dead.

"Cobo? Cobo?" Did her little brother really just hang up on her?

She pressed the On button a few times but got no ring tone. The phone she was using was no longer working for some reason. Maybe Cobo didn't hang up on her, after all. And then it hit her in her gut—someone else was in the house. Someone who had just disconnected the phone.

Her whole body froze. She couldn't bring herself to turn around.

"C'mon, Nikki," a voice said behind her. "What do you think you're doing?"

CHAPTER 48

LIZA

Upstairs, I am packing up my few things when my cell rings. It's a D.C. area code, but I don't recognize the number.

"Hello?" I hold my breath, waiting to see if it is a spam call.

"Hey, you," says a sweet voice. "It's Prentiss."

"Prentiss, what a surprise." I brace myself for questions. She is probably digging for dirt on what took place last night. "What's up?"

"So let me get straight to the point," she says, shifting into a more officious mode. "I'm calling as Zoe's lawyer. Detective Gaffney contacted me this morning. He'd like to set up a time to come to Washington and talk to Zoe. He said he can come Monday if that works."

"Is it bad that he called you and not me?"

"It's actually the smart thing for him to do. Zoe has counsel, and he knows it. And you will want counsel for this, Liza."

I stiffen. "Why? What for?"

"Nothing major, I didn't mean to scare you. But he told me that when they checked Chris de Groot's phone, he had been communicating with Emery's cell after she had died. He thinks that Zoe has had Emery's phone the whole time. If they wanted to, they could charge her with obstructing an investigation and lying to the police, but I didn't get the feeling they wanted to."

"Thank god."

"But they do need that phone."

"Of course. I understand." We make a plan to meet Monday afternoon, when Zoe will be off work.

After I hang up, I stand there, almost smiling in spite of myself. What a little snake. I remember that when the detective told us Emery's phone had not been found on the beach, my daughter sounded so innocent when she said she had no idea of its whereabouts. From downstairs, I hear the front door slam. I go to the window and watch Archer stride across the gravel driveway to his Tesla. Even from here, I can tell he's upset. Absentmindedly, I call Zoe, and I am surprised when she picks up.

"What's up?"

"How you doing this morning?"

"I'm okay, I guess. Dad's taking me to breakfast at Parkway Deli. I can't really talk."

"Listen, Detective Gaffney called. He's coming to D.C. to ask you some more questions."

"Ugh. Really? Do I have to?"

"Yes. You do."

"Fine. I'm just sick of talking about this."

"I get that. He also said he wants Emery's phone."

"Her phone?" Her tone is all innocence. But before she can lie to me, I push on.

"Zoe, he knows. He's seen the calls on Chris de Groot's phone. You're not in trouble, but the police need the phone. It's part of a murder investigation."

"Fine." She sighs, clearly defeated. "I was hoping I could keep it. I know it's stupid."

"It's not stupid. Not at all." I sit down on the bed. "You've been texting with Chris de Groot?"

"Yeah." She sighs loudly. "He used a fake name. Jericho. But I figured it out."

"Like his main character. Kurt Jericho."

"Exactly." There is pride in her voice. "And I figured out his real phone number, too. That's how I reached him."

"What do you mean, his *real* phone number?"

"I mean, Emery called him in the spring. Hold on." I hear some rustling. "Here we go—he told her not to use that number, and then he texted her from a different number."

"Can you send me his texts? I mean, now?"

"Sure." I hear the click of a screenshot and a few seconds later the ping of a text message. I zoom in on what she has sent me. I don't recognize the phone number. I begin to read the exchange of texts with Chris—first the ones from Emery and then the ones from Zoe pretending to be Emery. A hot sensation starts to spread across my face, and I can feel my heart speed up.

"You still there?" Zoe asks.

"Yeah, sorry. I was thinking of something Uncle Aaron said to me. About reading the Torah as carefully as you do a love letter."

"Ummm. Okay?"

"He meant that we should try to figure out the deeper meaning behind the written words, like when we read a letter." *Or, for that matter,* I think, *an email or a text message or a social media post.* "Does *see you later* mean your boyfriend plans to come by? Does signing off *love* mean he loves you? Or does he sign all letters like that?" I'm talking fast, the words tumbling out of my mouth, probably not making any sense to her. But it's clicking in my brain, thoughts exploding like the little bang-snaps we used to toss down in the street on the Fourth of July.

"Are you okay, Mom?"

"I will be, honey. I promise." We say goodbye, and I grab my bag and head back downstairs, my heart beating like a caged creature trying to escape. Shelby is the only one left in the kitchen. She's sitting at the counter with a mug of coffee and looking at a shelter magazine.

"Hey," she says when I come in.

I take my phone out of my bag. My hands shake as I pull up the text messages. My insides feel gelatinous. "Chris de Groot didn't send these texts, did he?"

"I'm sorry—what?" She shuts the magazine and looks up at me, a smile frozen on her face.

"Turns out, Zoe had Emery's phone the whole time."

She wiggles her eyebrows. "Wow."

I begin to read some of Chris's messages aloud.

"*Yr mom.* No vowel. No punctuation. *No bueno* with no caps?" I look up at her. "No grown man texts like this, Shel. Especially not a writer. But what I can't figure out is whose number this is. It's not yours. Did you get a burner phone?"

She chokes out a laugh. "Are you nuts? A burner phone? I'm not a drug dealer, Liza."

"What happens if I dial it?"

"If you do what?" The panic in her eyes is unmistakable.

But I'm already dialing.

Immediately, a pinging noise comes from the corner of the kitchen, where Shelby's camel leather bucket bag sits slouched on a chair.

CHAPTER 49

1994

Shelby popped her head out of the water and looked around but couldn't spot Todd.

Her heart sank. Neither Archer nor Chris was visible, either. It pissed her off. They were probably still playing drinking games inside. It was her birthday, and Todd would rather be with the guys than with her. And where the hell was Liza? Off with Nikki and some track friends, no doubt.

Self-pity began to bloom within her. She had been abandoned by her best friend and her boyfriend on her birthday. What was wrong with her? When her mother got angry, she sometimes told Shelby that she was *utterly unlovable*.

Her mom would apologize later, but still. That little voice took up residence in the back of her mind.

And here it was, whispering to her—*Utterly unlovable. That's why you're alone on your birthday.*

Shelby swam toward the shore and then began to wade in, the surf hitting the back of her legs, almost knocking her down. Alcohol could do this to her—uncork the resentment and insecurities she kept bottled up inside. Magnify the little voice.

As she marched up the sand, Shelby scanned the beach for any signs of Todd. She was already formulating her complaint in her head. It was her friggin' birthday. He could be so sweet when it was the two of them alone. So attentive. He would do this thing where he would trace each of her fingers with his pin-kie. Just the touch of his skin on the palm of her hand could make her crazy. They would lie side by side and talk about the future, what it would be like in college together, away from their parents' prying eyes. She had promised to sleep with him once they were in college, and he was patient. She had gotten really good at giving blow jobs, and he said that was enough, that he would wait.

But he had another side, a kind of casual cruelty, when the guys were around. He wasn't mean, exactly, but he blew her off. Ignored about half the things she said. Made little jokes that she didn't get but that would crack Chris up. She hated the way Chris smirked at her. He made that comment about the soft-freeze ice cream she was eating at Field Day at school. Some-thing about her impressive tongue work. Made her wonder if Todd had said something about her or if it was just Chris being a douche like usual.

And now, on her birthday, Todd was nowhere to be found.

She stopped short when she noticed a cluster of guys by the beach access. Wearing only her underwear, she was cold and drip-ping wet. All of a sudden, she was self-conscious. She grabbed a shirt from a pile of clothes on the beach and put it on. It was huge on her, the hem hitting her mid-thigh like a minidress.

She continued marching, feeling more indignant as it became clear it *was* Todd. And Archer and Chris. She was right.

"Hey!" she called as she grew close. "Hey, guys! What the hell?"

They all turned to her, and Todd started walking toward her.

"Where the hell have you been? It's my birthday, Todd." She knew how she sounded—the hysterical girlfriend—but she couldn't seem to stop herself. "You're supposed to be with me."

When he got closer, his face changed. She could tell that he knew something was wrong. He didn't like when she got too drunk. Caused a scene. Embarrassed him. Shelby's mother also got this way sometimes when she drank. Once, her mother yelled at her father at the country club, and he piled the kids into the car and pulled out of the parking lot, leaving his furious wife to find her own way home.

"Are you mad at me?" Shelby frowned. "Did I do something wrong?"

Todd shook his head. "No, it's not you." He looked like a little boy to her. Like he did in seventh grade when his stupid volcano erupted at the beginning of his presentation in science class.

Premature eruption! someone had yelled, and he had turned beet red.

"Are you okay?" she asked softly. He shook his head but didn't say anything. "Just tell me."

"I'm sorry, Shel. It's fucked up."

"What do you mean?" She took a step forward so their faces were inches apart. For her, it was just the two of them on the beach now. "What's fucked up? You can tell me, Todd."

He let out a little hiccup of a sob and then turned away.

"He doesn't mean anything," Archer said. Somehow he had appeared beside them without her noticing.

"Just tell me what's going on." She turned to Archer. "Maybe I can help."

"It's Whitney," Archer said.

Shelby groaned. "Oh god, what did she do now?"

"She's upset," Archer said. "She got really drunk. She was messing around with Chris in the dunes, and now she's upset. You know how it is."

Shelby nodded. They called this the "oopsies"—having drunk sex and then regretting it.

"And Nikki's talking about calling her dad. He's a cop, you know."

"Why? That's crazy."

"We could get in so much trouble," Todd said. "If my dad . . ." He didn't bother to finish the sentence. Todd's dad was a partner in one of the biggest lobbying firms on K Street. He and Todd's mom were always in the papers, and not just for chairing a gala or going to a ball, like Shelby's parents. His mom was a high-up political appointee in the Clinton administration. Something to do with education. There was only one rule in the Smythe house: don't do anything that would make the papers.

"Maybe I should go back—talk to her," Archer said.

"No, no. I'll do it," Shelby said. Her tone was annoyed, but she was secretly gratified. They needed her. "She'll listen to me."

The relief in their faces was palpable. She was used to people listening to her. She had three older brothers whom she loved to death, but she had to learn how to sweet-talk them and handle their big egos if she wanted to survive in that house. *Feminine wiles,* her mother called it. Worked on almost everyone, except her own parents. She had never had much sway with them. "I know what to say to her. Don't worry."

"You sure?" Todd asked. "We can go with you."

"This is a girl thing." She would clean up Chris's mess for Todd, and then he'd see—she was indispensable. "Just stay here. I'll be back before you know it."

CHAPTER 50

LIZA

I hang up. "If you have any respect for me at all, you're gonna tell me the truth."

She stares at me, unmoving.

"Truth bomb, Shelby. I need to know."

She walks to the fridge and takes out a bottle of wine that's half-full. After placing it with a clunk on the kitchen island, she takes two more mugs from the cabinet.

"It's nine thirty in the morning, Shelby."

"Yup. But if you drink it out of a coffee mug, it's okay." She pours the wine and takes a big swig.

"What the hell is going on?"

"It's an app called Hushed. You can get a second number to text from, using your phone, so people don't know it's you."

"So you pretended to be Chris?" My voice sounds shrill and strained. "Is that right?"

She nods. At least she isn't lying to me.

"Why?"

"Because—because I didn't want Emery to get anywhere near him. I mean, I didn't know about her whole DNA project, believe me." She lets out a strange, horselike laugh. "Trying to take Brody's Band-Aids. Can you believe it?"

I blink hard. Emery's subterfuge is the last thing I want to talk about. "Shelby, start at the beginning."

"When Emery came to me—you know, like I told you?—I didn't know exactly what she wanted. But I knew she was up to something. And I knew Chris was a loose cannon, to put it mildly. I wanted to keep them apart, but I couldn't tell her that. I couldn't let on that I knew who she was. So I gave her Chris's number, knowing full well he would never call her back. He never calls anyone back, right? And then I preemptively texted her. It's not evil; don't look at me like that."

"How did you know Emery was Whitney's daughter?"

She rolls her eyes. "C'mon. You can't hide a secret like that. Geoff told me. He knew right away."

I suck in my breath. "You lied to my face when I told you I had found out at the funeral. When I told you how I saw the necklace. You acted shocked."

"What was I supposed to say? That I knew already?"

"Yes! Exactly. It's called the truth."

"Please! You would have been so mad that I hadn't told you before."

"Why didn't you? Just tell me as soon as you figured it out?"

"Seriously?" Now she's the one who sounds hysterical, as if I am attacking her. "You would have wanted to meet her. I know you, Liza. And then what? She would have told you that Todd, Archer, and Chris were involved in something awkward twenty-eight years ago involving her mother."

"Something awkward? It was sexual assault, Shelby. It wasn't wearing the same dress as another girl at prom. Do you even get that?" I squeeze the base of my nose and shut my eyes for a second. I feel a monster headache coming on. Over the last year, there were dozens of times she could have told me. But she never wanted to. Never planned to. "You should have told me, Shelby."

She purses her lips and closes her eyes for a moment as if remembering something painful. "I couldn't. For one thing, I swore to Todd that I wouldn't. And, honestly, I just didn't think you'd understand."

"What do you mean?" She's right, of course, but I want to hear what she was thinking. I want to hear how my best friend justifies lying to me for decades.

"Look, don't take this the wrong way. I love you, but everything is so black and white with you. I mean, look at Daniel."

"Daniel?" His name is like a splash of icy water. "What's he got to do with this?"

"He cheated on you once. And that was it. Poof. Marriage over."

"It wasn't once. He was having an affair."

"Okay, but just one affair. And it was like he was dead to you. It was just over."

I can't believe I'm hearing this. Blood thumps in my head. "Things weren't good with me and Daniel for years. Anyway, this isn't about my marriage."

"I'm just trying to explain. Do you know how many times Todd has cheated on me? 'Cause I've lost count."

I open my mouth to speak but say nothing. What can I say? That I'm shocked that he continued to cheat on her over the years? I have no shock left to give. Of the recent revelations about Todd, his ongoing cheating is the least disturbing.

"Okay, Todd cheated. So what?"

"The point is, when I love someone, I don't give up on them. No matter how flawed they are. But you do, Liza. You judge people."

A harsh sound erupts from my throat. "This isn't about me being judgmental. You're a liar. You covered up a gang rape, Shelby—"

"Gang rape?" She lets out a sputtering laugh. "Don't be so dramatic. It was a stupid, drunken mistake, not some violent crime. They didn't throw her crying across a pool table like in that movie *The Accused*."

"It was more like that than you are willing to admit. And you covered it up. You pretended to be Chris de Groot. To what end? To protect your husband. To protect the life you have."

"We all agreed not to tell you. We wanted to protect you."

"Protect me?" I grab my phone and scroll through to the most recent messages, the ones that Zoe sent from Emery's phone after Emery's death. "You warned my daughter she could end up like Emery. Do you realize how fucked up that is?"

"I was *trying* to scare her, Liza. I wanted her as far away from Chris de Groot as possible. And I was right. Look at what he did."

I continue to scroll through the texts. "So what—you, pretending to be Chris, told Emery to meet you that night at the lighthouse? Then, Emery gets a text from your fake phone number saying, *I'm right behind you.*" I look up. "I don't get it. We were together that night. So who met her? Who texted, *I'm right behind you?*"

Shelby doesn't answer. She crosses her arms in front of her, but her whole body is trembling. I think back on that night at the Corkboard. Archer and Todd meeting us for a drink before they headed out to meet with Chris. "You can't have met Emery at the beach. You were with me and Prentiss at the Corkboard."

Shelby bites down on her lower lip and stares at me.

Another detail from Sunday night comes back to me. "Todd took your phone when he left the bar. By mistake. At least, that's what you said. You guys switched phones."

She turns her head, her hair falling like a curtain so I can't see her face.

"Shelby, did Todd take your cell phone on purpose that night? Did you guys plan that?"

I lay my hands flat on the cold marble island. I'm at the edge of something so awful. I'm afraid to move forward, but I can't back away. "Is Todd the one who met Emery that night? Did Todd . . . Did he hurt her?"

Shelby blinks back tears. "It was an accident. Nobody meant to hurt her, Liza. But what's the point of ruining so many lives over a misunderstanding? I'm not saying it's right, but wouldn't you do it for Zoe? If she made that kind of mistake?"

Her words tumble out of her, and I struggle to piece together their meaning. "Are you saying Todd hurt Emery? Because she was going to go public?"

"It was an accident. He just wanted to talk to her."

"An accident? How do you accidentally drown someone?" Shelby does not answer, so I continue, "Because it wasn't an accident, was it? Otherwise, you two wouldn't have covered it up. You wrote that suicide note, didn't you?"

"Let me explain it to you, Liza," Shelby pleads. "Maybe if I explain it to you, you'll understand. Emery wanted to destroy us!"

"Do you have any idea how depraved all this is?" I am yelling now. "You killed a child to hide your husband's involvement in a rape. I don't even know who you are."

"You won't tell the police, will you?" She stands up. "I'm your best friend."

"Do you realize what you have done? What you are a part of? Because it doesn't feel like you understand the enormity of it."

Shelby bites down on her lower lip, looking like a little girl who has been caught sneaking cookies. Tears well up in her eyes. "We can make this all go away, Liza." She reaches across the island and takes my hands in hers. "This can all be on Chris. He was a total creep. We just need to get our stories straight. Don't you see? Then we can all just move on with our lives, get back to normal. It'll be such a relief to have all this behind us. You have no idea how hard it's been for me, all these years, not being able to tell you. You're my best friend." She lets out a sob. "And I love you so much. It's been like this horrible monster that's following me all the time, lurking in the shadows. I wanted to tell you so many times. I really did. But I was afraid of what you'd say or do. I was afraid of losing you. You were so close with Nikki, and when she died, you were so upset."

"Nikki?" I blink, confused about why she is mentioning Nikki all of a sudden.

Shelby walks to the corner and grabs her bag from the chair. She plops it on the counter and rummages inside.

"What's going on?" I ask.

She reaches across the counter and grabs my hand. "I couldn't tell you," she whispers before pressing something cold into my open palm. "I just couldn't. I was afraid you'd hate me."

For a millisecond, we stay like that, her flesh pressed against mine. When she withdraws her hand, the glint of gold sends a shiver through me.

The room swims.

I stare at the small gold compass, a diamond beside the letter *N*.

"Shelby," I whisper. "What did you do?"

CHAPTER 51

1994

Shelby walked back to her beach house as quickly as she could, yanking the T-shirt down, but it barely covered her thighs. Steeling herself for the stares of people, she hurried across Route 1. But no one gave her a second glance. She was just another drunk girl during Beach Week.

She would convince Nikki that it was all a misunderstanding. Nikki was obviously upset, but she would get it once Shelby explained. Shelby wasn't a huge fan of Chris's, but if Nikki called her dad—who was a cop, no less—everyone would get in so much trouble.

And that would be a nightmare. Her own parents would get over it, but not Todd's. His father would kill him. He already thought Shelby wasn't good enough for his son. He was from Boston, had gone to Yale, and she knew he thought the Covingtons were new money, basically Beverly Hillbillies. He would blame Shelby. She was sure of it. *No*, Shelby thought, *I have to make this disappear.*

Not only would Beach Week be ruined, her whole life could be.

And for what? For Whitney?

Shelby found the front door of her house locked and no spare key in the frog. She walked around the back to the sliding door and tried it. It opened. They must not have latched it this afternoon. She felt stupid for leaving it open and lucky at the same time. She walked in and stood in the dining room, feeling dizzy from the drinking and from rushing to get here.

Nikki obviously didn't get it. Whitney was a slut. It was no big deal; it wasn't like they judged her for it. But she shouldn't be able to destroy people's lives. Shelby would talk some sense into Nikki. Explain it to her.

Someone was speaking in a low voice nearby. Shelby walked briskly into the kitchen, where she saw that the phone was missing from the base. Her stomach lurched. Nikki was obviously already calling her dad. Shelby grabbed the short cord that went from the base of the phone into the phone jack on the wall and yanked it hard.

There was no sign of Nikki anywhere. Shelby took a few steps in the living room and saw Nikki standing there, her back to her, fussing with the dead phone.

"C'mon, Nikki," Shelby said. "What do you think you're doing?"

"I'm calling my dad," Nikki said and dropped the hand holding the phone by her side. "I'm allowed to call my dad."

"Why aren't you at the beach like everyone else?"

"They raped her, Shelby." The words hit Shelby like little pellets. "They raped Whitney. All of them. They took turns."

Shelby stumbled back as if pushed. "Why would you say that?"

"Because it's true."

"That's a lie. Todd wouldn't do that."

"It's not a lie. I saw it with my own eyes."

Shelby let out a sharp laugh. "Yeah, right. You saw Todd raping someone? Bullshit."

"Fine, I didn't actually see it, but that's what Whitney said. She said that they all took turns."

Shelby's face flushed with anger. "And you believe her?" She was shouting, but she didn't care. Who did this girl think she was? Saying these things about Todd, about Archer. "Whitney

318 AGGIE BLUM THOMPSON

is a slut. A completely drunk slut. And a drama queen. She lies, you know. About a lot of things." She took a deliberate breath in an attempt to calm down. "You know Archer; you know Todd. They would never do that."

"We'll see what the police say."

"No, we won't." The rage boiled up within Shelby. There was a right way to handle things. You didn't just go calling the police every time some girl got drunk and regretted having sex. "This is her fault, too, you know." Shelby's hands clenched and unclenched.

"So what's the deal?" Nikki said, jutting her chin at the phone. "You're not going to let me call my parents?"

"This is my house." Shelby crossed her arms. "My rules."

"Fine. I'll make the call somewhere else." Nikki dropped the phone, and it clattered on the floor. She marched past her, through the kitchen and the dining room, and continued out the open sliding doors onto the patio.

"You're an ungrateful bitch, you know that?" Shelby screamed after her. "We invite you into our lives. We let you join our group. And this is how you repay us."

Nikki spun around. Shelby couldn't really make out her features in the dark, but Nikki's white T-shirt almost glowed. "Oh, that's how it is, huh? I'm supposed to be grateful you let me tag along to Beach Week, and in exchange, I'm not supposed to say anything when someone gets hurt? Sorry, that's not how I was raised."

Nikki turned, and the white T-shirt began floating away. Shelby rushed after her through the open door. Outside, she caught up to Nikki and grabbed a fistful of her shirt.

"Let go of me." Nikki ripped her shirt free from Shelby's grip. "You can't stop me. I'll go to the gas station and call my dad. And there's not a goddamn thing you can do about it."

Nikki began walking away again, fast, almost a run. And something hot exploded in Shelby.

There's not a goddamn thing you can do about it.

The words shot through her bloodstream like a flame chasing down a line of gasoline.

There's not a goddamn thing you can do about it.

Who the hell did this girl think she was? She was a nobody. From Wheaton. She was only at Beach Week because Liza felt sorry for her. Didn't she know that? She didn't belong here.

It was obvious. Nikki was jealous. She wanted their lives, and it made her want to destroy them.

Rage invaded every molecule of her body, saturated every pore on her skin. It was as if every little slight, every insult she had ever experienced—the comments about her weight and lovability from her mother, the incessant teasing from her brothers, her father's dismissal of her as being anything more than an ornament—was like a snowflake. Individually insignificant, but once amassed, the cumulative effect was that of a blizzard. And that blizzard of rage powered her forward.

Shelby charged after Nikki, a guttural howl escaping her as she ran. Nikki looked back and then broke into a run. She was rounding the corner of the house now. She'd be on the road soon, and then gone.

A burst of strength propelled Shelby forward onto the grass. As she tripped, she gripped Nikki's legs. The girl tumbled onto the ground before her. Shelby crawled up upon her like a giant insect. She sat on Nikki's chest, panting. Nikki reached up and grabbed at Shelby's throat, enclosing her neck in her small hands.

With a fierce tug, Nikki ripped Shelby's necklace off and tossed it onto the dark lawn.

"Bitch." Shelby gasped for breath. She tried to claw the hands from around her throat. But she could not pry them off. She fell forward, one hand hitting the grass. The other grazed a concrete brick.

Shelby gripped the heavy brick with both hands, and hoisted it above her head. She brought it down onto Nikki's skull. It grazed her forehead, and Nikki began to scream. Her eyes widened in terror. She dropped her hands from Shelby's neck. Again, Shelby lifted the brick, and again she drove it into Nikki's head.

Nikki stopped screaming.

Shelby kneeled over her, out of breath. "Nikki?" she whispered. She wasn't sure why she was whispering. Blood was pouring out of a wide gash in Nikki's head. Shelby's stomach lurched. Nikki's eyes were rolled back in her head, and her mouth was open as if in mid-scream.

Shelby got up, dizzy. She put her hand to her mouth and barely had time to turn away before vomiting. The alcohol shot out of her with force. She put her hands on her knees and stayed that way, heaving. Finally, Shelby straightened up, but she did not look back at Nikki. What should she do next? Her mind was murky, like the brackish water she could smell, so close by. She should take her pulse. But inside, she felt she knew the truth.

Nikki was dead.

And she had killed her.

Shelby had promised Todd and Archer that she would clear everything up and make it okay. And instead, this is what happened. How could she explain this? What could she say that would make this okay? Maybe she could go back to the beach. Just jump in the ocean and swim. When they discovered Nikki's body the next day, she could act surprised. They would blame an intruder. A psychopath.

A hand touched her shoulder. She screamed.

"It's okay, Shelby." She turned to see Coach Estes standing there, Chris de Groot beside him in the shadows. Where had they come from?

"Are you all right?" Coach Estes asked. "Are you hurt?"

"No." Shelby shook her head, unable to look at either of them. Tears burst from Shelby's eyes. She fell into Coach Estes's arms, blubbering. She told him everything. How she had been swimming with everyone and went looking for Todd. How there had been some kind of incident and how Shelby had come back here to talk some sense into Nikki, who was falsely accusing Todd and Archer of rape. And that she had walked in on her calling the police. She was going to report them all. "But what she was saying about them is not true. And then she fell. It was an accident."

He nodded, not contradicting her, even though she sensed he had seen it all. Instead, he walked over to Nikki and bent down. Fascinated, she watched him carefully pull off the girl's shorts, and then pull her shirt down, over her narrow hips, avoiding her bleeding head. Each time he pulled Nikki's arm through a sleeve and let the limb drop with a thud in the grass, Shelby shuddered. The tears spilled out of her eyes. She was looking at a dead girl. Her friend. And it was her fault, wasn't it?

"What are you doing?" Shelby asked, her voice barely above a whisper.

Geoff got up and walked over, shoving Nikki's clothing at her. "Take these, go back to the beach, leave them with the rest of the clothes, and get back in the water. Nikki went swimming with you. You saw her get in the water."

"Uh-huh." Shelby nodded. "She was going to go in, but then she wandered off—"

"No, Shelby, look at me. Nikki went swimming with you, got it? You saw her get in the water, and she never got out. Now go."

She started to back away. "What about Nikki?"

"I'll take care of Nikki. Just go. Hurry."

"You think people will believe me? Just because I say it?"

He nodded. "You're Shelby Covington, aren't you? They'll believe you. Wait, hold on a sec."

He went back to Nikki's body and then returned, pressing a small gold chain into her hand. "Leave this with the clothing."

Shelby took the necklace and the clothes in her arms and ran back to the beach. She dumped the clothes by another pile, then stripped off the T-shirt she was wearing. On top of Nikki's clothes, she lay the necklace that she had given to her just a few hours earlier. But she couldn't seem to walk away. Finally, she grabbed it and put it around her own neck. She'd designed these. Paid for these. And hers was gone.

No one would notice in the dark, anyway, that the diamond was on the *N* and not the *S*.

She ran down to the water and dove under, relishing how the icy cold numbed her, cleansed her. She had been dipped into a cold lake at her grampy's farm in the foothills of the Blue Ridge Mountains when she was nine, emerging reborn. She told herself this was a baptism, too. The water would cleanse her of her sins. And when she broke the water, she wouldn't be guilty anymore. When she did resurface, her friends and classmates were bobbing all around her.

She was just another figure in the dark, treading water.

She watched people splash their way to the shore until there were just a handful of swimmers left in the ocean. Then she got out, too. Dazed, she went in search of her clothing.

Liza walked up to her. "Where's Nikki?" she asked. Shelby winced. Liza had noticed Nikki was gone, but not that Shelby had been absent. It hurt.

Shelby plastered a smile on her face. "Isn't she here?" she responded. Could Liza tell she was lying?

Liza spun around and looked in the direction of the house. "Maybe she went inside."

But Nikki wasn't inside. And after all the clothing on the beach had been claimed, Liza found Nikki's shorts and shirt crumpled in a lonely pile. Shelby didn't have to say anything. She didn't have to say, *I saw her go in.* Others said it. They took the baton and ran with it. They ran up and down the beach calling Nikki's name. Shrieking it into the night air.

Panic threatened to overtake Shelby. What had she done? Looking at her face, Liza nodded. "I'm freaking out, too."

Todd found Shelby and wrapped her in his arms. "Where is

she?" he whispered in her ear. "We saw you come back without her."

But Shelby couldn't open her mouth to speak. Her teeth chattered with cold.

"We should call 9–1–1," someone said.

Shelby pulled her head back from Todd's chest. Her fingers grazed the delicate chain around her sore neck. "Yeah. We should call 9–1–1."

CHAPTER 52

LIZA

Once Shelby has finished telling her story, neither of us speaks. Anything I say will only minimize the horror of what she has just confessed to. My head aches, overwhelmed by trying to maneuver between the facts of that night so long ago and the extreme duplicity of the woman before me. Of my best friend.

Shelby never wanted to discuss Nikki. Whenever I brought her up, Shelby would get upset. Not because she was grieving, I realize now, but because she didn't want me asking too many questions. The thought infuriates me, how she emotionally manipulated me. All those years, Todd and Shelby harbored this secret.

"What about the night Emery died?" I ask. "Did Todd go to the beach planning to hurt Emery?"

"Of course not."

I spin around to see Todd has entered the room. My back stiffens.

"I went there to reason with her."

"Was Archer with you?"

"No. He went back to D.C. He doesn't know anything about this. After we went to Chris's house and found him passed out, Archer went back to D.C."

"And what—you told Emery to meet you at the lighthouse? Pretending to be Chris?"

"I thought I could reason with her."

"So what happened? How did she drown?"

He stiffens. "I'm not going to apologize for protecting my family."

"So what happened, Todd? How did Emery die?"

"She wanted to destroy us," he hisses through clenched teeth, making it sound like Emery was some kind of axe-wielding psychopath. I get up, suddenly sickened by being in the same room with them.

"Did you hurt her, Todd?"

"In six months, this can all be forgotten. A horrible nightmare that ended," Shelby says, walking over to Todd and looping her arm through his. "We can get through this, Liza. I love you. You're like a sister to me. We're family."

In her tone, I find only cool detachment, and in her expression, calculation. All these years, I realize, I made the mistake of pegging Shelby as a weak, unfulfilled stay-at-home mom. I was so wrong. She and Todd are the cocaptains of their own ship, navigating treacherous waters together. This is just another storm to endure. She sees sunny skies ahead.

"I need to hear it from Todd. What really happened."

"I tried to reason with her. She wanted to drag the whole mess into the light. Pick through it publicly for the whole world to see and judge. She was planning to make a podcast!" He laughs bitterly. "Can you imagine the audacity?"

"So what did you do?"

He runs his hands through his hair. "I panicked. I snapped."

"And you drowned her?"

"I didn't mean to. We were tussling in the water."

"Tussling?" I yell. "She weighed about one twenty, one thirty, tops. And you're what? Six two? One ninety? You killed her, Todd."

"Please, Liza, please." Shelby's face is contorted with fear. "Before you do anything that can't be undone, think it through."

Her voice cracks, and she begins crying. "Nothing can bring Emery back."

"She's right," Todd says. "What's done is done. Telling the police isn't going to bring her back. All it will do is cause more pain for everyone. Chris is dead. Don't you see? It can all end now."

"Think of Zoe," Shelby says. "How awful it will be for her. To have all this in the papers?"

I'm speechless. It feels like a fever dream, the kind with enough ties to reality that you question if you're asleep or not. In front of me are two people I've known almost all my life, who I would have sworn a week ago were the same as I am. Family-oriented, honest, caring. I've seen Todd stop to pick up other people's trash on the sidewalk. But they're actually monsters, inside the skin of those two people.

"Is it money? Is that what you want?" Todd asks. "A nicer house? We can take care of you."

Shelby nods earnestly. "And Zoe will be taken care of."

"You can't think . . ." But I don't even know how to finish that sentence. They *do* think. That's what I can't fathom. Together, they have convinced themselves that they're not guilty of anything, that they're actually the heroes in this sordid tale. And that money can sand off any of the rough edges of their story, quell any doubts. Something occurs to me.

"What about that suicide note on Instagram? You didn't do that, Todd." I turn to Shelby. "Was it you? No. You were with me the whole night. So who helped you with Instagram?"

It dawns on me. "Kinsey. Kinsey helped you. Or was it Brody?"

"Drop it, Liza." Shelby stares me down defiantly, crossing her arms. "It's time to stop talking. We need an answer. Are you going to the police or not?"

Todd turns to Shelby. "It's too late," he says under his breath. "She knows everything. She's going to tell the police."

The calm in his voice sends a chill through me. I take a step backward toward the front door. Every cell in my body is screaming *run*. "Walnut?" I call, my voice cracking. I jiggle Shelby's keys to attract him.

"Stop right there, Liza."

"No." I shake my head. Walnut trots into the room. "I have to go. We have to get home." I spin around, and I'm inches from the door when Todd comes up behind me and body-slams me against the wall. Pain radiates through my right hip. I roll my back against the wall, wincing. He is right in front of me, his jaw set tight, blue eyes shining with rage. He flings open the door and pushes me outside.

"What are you doing?" I ask as he pulls me down the stair so quickly I have no choice but to stumble alongside him. I click the car fob as we hurry past Shelby's SUV as if that can somehow save me, but all it does is unlock the doors with an anemic beep.

I peek over Todd's shoulder to see Shelby moving, very slowly. She is letting this happen.

I'm alone in this fight.

We are heading back to the dock. The same dock that Chris de Groot pulled me to last night. Only today, yellow police tape festoons the tops of the dock pilings. I claw at whatever body parts of Todd's I can reach. I feel sick, realizing he shot Chris last night to shut him up, not to protect me.

But Todd is so much bigger and stronger than I am, and I'm unable to stop him from dragging me back there.

"Get the boat ready," he calls over his shoulder to Shelby. He stops at the edge of the dock and rips the police tape down so we can pass. Gripping my upper arm, we walk out halfway and stop. A long, white sculling boat bobs in the water at the end of the dock. Both Brody and Todd are rowers, and Todd's taken me out a few times over the years. But there's no way I'm getting in that boat with him today.

But what can I do?

I go limp, letting my limbs go slack like a marionette's. Taken by surprise, Todd dips down.

"Get up, Liza." His voice is gruff, a growl. But I will myself to sink into the hard wooden planks. Todd falls to his knees for better leverage. He tries to pull me up by my shoulders, but I am languid, loose. When he gets close enough, I see my chance. I bend my right pointer finger so the knuckle sticks out above my fist and jam it as hard as I can into his left eye. It sinks in with a sickening ease that makes me want to retch.

He doubles over and howls, hand to his face. I scramble to my feet. Seconds later, he yanks me back down by my hair onto the dock. "Fucking bitch!"

He releases my hair and grabs my legs. Walking backward, he pulls me down the rough wooden dock. My throat is so tight that when I try to yell, what comes out is a weak yelp. My mouth open wide, I gulp for air.

Thump, thump.

As my head hits the dock again and again, sharp spikes of pain pierce my skull as if it's about to shatter into a million pieces.

And then a rush of something going by me. A loud yowl. Todd drops my legs.

I sit up to see Walnut gripping Todd's calf in his mouth, his black lips pulled back in a beautiful grimace that bares his white teeth.

From my position, I lean over the edge of the dock to grab one of the oars from the boat, almost falling into the water in the process. I rise just as Todd shakes Walnut free. The oar is heavy, but I commit all my strength to raising it over my right shoulder, up high like I've watched Ryan Zimmerman do a thousand times when he is at bat. I swing hard and fast at Todd's head.

The oar makes contact; I can feel the satisfying *thwack* in my bones. The reverberation sends me stumbling back. Todd collapses in front of me. He doesn't move. Only then do I sink to the dock, exhausted. Walnut rushes to me, and I grip him tightly as tears stream down my face.

Shelby runs past me and throws herself onto Todd's prone body. Sobbing, she pulls at him, calling his name.

I take out my phone and dial 9–1–1 and explain everything to them. Once I am sure that an ambulance and police are on their way, I hang up. The edges of my vision are blackening, my eyes are heavy, and I worry that I might not be conscious much longer. The images in front of me swim.

The sun glinting off the clear blue water.

The yellow police tape flapping in the breeze.

A woman bent over, tending a fallen man.

Shelby sits up and looks straight at me, rage contorting her pretty little features into a mask of hatred.

"Couldn't you just keep one little secret?" she asks. "How are you going to live with yourself?"

CHAPTER 53

ZOE

Walnut leads the way as I climb the stairs with the tray, trying not to spill the coffee.

I push my mom's bedroom door open with my hip.

"Good morning," I say, setting the tray down. "I brought you coffee and a yogurt. I hope I made it right."

"That's so sweet, honey. You didn't have to do that. I could have come down."

"It's okay. You're supposed to rest, right? Isn't that what the doctor said?" I feel proud that none of the panic I felt yesterday at the hospital has crept into my voice.

"Last night must have been really scary for you," she says.

"It was fine." But it wasn't. I still haven't processed everything that happened. I slept in, and around eleven, my dad woke me up to tell me he was going out to Rehoboth because Mom was in the hospital. I insisted on going. When we got there, we waited for what seemed like an eternity. Dad kept saying she was all right, that they were just doing some tests. But it was hard not to think the worst. And it was weird that Shelby wasn't responding to my texts. That's before I knew what happened. My dad didn't tell me why—not then, anyway.

Finally, a doctor came out and told us that my mom had experienced a concussion. "Don't be alarmed when you see her," the doctor told us. "We had to shave the back of her head to clean out a wound. But you can't really tell; her hair covers it."

My mom leans over and dips a cookie in the tea. "Come sit," she says and pats the bed. "Did you see my new undercut?" She flips her hair to show me the shaved part on the back of her head.

I wince at the sight of the bandage. "Yeah. Cool."

"Oh, honey. Sorry. I was just trying to be funny. This all must have been so upsetting for you."

I try to smile. "I'm okay. Can you tell me what happened at Shelby's? Is it true that Todd attacked you?"

"You heard that, huh?"

"Yeah. Dad was talking to someone on the phone last night, after we took you home from the hospital and tucked you into bed. I heard him say that the police arrested Todd. Is that true?"

She leans back and shuts her eyes a moment. "Yes. Todd attacked me. I'm sorry that I don't know anything about his being arrested. But I am sure we will find out soon. And I promise I will tell you every single detail later today. But for now, can you just sit with me?" She pats the bed again, and this time I sit beside her. When I am closer, she touches the necklace around my neck. For a second, I think I'm going to be in trouble.

"I found it in your jewelry box," I say, rubbing the small gold compass between my fingers. "I hope that's all right."

"Of course."

"It reminds me of Emery," I say. "You know, how the diamond is next to the *E*?"

"I hadn't thought of that. That's very sweet." She takes my hand and squeezes it. "I wanted to say something."

"Okay."

"I'm sorry I didn't listen to you before," she says. "About so many things. About Emery. You tried to tell me, and I wouldn't listen."

I'm a little taken aback. Not in a bad way, just surprised. "It's okay. So you believe me now?"

"I do."

"Did Todd kill her?" My mom closes her eyes tightly but does not respond. "Mom. Please. I need to know."

"He was involved. The police will be sorting out the details. Maybe we will learn more when Detective Gaffney comes by to pick up Emery's phone and talk to you. But it's important that you know I'm so sorry."

"It's okay, Mom. Really."

"It's not okay, but I am going to try to do better. First thing tomorrow morning, I am going to give Washington Prep my two weeks' notice. I won't be working there anymore."

I feel my eyes widen. "Really? Does that mean I don't have to go back in the fall?"

She laughs. "Not only does it mean you don't *have* to go back, it means you *can't* go back, because we can't afford it without my employee discount."

"Yay." I give her a quick hug. "Does that mean I'll go to Wilson?" I ask, referring to the D.C. public school we are zoned for.

"Maybe. If we still live in this part of D.C."

I pull back and give her a look. "Where else would we live?"

She sighs. "Oh, I don't know. I'm thinking maybe it's time to sell the house. It's a lot of work to keep up. A modern apartment or condo building sounds nice."

"Maybe one with a pool?"

"Maybe."

"You know," I say, poking her on the shoulder, "there are a lot of new apartments in downtown Bethesda, and if we lived there, I could walk to B-CC."

"Hmmm. . . . Bethesda–Chevy Chase High School? That's a pretty big school, you know."

"I don't mind."

"I like seeing you smile. I want you to be happy."

I roll my eyes. But the truth is that I want that, too. To be happy. But it's so hard to find good in a world where violence and cruelty are everywhere. My best friend is dead, and someone I've known all my life was involved, maybe responsible. "It's not that simple," I say. "You can't just decide to be happy."

"True. But you can remind yourself that there are good things in life."

I'm about to disagree when I stop myself. Her words remind me of Emery. I straighten up. "Do you still have that laminator?"

My mom's eyes widen. "Sure. It's probably on the top shelf in the hall closet. I haven't taken that thing down since I made Valentine's bingo for your fifth-grade class. There was a time when I used it constantly."

"I remember," I say. "You laminated everything—chore charts, snack suggestions, and how to fix the toilet. You know, the one that used to run all the time? It made Dad crazy, these little laminated signs all over the house."

My mom laughs, and I do, too.

"What do you want to laminate?" she asks.

"Hold on. I'll show you." I go to my room and come back with the half-finished Wheel of Joy that Emery made for me.

She takes it as tenderly as scooping up a robin's egg in the spring. "What is it?" she asks.

"It's a Wheel of Joy," I say, feeling nervous. Maybe she will think this is stupid. "Emery made it for me."

"I see." My heart gallops as she begins to read aloud as if she is reading my diary. And in a way, she is.

My mom letting me eat a whole bag of marshmallows when my hamster died.

Going to a Nats game on the Fourth of July with my dad.

Visiting Ojiichan and Obaachan in Hawaii and eating yomogi mochi for the first time.

"This is awesome." She looks up at me and sniffles.

"Mom, please. Don't cry."

"I'm not going to," she says and wipes at her nose with the back of her hand. "Are you going to finish painting it?"

"Well, I was going to paint the rest, but then I thought, you know, why not leave it the way it is? Not everything has to be perfect."

"Come here." My mom holds her arms out, and I lean down to let her hug me. "You're absolutely right, honey. Not everything has to be perfect."

LIZA

When the automatic coffee maker beeps, I roll out of bed and plod down the hallway to the kitchen. I've come to enjoy not having stairs. Although the kitchen in the apartment is even tinier than my old one, it's shiny and new with a dishwasher that works. In fact, the whole building is shiny and new. Our small balcony overlooks a cobbled pedestrian alley in downtown Bethesda that is lined with shops. When the weather warms up, Zoe and I are going to plant geraniums out there. For now, the only greenery is a teeny Christmas tree on a table, right next to the menorah.

With coffee in hand, I head back to my bedroom and get dressed for Walnut's walk. I'm getting better at not thinking about the past every waking minute of my day. During the week, I'm busy with my new job as an editor at *AARP: The Magazine*. The pay is less than my old job, but the benefits are decent.

However occupied my mind is during work hours, in my alone time, the thoughts come barreling in.

No one ever found the paternity test that Chris de Groot claimed he had. The hospital kept no record of it. The only recourse would be to exhume little baby Henry, but Whitney's parents expressed no interest in disturbing his grave. I don't blame them for wanting to move on. But it means we will never know who the father is—Archer, Chris, or Todd.

Prentiss told me that Todd, who pleaded guilty to assaulting me, will be out of prison in less than two months. This whole ordeal inspired her to get back into law, and to my surprise, she took a position with the Mid-Atlantic Innocence Project. She's pretty plugged in to the criminal justice system, and she gave me a heads-up that he was to be released early for good behavior from the medium-security prison where he's been serving time.

I can only hope that he won't be out for long. That charges in Emery's death will be brought soon. The police insist the investigation is active and ongoing, but apparently, Todd confessing to me in his kitchen is not enough to bring charges. It takes time to build a case, Detective Gaffney told me, especially since Emery's body showed no signs of trauma. He talked to me about cell phone records, geolocation, eyewitnesses. Todd, and anyone else involved, will face their day in court, he assured me. Be patient.

Shelby murdered Nikki. But this many years later, there is no physical evidence that directly ties her to Nikki's death, and few witnesses left that could be helpful. Me of course, and Archer. And Geoff Estes, who is gone. After recovering from a head wound, he has moved to Switzerland, a country that has refused extradition requests in the past.

The crack in Nikki's skull backs up what Shelby confessed to me about the concrete brick, Gaffney said, but the police need time to build a strong case against her.

"Just because you don't hear from us," he said, "doesn't mean we're not working on it. Because we are. We are not letting this go."

That makes me feel better, but it infuriates me that in the world's eyes, the only thing the Smythes were found guilty of was bad judgment, of having been friends with Chris de Groot. (And of course, Todd assaulting me.)

Prentiss is one of the few people, Cobo being the other, to whom I can talk about the frustration of seeing Shelby and Todd moving on with their lives. "But you want the investigation done thoroughly," Prentiss always reminds me. "You don't want to risk an acquittal or having the case overturned. It's worth waiting."

"Isn't justice delayed, justice denied?" I asked her.

"This isn't justice delayed, though. This is the time needed to build a strong enough case to get a conviction. Be patient."

Patience does not come easily to me. Especially since I know Shelby is out there enjoying life. She moved down to Palm Beach, Florida, and Kinsey is going to the University of Miami. Occasionally, late at night, I will stalk Shelby's public Facebook page. I'll peer into her tanned face and bright white smile and wonder if she ever feels a twinge of guilt. I doubt it.

According to the bio on her page, Shelby runs a Bible study class, is a proud Hurricanes mom, a Gemini, and part of a local Peloton team—an Adrian devotee, whatever that means.

Murderer is not one of the words she uses to describe herself.

I don't know any more than what she posts on Facebook, because I don't accept her calls and I don't read her letters.

She has hundreds of new Facebook friends—almost all of them from Florida. And yes, I checked. Shelby is one of those gold-plated girls. Not a trendsetter, not on the cutting edge of anything, but so joyful and confident that you can't help but be drawn to her. She's always had that kind of power. She could have done so much good with it.

In a different family, she would have been encouraged to run for office or to be a leader in some way. But not in her family.

For her role in posting the fake suicide note that fateful night, Kinsey received no punishment, at least not yet. I've been told conspiracy charges may be coming. We'll see. Kinsey is technically in college now, but her real hustle is on Instagram as an influencer hawking powdered "cleanses" and lash extensions.

And Brody? He's gone. Instead of going to Clemson in the fall, he's taking a gap year in Tanzania, constructing water catchment systems. Sometimes Zoe shows me a picture from his private Instagram. Nothing in those photos suggests he was once a

Ledge Boy or even son of Todd and Shelby Smythe. According to Zoe, he and Shelby do not follow each other.

And so it goes. I always knew money could protect you against life's harsh blows, but it felt abstract to me until I witnessed it up close. Prentiss has helped me to not be cynical. It's not just about being afraid to take on the Smythes. On the contrary. "The DA's office won't take on a couple like the Smythes until they have an airtight case. But they want to, believe me," she said. "The detectives and prosecutor working on this are salivating at the chance to show the world that money does not put you above the law."

In the meantime, at least now I know the truth, and so does Cobo. He wants to bring a civil suit, but will give the police a chance to bring a criminal one first. Bringing a civil suit first might jeopardize the chances of a criminal trial.

It's not only the Smythes who have left D.C.

I believed Archer when he said he never knew how Nikki died. I have to believe him—it is too painful to think that he knew all along. He's in California now, working as a producer. He is out of the news business and into the world of make-believe. It suits him. He emails me occasionally, as part of a big blast that he sends to a distribution list called "D.C. Crew" with news of his success. He's adapting a lesser-known Patricia Highsmith novel, *The Sweet Sickness,* into a series for TV.

I read the book in college, and the only scene I really remember is when the main character, a psychopath, goes to an Italian restaurant and orders two dinners—one for himself and one for a woman with whom he has an imaginary relationship. Is that the way Archer feels? That his relationship with Todd and Shelby turned out to be a figment of his imagination? It's how I feel some days.

About a month ago, he texted me a screenshot of a casting call for a female lead whose *"exceptional hotness makes it hard to believe that she has any brains. Also has a black belt in karate."*

There's gotta be a good name for a band in there somewhere, he texted. *Black Belt? Exceptional Hotness?*

I didn't respond.

Archer and Todd are rapists. But as they move into their new communities, and on with their new lives, they will bear no scarlet letter to identify them as such. We are surrounded by such men, who committed these acts in their youth and never paid any price. They've grown up, married, become fathers, bosses. They're behind us in the line at Starbucks, lifting a beer at the neighborhood barbecue, in the cubicle next to ours at work.

At first, I felt a deep anger mixed with shame about my years of ignorance. My whole life felt like a lie. I went into a cleaning frenzy when I was getting the house ready to put on the market. I threw away anything that reminded me of the four of us, including all the photos of vacations, birthdays, and parties going back thirty years. I didn't want to be reminded of such evil and how closely intertwined I was with them. Because what did that make me?

But recently, I'm starting to think it's more complicated than that. When I first read *Night* by Elie Wiesel as a teenager, I came to my dad, my eyes swollen from crying, and said the Germans were evil. My father told me that was too simple. There are no good people, and there are no evil people, he said, just people. Sometimes we do good things, and sometimes we do evil things.

If you label people as evil, you don't just deny them their full humanity—you ignore the fact that the ability to do evil lies within everybody. Even the so-called good people. We have to stay vigilant, he said, and not delude ourselves into thinking we are the good ones.

Sometimes I think about Brody and Kinsey. How much did they know? How deeply were they involved? Did Shelby sit them down one day and say, *Hey, kids, let me tell you a story about a couple of crimes from three decades ago?*

They are the next generation, and I worry that like Todd and

Shelby, the lesson they take with them as they head out in the world is to prioritize a robust but unexamined self-preservation at all costs. A sense of entitlement that does not stop even when others get hurt. Certainly their parents are not chagrined by what they did. Which is why it is so important to me that they do get charged in the deaths of Emery and Nikki.

It reminds me of a John Steinbeck quote: "It isn't that the evil thing wins—it never will—but that it doesn't die."

Once dressed, I pause outside Zoe's door.

"I can hear you breathing," she says.

I crack open the door, smiling. "Just heading out for my walk. What are you doing today?"

"I'm probably going to hang out with Frances today. Or Cloud."

"That's fine." I've met both of them. Frances is a chatty girl who does stage crew with Zoe at Bethesda–Chevy Chase High School, while Cloud is a bit more mysterious—shy, gender-neutral, also interested in theater.

Zoe is happier than I have seen her in a long time. It turns out a large public school didn't swallow her up and spit her out. She's found her people. She still has moments of darkness and sadness about what happened. I've offered therapy, but she refuses, opting for a twice-monthly check-in with Uncle Aaron.

I pull on boots, a jacket, and a hat. My phone says it's a blustery thirty-six degrees outside. Walnut and I take the stairs down to the ground floor and wave at the receptionist. Outside, the wind is whipping around the corner of the building, and we huddle against a wall to wait. In a few minutes, a man in a peacoat with the collar popped up comes toward us, a frisky terrier mix straining at the leash.

"New coat?" I ask. "I like it."

Cobo leans in and kisses me. "Thanks, but I should've worn a hat. Actually, I need a new one."

"There's a few shops around the corner." We wait for the dogs to say hello. His rescue, Ginger, jumps up and down, sniffs at Walnut, and spins around while my pup stands there stoically, enduring it.

"Let's get coffee first," Cobo says. We turn left and walk side by side.

At first, we spent hours together going over every little detail. What really happened. How the Smythes shouldn't get away with this, but they would. What should have happened instead. We fell into bed like two injured animals licking each other's wounds.

On one of those last, beautiful September evenings, we had pupusas at Los Charros in Wheaton. "I don't want to do this anymore," Cobo said. My stomach clenched immediately, and I steeled myself, but I needn't have. "I want to move forward with you. Not just talk about the hurt. Let's try something—no talking about what happened for one month."

"Fine," I said, raising my margarita. "I'll drink to that."

And surprisingly, it has not been hard to do. One month has turned into two, and then three.

At Quartermaine, I hold the dogs and wave hi to Yonas while Cobo goes in and gets us drinks. I can't lie to myself that losing Shelby has been easy. I imagine it's what it feels like to lose a sister. Sometimes my hands pick up my phone to text her before I realize that she is no longer in my life. That moment of remembering is a sucker punch, taking the wind right out of me, like an amputee who still vividly perceives their lost limb.

I don't think I will ever make a friend like Shelby again. One who knows me inside and out. Trust is a fragile thing. Once shattered, it may be impossible to reconstitute.

My phone pings, and I see Zoe has texted me.

Can I sleep over at Cloud's house tonight?

My finger hovers over the keypad. I've met their mom. Lolly is a single mother who lives not too far from us in a small, brick house near the high school. There's no logical reason to say no.

It's wonderful Zoe's making friends. I like Lolly, who is a history professor at George Washington University. Maybe we will even become friends.

Before you ask about the SITCH—their mom will be home.

I can't help but grin. Zoe knows I'm nervous. That it's everything I can do just to let her leave our apartment in the morning.

But where there is no trust, there can be no love.

Sounds good, I type. *I trust you.*

ACKNOWLEDGMENTS

My deepest thanks go to my editor, Kristin Sevick, whose enthusiasm, sharp eyes, and editorial skill helped make this book what it is. And a big thank-you to everyone at Forge/Macmillan who helped bring this book out into the world.

To my wonderful agent—Katie Shea Boutillier at the Donald Maass Literary Agency—thank you for all your support.

I could not have written this during lockdown without the love and support of my friends. I won't try to name you all, but you know who you are and why this was such a tough year for me, so thank you. To my early readers—Janelle Wong, who read with a keen eye, and Julie Coe, for those countless walks through the neighborhood—a huge thanks. And thank you to the whip-smart women in my book club, and to the Five Families, who are always ready with a signature cocktail.

To Assistant U.S. Attorney Steve Snyder, thank you for once again being generous enough to take the time to provide insight into your profession. Thank you to Chris Watanabe, for explaining sukiyaki to me, among other things.

I will never forget writing this book during year one of the pandemic lockdown—trying to suss out quiet spots while my kids attended Zoom classes and my husband worked from the kitchen. I feel so lucky to have such a warm and loving family—thank you, Luca and Roxy, for bringing so much joy to my life. I am especially indebted to my husband, John Thompson, who once again proved he is not just a kick-ass line editor but an all-around awesome human being.